H

She wanted to kiss him. . .he looked rough and restless and disheveled, the way a man might after a night of wild sex. But just what kind of lover would Douglas Lord be? Ruthless. She felt her heart thud a little faster at the thought. He smelled of tobacco and sweat. He looked like a man who lived on the edge and liked it. She'd like to feel that clever, interesting mouth on hers—but not yet. Once she'd kissed him she might forget that she had to stay one step ahead of him.

'The thing is,' she murmured, letting her hands stray into his hair when their lips were only a breath apart, 'Uncle Maxie can get a passport for you and two thirty-day visas to Madagascar for both of us within twenty-four hours.'

'How?'

Whitney noted with amused annoyance just how quickly his seductive tone became businesslike. 'Connections, Douglas,' she said blithely. 'What're partners for?'

He shot her an appraising look. Damn if she wasn't becoming handy. If he weren't careful, she'd become indispensable. . .

**Nora Roberts** is the best-selling author of over seventy-five novels, including a string of international best-sellers. A prolific and popular writer, she has a large and devoted following on both sides of the Atlantic, with more than 25 million copies of her books in print and translations into 26 languages. She was the first author to be inducted into the *Romance Writers of America* Hall of Fame and has won numerous awards for her writing, including a Lifetime Achievement award from America's *Romantic Times* magazine. Nora Roberts lives with her husband and family in Maryland, USA.

By the same author in *Worldwide* paperbacks:

SWEET REVENGE
NORA ROBERTS — A COLLECTION

# HOT ICE

## NORA ROBERTS

**WORLDWIDE BOOKS**
LONDON · SYDNEY · TORONTO

*First published in Hardback in 1988
by Worldwide Books
Eton House, 18-24 Paradise Road, Richmond, Surrey
TW9 1SR*

*First published in Paperback 1989
This edition published 1994
Published by arrangement with Bantam Books, Inc.*

*Australian copyright 1988
Philippine copyright 1988*

© Nora Roberts 1987

ISBN 0 373 59375 9

*11-9406*

*Printed in Great Britain by
BPC Paperbacks Ltd*

To Bruce,
for showing me that being in love
is the ultimate adventure

# CHAPTER ONE

He was running for his life. And it wasn't the first time. As he raced by Tiffany's elegant window display, he hoped it wouldn't be his last. The night was cool with April rain slick on the streets and sidewalk. There was a breeze that even in Manhattan tasted pleasantly of spring. He was sweating. They were too damn close.

Fifth Avenue was quiet, even sedate at this time of night. Streetlights intermittently broke the darkness; traffic was light. It wasn't the place to lose yourself in a crowd. As he ran by Fifty-third, he considered ducking down into the subway below the Tishman Building—but if they saw him go in, he might not come back out.

Doug heard the squeal of tires behind him and whipped around the corner of Cartier's. He felt the sting in his upper arm, heard the muffled pop of a silenced bullet, but never slackened his pace. Almost at once, he smelled the blood. Now they were getting nasty. And he had the feeling they could do a lot worse.

But on Fifty-second Street were people—a group here and there, some walking, some standing. Here, there was noise—raised voices, music. His labored breathing went unnoticed. Quietly he stood behind a redhead who was four or five inches taller than his own six feet—and half again as wide. She was swaying to the music that poured out of her portable stereo. It was like hiding behind a tree in a windstorm. Doug took the opportunity to catch his breath and check his

wound. He was bleeding like a pig. Without giving it a
thought, he slipped the striped bandana out of the
redhead's back pocket and wrapped it around his arm.
She never stopped swaying—he had very light fingers.

It was more difficult to kill a man outright when
there was a crowd, he decided. Not impossible, just
harder. Doug kept his pace slow and faded in and out
of the packs of people while he kept his eyes and ears
open for the discreet black Lincoln.

Near Lexington he saw it pull up a half block away,
and he saw the three men in trim dark suits get out.
They hadn't spotted him yet, but it wouldn't be long.
Thinking fast, he scanned the crowd he'd merged with.
The black leather with the two dozen zippers might
work.

'Hey.' He grabbed the arm of the boy beside him.
'I'll give you fifty bucks for your jacket.'

The boy with pale spiked hair and a paler face
shrugged him off. 'Fuck off. It's leather.'

'A hundred then,' Doug muttered. The three men
were getting closer all the time.

This time the boy took more interest. He turned his
face so that Doug saw the tiny tattooed vulture on his
cheek. 'Two hundred and it's yours.'

Doug was already reaching for his wallet. 'For two
hundred I want the shades too.'

The boy whipped off the wraparound mirrored sunglasses. 'You got 'em.'

'Here, let me help you off with that.' In a quick
move, Doug yanked the boy's jacket off. After stuffing
bills in the boy's hand he pulled it on, letting out a hiss
of breath at the pain in his left arm. The jacket smelled,
not altogether pleasantly, of its previous owner. Ignoring it, Doug tugged the zipper up. 'Look, there're three
guys in undertaker suits coming this way. They're

scouting out for extras for a Billy Idol video. You and your friends here should get yourselves noticed.'

'Oh yeah?' And as the boy turned around with his best bored-teenager's look on his face, Doug was diving through the nearest door.

Inside, wallpaper shimmered in pale colors under dimmed lights. People sat at white linen-covered tables under art-deco prints. The gleam of brass rails formed a path to more private dining rooms or to a mirrored bar. With one whiff, Doug caught the scent of French cooking—sage, burgundy, thyme. Briefly he considered hustling his way past the maitre d' to a quiet table, then decided the bar was better cover. Affecting a bored look, he stuck his hands in his pockets and swaggered over. Even as he leaned on the bar, he was calculating how and when to make his exit.

'Whiskey.' He pushed the wraparound shades more firmly onto his nose. 'Seagram's. Leave the bottle.'

He stood hunched over it, his face turned ever so slightly toward the door. His hair was dark, curling into the collar of the jacket; his face was clean-shaven and lean. His eyes, hidden behind the mirrored glasses, were trained on the door as he downed the first fiery taste of whiskey. Without pausing, he poured a second shot. His mind was working out all the alternatives.

He'd learned to think on his feet at an early age, just as he'd learned to use his feet to run if that was the best solution. He didn't mind a fight, but he liked to have the odds in his favor. He could deal straight, or he could skim over the finer points of honesty— depending on what was the most profitable.

What he had strapped to his chest could be the answer to his taste for luxury and easy living—the taste he'd always wanted to cultivate. What was outside, combing the streets for him, could be a quick end to living at all. Weighing one against the other, Doug opted to shoot for the pot of gold.

The couple beside him were discussing the latest Mailer novel in earnest voices. Another group tossed around the idea of heading to a club for jazz and cheaper booze. The crowd at the bar was mostly single, he decided, here to drink off the tension of a business day and show themselves to other singles. There were leather skirts, three-piece suits, and high-topped sneakers. Satisfied, Doug pulled out a cigarette. He could have chosen a worse place to hide.

A blonde in a dove gray suit slid onto the stool beside him and flicked her lighter at the end of his cigarette. She smelled of Chanel and vodka. Crossing her legs, she downed the rest of her drink.

'Haven't seen you in here before.'

Doug gave her a brief look—enough to take in the slightly blurred vision and the predatory smile. Another time, he'd have appreciated it. 'No.' He poured another shot.

'My office is a couple of blocks from here.' Even after three Stolichnayas, she recognized something arrogant, something dangerous in the man beside her. Interested, she swiveled a little closer. 'I'm an architect.'

The hair on the back of his neck stood up when they walked in. The three of them looked neat and successful. Shifting, he looked over the blonde's shoulder as they separated. One of them stood idly by the door. The only way out.

Attracted rather than discouraged by his lack of response, the blonde laid a hand on Doug's arm. 'And what do you do?'

He let the whiskey lie in his mouth for just a moment before he swallowed and sent it spreading through his system. 'I steal,' he told her because people rarely believe the truth.

She smiled as she took out a cigarette, then handed him her lighter and waited for Doug to flick it on for her. 'Fascinating, I'm sure.' She blew out a quick, thin stream of smoke and plucked the lighter from his fingers. 'Why don't you buy me a drink and tell me all about it?'

A pity he'd never tried that line before since it seemed to work so well. A pity the timing was all wrong, because she filled out the little suit neater than a CPA filled out a 1099. 'Not tonight, sugar.'

Keeping his mind on business, Doug poured more whiskey and stayed out of the light. The impromptu disguise might work. He felt the pressure of a gun barrel against his ribs. Then again, it might not.

'Outside, Lord. Mr Dimitri's upset that you didn't keep your appointment.'

'Yeah?' Casually, he swirled the whiskey in his glass. 'Thought I'd have a couple of drinks first, Remo—must've lost track of time.'

The barrel dug into his ribs again. 'Mr Dimitri likes his employees to be prompt.'

Doug downed the whiskey, watching in the mirror behind the bar as the two other men took position behind him. Already the blonde was backing off to look for an easier mark. 'Am I fired?' He poured another glass and figured the odds. Three to one—they were armed, he wasn't. But then, of the three of them, only Remo had what could pass for a brain.

'Mr Dimitri likes to fire his employees in person.' Remo grinned and showed perfectly capped teeth under a pencil-thin moustache. 'And he wants to give you real special attention.'

'Okay.' Doug placed one hand on the whiskey bottle, the other on the glass. 'How about a drink first?'

'Mr Dimitri doesn't like drinking on the job. And you're late, Lord. Real late.'

'Yeah. Well, it's a shame to waste good booze.' Whirling, he tossed the whiskey into Remo's eyes and swung the bottle into the face of the suited man at his right. With the impetus of the swing, he ran headlong into the third man so that they fell backward onto the dessert display. Chocolate soufflé and rich French cream flew in a symphony of high-caloric rain. Wrapped around each other like lovers, they rolled into the lemon torte. 'Terrible waste,' Doug muttered and pushed a handful of strawberry mousse into the other man's face. Knowing the element of surprise would wear out quickly, Doug used the most expeditious means of defense. He brought his knee up hard between his opponent's legs. Then he ran.

'Put it on Dimitri's tab,' he called out as he pushed his way through tables and chairs. On impulse, he grabbed a waiter, then shoved him and his loaded tray in Remo's direction. Roast squab flew like a bullet. With one hand on the brass rail, he leapt over and scrambled for the door. He left the chaos behind him and broke into the street.

He'd bought some time, but they'd be behind him again. And this time, they'd be mean. Doug headed uptown on foot, wondering why the hell you could never find a cab when you needed one.

Traffic was light on the Long Island Expressway as Whitney headed into town. Her flight from Paris had landed at Kennedy an hour behind schedule. The back seat and trunk of her little Mercedes were crammed with luggage. The radio was turned up high so that the gritty strains of Springsteen's latest hit could ricochet through the car and out the open window. The two-week trip to France had been a gift to herself for finally working up the courage to break off her engagement to Tad Carlyse IV.

No matter how pleased her parents had been, she just couldn't marry a man who color-coordinated his socks and ties.

Whitney began to sing harmony with Springsteen as she tooled around a slower-moving compact. She was twenty-eight, attractive, moderately successful in her own career while having enough family money to back her up if things got really tough. She was accustomed to affluence and deference. She'd never had to demand either one, only expect them. She enjoyed being able to slip into one of New York's posher clubs late at night and find it filled with people she knew.

She didn't mind if the paparazzi snapped her or if the gossip columns speculated on what her latest outrage would be. She'd often explained to her frustrated father that she wasn't outrageous by design, but by nature.

She liked fast cars, old movies, and Italian boots.

At the moment, she was wondering if she should go home or drop in at Elaine's and see who'd been up to what in the past two weeks. She didn't feel jet lag, but a trace of boredom. More than a trace, she admitted. She was nearly smothered with it. The question was what to do about it.

Whitney was the product of new money, big money. She'd grown up with the world at her fingertips, but she hadn't always found it interesting enough to reach for. Where was the challenge? she wondered. Where was the—she hated to use the word—purpose? Her circle of friends was wide, and from the outside appeared to be diverse. But once you got in, once you really saw beneath the silk dresses or chinos, there was a sameness to these young, urbane, wealthy, pampered people. Where was the thrill? That was better, she thought. Thrill was an easier word to deal with than purpose. It wasn't a thrill to jet to Aruba if you only had to pick up the phone to arrange it.

Her two weeks in Paris had been quiet and soothing—and uneventful. Uneventful. Maybe that was the crux. She wanted something—something more than she could pay for with a check or credit card. She wanted action. Whitney also understood herself well enough to know she could be dangerous in this kind of mood.

But she wasn't in the mood to go home, alone, and unpack. Then again, she wasn't feeling much like a club crowded with familiar faces. She wanted something new, something different. She could try one of the new clubs that were always popping up. If she liked, she could have a couple of drinks and make conversation. Then, if the club interested her enough, she could drop a few words in the right places and make it the newest hot spot in Manhattan. The fact that she had the power to do so didn't astonish her, or even particularly please her. It simply was.

Whitney squealed to a halt at a red light to give herself time to make up her mind. It seemed like nothing was happening in her life lately. There wasn't any excitement, any, well, zing.

She was more surprised than alarmed when her passenger door was yanked open. One look at the black zippered jacket and wraparound glasses of the hitchhiker had her shaking her head. 'You aren't keeping up with fashion trends,' she told him.

Doug shot a look over his shoulder. The street was

clear, but it wouldn't be for long. He jumped in and slammed the door. 'Drive.'

'Forget it. I don't drive around with guys who wear last year's clothes. Take a walk.'

Doug stuck his hand in his pocket, using his forefinger to simulate the barrel of a gun. 'Drive,' he repeated.

She looked at his pocket, then back at his face. On the radio the disk jockey announced a full hour of blasts from the past. Vintage Stones began to pour out. 'If there's a gun in there, I want to see it. Otherwise, take off.'

Of all the cars he could've picked. . . Why the hell wasn't she shaking and pleading like any normal person would've done? 'Dammit, I don't want to have to use this, but if you don't throw this thing in gear and get moving, I'm going to have to put a hole in you.'

Whitney stared at her own reflection in his glasses. Mick Jagger was demanding that someone give him shelter. 'Bullshit,' she said, her diction exquisite.

Doug gave a moment's consideration to knocking her cold, dumping her out and taking the car. Another glance over his sholder showed him there wasn't much time to waste.

'Look, lady, if you don't get moving, there're three men in that Lincoln coming up behind us that'll do a lot of damage to your toy here.'

She looked in the rearview mirror and saw the big, black car slowing down as it approached. 'My father had a car like that once,' she commented. 'I always called it his funeral car.'

'Yeah—get in gear or it's going to be my funeral.'

Whitney frowned, watching the Lincoln in her rearview mirror, then impulsively decided to see what would happen next. She threw the car into first and zipped across the intersection. The Lincoln immediately picked up the pace. 'They're following.'

'Of course they're following,' Doug spat out. 'And if you don't step on it, they're going to crawl into the back seat and shake hands.'

Mostly out of curiosity, Whitney punched the gas and turned down Fifty-seventh. The Lincoln stayed with her. 'They're really following,' she said again, but with a grin of excitement.

'Can't this thing go any faster?'

She turned the grin on him. 'Are you kidding?' Before he could respond, she gunned the engine and was off like a shot. This was definitely the most interesting way to spend the evening she could imagine. 'Think I can lose them?' Whitney looked behind her, craning her neck to see if the Lincoln was still following. 'Ever see *Bullitt*? Of course, we don't have any of those nifty hills, but—'

'Hey, watch it!'

Whitney turned back around and, whipping the wheel, skimmed around a slower-moving sedan.

'Look.' Doug gritted his teeth. 'The whole purpose of this is to stay alive. You watch the road, I'll watch the Lincoln.'

'Don't be so snotty.' Whitney careened around the next corner. 'I know what I'm doing.'

'Look where you're going!' Doug grabbed the wheel, yanking it so that the fender missed a car parked at the curb. 'Damn idiot woman.'

Whitney lifted her chin. 'If you're going to be insulting, you'll just have to get out.' Slowing down, she swung toward the curb.

'For God's sake don't stop.'

'I don't tolerate insults. Now—'

'Down!' Doug hauled her sideways and pulled her

down to the seat just before the windshield exploded into spiderweb cracks.

'My car!' She struggled to sit up, but only managed to twist her head to survey the damage. 'Goddamn it, it didn't have a scratch on it. I've only had it for two months.'

'It's going to have a lot more than a scratch if you don't step on the gas and keep going.' From his crouched position, Doug twisted the wheel toward the street and peered cautiously over the dash. 'Now!'

Infuriated, Whitney stepped hard on the accelerator, moving blindly into the street while Doug held onto the wheel with one hand and held her down with the other.

'I can't drive this way.'

'You can't drive with a bullet in your head either.'

'A bullet?' Her voice didn't crack with fear, but vibrated with annoyance. 'They're shooting at us?'

'They ain't throwing rocks.' Tightening his grip, he spun the wheel so that the car bumped into the curb and around the next corner. Frustrated that he couldn't take the controls himself, he took a cautious look behind. The Lincoln was still there, but they'd gained a few seconds. 'Okay, sit up, but keep low. And for Chrissake keep moving.'

'How'm I supposed to explain this to the insurance company?' Whitney poked up her head and tried to find a clear spot in the broken windshield. 'They're never going to believe someone was shooting at me and I've already got a filthy record. Do you know what my rates are?'

'The way you drive, I can imagine.'

'Well, I've had enough.' Setting her jaw, Whitney turned left.

'This is a one-way street.' He looked around helplessly. 'Didn't you see the sign?'

'I know it's a one-way street,' she muttered and pressed harder on the gas. 'It's also the quickest way across town.'

'Oh, Jesus.' Doug watched the headlights bearing down on them. Automatically he gripped the door handle and braced for the impact. If he was going to die, he thought fatalistically, he'd rather be shot, nice and clean through the heart, than be spread all over a street in Manhattan.

Ignoring the screams of horns, Whitney jerked the car to the right, then to the left. Fools and small animals, Doug thought as they breezed between two oncoming cars. God looked out for fools and small animals. He could only be grateful he was with a fool.

'They're still coming.' Doug turned in the seat to watch the progress of the Lincoln. Somehow it was easier if he didn't watch where he was going. They bounced from side to side as she maneuvered between cars, then with a force that threw him against the door, she turned another corner. Doug swore and grabbed for the wound on his arm. Pain began again with a low, insistent thud. 'Stop trying to kill us, will you? They don't need any help.'

'Always complaining,' Whitney tossed back. 'Let me tell you something, you're not a real fun guy.'

'I tend to get moody when somebody's trying to kill me.'

'Well, try to lighten up a bit,' Whitney suggested. She barreled around the next corner, skimming the curb. 'You're making me nervous.'

Doug flopped back in his seat and wondered why, with all the possibilities, it had to end this way—smashed into unrecognizable pulp in some crazy

woman's Mercedes. He could've gone quietly with
Remo and had Dimitri murder him with some ritual.
There'd have been more justice in that.

They were on Fifth again, moving south at what
Doug saw was better than ninety. As they went through
a puddle, water slushed up as far as the window. Even
now, the Lincoln was less than a half block behind.
'Dammit. They just won't shake loose.'

'Oh yeah?' Whitney set her teeth and gave the mirror
a quick check. She'd never been a gracious loser.
'Watch this.' Before Doug could draw a breath, she
whipped the Mercedes around in a tight U-turn and
headed dead-on for the Lincoln.

He watched with a kind of fascinated dread. 'Oh my
God.'

Remo, in the passenger seat of the Lincoln, echoed
the sentiment just before his driver lost courage and
steered toward the curb. The speed took them over it,
across the sidewalk and, with an impressive flourish,
through the plate-glass window of Godiva Chocolatiers. Without slackening pace, Whitney spun the
Mercedes around again and cruised down Fifth.

Dropping back in his seat, Doug let out a series of
long, deep breaths. 'Lady,' he managed to say, 'you
got more guts than brains.'

'And you owe me three hundred bucks for the
windshield.' Rather sedately, she pulled into the underground parking of a high rise.

'Yeah.' Absently, he patted his chest and torso to
see if he was all in one piece. 'I'll send you a check.'

'Cash.' After pulling into her space, Whitney turned
off the ignition and hopped out. 'Now, you can carry
my luggage up.' She popped the trunk before she
strolled toward the elevator. Maybe her knees were

shaking, but she'd be damned if she'd admit it. 'I want a drink.'

Doug looked back toward the entrance of the garage and calculated his chances on the street. Maybe an hour or so inside would give him the chance to outline the best plan. And, he supposed, he owed her. He started to haul out the luggage.

'There's more in the back.'

'I'll get it later.' He slung a garment bag over his shoulder and hoisted two cases. Gucci, he noted with a smirk. And she was bitching about a lousy three hundred.

Doug walked into the elevator and dumped the two cases unceremoniously on the floor. 'Been on a trip?'

Whitney punched the button for the forty-second floor. 'A couple of weeks in Paris.'

'Couple of weeks,' Doug glanced at the three bags. And she'd said there were more. 'Travel light, do you?'

'I travel,' Whitney said rather grandly, 'as I please. Ever been to Europe?'

He grinned, and though the sunglasses hid his eyes, she found the smile appealing. He had a well-shaped mouth and teeth that weren't quite straight. 'Few times.'

They measured each other in silence. It was the first opportunity Doug had had to really look at her. She was taller than he'd expected—though he wasn't altogether sure just what he'd expected. Her hair was almost completely hidden under an angled white fedora, but what he could see was as pale as the punk's he'd stopped on the street, though a richer shade. The brim of the hat shaded her face, but he could see a flawless ivory complexion over elegant bones. Her eyes were round, the color of the whiskey he'd downed earlier. Her mouth was naked and unsmiling. She smelled like something soft and silky you wanted to touch in a dark room.

She was what he'd have termed a stunner, though she didn't appear to have any obvious curves beneath the simple sable jacket and silk slacks. Doug had always preferred the obvious in women. Perhaps the flamboyant. Still, he didn't find it any real hardship to look at her.

Casually, Whitney reached in her snakeskin bag and drew out her keys. 'Those glasses are ridiculous.'

'Yeah. Well they served their purpose.' He took them off.

His eyes surprised her. They were very light, very clear and green. Somehow they were at odds with his face and his coloring—until you noticed how direct they were, and how carefully they watched, as if he were a man who measured everything and everyone.

He hadn't worried her before. The glasses had made him appear silly and harmless. Now, Whitney had her first stirrings of discomfort. Who the hell was he, and why were men shooting at him?

When the doors slid open, Doug bent to pick up the suitcases. Whitney glanced down and noticed the thin stream of red dripping down his wrist. 'You're bleeding.'

Doug looked down dispassionately. 'Yeah. Which way?'

She hesitated only a moment. She could be just as cavalier as he. 'To the right. And don't bleed on those cases.' Breezing past him, she turned the key in the lock.

Through annoyance and pain, Doug noticed she had quite a walk. Slow and loose with an elegant sort of swing. It made him conclude that she was a woman accustomed to being followed by men. Deliberately he came up alongside her. Whitney spared him a glance before she pushed open the door. Then, flicking on the lights, she walked inside and went directly to the bar. She chose a bottle of Remy Martin and poured generous amounts into two glasses.

Impressive, Doug thought as he took stock of her apartment. The carpet was so thick and soft he could be happy sleeping on it. He knew enough to recognize the French influence in her furnishings, but not enough to pin down the period. She'd used deep sapphire blue and mustard yellow to offset the stunning white of the carpet. He could spot an antique when he saw one, and he spotted quite a few in this room. Her romantic taste was as obvious to him as the Monet seascape on the wall. A damn good copy, he decided. If he just had the time to hock it, he could be on his way. It didn't take more than a cursory glance to make him realize he could fill his zippered pockets with handfuls of her fancy French whatnots to pawn for a first-class ticket that would get him far away from this burg. Trouble was, he didn't dare deal in any pawnshop in the city. Not now that Dimitri had his tentacles out.

Because the furnishings weren't of any use to him, he wasn't sure why they appealed. Normally he would have found them too feminine and formal. Perhaps after an evening of running, he needed the comfort of silk pillows and lace. Whitney sipped her cognac as she carried the glasses across the room.

'You can bring this into the bathroom,' she told him as she handed him his drink. Negligently she tossed the fur over the back of the sofa. 'I'll take a look at that arm.'

Doug frowned while he watched her walk away. Women were supposed to ask questions, dozens of them. Maybe this one just didn't have the brains to think of them. Reluctantly he followed her, and the trail of her scent. But she was classy, he admitted. There was no denying it.

'Take off that jacket and sit down,' she ordered, running water over a monogrammed washcloth.

Doug stripped off the jacket, gritting his teeth as he peeled it from his left arm. After carefully folding it and laying it on the lip of the tub, he sat on a ladder-back chair anyone else would have had in their living room. He looked down and saw the sleeve of his shirt was caked with blood. Swearing, he ripped it off and exposed the wound. 'I can do it myself,' he muttered and reached for the cloth.

'Be still.' Whitney began to wipe away the dried blood with the soapy warm cloth. 'I can't very well see how much damage was done until I clean it up.'

He sat back because the warm water was soothing and her touch was gentle. But while he sat back, he watched her. Just what kind of woman was she? he wondered. She drove like a nerveless maniac, dressed like *Harper's Bazaar*, and drank—he'd noticed she'd already knocked back her cognac—like a sailor. He'd have been more comfortable if she'd shown just a touch of the hysteria he'd expected.

'Don't you want to know how I got this?'

'Hmmm.' Whitney pressed a clean cloth to the wound to slow the new bleeding. Because he wanted her to ask, she was determined not to.

'A bullet,' Doug said with relish.

'Really?' Interested, Whitney removed the cloth to get a closer look. 'I've never seen a bullet wound before.'

'Terrific.' He swallowed more cognac. 'How do you like it?'

She shrugged before she slid back the mirrored door of the medicine cabinet. 'It's not terribly impressive.'

Frowning, he looked down at the wound himself. True, the bullet had only nicked him, but he had been shot. It wasn't every day a man got shot. 'It hurts.'

'Aw, well we'll bandage it all up. Scratches don't hurt nearly so much if you can't see them.'

He watched her root through jars of face cream and bath oils. 'You've got a smart mouth, lady.'

'Whitney,' she corrected. 'Whitney MacAllister.' Turning she offered her hand formally.

His lips curved. 'Lord, Doug Lord.'

'Hello, Doug. Now, after I fix this up, we'll have to discuss the damage to my car and the payment.' She went back to the medicine cabinet. 'Three hundred dollars.'

He took another swallow of cognac. 'How come you know it's three hundred?'

'I'm giving you the low end of the scale. You can't fix a spark plug in a Mercedes for less than three hundred.'

'I'll have to owe you. I spent my last two hundred on the jacket.'

'That jacket?' Amazed, Whitney twisted her head and stared at him. 'You look smarter.'

'I needed it,' Doug tossed back. 'Besides, it's leather.'

This time she laughed. 'As in genuine imitation.'

'What d'you mean, imitation?'

'That zippered monstrosity didn't come off any cow. Ah, here it is. I knew I had some.' With a satisfied nod, she took a bottle from the cabinet.

'That little sonofabitch,' Doug mumbled. He hadn't had the time or the opportunity to look too closely at his purchase before. Now, in the bright bathroom light, he saw it was nothing more than cheap vinyl. Two hundred dollars' worth. The sudden fire in his arm had him jerking. 'Goddamn it! What're you doing?'

'Iodine,' Whitney told him, smearing it on generously.

He settled down, scowling. 'It stings.'

'Don't be a baby.' Briskly, she wrapped gauze around his upper arm until the wound was covered. She snipped off tape, secured it, then gave it a final pat. 'There,' she said, rather pleased with herself. 'Good as new.' Still bent over, she turned her head and smiled at him. Their faces were close, hers full of laughter, his full of annoyance. 'Now about my car—'

'I could be a murderer, a rapist, a psychopath for all you know.' He said it softly, dangerously. She felt a tremor move up her back and straightened.

'I don't think so.' But she picked up her empty glass and went back into the living room. 'Another drink?'

Damn, she did have guts. Doug grabbed the jacket and followed her. 'Don't you want to know why they were after me?'

'The bad guys?'

'The—the bad guys?' he repeated on an astonished laugh.

'Good guys don't shoot at innocent bystanders.' She poured herself another drink, then sat on the sofa. 'So, by process of elimination I figure you're the good guy.'

He laughed again and dropped down beside her. 'A lot of people might disagree with you.'

Whitney studied him again over the rim of her glass. No, perhaps good was too concise a word. He looked more complicated than that. 'Well, why don't you tell me why those three men wanted to kill you.'

'Just doing their job.' Doug drank again. 'They work

for a man named Dimitri. He wants something I've got.'

'Which is?'

'The route to a pot of gold,' he said absently. Rising, he began to pace. Less than twenty dollars in cash nestled with an expired credit card in his pocket. Neither could buy his way out of the country. What he had carefully folded in a manila envelope was worth a fortune, but he had to buy himself a ticket before he could cash it in. He could lift a wallet at the airport. Better, he could try rushing on the plane, flashing his fake ID, and play the hard-bitten, impatient FBI agent. It had worked in Miami. But it didn't feel right this time. He knew enough to go with his instincts.

'I need a stake,' he muttered. 'A few hundred— maybe a thousand.' Thoughtfully, he turned back and looked at Whitney.

'Forget it,' she said simply. 'You already owe me three hundred dollars.'

'You'll get it,' he snapped. 'Dammit, in six months I'll buy you a whole car. Look at it as an investment.'

'My broker takes care of that.' She sipped again and smiled. He was very attractive in this mood, restless, anxious to move. His exposed arm rippled with muscle that was subtle and lean. His eyes were lit with enthusiasm.

'Look, Whitney.' He came back and sat on the arm of the sofa beside her. 'A thousand. That's nothing after what we've been through together.'

'It's seven hundred dollars more than what you already owe me,' she corrected him.

'I'll pay you back double within six months. I need to buy a plane ticket, some supplies. . .' He looked down at himself, then back at her with that quick, appealing grin. 'A new shirt.'

An operator, she thought, intrigued. Just what did a pot of gold mean to him? 'I'd have to know a lot more before I put my money down.'

He'd charmed women out of more than money. So, confidently, he took her hand between his, rubbing his thumb over her knuckles. His voice was soft, compelling. 'Treasure. The kind you only read about in fairy stories. I'll bring you back diamonds for your hair. Big, glittery diamonds.. They'll make you look like a princess.' He skimmed a finger up her cheek. It was soft, cool. For a moment, only a moment, he lost the thread of his pitch. 'Something else out of a fairy story.'

Slowly, he removed her hat, then watched in astonished admiration as her hair tumbled down, over her shoulders, over her arms. Pale as winter sunlight, soft as silk. 'Diamonds,' he repeated, tangling his fingers through it. 'Hair like this should have diamonds in it.'

She was caught up in him. Part of her would have believed anything he said, done anything he asked, as long as he continued to touch her in just that way. But it was the other part, the survivor, who managed to take control. 'I like diamonds. But I also know a lot of people who pay for them, and end up with pretty glass. Guarantees, Douglas.' To distract herself, she drank more cognac. 'I always want to see the guarantee—the certificate of value.'

Frustrated, he rose. She might look like a pushover, but she was as tough as they came. 'Look, nothing's stopping me from just taking it.' He snatched her purse off the sofa and held it out to her. 'I can walk out of here with this or we can make a deal.'

Standing, she plucked it out of his hands. 'I don't make deals until I know all the terms. You've got a hell of a nerve threatening me after I saved your life.'

'Saved my life?' Doug exploded. 'You damn near killed me twenty times.'

Her chin lifted. Her voice became regal and haughty. 'If I hadn't outwitted those men, getting my car damaged in the process, you'd be floating in the East River.'

The image was entirely too close to the truth. 'You've been watching too many Cagney movies,' he tossed back.

'I want to know what you have and where you intend to go.'

'A puzzle. I've got pieces to a puzzle and I'm going to Madagascar.'

'Madagascar?' Intrigued, she turned it over in her mind. Hot, sultry nights, exotic birds, adventure. 'What kind of puzzle? What kind of treasure?'

'My business.' Favoring his arm, he slipped on the jacket again.

'I want to see it.'

'You can't see it. It's in Madagascar.' He took out a cigarette as he calculated. He could give her enough, just enough to interest her and not enough to cause trouble. Blowing out smoke, he glanced around the room. 'Looks like you know something about France.'

Her eyes narrowed. 'Enough to order escargots and Dom Pérignon.'

'Yeah, I bet.' He lifted a pearl-encrusted snuffbox from the top of a curio cabinet. 'Let's just say the goodies I'm after have a French accent. An old French accent.'

She caught her bottom lip between her teeth. He'd hit a button. The little snuffbox he was tossing from hand to hand was two hundred years old and part of an extensive collection. 'How old?'

'Couple centuries. Look, sugar, you could back me.' He set the box down and walked to her again. 'Think

of it as a cultural investment. I take the cash, and I
bring you back a few trinkets.'

Two hundred years meant the French Revolution.
Marie and Louis. Opulence, decadence and intrigue.
A smile began to form as she thought it through.
History had always fascinated her, French history in
particular with its royalty and court politics, philos-
ophers and artists. If he really had something—and the
look in his eyes convinced her he did—why shouldn't
she have a share? A treasure hunt was bound to be
more fun than an afternoon at Sotheby's.

'Say I was interested,' she began as she worked out
her terms. 'What kind of a stake would be needed?'

He grinned. He hadn't thought she'd take the bait so
easily. 'Couple thousand.'

'I don't mean money.' Whitney dismissed it as only
the wealthy could. 'I mean how do we go about getting
it?'

'We?' He wasn't grinning now. 'There's no we.'

She examined her nails. 'No we, no money.' She sat
back, stretching her arms on the top of the sofa. 'I've
never been to Madagascar.'

'Then call your travel agent, sugar. I work alone.'

'Too bad.' She tossed her hair and smiled. 'Well, it's
been nice. Now if you'll pay me for the damages. . .'

'Look, I haven't got time to—' He broke off at the
quiet sound behind him. Spinning around, Doug saw
the door handle turn slowly—right, then left. He held
up a hand, signaling silence. 'Get behind the couch,'
he whispered while he scanned the room for the
handiest weapon. 'Stay there and don't make a sound.'

Whitney started to object, then heard the quiet rattle
of the knob. She watched Doug pick up a heavy
porcelain vase.

'Get down,' he hissed again as he switched off the

lights. Deciding to take his advice, Whitney crouched behind the sofa and waited.

Doug stood behind the door, watching as it opened slowly, silently. He gripped the vase in both hands and wished he knew how many of them he had to go through. He waited until the first shadow was completely inside, then lifting the vase over his head, brought it down hard. There was a crash, a grunt, then a thud. Whitney heard all three before the chaos began.

There was a shuffle of feet, another splinter of glass—her Meissen tea set if the direction of the sound meant anything—then a man cursed. A muffled pop was followed by another tinkle of glass. A silenced bullet, she decided. She'd heard the sound on enough late-night movies to recognize it. And the glass—twisting her head she saw the hole in the picture window behind her.

The super wasn't going to like it, she reflected. Not one bit. And she was already on his list since the last party she'd given had gotten slightly out of hand. Damn it, Douglas Lord was bringing her a great deal of trouble. The treasure—she drew her brows together—the treasure better be worth it.

Then, it was quiet, entirely too quiet. Over the silence all she could hear was the sound of breathing.

Doug pressed back into the shadowy corner and held on to the ·45. There was one more, but at least he wasn't unarmed now. He hated guns. A man who used them generally ended up being on the wrong end of the barrel too often for comfort.

He was close enough to the door to slip through it and be gone, maybe without notice. If it hadn't been for the woman behind the couch, and the knowledge that he'd gotten her into this, he'd have done it. The fact that he couldn't only made him furious with her.

He might, just might, have to kill a man to get out. He'd killed before, was aware he was likely to do so again. But it was a part of his life he could never examine without guilt.

Doug touched the bandage on his arm and his fingers came away wet. Damn, he couldn't stand there waiting and bleeding to death. Moving soundlessly, he edged along the wall.

Whitney had to cover her mouth to hold back all sound as the shadow crouched at the end of the sofa. It wasn't Doug—she saw immediately that the neck was too long and the hair too short. Then she caught the flicker of movement to her left. The shadow turned toward it. Before she had time to think, Whitney pulled off her shoe. Holding the good Italian leather in one hand, she aimed the three-inch heel at the shadow's head. With all the strength she could muster, she brought it down.

There was a grunt, then a thud.

Amazed at herself, Whitney held up her shoe in triumph. 'I got him!'

'Sweet Jesus,' Doug muttered as he dashed across the room, grabbing her hand and dragging her along with him.

'I knocked him cold,' she told Doug as he streaked toward the stairway. 'With this.' She wiggled the shoe that was crushed between his hand and hers. 'How did they find us?'

'Dimitri. Traced your plates,' he said, enraged with himself for not considering it before. Streaking down the next flight of stairs he started making new plans.

'That fast?' She gave a quick laugh. Adrenaline was pumping through her. 'Is this Dimitri a man or a magician?'

'He's a man who owns other men. He could pick up

the phone and have your credit rating and your shoe size in a half hour.'

So could her father. That was business, and she understood business. 'Look, I can't run lopsided, give me a couple of seconds.' Whitney pulled her hand from his and put on her shoe. 'What're we going to do now?'

'We've got to get to the garage.'

'Down forty-two flights?'

'Elevators don't have back doors.' With this he grabbed her hand and began to jog down the steps again. 'I don't want to come out near your car. He's probably got somebody watching it just in case we get that far.'

'Then why're we going to the garage?'

'We still need a car. I've got to get to the airport.'

Whitney slung the strap of her purse over her head so that she could grip the rail for support as they ran. 'You're going to steal one?'

'That's the idea. I'll drop you off at a hotel—register under some other name, then—'

'Oh no,' she interrupted, noting gratefully that they were passing the twentieth floor. 'You're not dumping me in any hotel. Windshield, three hundred, plate-glass window, twelve hundred. Dresden vase circa 1865, twenty-two seventy-five.' She retrieved her purse, dug a notebook out of it, and never missed a beat. The minute she caught her breath, she'd start an accounting. 'I'm going to collect.'

'You'll collect,' he said grimly. 'Now, save your breath.' She did, and began to work out her own plan.

By the time they'd reached the garage level, she was winded enough to lean breathlessly against the wall while he peered through a crack in the door. 'Okay, the closest one is a Porsche. I'll go out first. Once I'm in the car, you follow. And keep down.'

He slipped the gun back out of his pocket. She caught the look in his eye, a look of—loathing? she wondered. Why should he look down at a gun as though it were something vile? She'd thought a gun would fit easily into his hand, the way a gun did for a man who hung out in dim bars and smoky hotel rooms. But it didn't fit easily. It didn't fit at all. Then he went through the door.

Who was Doug Lord really? Whitney asked herself. Was he a hood, a con, a victim? Because she sensed he was all three, she was fascinated and determined to find out why.

Crouched, Doug took out what looked like a pen-knife. Whitney watched as he fiddled with the lock for a moment, then quietly opened the passenger door. Whatever he was, Whitney noted, he was good at breaking and entering. Leaving that for later, she crept through the door. He was already in the driver's seat and working with wires under the dash when she climbed inside.

'Damn foreign cars,' he muttered. 'Give me a Chevy any day.'

Wide-eyed with admiration, Whitney heard the engine spring to life. 'Can you teach me how to do that?'

Doug shot her a look. 'Just hold on. This time, I'm driving.' Throwing the Porsche into reverse, he peeled out of the space. By the time they reached the garage entrance, they were doing sixty. 'Got a favorite hotel?'

'I'm not going to a hotel. You're not getting out of my sight, Lord, until your account has a zero balance. Where you go, I go.'

'Look, I don't know how much time I have.' He kept a careful eye on the rearview mirror as he drove.

'What you don't have any of is money,' she reminded

him. She had her book out now and began to write in neat columns. 'And you're currently in to me for a windshield, an antique porcelain vase, a Meissen tea set—eleven-fifty for that—and a plate-glass window—maybe more.'

'Then another thousand isn't going to matter.'

'Another thousand always matters. Your credit's only good as long as I can see you. If you want a plane ticket you're taking on a partner.'

'Partner?' He turned to her, wondering why he didn't just take her purse and shove her out the door. 'I never take on partners.'

'You do this time. Fifty-fifty.'

'I've got the answers.' The truth was he had the questions, but he wasn't going to worry about details.

'But you don't have the stake.'

He swung on to FDR Drive. No, dammit, he didn't have the stake, and he needed it. So, for now, he needed her. Later, when he was several thousand miles from New York, they could negotiate terms. 'Okay, just how much cash have you got on you?'

'A couple hundred.'

'Hundred? Shit.' He kept his speed to a steady fifty-five now. He couldn't afford to get pulled over. 'That won't take us farther than New Jersey.'

'I don't like to carry a lot of cash.'

'Terrific. I've got papers worth millions and you want to buy in for two hundred.'

'Two hundred, plus the five thousand you owe me. And—' She reached into her purse. 'I've got the plastic.' Grinning, she held up a gold American Express card. 'I never leave home without it.'

Doug stared at it, then threw back his head and laughed. Maybe she was more trouble than she was worth, but he was beginning to doubt it.

\* \* \*

The hand that reached for the phone was plump and very white. At the wrist, white cuffs were studded with square sapphires. The nails were buffed to a dull sheen and neatly clipped. The receiver itself was white, pristine, cool. Fingers curled around it, three elegantly manicured ones and a scarred-over stub where the pinky should have been.

'Dimitri.' The voice was poetry. Hearing it, Remo began to sweat like a pig. He drew on his cigarette and spoke quickly, before exhaling.

'They gave us the slip.'

Dead silence. Dimitri knew it was more terrifying than a hundred threats. He used it five seconds, ten. 'Three men against one and a young woman. How inefficient.'

Remo pulled the tie loose from his throat so he could breathe. 'They stole a Porsche. We're following them to the airport now. They won't get far, Mr Dimitri.'

'No, they won't get far. I have a few calls to make, a few. . .buttons to push. I'll meet you in a day or two.'

Remo rubbed his hand over his mouth as his relief began to spread. 'Where?'

There was a laugh, soft, distant. The sense of relief evaporated like sweat. 'Find Lord, Remo. I'll find you.'

# CHAPTER TWO

His arm was stiff. When Doug rolled over he gave a little grunt of annoyance at the discomfort and absently pushed at the bandage. His face was pressed into a soft feather pillow covered by a linen case that had no scent. Beneath him, the sheet was warm and smooth. Gingerly flexing his left arm, he shifted on to his back.

The room was dark, deceiving him into thinking it was still night until he looked at his watch. Nine-fifteen. Shit. He ran a hand over his face as he pushed himself up in bed.

He should be on a plane halfway to the Indian Ocean instead of lying around in a fancy hotel room in Washington. A dull, fancy hotel room, he remembered as he thought of the fussy, red-carpeted lobby. They'd arrived at one-ten and he hadn't even been able to get a drink. The politicians could have Washington, he'd take New York.

The first problem was that Whitney held the purse strings, and she hadn't given him a choice. The next problem was, she'd been right. He'd only been thinking of getting out of New York, she'd been thinking of details like passports.

So, she had connections in DC, he thought. If connections could cut through paperwork, he was all for it. Doug glanced around the high-priced room that was hardly bigger than a broom closet. She'd charge him for the room, too, he realized, narrowing his eyes at the connecting door. Whitney MacAllister had a mind like a CPA. And a face like. . .

With a half grin he shook his head and lay back. He'd better keep his mind off her face, and her other attributes. It was her money he needed. Women had to wait. Once he had what he was going for, he could swim neck-deep in them if he wanted.

The image was pleasant enough to keep him smiling for another minute. Blondes, brunettes, redheads, plump, thin, short and tall. There was no point in being too discriminating, and he intended to be very generous with his time. First, he had to get the damn passport and visa. He scowled. Damn bureaucratic bullshit. He had a treasure waiting for him, a professional bone breaker breathing down his neck, and a crazy woman in the room next door who wouldn't even buy him a pack of cigarettes without marking it down in the little notebook she kept in her two-hundred-dollar snakeskin bag.

The thought prompted him to reach over to pluck a cigarette from the pack on the nightstand. He couldn't understand her attitude. When he had money to spend, he was generous with it. Maybe too generous, he decided with a half laugh. He certainly never had it for long.

Generosity was part of his nature. Women were a weakness, especially small, pouty women with big eyes. No matter how many times he'd been taken by one, he invariably fell for the next. Six months before, a little waitress named Cindy had given him two memorable nights and a sob story about a sick mother in Columbus. In the end, he'd parted company with her—and with five grand. He'd always been a sucker for big eyes.

That was going to change, Doug promised himself. Once he had his hands on the pot of gold, he was going to hold on to it. This time he was going to buy that big splashy villa in Martinique and start living his life the way he'd always dreamed. And he'd be generous with his servants. He'd cleaned up after enough rich people to know how cold and careless they could be with servants. Of course, he'd only cleaned up after them until he could clean them out, but that didn't change the bottom line.

Working for the wealthy hadn't given him his taste for rich things. He'd been born with it. He just hadn't been born with money. Then again, he felt he'd been better off being born with brains. With brains and certain talents you could take what you needed—or wanted—from people who barely noticed the sting. The job kept the adrenaline going. The result, the money, just let you relax until the next time.

He knew how to plan for it, how to plot, how to scheme. And he also knew the value of research. He'd been up half the night going over every scrap of information he could decipher in the envelope. It was a puzzle, but he had the pieces. All he needed to put them all together was time.

The neatly typed translations he'd read might have just been a pretty story to some, a history lesson to others—aristocrats struggling to smuggle their jewels and their precious selves out of revolution-torn France. He'd read words of fear, of confusion, and of despair. In the plastic-sealed originals, he'd seen hopelessness in the handwriting, in words he couldn't read. But he'd also read of intrigue, of royalty, and of wealth. Marie Antoinette. Robespierre. Necklaces with exotic names hidden behind bricks or concealed in wagon-loads of potatoes. The guillotine, desperate flights across the English Channel. Pretty stories steeped in history and colored with blood. But the diamonds, the emeralds, the rubies the size of hen's eggs had been real too.

Some of them had never been seen again. Some had been used to buy lives or a meal or silence. Others had traveled across oceans. Doug worked the kinks out of his arm and smiled. The Indian Ocean—trade route for merchants and pirates. And on the coast of Madagascar, hidden for centuries, guarded for a queen, was the answer to his dreams. He was going to find it, with the help of a young girl's journal and a father's despair. When he did, he'd never look back.

Poor kid, he thought, imagining the young French girl who'd written out her feelings two hundred years before. He wondered if the translation he'd read had really keyed in on what she'd gone through. If he could read the original French. . . He shrugged and reminded himself she was long dead and not his concern. But she'd just been a kid, scared and confused.

*Why do they hate us?* she'd written. *Why do they look at us with such hate? Papa says we must leave Paris and I believe I will never see my home again.*

And she never had, Doug mused, because war and politics go for the big view and trample all over the little guy. France during the Revolution or a steamy pit of a jungle in Nam. It never changed. He knew just what it felt like to be helpless. He wasn't going to feel that way ever again.

He stretched and thought of Whitney.

For better or worse, he'd made a deal with her. He never turned his back on a deal unless he was sure he could get away with it. Still, it grated to have to depend on her for every dollar.

Dimitri had hired him to steal the papers because he was, Doug admitted honestly as he sucked in smoke, a very good thief. Unlike Dimitri's standard crew, he'd never considered that a weapon made up for wit. He'd always preferred living by the latter. Doug knew it was his reputation for doing a smooth, quiet job that had earned him the call from Dimitri to lift a fat envelope from a safe in an exclusive co-op off Park Avenue.

A job was a job, and if a man like Dimitri was willing to pay five thousand for a bunch of papers, a great many with faded and foreign writing, Doug wasn't going to argue. Besides, he'd had some debts to pay.

He'd had to get by two sophisticated alarm systems and four security guards before he could crack the little gem of a wall safe where the envelope was stored. He had a way with locks and alarms. It was—well, a gift, Doug decided. A man shouldn't waste his God-given talents.

The thing was, he'd played it straight. He'd taken nothing but the papers—though there'd been a very interesting-looking black case in the safe along with it. He never considered that taking them out to read them was any more than covering his bets. He hadn't expected to be fascinated by the translations of letters or a journal or documents that stretched back two hundred years. Maybe it had been his love of a good story, or his respect for the written word that had touched off his imagination as he had skimmed over the papers. But fascinated or not, he would have turned them over. A deal was a deal.

He'd stopped in a drugstore and bought adhesive. Strapping the envelope to his chest had just been a precaution. New York, like any city, was riddled with dishonest people. Of course, he'd arrived at the East-Side playground an hour early and had hidden. A man stayed alive longer if he watched his ass.

While sitting behind the shrubbery in the rain, he'd thought over what he'd read—the correspondence, the documents, and the tidy list of gems and jewels. Whoever had collected the information, translated it so meticulously, had done so with the dedication of a professional librarian. It had passed through his mind briefly that if he'd had the time and opportunity, he'd have followed up on the rest of the job himself. But a deal was a deal.

Doug had waited with every intention of turning over the papers and collecting his fee. That had been before he'd learned that he wasn't going to get the five thousand Dimitri had agreed on. He was going to get a two-dollar bullet in the back and a burial in the East River.

Remo had arrived in the black Lincoln with two other men dressed for business. They'd calmly debated the most efficient way to murder him. A bullet in the brain seemed to be the method agreed on, but they were still working out the 'when' and 'where' as Doug crouched behind bushes six feet away. It seemed Remo had been fussy about getting blood on the Lincoln's upholstery.

At first Doug had been angry. No matter how many times he'd been double-crossed—and he'd stopped counting—it always made him angry. Nobody was honest in this world, he'd thought as the adhesive pulled a bit at his skin. Even while he'd concentrated on getting out in one piece, he had begun to consider his options.

Dimitri had a reputation for being eccentric. But he also had a reputation for picking winners, from the right senator to keep on the payroll to the best wine to stock in the cellar. If he wanted the papers badly enough to snip off a loose end named Doug Lord, they must be worth something. On the spot, Doug decided the papers were his and his fortune was made. All he had to do was live to claim it.

In reflex he touched his arm now. Stiff, yes, but

already healing. He had to admit crazy Whitney
MacAllister had done a good job there. He blew smoke
between his teeth before he crushed out the cigarette.
She'd probably charge him for it.

He needed her for the moment, at least until they
were out of the country. Once he got to Madagascar,
he'd ditch her. A slow, lazy grin covered his face. He'd
had some experience in outmaneuvering women.
Sometimes he succeeded. His only regret was that he
wouldn't get to see her stomp and swear when she
realized he'd given her the slip. Picturing those clouds
of pale, sunlit hair he thought it was almost too bad he
had to double-cross her. He couldn't deny he owed
her. Even as he sighed and began to think kindly of
her, the connecting door burst open.

'Still in bed?' Whitney crossed to the window and
pulled open the drapes. She waved a hand fussily in
front of her face in an attempt to clear the haze of
smoke. He'd been up for awhile, she decided. Smoking
and plotting. Well, she'd been doing some figuring
herself. When Doug swore and squinted, she merely
shook her head. 'You look terrible.'

He was vain enough to scowl. His chin was rough
with a night's coarse growth of beard, his hair was
unruly, and he'd have killed for a toothbrush. She, on
the other hand, looked as though she'd just walked out
of Elizabeth Arden's. Naked in the bed with the sheet
up to his waist, Doug felt at a disadvantage. He didn't
care for that sensation.

'You ever knock?'

'Not when I'm paying for the room,' she said easily.
She stepped over the tangle of jeans on the floor.
'Breakfast is on its way up.'

'Great.'

Ignoring his sarcasm, Whitney made herself at home

by sitting on the bottom of the bed and stretching out her legs.

'Make yourself comfortable,' Doug said expansively.

Whitney only smiled and shook back her hair. 'I got in touch with Uncle Maxie.'

'Who?'

'Uncle Maxie,' Whitney repeated, giving her nails a quick check. She really needed a manicure before they left town. 'Actually, he's not my uncle, I just call him my uncle.'

'Oh, that kind of uncle,' Doug said, a half sneer on his face.

Whitney spared him a mild glance. 'Don't be crude, Douglas. He's a dear friend of the family's. Perhaps you've heard of him. Maximillian Teebury.'

'Senator Teebury?'

She spread her fingers for a last examination. 'You do keep up with current events.'

'Look, smartass.' Doug grabbed her arm so that she tumbled half into his lap. Whitney only smiled up at him, knowing she still held all the aces. 'Just what does Senator Teebury have to do with anything?'

'Connections.' She ran a finger down his cheek, clucking her tongue at the roughness. But roughness, she discovered, had its own primitive appeal. 'My father always says you can do without sex in a pinch, but you can't do without connections.'

'Yeah?' Grinning, he lifted her up so that her face was close to his and her hair streamed down to the sheets. Again he caught the drift of her scent that meant wealth and class. 'Everybody has different priorities.'

'Indeed.' She wanted to kiss him. He looked rough and restless and disheveled, the way a man might after a night of wild sex. Just what kind of a lover would

Douglas Lord be? Ruthless. She felt her heart thud a little faster at the thought. He smelled of tobacco and sweat. He looked like a man who lived on the edge and enjoyed it. She'd like to feel that clever, interesting mouth on hers—but not yet. Once she'd kissed him she might forget that she had to stay one step ahead of him. 'The thing is,' she murmured, letting her hands stray into his hair when their lips were only a breath apart, 'Uncle Maxie can get a passport for you and two thirty-day visas to Madagascar within twenty-four hours.'

'How?'

Whitney noted with amused annoyance just how quickly his seducing tone became businesslike. 'Connections, Douglas,' she said blithely. 'What're partners for?'

He shot her a considering look. Damn if she wasn't becoming handy. If he wasn't careful, she'd be indispensable. The last thing a smart man needed was an indispensable woman who had eyes like whiskey and skin like the underside of petals. Then it hit him that they'd be on their way by that time the next day. Letting out a quick whoop, he rolled on top of her. Her hair fanned over the pillow. Her eyes, half-wary, half-laughing, met his.

'Let's find out, partner,' he suggested.

His body was hard, like his eyes could be, like his hand as it cupped her face. It was tempting. He was tempting. But it was always vital to weigh advantage against disadvantage. Before Whitney could decide whether to agree or not, there was a knock at the door. 'Breakfast,' she said cheerfully, wiggling out from under him. If her heart was beating a bit too fast, she wasn't going to dwell on it. There was too much to do.

Doug folded his arms behind his head and leaned

back on the headboard. Maybe desire was eating a hole in his stomach, or maybe it was just hunger. Maybe it was both. 'Let's have it in bed.'

Whitney gave her opinion of his suggestion by ignoring it. 'Good morning,' she said brightly to the waiter as he wheeled in the tray.

'Good morning, Ms MacAllister.' The young, square-built Puerto Rican didn't even glance at Doug. His eyes were all for Whitney. With considerable charm, he handed her a pink rosebud.

'Why, thank you, Juan. It's lovely.'

'I thought you'd like it.' He flashed her a quick grin, showing a mouthful of strong, even teeth. 'I hope your breakfast's okay. I brought up the toiletries and the paper you asked for.'

'Oh, that's wonderful, Juan.' She smiled at the dark stud of a waiter, Doug noted, with a lot more sweetness than she'd bothered to show him. 'I hope it wasn't too much trouble.'

'Oh, no, never for you, Ms MacAllister.'

Behind the waiter's back, Doug silently mimicked his words and soulful expression. Whitney only arched a brow, then signed the check with a flourish. 'Thank you, Juan.' She reached into her bag and pulled out a twenty. 'You've been a big help.'

'A pleasure, Ms MacAllister. You just call me if there's anything else I can do.' The twenty disappeared into his pocket with the speed and discretion of long practice. 'Enjoy your breakfast.' Still smiling, he backed his way out of the door.

'You love them to grovel, don't you?'

Whitney turned a cup right side up and poured coffee. Casually, she waved the rosebud under her nose. 'Put some pants on and come eat.'

'And you were damn generous with the little bit of

cash we've got.' She said nothing, but he saw she was drawing out her little notepad. 'Just hold on, it was you overtipped the waiter, not me.'

'He got you a razor and a toothbrush,' she said mildly. 'We'll split the tip because your hygiene's of some concern to me at the moment.'

'That's big of you,' he grumbled. Then, because he wanted to see just how far he could push her, he climbed slowly out of bed.

She didn't gasp, she didn't flinch, she didn't blush. She merely gave him one long, measuring survey. The white bandage on his arm was a stark contrast against his dark-toned skin. God, he had a beautiful body, she thought as her pulse began a slow, dull thud. Lean, sleek, and subtly muscled. Naked, unshaven, half-smiling, he looked more dangerous and more appealing than any man she'd ever come across. She wouldn't give him the satisfaction of knowing it.

Without taking her eyes from him, Whitney lifted her coffee cup. 'Stop bragging, Douglas,' she said mildly, 'and put your pants on. Your eggs are getting cold.'

Damn, she was a cool one, he thought as he grabbed up his jeans. Just once, he was going to see her sweat. Flopping down in the chair across from her, Doug began to stuff himself with hot eggs and crisp bacon. At the moment he was too hungry to calculate what the luxury of room service was costing him. Once he found the treasure, he could buy his own damn hotel.

'Just who are you, Whitney MacAllister?' he demanded over a full mouth.

She added a dash of pepper to her own eggs. 'In what way?'

He grinned, pleased that she wouldn't give easy answers. 'Where do you come from?'

'Richmond, Virginia,' she said, lapsing so quickly into a smooth Virginia accent one would've sworn she'd had one all along. 'My family's still there, on the plantation.'

'Why'd you move to New York?'

'Because it's fast.'

He reached for toast, scrutinizing the basket of jellies. 'What do you do there?'

'Whatever I like.'

He looked into her sultry, whiskey-colored eyes and believed it. 'Do you have a job?'

'No, I have a profession.' She lifted a piece of bacon between her fingers and nibbled. 'I'm an interior designer.'

He remembered her apartment, the feeling of elegance, the melding of colors, the uniqueness. 'A decorator,' he mused. 'You'd be a good one.'

'Naturally. And you?' She poured them both more coffee. 'What do you do?'

'A lot of things.' He reached for the cream, watching her. 'Mostly I'm a thief.'

She remembered the ease with which he had stolen the Porsche. 'You'd be a good one.'

He laughed, enjoying her. 'Naturally.'

'This puzzle you mentioned. The papers.' She tore a piece of toast in two. 'Are you going to show them to me?'

'No.'

She narrowed her eyes. 'How do I know you have them? How do I know that if you do have them they're worth my time, not to mention my money?'

He seemed to consider a moment, then offered her the basket of jellies. 'Faith?'

She chose strawberry preserves and spread them on

generously. 'Let's try not to be ridiculous. How'd you get them?'

'I—acquired them.'

Biting into the toast, she watched him over it. 'Stole them.'

'Yeah.'

'From the men who were chasing you?'

'For the man they work for,' Doug corrected her. 'Dimitri. Unfortunately, he was going to double-cross me, so all bets were called off. Possession's nine-tenths of the law.'

'I suppose.' She considered for a moment the fact that she was breakfasting with a thief who was in possession of a mysterious puzzle. She supposed she'd done more unusual things in her life. 'All right, let's try this. What form is this puzzle in?'

Doug considered giving her another nonanswer, then caught the look in her eyes. Cool, unflappable determination. He'd better give her something, at least until he had the passport and a ticket. 'I've got papers, documents, letters. I told you it went back a couple hundred years. There's enough information in the papers I have to lead me right to the pot of gold, a pot of gold nobody even knows is there.' When another thought occurred to him, he frowned at her. 'You speak French?'

'Of course,' she said, and smiled. 'So some of the puzzle's in French.' When he said nothing she steered him back again. 'Why doesn't anyone know about your pot of gold?'

'Anyone who did is dead.'

She didn't like the way he said it, but she wasn't about to back off now. 'How do you know it's genuine?'

His eyes became intense, the way they could when you least expected it. 'I feel it.'

'And who's this man who's after you?'

'Dimitri? He's a first-class businessman—bad business. He's smart, he's mean, he's the kind of guy who knows the Latin name for the bug he's picking the wings off. If he wants the papers, they're worth a hell of a lot. One hell of a lot.'

'I guess we'll find that out in Madagascar.' She picked up the *New York Times* Juan had delivered. She didn't like the way Doug had described the man who was after him. The best way to avoid thinking about it was to think of something else. Opening the paper she caught her breath, then let it out again. 'Oh, shit.'

Intent on finishing his eggs, Doug gave her an absent 'Hmmm?'

'I'm in for it now,' she predicted, rising and tossing the open paper on to his plate.

'Hey, I'm not finished.' Before he could push the paper aside, he saw Whitney's picture smiling up at him. Above the picture was a splash of headline.

## ICE-CREAM HEIRESS MISSING

'Ice-cream heiress,' Doug muttered, skimming down to the text before he fully took it in. 'Ice cream. . .' His mouth fell open as he dropped the paper. 'Mac-Allister's ice cream? That's you?'

'Indirectly,' Whitney told him, pacing the room as she tried to work out the best plan. 'It's my father.'

'MacAllister's ice cream,' Doug repeated. 'Sonofa-bitch. He makes the best damn fudge ripple in the country.'

'Of course.'

It hit him then that she wasn't just a classy decorator

but the daughter of one of the richest men in the country. She was worth millions. *Millions*. And if he was caught with her, he'd be up on kidnapping charges before he could ask for his court appointed lawyer. Twenty years to life, he thought, dragging a hand through his hair. Doug Lord sure knew how to pick 'em.

'Look, sugar, this changes things.'

'It certainly does,' she muttered. 'Now I have to call Daddy. Oh, and Uncle Maxie, too.'

'Yeah.' He scooped up the last forkful of eggs, deciding he'd better eat while he had the chance. 'Why don't you figure out my bill, and we'll—'

'Daddy is going to think I'm being held for ransom or something.'

'Exactly.' He grabbed the last piece of toast. Since she'd figure out a way for him to pay for the meal, he might as well enjoy it. 'And I don't want to end up with a cop's bullet in my head either.'

'Don't be ridiculous.' Whitney dismissed him with a wave of the hand while she refined her plan of approach. 'I'll get around Daddy,' she murmured. 'I've been doing it for years. I should be able to get him to wire me some money while I'm at it.'

'Cash?'

She shot him a long, appraising look. 'That certainly got your attention.'

He set the toast aside. 'Look, gorgeous, if you know how to get around your old man, who'm I to argue? And, while the plastic's nice, and the cash you can get with the plastic's nice, a little extra of the green stuff would help me sleep a lot easier.'

'I'll take care of it.' She walked to the connecting doors, then paused. 'You really could use a shower and a shave, Douglas, before we go shopping.'

He stopped in the act of rubbing his chin. 'Shopping?'

'I'm not going to Madagascar with one blouse and one pair of slacks. And I'm certainly not going anywhere with you wearing a shirt with only one sleeve. We'll do something about your wardrobe.'

'I can pick out my own shirts.'

'After seeing that fascinating jacket you had on when we met, I have my doubts.' With this, she closed the door between them.

'It was a disguise,' he yelled at her, then stormed off toward the bathroom. Damn woman always had to have the last word.

But he had to admit, she had taste. After a two-hour shopping whirlwind, he was carrying more packages than he cared to, but the cut of his shirt helped conceal the slight bulge of the envelope that was again strapped to his chest. And he liked the way the loose linen felt against his skin. The same way he liked the way Whitney's hips moved under the thin white dress. Still, there was no use being too agreeable.

'What the hell am I going to do with a suit tramping around in a forest in Madagascar?'

She glanced over and adjusted the collar of his shirt. He'd fussed about wearing baby blue, but Whitney reaffirmed her opinion that it was an excellent color for him. Oddly enough, he looked as though he'd been born wearing tailored slacks. 'When one travels, one should be prepared for anything.'

'I don't know how much walking we're going to have to do, sugar, but I'll tell you this. You're carrying your own gear.'

She tipped down her new signature sunglasses. 'A gentleman to the last.'

'You bet.' He stopped beside a drugstore and shifted

the packages under one arm. 'Look, I need some things in here. Give me a twenty.' When she only lifted a brow, he swore. 'Come on, Whitney, you're going to mark it down in your damn account book anyway. I feel naked without any cash.'

She gave him a sweet smile as she reached in her purse. 'It didn't bother you to be naked this morning.'

Her lack of reaction to his body still irked. He plucked the bill from her hand. 'Yeah, we'll take that up again sometime. I'll meet you upstairs in ten minutes.'

Pleased with herself, Whitney crossed to the hotel and breezed through the lobby. She was having more fun annoying Doug Lord than she'd had in months. She shifted the smart leather tote she'd bought to the other hand and pushed the button for her floor.

Things were looking good, she decided. Her father had been relieved that she was safe and not displeased that she was leaving the country again. Laughing to herself, Whitney leaned back against the wall. She supposed she had given him a few bad moments in the past twenty-eight years, but she was just made that way. In any case, she'd spun fact and fiction together until her father had been satisfied. With the thousand dollars he was wiring to Uncle Maxie that afternoon, she and Doug would be on solid ground before they took off for Madagascar.

Even the name appealed to her. Madagascar, she mused as she strolled down the hall toward her room. Exotic, new, unique. Orchids and lush greens. She wanted to see it all, experience it, as much as she wanted to believe the puzzle Doug talked about led to that pot of gold.

It wasn't the gold itself that drew her. She was too accustomed to wealth to have her heartbeat quicken at the thought of more. It was the thrill of looking, of finding, that attracted her. Oddly enough, she understood better than Doug that he felt the same.

She was going to have to learn a great deal more about him, she decided. From the way he'd discussed cut and material with the salesclerk, he wasn't a stranger to the finer things. He could've passed for one of the casually rich in a classic-cut linen shirt—unless you looked at his eyes. Really looked. Nothing casual there, Whitney thought. They were restless, wary, and hungry. If they were going to be partners, she had to find out why.

As she unlocked the door, it occurred to her that she had a few minutes alone, and that maybe, just maybe, Doug had stashed the papers in his room. She was putting up the money, Whitney told herself. She had every right to see what she was financing. Still, she moved quietly, keeping an ear out for Doug's return as she crossed to the connecting doors. She caught her breath, then with a hand to her heart, laughed.

'Juan, you scared me to death.' She stepped inside, looking beyond where the young waiter sat to the still-littered table. 'Did you come to pick up the breakfast dishes?' She didn't have to put off her quick search because of him, she decided and began to poke through Doug's dresser. 'Is the hotel busy this time of year?' she asked conversationally. 'It's cherry-blossom time, isn't it? That always brings in the tourists.'

Frustrated that the dresser was empty, she scanned the room. Maybe the closet. 'What time does the maid usually come in, Juan? I could use some extra towels.' When he continued to stare silently at her she frowned. 'You don't look well,' she told him. 'They work you too hard. Maybe you should. . .' She touched a hand to his shoulder and slowly, bonelessly, he slumped to her feet, leaving a smear of blood on the back of the chair.

She didn't sceam because her brain and her vocal cords had frozen. Eyes wide, mouth working, she backed up. She'd never seen death before, never smelled it, but she recognized it. Before she could run from it, a hand clamped over her arm.

'Very pretty.'

The man whose face was inches from hers held a gun under her chin. One cheek was badly scarred, jagged, as from a broken bottle or a blade. Both his hair and his eyes were the color of sand. The barrel of the gun was like ice on her skin. Grinning, he skimmed the gun down her throat.

'Where's Lord?'

Her gaze darted down to the crumpled body inches away from her feet. She could see the red stain spread over the white back of his jacket. Juan would be no help, and he'd never spend the twenty-dollar tip she'd given him only hours before. If she wasn't careful, very, very careful, she'd end up the same way.

'I asked you about Lord.' The gun pushed her chin up a little higher.

'I lost him,' she said, thinking fast. 'I wanted to get back here and find the papers.'

'Double-cross.' He toyed with the ends of her hair and made her stomach roll. 'Smart too.' The fingers tightened, jerking her head back. 'When's he coming back?'

'I don't know.' She winced at the pain and struggled to keep her mind clear. 'Fifteen minutes, maybe a half hour.' Any minute, she thought desperately. He could walk in any minute and then they both would be dead. Another glance at the body sprawled at her feet and her eyes filled. Whitney swallowed hard, knowing she couldn't afford tears. 'Why did you kill Juan?'

'Wrong place at the wrong time,' he said with a grin. 'Just like you, pretty lady.'

'Listen. . .' It wasn't difficult to keep her voice low, if she'd tried to speak above a whisper her teeth would have chattered. 'I don't have any allegiance to Lord. If you and I could find the papers, then. . .' She let the sentence trail off, moistening her lips with her tongue. He watched the gesture before he ran his gaze down her body.

'Not much tit,' he said with a sneer, then stepped back, gesturing with the gun. 'Maybe I should see more of what you're offering.'

She toyed with the top button of her blouse. She'd gotten his mind off killing her for the moment, but this wasn't much of a bargain. Inching back as she moved to the next button, she felt her hips bump into the table. As if to steady herself, she rested a palm on it, keeping her gaze on his sand-colored eyes. She felt cool stainless steel brush her fingertips.

'Maybe you should help me,' she whispered and forced herself to smile.

He inclined his head as he set the gun on the dresser. 'Maybe I should.' Then his hands were on her hips, moving slowly up her body. Whitney gripped the handle in her fist and plunged the fork into the side of his throat.

Blood spurting, squealing like a pig, he jumped back. As he reached for the handle himself, she picked up the leather tote and swung it with all the force she had. She didn't look to see how deep she'd driven the prongs into him. She ran.

In high good humor after a brief flirtation with the

checkout girl, Doug started to swing into the lobby. Running full steam, Whitney barreled into him.

He juggled tottering packages. 'What the hell—'

'Run!' she shouted, and without waiting to see if he took her advice, raced out of the hotel.

Swearing and fumbling with packages, he drew up alongside her. 'What for?'

'They've found us.'

A glance over his shoulder showed him Remo and two others just hustling out of the hotel. 'Ah, shit,' Doug muttered, then grabbing Whitney's arm, he dragged her through the first door he came to. They were greeted by the quiet strains of harp music and a stiff-backed maitre d'.

'You have a luncheon reservation?'

'Just looking for friends,' Doug told him, nudging Whitney along.

'Yes, I hope we're not too early.' She batted her eyes at the maitre d' before scanning the restaurant. 'I do hate being early. Ah, there's Majorie now. My, my, she's put on weight.' With Whitney leaning conspiratorially toward Doug, they moved past the maitre d'. 'Be sure to compliment her on that horrid outfit, Rodney.'

Skirting through the restaurant, they made a direct line for the kitchen. 'Rodney?' he complained in undertones.

'It just came to me.'

'Here.' Thinking fast, he shoved the boxes and bags into Whitney's tote, then slung the whole business over his shoulder. 'Let me do the talking.'

In the kitchen they made their way around counters and ranges and cooks. Moving as quickly as he thought prudent, Doug aimed for the back door. A white-aproned bulk, three feet wide, stepped in front of him.

'Guests are not permitted in the kitchen.'

Doug looked up at the chef's hat at least a foot above his own head. It reminded him how much he hated physical altercations. You didn't get so many bruises when you used your head. 'One minute, one minute,' Doug said fussily and turned to the pot simmering at his right. 'Sheila, this has the most *divine* scent. Superb, sensuous. Four stars for the scent.'

Catching on, she drew her pad out of her bag. 'Four stars,' she repeated, scribbling.

Picking up the ladle, Doug held it under his nose, closed his eyes and sampled. 'Ah.' He drew the word out so dramatically Whitney had to choke down a giggle. '*Poisson Véronique*. Magnificent. Absolutely magnificent. Definitely one of the top contenders in the contest. Your name?' he demanded from the chef.

The white-aproned bulk preened. 'Henri.'

'Henri,' he repeated, waving a hand at Whitney. 'You'll be notified within ten days. Come, Sheila, don't dawdle. We have three more stops to make.'

'My money's on you,' Whitney told Henri as they walked out the back door.

'Okay.' Doug gripped her arm hard when they stood in the alley. 'Remo's only half-stupid so we've got to get out fast. Which way to Uncle Maxie's?'

'He lives in Virginia, Roslyn.'

'All right, we need a cab.' He started forward, then pushed Whitney back against the wall so quickly she lost her breath. 'Dammit, they're already out there.' He took a moment, knowing the alley wouldn't be safe for long. In his experience, alleys were never safe for long. 'We'll have to go the other way, which means going over a few walls. You're going to have to keep up.'

The image of Juan was still fresh in her mind. 'I'll
keep up.'

'Let's go.'

They started out side by side then swerved to the
right. Whitney had to scramble over boxes to make it
over the first fence and her leg muscles sang out in
surprise on the landing. She kept running. If he had a
pattern to his flight, she couldn't find it. He zigzagged
down streets, through alleys, and over fences until her
lungs burned from the effort of keeping the pace. The
floaty skirt of her dress caught on some chain link and
tore jaggedly at the hem. People stopped to look at
them in surprise and speculation as they never would've
done in New York.

Always, he seemed to have one eye looking over his
shoulder. She had no way of knowing he'd lived that
way most of his life and had often wondered if he'd
ever live any other way. When he dragged her down
the stairs toward Metro Center, she had to grip the rail
to keep from plunging head first.

'Blue lines, red lines,' he muttered. 'Why do they
have to screw things up with colors?'

'I don't know.' Breathless, she leaned against the
information board. 'I've never ridden the Metro
before.'

'Well, we're fresh out of limos. Red line,' he
announced and grabbed her hand again. He hadn't lost
them. Doug could still smell the hunt. Five minutes, he
thought. He only wanted a five-minute lead. Then
they'd be on one of those speedy little trains and gain
more time.

The crowd was thick and babbling in a half dozen
languages. The more people the better, he decided as
he inched his way along. He glanced over his shoulder
when they stood at the edge of the platform. His gaze

met Remo's. He saw the bandage on the tanned cheek. Compliments of Whitney MacAllister, Doug thought and couldn't resist tossing back a grin. Yeah, he owed her for that, he decided. If for nothing else, he owed her for that.

It was all timing now, he knew, as he pulled Whitney on to the train. Timing and luck. It was either with them or against them. Sandwiched between Whitney and a sari-clad Indian woman, Doug watched Remo fight his way through the crowd.

When the doors closed, he grinned and gave the frustrated man outside a half salute. 'Let's find a seat,' he said to Whitney. 'There's nothing like public transportation.'

She said nothing as they worked their way through the car, and still nothing when they found a space nearly big enough for both of them. Doug was too busy alternately cursing and blessing his luck to notice. In the end, he grinned at his own reflection in the glass to his left.

'Well, the sonofabitch might've found us, but he's going to have a hell of a lot of explaining to do to Dimitri about losing us again.' Satisfied, he draped his arm over the back of the bright orange seat. 'How'd you spot them anyway?' he asked absently while he plotted out his next move. Money, passport, and airport, in that order, though he had to fit in a quick trip to the library. If Dimitri and his hounds showed up in Madagascar, they'd just lose them again. He was on a roll. 'You've got a sharp eye, sugar,' he told her. 'We'd've been in a bad way if there'd been a welcoming committee back in the hotel room.'

Adrenaline had carried her through the streets. The need to survive had driven her hard and fast until the moment she'd sat down. Drained, Whitney turned her head and stared at his profile. 'They killed Juan.'

'What?' Distracted, he glanced over. For the first time he noticed that her skin was bloodless and her eyes blank. 'Juan?' Doug drew her closer, dropping his voice to a whisper. 'The waiter? What're you talking about?'

'He was dead in your room when I went back. There was a man waiting.'

'What man?' Doug demanded. 'What'd he look like?'

'His eyes were like sand. He had a scar down his cheek, a long, jagged scar.'

'Butrain,' Doug mumbled. Some of Dimitri's excess slime and as mean as they came. He tightened his grip on Whitney's shoulder. 'Did he hurt you?'

Her eyes, dark as aged whiskey, focused on his again. 'I think I killed him.'

'What?' he stared at the elegant, fine-boned face. 'You killed Butrain? How?'

'With a fork.'

'You—' Doug stopped, sat back, and tried to take it in. If she hadn't been looking at him with big, devastated eyes, if her hand hadn't been like ice, he'd have laughed out loud. 'You're telling me you did in one of Dimitri's apes with a fork?'

'I didn't stop to take his pulse.' The train pulled up at the next stop and, unable to sit still, Whitney rose and pushed her way off. Swearing and struggling through bodies, Doug caught up with her on the platform.

'Okay, okay, you'd better tell me the whole thing.'

'The whole thing?' Abruptly enraged, she turned on him. 'You want to hear the whole thing? The whole bloody thing? I walk back into the room and there's that poor, harmless boy dead, blood all over his starched white coat, and some creep with a face like a road map's holding a gun to my throat.'

Her voice had risen so that passersby turned to listen or to stare.

'Keep it down,' Doug muttered, dragging her toward another train. They'd ride, it didn't matter where, until she was calm and he had a more workable plan.

'You keep it down,' she shot back. 'You got me into this.'

'Look, honey, you can take a walk any time you want.'

'Sure, and end up with my throat slit by someone who's after you and those damn papers.'

The truth left him little defense. Shoving her down into a corner seat, he squeezed in beside her. 'Okay, so you're stuck with me,' he said under his breath. 'Here's a news flash—listening to you whine about it gets on my nerves.'

'I'm not whining.' She turned to him with eyes suddenly drenched and vulnerable. 'That boy's dead.'

Anger drained and guilt flared. Not knowing what else to do, he put his arm around her. He wasn't used to comforting women. 'You can't let it get to you. You're not responsible.'

Tired, she let her head rest on his shoulder. 'Is that how you get through life, Doug, by not being responsible?'

Curling his fingers into her hair, he watched their blurred twin images in the glass. 'Yeah.'

They lapsed into silence with both of them wondering if he were telling the truth.

# CHAPTER THREE

She had to snap out of it. Doug shifted in his first-class seat and wished he knew how to shake the grief out of her. He thought he understood wealthy women. He'd worked for—and on—plenty of them. It was just as true, he supposed, that plenty of them had worked on him. The trouble was, had always been, that he invariably fell just a little bit in love with any woman he spent more than two hours with. They were so, well, feminine, he decided. Nobody could sound more sincere than a soft-smelling, soft-skinned woman. But he'd learned through experience that women with big bank accounts generally had hearts of pure plastic. The minute you were about ready to forget the diamond earrings in favor of a more meaningful relationship, they dumped all over you.

Callousness. He thought that was the worst failing of the rich. The kind of callousness that made them step all over people with the nonchalance of a child stomping on a beetle. For recreation, he'd choose a waitress with an easy laugh. But when it was business, Doug went straight to the bank balance. A woman with a hefty one was an invaluable cover. You could get through a lot of locked doors with a rich woman on your arm. They came in varieties, certainly, but generally could be slapped with a few basic labels. Bored, vicious, cold, or silly came to mind. Whitney didn't seem to qualify for any one of those labels. How many people would have remembered the name of a waiter, much less mourned for him?

They were on their way to Paris out of Dulles International. Enough of a detour, he hoped, to throw Dimitri off the scent. If it bought him a day, a few hours, he'd use it. He knew, as anyone in the business knew, of Dimitri's reputation for dealing with those who attempted to cross him. A traditional man, Dimitri preferred traditional methods. Men like Nero would have appreciated Dimitri's flare for slow, innovative torture. There had been murmurs about a basement room in Dimitri's Connecticut estate. Supposedly it was filled with antiques—the sort from the Spanish Inquisition. Rumor had it that there was a top-grade studio as well. Lights, camera, action. Dimitri was credited for enjoying replays of his more gruesome work. Doug wasn't going to find himself in the spotlight in one of Dimitri's performances, nor was he going to believe the myth that Dimitri was omnipotent. He was just a man, Doug told himself. Flesh and blood. But even at thirty thousand feet, Doug had the uneasy sensation of a fly being toyed with by a spider.

Taking another drink, he pushed that thought aside. One step at a time. That's how he'd play it, and that's how he'd survive.

If he'd had the time, Doug would have taken Whitney to the Hotel de Crillon for a couple of days. It was the only place he stayed in Paris. There were cities he'd settle for a motel with a cot, and cities where he wouldn't sleep at all. But Paris. His luck had always held in Paris.

He made it a point to arrange a trip twice a year, for no other reason than the food. As far as Doug was concerned no one cooked better than the French, or those educated in France. Because of that, he had managed to bluff his way into several courses. He'd learned the French way, the *correct* way to prepare an omelette at the Cordon Bleu. Of course, he kept a low profile on that particular interest. If word got out that he'd worn an apron and whisked eggs, he'd lose his reputation on the streets. Besides, it would be embarrassing. So he always covered his trips to Paris for cooking interests with business.

A couple of years back, he'd stayed there for a week, playing the wealthy playboy and riffling the rooms of the rich. Doug remembered he'd hocked a very good sapphire necklace and paid his bill in full. You never knew when you'd want to go back.

But there wasn't time on this trip for a quick course in soufflés or a handy piece of burglary. There would be no sitting still in one place until the game was over. Normally he preferred it that way—the chase, the hunt. The game itself was more exciting than the winning. Doug had learned that after his first big job. There'd been the tension and pressure of planning, the rippling thrill and half terror of execution, then the rushing excitement of success. After that, it was simply another job finished. You looked for the next. And the next.

If he'd listened to his high-school counselor, he'd probably be a very successful lawyer right now. He'd had the brains and the glib tongue. Doug sipped smooth scotch and was grateful he hadn't listened.

Imagine, Douglas Lord, Esquire, with a desk piled with papers and luncheon meetings three days a week. Was that any way to live? He skimmed another page of the book he'd stolen from a Washington library before they'd left. No, a profession that kept you in an office owned you, not the other way around. So, his IQ topped his weight, he'd rather use his talents for something satisfying.

At the moment, it was reading about Madagascar,

its history, its topography, its culture. By the time he finished this book, he'd know everything he needed to know. There were two other volumes in his case he'd save for later. One was a history of missing gems, the other a long, detailed history of the French Revolution. Before he found the treasure, he'd be able to see it, and to understand it. If the papers he'd read were fact, he had pretty Marie Antoinette and her penchant for opulence and intrigue to thank for an early retirement. The Mirror of Portugal diamond, the Blue Diamond, the Sancy—all fifty-four carats of it. Yeah, French royalty had had great taste. Good old Marie hadn't rocked tradition. Doug was grateful for it. And for the aristocrats who had fled their country guarding the crown jewels with their lives, holding them in secret until the royal family might rule France again. . .

He wouldn't find the Sancy in Madagascar. Doug was in the business and knew the rock was now in the Astor family. But the possibilities were endless. The Mirror and the Blue had dropped out of sight centuries before. So had other gems. The Diamond Necklace Affair—the straw that had broken the peasants' back—was riddled with theory, myth, and speculation. Just what had become of the necklace that had ultimately ensured Marie of not having a neck to wear it on?

Doug believed in fate, in destiny, and just plain luck. Before it was over, he was going to be knee-deep in sparkles—royal sparkles. And screw Dimitri.

In the meantime, he wanted to learn all he could about Madagascar. He was going far off his own turf—but so was Dimitri. If Doug could beat his adversary in anything, he prided himself on being able to top him in intelligent research. He read page after page and tallied fact after fact. He'd find his way around the little island in the Indian Ocean the same way he went from East-Side to West-Side Manhattan. He had to.

Satisfied, he set the book aside. They'd been at cruising altitude for two hours. Long enough, Doug decided, for Whitney to brood in silence.

'Okay, knock it off.'

She turned and gave him a long, neutral look. 'I beg your pardon?'

She did it well, Doug reflected. The ice-bitch routine peculiar to women with money or guts. Of course, he was learning that Whitney had both. 'I said knock it off. I can't stand a pouter.'

'A pouter?'

Because her eyes were slits and she'd hissed the words, he was satisfied. If he made her angry, she'd snap out of it all the quicker. 'Yeah. I'm not crazy about a woman who runs her mouth a mile a minute, but we should be able to come up with something in between.'

'Should we? How lovely that you have such definite requirements.' She took a cigarette from the pack he'd tossed on the arm between them and lit it. He'd never known the gesture could be so haughty. It helped amuse him.

'Let me give you lesson one before we go any further, sweetie.'

Deliberately, and with a quiet kind of venom, Whitney blew smoke in his face. 'Please do.'

Because he recognized pain when he saw it, he gave her another minute. Then his voice was flat and final. 'It's a game.' He took the cigarette from her fingers and drew on it. 'It's always a game, but you go into it knowing there are penalties.'

She stared at him. 'Is that what you consider Juan? A penalty?'

'He was in the wrong place at the wrong time,' he told her, unknowingly echoing Butrain's words. But she heard something else. Regret? Remorse? Though she couldn't be sure, it was something. She held on to it. 'We can't go back and change what happened, Whitney. So we go on.'

She picked up her neglected drink. 'Is that what you do best? Go on?'

'If you want to win. When you have to win, you can't look back very often. Tearing yourself up over this isn't going to change anything. We're one step ahead of Dimitri, maybe two. We've got to stay that way because it's a game, but you play it for keeps. If we don't stay ahead, we're dead.' As he spoke, he laid a hand over hers, not for comfort, but to see if it was steady. 'If you can't take it, you'd better think about backing off now because we've got a hell of a long way to go.'

She wouldn't back off. Pride was the problem, or the blessing. She'd never been able to back off. But what about him? she wondered. What made Douglas Lord run? 'Why do you do it?'

He liked the curiosity, the spark. As he settled back he was satisfied she'd gotten over the first hump. 'You know, Whitney, it's a hell of a lot sweeter to win the pot at poker with a pair of deuces than with a flush.' He blew out smoke and grinned. 'One hell of a lot sweeter.'

She thought she understood and studied his profile. 'You like the odds against you.'

'Long shots pay more.'

She sat back, closed her eyes, and was silent so long he thought she dozed. Instead, Whitney was going

back over everything that had happened, step by step.
'The restaurant,' she asked abruptly. 'How did you pull
that off?'

'What restaurant?' He was studying the different
tribes of Madagascar in his book and didn't bother to
look up.

'In Washington, when we were running for our lives
through the kitchen and that enormous man in white
stepped in front of you.'

'You just use the first thing that comes to your mind,'
he said easily. 'It's usually the best.'

'It wasn't just what you said.' Unsatisfied, Whitney
shifted in her seat. 'One minute you're a frantic man
off the streets, and the next a snooty food critic saying
all the right things.'

'Baby, when your life's on the line, you can be
anything.' Then he looked up and grinned. 'When you
want something bad enough, you can be anything.
Usually I like to case a job from the inside. All you
have to do is decide if you're going in the front door or
the servants' entrance.'

Interested, she signaled for another drink for each of
them. 'Meaning?'

'Okay, take California. Beverly Hills.'

'No, thanks.'

Ignoring her, Doug began to reminisce. 'First you
have to decide which one of those nifty mansions you
want to take. A few discreet questions, a little legwork,
and you home in on one. Now, front door or back?
That might depend on my own whim. Getting in the
front's usually easiest.'

'Why?'

'Because money wants references for servants, not
from guests. You need a stake, a few thousand. Check
into the Wilshire Royal and rent a Mercedes, drop a

few names—of people you know are out of town. Once you get into the first party, you're set.' With a sigh, he drank. 'Boy, they do like to wear their bank accounts around their necks in the Hills.'

'And you just walk right in and pluck them off?'

'More or less. The tough part is not to be greedy—and to know who's wearing rocks and who's wearing glass. Lot of bullshit in California. Basically, you just have to be a good mimic. Rich people are creatures more of habit than imagination.'

'Thanks.'

'You dress right, make sure you're seen at the right places—with a few of the right people—and nobody's going to question your pedigree. The last time I used that routine, I checked into the Wilshire with three thousand dollars. I checked out with thirty grand. I like California.'

'Sounds to me like you can't go back anytime soon.'

'I've been back. I tinted my hair, grew a little moustache, and wore jeans. I pruned Cassie Lawrence's roses.'

'Cassie Lawrence? The professional piranha who disguises herself as a patron of the arts?'

A perfect description. 'You've met?'

'Unfortunately. How much did you take her for?'

From the tone, Doug decided Whitney would've been pleased he'd had quite a haul. He also decided not to tell her he'd had a breeze casing the inside because Cassie had enjoyed watching him weed her azaleas without a shirt. She'd practically eaten him alive in bed. In return, he'd lifted an ornate ruby necklace and a pair of diamond earrings as big as Ping-Pong balls.

'Enough,' Doug answered at length. 'I take it you don't like her.'

'She has no class.' It was said simply, from a woman who did. 'Did you sleep with her?'

He choked on his drink, then set it down carefully. 'I don't think—'

'So you did.' A bit disappointed, Whitney studied him. 'I'm surprised I didn't see the scars.' She studied him another moment, thoughtful, quiet. 'Don't you find that sort of thing demeaning?'

He could've strangled her without a qualm. True, there were times he slept with a mark and enjoyed himself—and made certain the mark enjoyed herself as well. Payment for payment. But as a rule, he found using sex as close to ugly as he wanted to get. 'A job's a job,' he said briefly. 'Don't tell me you've never slept with a client.'

She lifted a brow at him, the way an amused woman could. 'I sleep with whom I choose,' she told him in a tone that stated she chose well.

'Some of us weren't born with choices.' Opening his book again, he stuck his nose in it and fell silent.

She wasn't going to make him feel guilty. Guilt was something he avoided more scrupulously than the police or a furious mark. The minute you let guilt start sucking at you, you were finished.

Funny, it didn't seem to bother her a bit that he stole for a living. It didn't bother her that he stole particularly from her class. She'd never blinked an eye at that. In fact, it was more than likely that he'd relieved some of her friends of excess personal property. She wasn't the least concerned.

Just what kind of woman was she anyway? He thought he understood her thirst for adventure, for excitement and taking chances. He'd lived his life on little else. But it didn't fit those cool, moneyed looks.

No, she hadn't missed a beat when he'd told her he

was a thief, but she'd looked at him with derision, and yes, dammit, pity, when she'd discovered he'd slept with a West-Coast shark for a handful of glitter.

And where had the glitter gotten him? Thinking back, Doug remembered he'd dumped the rocks on a fence in Chicago within twenty-four hours. After a routine haggle over price, a whim had taken him to Puerto Rico. Within three days, Doug had lost all but two thousand in the casinos. What had the glitter gotten him? he thought again, then grinned. One hell of a weekend.

Money just didn't stick to him. There was always another game, a sure thing at the track or a big-eyed woman with a sob story and a breathy voice. Still, Doug didn't consider himself a sucker. He was an optimist. He'd been born one and remained one even after more than fifteen years in the business. Otherwise, the kick would have gone out of it and he might as well be a lawyer.

Hundreds of thousands of dollars had passed through his hands. The operative words were passed through. This time would be different. It didn't matter that he'd said so before, this time *would* be different. If the treasure was half as big as the papers indicated, he'd be set for life. He'd never have to work again—except for an occasional job to keep in shape.

He'd buy a yacht and sail from port to port. He'd head for the south of France, bake in the sun, and watch women. He'd keep one step ahead of Dimitri for the rest of his life. Because Dimitri, as long as he lived, would never let up. That, too, was part of the game.

But the best part was the doing, the planning, the maneuvering. He'd always found it more exciting to anticipate the taste of champagne than to finish the bottle. Madagascar was only hours away. Once there he could start applying everything he'd been reading along with his own skills and experience.

He'd have to pace himself to keep ahead of Dimitri—but not so far ahead he ran into Dimitri on the other end. The trouble was that he wasn't sure how much his former employer knew about the contents of the envelope. Too much, he thought, absently touching a hand to his chest where it was still strapped. Dimitri was bound to know plenty because he always did. No one had ever crossed him and lived to enjoy it. Doug knew if he sat still too long he'd feel hot breath on the back of his neck.

He'd just have to play it by ear. Once they were there. . . He glanced over at Whitney. She was kicked back in her seat, eyes closed. In sleep she looked cool and serene and untouchable. Need stirred inside him, the need he'd always had for the untouchable. This time he'd just have to smother it.

It was strictly business between them, Doug mused. All business. Until he could talk her out of some cold cash and gently ditch her along the way. Maybe she'd been more help than he'd anticipated so far, but she was a type he understood. Rich and restless. Sooner or later, she'd become bored with the whole scheme. He had to get the cash before she did.

Certain he would, Doug pressed the button to release his seat back. He shut the book. What he'd read he wouldn't forget. His gift for recall would have breezed him through law school or any other profession. He was satisfied that it helped in the career he'd chosen. He never needed notes when he cased a job because he didn't forget. He never hit the same mark twice because names and faces stayed with him.

Money might slip through his fingers but details didn't. Doug took it philosophically. You could always get more money. Life would be pretty dull if you put it all in stocks and bonds instead of on the wheel or the horses. He was satisfied. Because he knew the next few days would be long and hard, he was even better than satisfied. It was more exciting to find a diamond in a garbage heap than in a display cabinet. He was looking forward to digging.

Whitney slept. It was the movement of the plane beginning its long descent that woke her. Thank God, was her first thought. She was thoroughly sick of planes. If she'd been traveling alone, she'd have taken the Concorde. Under the circumstances, she hadn't been willing to pick up the extra fare for Doug. His account in her little book was growing, and while she fully intended to collect every penny, she knew he fully intended she wouldn't.

To look at him now, you'd think he was as sincere as a first-year Boy Scout. She studied him as he slept, his hair mussed from travel, his hands closed over the book on his lap. Anyone would've taken him for an ordinary man of some means on his way to a European vacation. That was part of his skill, she decided. The ability to blend in with any group he chose would be invaluable.

Just what group did he belong to? The sleazy, hard-edged members of the underworld who dealt in dark alleys? She remembered the look in his eyes when he'd asked about Butrain. Yes, she was sure he'd seen his share of dark alleys. But belong? No, it didn't quite fit.

Even in the short time she'd known him she was certain he simply didn't belong. He was a maverick, perhaps not always wise, but always restless. That was part of the appeal. He was a thief, but she thought he had a certain code of honor. A court might not recognize it, but she did. And respected it.

He wasn't hard. She'd seen in his eyes when he spoke of Juan that he wasn't hard. He was a dreamer. She'd seen that in his eyes when he spoke of the treasure. And he was a realist. She'd heard that in his voice when he spoke of Dimitri. A realist knew enough to fear. He was too complex to belong. And yet. . .

He'd been Cassie Lawrence's lover. Whitney knew the West-Coast diamond ate men for breakfast. She was also very discriminating about whom she chose to share her sheets. What had Cassie seen? A young, virile man with a hard body? Perhaps that had been enough, but Whitney didn't think so. Whitney had seen for herself that morning in Washington just how attractive Doug Lord was, from head to foot. And she'd been tempted. By more than his body, she admitted. Style. Doug Lord had his own style, and it was that, she believed, that helped him over the threshold of homes in Beverly Hills or Bel Air.

She'd thought she understood him until he'd been embarrassed by her remark about Cassie. Embarrassed and angry when she'd expected a shrug and an offhand remark. So, he had feelings, and values, she mused. It made him more interesting and likable if it came to that.

Likable or not, she was going to find out more about this treasure and soon. She had too much money invested to move much further blindly. She'd gone with him on impulse and stayed through necessity. Instinctively she knew she was safer with him than without. Safety and impulse aside, Whitney was too much a businesswoman to invest in unnamed stock. Before too much more time had passed, she'd have a look at what he hoarded. She might like him, even understand him to a point, but she didn't trust him. Not an inch.

As he drifted awake, Doug came to the same conclusion about Whitney. He was going to keep the envelope close to his skin until he had the treasure in his hand.

As the plane began its final descent, they brought their chairs back up, smiled at each other, and calculated.

By the time they'd struggled with luggage and passed through customs, Whitney was more than ready to be horizontal in a stationary bed.

'Hotel de Crillon,' Doug told the cab driver and Whitney sighed.

'I apologize for ever doubting your taste.'

'Sugar, my problem's always been twenty-four-carat taste.' He brushed at the ends of her hair more in reflex than design. 'You look tired.'

'It hasn't been a restful forty-eight hours. Not that I'm complaining,' she added. 'But it's going to feel marvelous to stretch out for the next eight.'

He merely grunted and watched Paris whiz by. Dimitri wouldn't be far behind. His network of information was every bit as extensive as Interpol's. Doug could only hope the few curves he had thrown would be enough to slow down the chase.

As he thought, Whitney struck up a conversation with the driver. Because it was in French, Doug couldn't understand, but he caught the tone. Light, friendly, even flirtatious. Odd, he reflected. Most of the women he knew who'd grown up with portfolios never really saw the people who served them. It was one of the reasons he'd found it so easy to steal from them. The rich were insular, but no matter how often the less endowed said so, the rich weren't unhappy. He'd bullshitted his way into their circle often enough to know that money could buy happiness. It just cost a bit more every year.

'What a cute little man.' Whitney stepped on to the

curb and breathed in the scent of Paris. 'He said I was the most beautiful woman to sit in his cab in five years.'

Doug watched her pass bills to the doorman before she breezed into the hotel. 'And earned himself a fat tip, I'll bet,' he muttered. The way she tossed money around, they'd be broke again before they landed in Madagascar.

'Don't be such a cheapskate, Douglas.'

He ignored that and took her arm. 'You read French as well as you speak it?'

'Need some help reading the menu?' she began, then stopped. '*Tu ne parle pas français, mon cher?*' While he studied her in silence, she smiled. 'Fascinating. I should have caught on before that everything wasn't translated.'

'Ah, Mademoiselle MacAllister!'

'Georges.' She sent the desk clerk a smile. 'I couldn't stay away.'

'Always a pleasure to have you back.' His eyes lit again as he spotted Doug over her shoulder. 'Monsieur Lord. Such a surprise.'

'Georges.' Doug met Whitney's speculative look briefly. 'Mademoiselle MacAllister and I are traveling together. I hope you have a suite available.'

Romance bloomed in Georges' head. If he hadn't had a suite, Georges would have been tempted at that moment to vacate one. 'But of course, of course. And your papa, mademoiselle, he is well?'

'Very well, thank you, Georges.'

'Charles will take your bags. Enjoy your stay.'

Whitney pocketed her key without glancing at it. She knew the beds in the Crillon were soft and seductive. The water in the taps was hot. A bath, a little caviar from room service, and a bed. In the morning she'd have a few hours in the beauty salon before they took the last leg of the journey.

'I take it you've stayed here before.' Whitney slipped into the elevator and leaned against the wall.

'From time to time.'

'A profitable place, I assume.'

Doug only smiled at her. 'The service is excellent.'

'Hmmm.' Yes, she could see him here, sipping champagne and nibbling pâté. Just as she could see him running through alleys in DC. 'How lucky for me we've never crossed paths here before.' When the doors opened, she strolled out ahead. Doug took her arm and steered her to the left. 'The ambience is important, I suppose, in your business,' she added.

He allowed his thumb to brush over the inside of her elbow. 'I have a taste for rich things.'

She only gave him an easy smile that said he wouldn't sample her until she was ready.

The suite was no less than she expected. Whitney let the bellman fuss a few moments, then eased him out with a tip. 'So. . .' She plopped down on the sofa and kicked off her shoes. 'What time do we leave tomorrow?'

Instead of answering, he took a shirt from his suitcase, balled it up until it wrinkled, then tossed it over a chair. As Whitney watched, he took various articles of clothing out and draped them here and there throughout the suite.

'Hotel rooms are so impersonal until you have your own things around, aren't they?'

He mumbled something and dropped socks on the carpet. It wasn't until he moved to her cases that she objected.

'Just a minute.'

'Half the game's illusion,' he told her and tossed a

pair of Italian heels into a corner. 'I want them to think we're staying here.'

She grabbed a silk blouse out of his hands. 'We are staying here.'

'Wrong. Go hang a couple of things in the closet while I mess up the bathroom.'

Left with the blouse in her hands, Whitney tossed it down and followed him. 'What are you talking about?'

'When Dimitri's muscle gets here, I want them to think we're still around. It might only buy us a few hours, but it's enough.' Systematically, he went through the big, plush bath unwrapping soap and dropping towels. 'Go get some of your face junk. We'll leave a couple bottles.'

'Oh no we won't. What the hell am I supposed to do without it?'

'We ain't going to the ball, sugar.' He went into the master bedroom and tumbled the covers. 'One bed'll do,' he muttered. 'They wouldn't believe we weren't sleeping together anyway.'

'Are you padding your ego or insulting mine?'

He pulled out a cigarette, lit up, and blew out smoke, all without taking his eyes off her. For a moment, just a moment, she wondered what he was capable of. And if she'd like it after all. Saying nothing, he strode back into the next room and began to rifle her cases.

'Damn it, Doug, those are my things.'

'You'll get them back, for Chrissake.' Choosing a handful of cosmetics at random, he started back to the bath.

'That moisturizer costs me sixty-five dollars a bottle.'

'For this?' Interested, he turned the bottle over. 'And I thought you were practical.'

'I'm not leaving this room without it.'

'Okay.' He tossed it back to her and dumped the rest

on the vanity. 'This'll do.' As he passed through the suite again, he stubbed out the half-smoked cigarette and lit another. 'We've got just about enough,' he decided as he crouched down to close Whitney's case. A little swatch of lace caught his eye. He lifted out a pair of sheer bikini briefs. 'You fit in these?' He could see her in them. He knew better than to let his imagination go in that direction, but he could see her in them and nothing else.

She resisted the urge to snatch them out of his hand. That was easy. The pressure that formed low in her stomach as he brushed his fingers over the material wasn't as easily controlled. 'When you've finished playing with my underwear, why don't you tell me what's going on?'

'We check in.' After a moment, Doug tossed the little excuse of lace back in her bag. 'Then we take our bags down the service elevator and get back to the airport. Our flight leaves in an hour.'

'Why didn't you tell me before?'

He snapped her bag closed. 'Didn't come up.'

'I see.' Whitney took a stroll around the suite until she thought her temper might hold. 'Let me explain something to you. I don't know how you worked before, and it isn't important. This time'—she turned back to face him—'this time, you've got a partner. Whatever little plans you have in your head are half mine.'

'You don't like the way I work, you can back out right now.'

'You owe me.' When he started to object, she took a step closer, drawing her book from her purse as she moved. 'Should I read off the list?'

'Screw your list. I've got gorillas on my ass. I can't worry about accounting.'

'You'd better worry about it.' Still calm, she dropped the book back into her purse. 'Without me you'll go treasure hunting with empty pockets.'

'Sugar, a couple hours in this hotel and I'd have enough money to take me anywhere I wanted to go.'

She didn't doubt it, but her gaze remained level with his. 'But you don't have time to play cat burglar and we both know it. Partners, Douglas, or you fly to Madagascar with eleven dollars in your pocket.'

Damn her for knowing what he had, almost to the penny. He crushed out his cigarette, then picked up his own bag. 'We've got a plane to catch. Partner.'

Her smile came slowly, and with such a gleam of satisfaction he was tempted to laugh. Whitney slipped on her shoes and picked up a tote bag. 'Get that case, will you?' Before he could swear at her, she was moving to the door. 'I only wish I'd had time for a bath.'

Because of the ease with which they rode the service elevator down and walked out of the hotel, Whitney imagined he'd used that escape route before. She decided she could drop a letter to Georges in a few days and ask him to store her things until she could pick them up. She hadn't even had a chance to wear that blouse yet. And the color was very flattering.

All in all it seemed like a waste of time to her, but she was willing to humor Doug, for the moment. Besides, in the mood he was in they were better off in a plane than sharing a suite. And she wanted some time to think. If the papers he had, or some of them at any rate, were in French, then it was obvious he couldn't read them. She could. A smile touched her lips. He wanted to ditch her, she wasn't fool enough to think otherwise, but she'd just made herself even more useful. All she had to do now was persuade him to let her do some translating.

Still, she wasn't in the best of moods herself when they pulled up at the airport. The thought of going through customs again, of boarding another plane, was enough to make her snarl.

'It seems we could've checked into a second-class hotel and had a few hours.' Sweeping back her hair, she thought of the bath again. Hot, steamy, fragrant. 'I'm beginning to think you're paranoid about this Dimitri. You treat him as though he's omnipotent.'

'They say he is.'

Whitney stopped and turned. It was the way he said it, as though he half believed it, that made her flesh crawl. 'Don't be ridiculous.'

'Cautious.' He scanned the terminal as they walked. 'You're better off walking around a ladder than under it.'

'The way you talk about him, you'd think he wasn't human.'

'He's flesh and blood,' Doug murmured, 'but that doesn't make him human.'

The shiver skimmed along her skin again. Turning toward Doug, she jolted into someone and dropped her bag. With an impatient mutter, she bent to pick it up. 'Look, Doug, no one could possibly have caught up with us already.'

'Shit.' Grabbing her arm, he yanked her into a gift shop. With another shove, she was up to her eyes in T-shirts.

'If you wanted a souvenir—'

'Just look, sweetheart. You can apologize later.' With a hand on the back of her neck, he steered her head to the left. After a moment, Whitney recognized the tall, dark man who'd chased them in Washington. The moustache, the little white bandage on his cheek. She didn't need to be told that the two men with him belonged to Dimitri. And where was Dimitri himself? She caught herself sliding down lower and swallowing.

'Is that—'

'Remo.' Doug mumbled the word. 'They're faster than I thought they'd be.' He rubbed a hand over his mouth and swore. He didn't like the feeling that the web was widening at Dimitri's leisure. If he and Whitney had strolled another ten yards, they'd have walked into Remo's arms. Luck was the biggest part of the game, he reminded himself. It was what he liked the best. 'It'll take them a while to track down the hotel. Then they'll sit and wait.' He grinned a little, nodding. 'Yeah, they'll wait for us.'

'How?' Whitney demanded. 'For God's sake how could they be here already?'

'When you're dealing with Dimitri, you don't ask how. You just look over your shoulder.'

'He'd need a crystal ball.'

'Politics,' Doug said. 'Remember what your old man told you about connections? If you had one in the CIA and you made a call, pushed a button, you could be on top of someone without leaving your easy chair. A call to the Agency, to the Embassy, to Immigration, and Dimitri had a handle on our passports and visas before the ink was dry.'

She moistened her lips and tried to pretend her throat hadn't gone dry. 'Then he knows where we're going.'

'You bet your ass. All we have to do is stay one step ahead. Just one.'

Whitney let out a little sigh when she realized her heart was thumping. The excitement was back. If she gave herself time it would smother the fear. 'Looks like you know what you're doing after all.' When he turned his head to scowl at her she gave him a quick, friendly kiss. 'Smarter than you look, Lord. Let's go to Madagascar.'

Before she could rise, he caught her chin in his hand. 'We're going to finish this there.' His fingers tightened briefly, but long enough. 'All of this.'

She met him look for look. They had too far to go to give in now. 'Maybe,' she said. 'But we have to get there first. Why don't we catch that plane?'

Remo picked up a silky bit of fluff Whitney would have called a nightgown. He balled it into his fist. He'd have his hands on Lord and the woman before morning. This time they wouldn't slip through his fingers and make him look like a fool. When Doug Lord walked back in the door he'd put a bullet between his eyes. And the woman—he'd take care of the woman. This time . . . slowly he ripped the gown in half. The silk tore with hardly a whisper. When the phone rang, he jerked his head, signaling the other men to flank the door. Using the tip of his thumb and finger, Remo lifted the receiver. When he heard the voice, his sweat glands opened.

'You've missed them again, Remo.'

'Mr Dimitri.' He saw the other men look over and turned his back. It was never wise to let fear show. 'We've found them. As soon as they come back, we'll—'

'They won't be back.' With a long, smooth sigh, Dimitri blew out smoke. 'They've been spotted at the airport, Remo, right under your nose. The destination is Antananarivo. Your tickets are waiting for you. Be prompt.'

# CHAPTER FOUR

Whitney pushed open the wooden shutters on the window and took a long look at Antananarivo. It didn't, as she'd thought it would, remind her of Africa. She'd spent two weeks once in Kenya and remembered the heady morning scent of meat smoking on sidewalk grills, of towering heat and a cosmopolitan flair. Africa was only a narrow strip of water away, but Whitney saw nothing from her window that resembled what she remembered of it.

Nor did she find a tropical island flair. She didn't sense the lazy gaiety she'd always associated with islands and island people. What she did sense, though she wasn't yet sure why, was a country completely unique to itself.

This was the capital of Madagascar, the heart of the country, city of open-air markets and hand-drawn carts existing in complete harmony and total chaos alongside high-rise office buildings and sleek modern cars. It was a city, so she expected the habitual turmoil that brewed in cities. Yet what she saw was peaceful: slow, but not lazy. Perhaps it was just the dawn, or perhaps it was inherent.

The air was cool with dawn so that she shivered, but didn't turn away. It didn't have the smell of Paris, or Europe, but of something riper. Spice mixed with the first whispers of heat that threatened the morning chill. Animals. Few cities carried even a wisp of animal in their air. Hong Kong smelled of the harbor and London

of traffic. Antananarivo smelled of something older
that wasn't quite ready to fade under concrete or steel.

There was a haze as heat hovered above the cooler
ground. Even as she stood, Whitney could feel the
temperature change, almost degree by degree. In
another hour, she thought, the sweat would start to
roll and the air would smell of that as well.

She had the impression of houses stacked on top of
houses, stacked on top of more houses, all pink and
purple in the early light. It was like a fairy tale: sweet
and a little grim around the edges.

The town was all hills, hills so steep and breathless
that stairs had been dug, built into rock and earth to
negotiate them. Even from a distance they seemed
worn and old and pitched at a terrifying angle. She saw
three children and their dog heedlessly racing down
and thought she might get winded just watching them.

She could see Lake Anosy, the sacred lake, steel
blue and still, ringed by the jacaranda trees that gave it
the exotic flair she'd dreamed of. Because of the
distance, she could only imagine the scent would be
sweet and strong. Like so many other cities, there were
modern buildings, apartments, hotels, a hospital, but
sprinkled among them were thatched roofs. A stone's
throw away were rice paddies and small farms. The
fields would be moist and glitter in the afternoon sun.
If she looked up toward the highest hill, she could see
the palaces, glorious in the dawn, opulent, arrogant,
anachronistic. She heard the sound of a car on a wide
avenue below.

So they were here, she thought, stretching and
drawing in the cool air. The plane trip had been long
and tedious, but it had given her time to adjust to what
had happened and to make some decisions of her own.
If she were honest, she had to admit that she'd made

her decision the moment she'd stepped on the gas and started her race with Doug. True, it had been an impulse, but she'd stick by it. If nothing else, the quick stop in Paris had convinced her that Doug was smart and she was in for the count. She was thousands of miles away from New York now, and the adventure was here.

She couldn't change Juan's fate, but she could have her own personal revenge by beating Dimitri to the treasure. And laughing. To accomplish it, she needed Doug Lord and the papers she'd yet to see. See them she would. It was a matter of learning how to get around Doug.

Doug Lord, Whitney mused, stepping away from the window to dress. Who and what was he? Where did he come from and just where did he intend to go?

A thief. Yes, she thought he was a man who might lift stealing to the level of a profession. But he wasn't a Robin Hood. He might steal from the rich, but she couldn't picture him giving to the poor. Whatever he—acquired, he'd keep. Yet she couldn't condemn him for it. For one, there was something about him, some flash she'd seen right from the beginning. A lack of cruelty and a dash of what was irresistible to her. Daring.

Then, too, she'd always believed if you excelled at something, you should pursue it. She had an idea that he was very good at what he did.

A womanizer? Perhaps, she thought, but she'd dealt with womanizers before. Professional ones who could speak three languages and order the best champagne were less admirable than a man like Doug Lord who would womanize in all good humor. That didn't worry her. He was attractive, even appealing when he wasn't arguing with her. She could handle the physical part of it. . .

Though she could remember what it was like to lie beneath him with his mouth a teasing inch above hers. There'd been a pleasant, breathless sort of sensation she'd have liked to explore a bit further. She could remember what it was like to wonder just how it would feel to kiss that interesting, arrogant mouth.

Not as long as they were business partners, Whitney reminded herself as she shook out a skirt. She'd keep things on the practical sort of level she could mark down in her notebook. She'd keep Doug Lord at a careful distance until she had her share of the winnings in her hand. If something happened later, then it happened. With a half smile, she decided it might be fun to anticipate it.

'Room service.' Doug breezed in, carrying a tray. He checked a moment, taking a brief but thorough look at Whitney who stood by the bed in a sleek, buff-colored teddy. She could make a man's mouth water. Class, he thought again. A man like him had better watch his step when he started to have fantasies about class. 'Nice dress,' he said easily.

Refusing to give him any reaction, Whitney stepped into the skirt. 'Is that breakfast?'

He'd break through that cool eventually, he told himself. In his own time. 'Coffee and rolls. We've got things to do.'

She drew on a blouse the color of crushed raspberries. 'Such as?'

'I checked the train schedule.' Doug dropped into a chair, crossed his ankles on the table and bit into a roll. 'We can be on our way east at twelve-fifteen. Meantime we've got to pick up some supplies.'

She took her coffee to the dresser. 'Such as?'

'Backpacks,' he said, watching the sun rise over the city outside. 'I'm not lugging that leather thing through the forest.'

Whitney took a sip of coffee before picking up her brush. It was strong, European style, and thick as mud. 'As in hiking?'

'You got it, sugar. We'll need a tent, one of those new lightweight ones that fold up to nothing.'

She drew the brush in a long, slow stroke through her hair. 'Anything wrong with hotels?'

With a quick smirk, he glanced over, then said nothing at all. Her hair looked like gold dust in the morning light. Fairy dust. He found it difficult to swallow. Rising, he paced over to the window so that his back was to her. 'We'll use public transportation when I think it's safe, then go through the back door. I don't want to advertise our little expedition,' he muttered. 'Dimitri isn't going to give up.'

She thought of Paris. 'You've convinced me.'

'The less we use public roads and towns, the less chance he has of picking up our scent.'

'Makes sense.' Whitney wound her hair into a braid and secured the end with a swatch of ribbon. 'Are you going to tell me where we're going?'

'We'll travel by rail as far as Tamatave.' He turned, grinning. With the sun at his back he looked more like a knight than a thief. His hair fell to his collar, dark, a bit unruly. There was a light of adventure in his eyes. 'Then, we go north.'

'And when do I see what it is that's taking us north?'

'You don't need to. I've seen it.' But he was already calculating how he could get her to translate pieces for him without giving her the whole.

Slowly, she tapped her brush against her palm. She wondered how long it would be before she could translate some of the papers, and keep a few snatches of information to herself. 'Doug, would you buy a pig in a poke?'

'If I liked the odds.'

With a half smile, she shook her head. 'No wonder you're broke. You have to learn how to hang on to your money.'

'I'm sure you could give me lessons.'

'The papers, Douglas.'

They were strapped to his chest again. The first thing he was going to buy was a knapsack where he could store them safely. His skin was raw from the adhesive. He was certain Whitney would have some pretty ointment that would ease the soreness. He was equally sure she'd mark the cost of it in her little notebook.

'Later.' When she started to speak again, he held up a hand. 'I've got a couple of books along you might like to read. We've got a long trip and plenty of time. We'll talk about it. Trust me, okay?'

She waited a moment, watching him. Trust, no, she wasn't foolish enough to feel it. But as long as she held the purse strings, they were a team. Satisfied, she swung her handbag strap over her shoulder and held out her hand. If she were going on a quest, she'd just as soon it be with a knight who had some tarnish on him. 'Okay, let's go shopping.'

Doug led her downstairs. As long as she was in a good mood, he might as well make his pitch. Companionably, he swung an arm around her shoulder. 'So, how'd you sleep?'

'Just fine.'

On their way through the lobby, he plucked a small purple blossom from a vase and tucked it behind her ear. Passion-flower—he thought it might suit her. Its scent was strong and sweet, as a tropical flower's should be. The gesture touched her, even as she distrusted it. 'Too bad we don't have much time to play tourist,' he said conversationally. 'The Queen's Palace is supposed to be something to see.'

'You have a taste for the opulent?'

'Sure. I always figured it was nice to live with a little flash.'

She laughed, shaking her head. 'I'd rather have a feather bed than a gold one.'

'"They say that knowledge is power. I used to think so, but I now know that they meant money."'

She stopped in her tracks and stared at him. What kind of a thief quoted Byron? 'You continue to surprise me.'

'If you read you're bound to pick up something.' Shrugging, Doug decided to steer away from philosophy and back to practicality. 'Whitney, we agreed to divide the treasure fifty-fifty.'

'After you pay me what you owe me.'

He gritted his teeth on that. 'Right. Since we're partners, it seems to me we ought to divide the cash we have fifty-fifty.'

She turned her head to give him a pleasant smile. 'Does it seem like that to you?'

'A matter of practicality,' he told her breezily. 'Suppose we got separated—'

'Not a chance.' Her smile remained pleasant as she tightened her hold on her purse. 'I'm sticking to you like an appendage until this is all over, Douglas. People might think we're in love.'

Without breaking rhythm, he changed tactics. 'It's also a matter of trust.'

'Whose?'

'Yours, sugar. After all, if we're partners, we have to trust each other.'

'I do trust you.' She draped a friendly arm around his waist. The mist was burning off and the sun was climbing. 'As long as I hold the bankroll—sugar.'

Doug narrowed his eyes. Classy wasn't all she was, he thought grimly. 'Okay then, how about an advance?'

'Forget it.'

Because choking her was becoming tempting, he broke away to face her down. 'Give me one reason why you should hold all the cash?'

'You want to trade it for the papers?'

Infuriated, he spun away to stare at the whitewashed house behind him. In the dusty side yard, flowers and vines tangled in wild abandon. He caught the scents of breakfast cooking and overripe fruit.

There was no way he could give her the slip as long as he was broke. There was no way he could justify lifting her purse and leaving her stranded. The alternative left him exactly where he was—stuck with her. The worst of it was he was probably going to need her. Sooner or later he'd need someone to translate the correspondence written in French, for no other reason than his own nagging curiosity. Not yet, he thought. Not until he was on more solid ground. 'Look, dammit, I've got eight dollars in my pocket.'

If he had much more, she reflected, he'd dump her without a second thought. 'Change from the twenty I gave you in Washington.'

Frustrated, he started down a set of steep stairs. 'You've got a mind like a damn accountant.'

'Thanks.' She hung on to the rough wooden rail and wondered if there were any other way down. She shielded her eyes and looked. 'Oh look, what's that, a bazaar?' Quickening her pace, she dragged Doug back with her.

'Friday market,' he grumbled. 'The zoma. I told you that you should read the guidebook.'

'I'd rather be surprised. Let's take a look.'

He went along because it was as easy, and perhaps cheaper, to buy some of the supplies in the open market as it was to buy them in one of the shops. There was time before the train left, he thought with a quick check of his watch. They might as well enjoy it.

There were thatch-roofed structures and wooden stalls under wide white umbrellas. Clothes, fabrics, gemstones were spread out for the serious buyer or the browser. Always a serious buyer, Whitney spotted an interesting mix of quality and junk. But it wasn't a fair, it was business. The market was organized, crowded, full of sound and scent. Wagons drawn by oxen and driven by men wrapped in white lambas were crammed with vegetables and chickens. Animals clucked and mooed and snorted in varying degrees of complaint as flies buzzed. A few dogs milled around, sniffing, and were shooed away or ignored.

She could smell feathers and spice and animal sweat. True, the roads were paved, there were sounds of traffic and not too far away the windows of a first-class hotel glistened in the burgeoning sun. A goat shied at a sudden noise and pulled on his tether. A child with mango juice dripping down his chin tugged on his mother's skirt and babbled in a language Whitney had never heard. She watched a man in baggy pants and a peaked hat point and count out coins. Caught by two scrawny legs, a chicken squawked and struggled to fly. Feathers drifted. On a rough blanket was a spread of amethysts and garnets that glinted dully in the early sun. She started to reach out, just to touch, when Doug pulled her to a display of sturdy leather moccasins.

'There'll be plenty of time for baubles,' he told her

and nodded toward the walking shoes. 'You're going
to need something more practical than those little strips
of leather you're wearing.'

With a shrug, Whitney looked over her choices.
They were a long way from the cosmopolitan cities she
was accustomed to, a long way from the playgrounds
the wealthy chose.

Whitney bought the shoes, then picked up a hand-
made basket, instinctively bargaining for it in flawless
French.

He had to admire her, she was a born negotiator.
More, he liked the way she had fun arguing over the
price of a trinket. He had a feeling she'd have been
disappointed if the haggling had gone too quickly or
the price had dropped too dramatically. Since he was
stuck with her, Doug decided to be philosophical and
make the best of the partnership. For the moment.

'Now that you've got it,' Doug said, 'who's going to
carry it?'

'We'll leave it in storage with the luggage. We'll
need some food, won't we? You do intend to eat on
this expedition?' Eyes laughing, she picked up a mango
and held it under his nose.

He grinned and chose another, then dropped both in
her basket. 'Just don't get carried away.'

She wandered through the stalls, joining in the
bargaining and carefully counting out francs. She fingered a necklace of shells, considering it as carefully as
she would a bauble of Cartier's. In time, she found
herself filtering out the strange Malagasy and listening,
answering, even thinking in French. The merchants
traded in a continual stream of give and take. It seemed
they were too proud to show eagerness, but Whitney
hadn't missed the marks of poverty on many.

How far had they come, she wondered, traveling in

wagons? They didn't seem tired, she thought as she
began to study the people as closely as their wares.
Sturdy, she would have said. Content, though there
were many without shoes. The clothes might be dusty,
some worn, but all were colorful. Women braided and
pinned and wound their hair in intricate, timely
designs. The zoma, Whitney decided, was as much a
social event as a business one.

'Let's pick up the pace, babe.' There was an itch
between his shoulder blades that was growing more
nagging. When Doug caught himself looking over his
shoulder for the third time, he knew it was time to
move on. 'We've got a lot more to do today.'

She dropped more fruit in the basket with vegetables
and a sack of rice. She might have to walk and sleep in
a tent, Whitney thought, but she wouldn't go hungry.

He wondered if she knew just what a startling
contrast she made among the dark merchants and
solemn-faced women with her ivory skin and pale hair.
There was an unmistakable air of class about her even
as she stood bargaining for dried peppers or figs. She
wasn't his style, Doug told himself, thinking of the
sequins-and-feathers type he normally drifted to. But
she'd be a hard woman to forget.

On impulse he picked up a soft cotton lamba and
draped it over her head. When she turned, laughing,
she was so outrageously beautiful he lost his breath. It
should be white silk, he thought. She should wear
white silk, cool, smooth. He'd like to buy her yards of
it. He'd like to drape her in it, in miles of it, then
slowly, slowly strip it from her until it was only her
skin, just as soft, just as white. He could watch her
eyes darken, feel her flesh heat. With her face beneath
his hands, he forgot she wasn't his style.

She saw the change in his eyes, felt the sudden

tension in his fingers. Her heart began a slow, insistent thudding against her ribs. Hadn't she wondered what he'd be like as a lover? Wasn't she wondering now when she could feel desire pouring out of him? Thief, philosopher, opportunist, hero? Whatever he was, her life was tangled with his and there was no going back. When the time came, they'd come together like thunder, no pretty words, no candlelight, no sheen of romance. She wouldn't need romance because his body would be hard, his mouth hungry, and his hands would know where to touch. Standing in the open market, full of exotic scents and sound, she forgot that he'd be easy to handle.

Dangerous woman, Doug realized as he deliberately relaxed his fingers. With the treasure almost within reach and Dimitri like a monkey on his back, he couldn't afford to think of her as a woman at all. Women—big-eyed women—had always been his downfall.

They were partners. He had the papers, she had the bankroll. That was as complicated as things were going to get.

'You'd better finish up here,' he said calmly enough. 'We have to see about the camping supplies.'

Whitney let out a quiet, cleansing breath and reminded herself he was already into her for over seven thousand dollars. It wouldn't pay to forget it. 'All right.' But she bought the lamba, telling herself it was simply a souvenir.

By noon they were waiting for the train, both of them carrying knapsacks carefully packed with food and gear. He was restless, impatient to begin. He'd risked his life and gambled his future on the small bulge of papers taped to his chest. He'd always played the odds, but this time, he held the bank. By summer, he'd be dripping in money, lying on some hot foreign beach sipping rum while some dark-haired, sloe-eyed woman rubbed oil over his shoulder. He'd have enough money to ensure that Dimitri would never find him, and if he wanted to hustle, he'd hustle for pleasure, not for his living.

'Here it comes.' Feeling a fresh surge of excitement, Doug turned to Whitney. With the shawl draped over her shoulders, she was carefully writing in her notepad. She looked cool and calm, while his shirt was already beginning to stick to his shoulder blades. 'Will you quit scrawling in that thing?' he demanded, taking her arm. 'You're worse than the goddamn IRS.'

'Just adding on the price of your train ticket, partner.'

'Jesus. When we get what we're after, you'll be knee-deep in gold and you're worried about a few francs.'

'Funny how they add up, isn't it?' With a smile, she dropped the pad back in her purse. 'Next stop. Tamatave.'

A car purred to a halt just as Doug stepped on to the train behind Whitney.

'There they are.' Jaw set, Remo reached beneath his jacket until his palm fit over the butt of his gun. The fingers of his other hand brushed over the bandage on his face. He had a personal score to settle with Lord now. It was going to be a pleasure. A small hand with the pinky only a stub closed with steely strength on his arm. The cuff was still white, studded this time with hammered gold ovals. The delicate hand, somehow elegant despite the deformity, made the muscles in Remo's arm quiver.

'You've let him outwit you before.' The voice was quiet and very smooth. A poet's voice.

'This time he's a dead man.'

There was a pleasant chuckle followed by a trail of expensive French tobacco smoke. Remo didn't relax or offer any excuses. Dimitri's moods could be deceiving and Remo had heard him laugh before. He'd heard him give that same mild, pleasant laugh as he'd seared the bottom of a victim's feet with blue flame from a monogrammed cigarette lighter. Remo didn't move his arm, nor did he open his mouth.

'Lord's been a dead man since he stole from me.' Something vile slipped into Dimitri's voice. It wasn't anger, but more power, cool and dispassionate. A snake doesn't always spew venom in fury. 'Get my property back, then kill him however you please. Bring me his ears.'

Remo gestured for the man in the back seat to get out and purchase tickets. 'And the woman?'

There was another stream of tobacco smoke as Dimitri thought it through. He'd learned years before that decisions made rashly leave a jagged trail. He preferred the smooth and the clean. 'A lovely woman and clever enough to sever Butrain's jugular. Damage her as little as possible and bring her back. I'd like to talk with her.'

Satisfied, he sat back, idly watching the train through the smoke glass of the car window. It amused and satisfied him to smell the powdery scent of fear drifting from his employees. Fear, after all, was the most elegant of weapons. He gestured once with his mutilated hand. 'A tedious business,' he said when Remo closed the car door. His sigh was delicate while he touched a scented silk handkerchief to his nose. The smell of dust and animal annoyed him. 'Drive back to the hotel,' he instructed the silent man at the wheel. 'I want a sauna and a massage.'

* * *

Whitney positioned herself next to a window and prepared to watch Madagascar roll by. As he had off and on since the previous day, Doug had his face buried in a guidebook.

'There are at least thirty-nine species of lemur in Madagascar and more than eight hundred species of butterflies.'

'Fascinating. I had no idea you were so interested in fauna.'

He looked over the top of the book. 'All the snakes are harmless,' he added. 'Little things like that are important to me when I'm sleeping in a tent. I always like to know something about the territory. Like the rivers here are full of crocs.'

'I guess that kills the idea of skinny dipping.'

'We're bound to run into some of the natives. There are several distinct tribes, and according to this everybody's friendly.'

'That's good news. Do you have a projection as to how long it should be before we get to where "X" marks the spot?'

'A week, maybe two.' Leaning back, he lit a cigarette. 'How do you say diamond in French?'

'*Diamant*.' Narrowing her eyes, she studied him. 'Did this Dimitri have anything to do with stealing diamonds out of France and smuggling them here?'

Doug smiled at her. She was close, but not close enough. 'No. Dimitri's good, but he didn't have anything to do with this particular heist.'

'So it is diamonds and they were stolen.'

Doug thought of the papers. 'Depends on your point of view.'

'Just a thought,' Whitney began, plucking the cigarette from him for a drag. 'But have you ever considered what you'd do if there was nothing there?'

'It's there.' He blew out smoke and watched her with his clear, green eyes. 'It's there.'

As always she found herself believing him. It was impossible not to. 'What are you going to do with your share?'

He stretched his legs on to the seat beside her and grinned. 'Wallow in it.'

Reaching in the bag, she plucked out a mango and tossed it to him. 'What about Dimitri?'

'Once I have the treasure, he can fry in hell.'

'You're a cocky sonofabitch, Douglas.'

He bit into the mango. 'I'm going to be a rich cocky sonofabitch.'

Interested, she took the mango for a bite of her own. She found it sweet and satisfying. 'Being rich's important?'

'Damn right.'

'Why?'

He shot her a look. 'You're speaking from the comfort of several billion gallons of fudge ripple.'

She shrugged. 'Let's just say I'm interested in your outlook on wealth.'

'When you're rich and you play the horses and lose, you get ticked off because you lost, not because you blew the rent money.'

'And that's what it comes down to?'

'Ever worried about where you were going to sleep at night, sugar?'

She took another bite of fruit before handing it back to him. Something in his voice had made her feel foolish. 'No.'

She lapsed into silence for a time as the train rumbled on, stopping at stations while people filed on or filed off. It was already hot, almost airless inside. Sweat, fruit, dust, and grime hung heavily. A man in a white

panama a few seats forward mopped at his face with a
large bandana. Because she thought she recognized
him from the zoma, Whitney smiled. He only pocketed
the bandana and went back to his newspaper. Idly
Whitney noticed it was English before she turned back
to a study of the landscape.

Grassy rolling hills raced by, almost treeless. Small
villages or settlements were huddled here and there
with thatch-roofed houses and wide barns positioned
near the river. What river? Doug had the guidebook
and could certainly tell her. She was beginning to
understand he could give her a fifteen-minute lecture
on it. Whitney preferred the anonymity of dirt and
water.

She saw no crisscross of telephone wires or power
poles. The people living along these endless, barren
stretches would have to be tough, independent, self-
sufficient. She could appreciate that, admire it, without
putting herself in their place.

Though she was a woman who craved the city with
its crowds and noise and pulse, she found the quiet and
vastness of the countryside appealing. She'd never
found it difficult to value both a wildflower and a full-
length chinchilla. They both brought pleasure.

The train wasn't quiet. It rumbled and moaned and
swayed while conversation was a constant babble. It
smelled, not too unpleasantly as air drifted through the
windows, of sweat. The last time she'd ridden a train
had been on impulse, she recalled. She'd had an air-
conditioned roomette that smelled of powder and
flowers. It hadn't been nearly as interesting a ride.

A woman with a thumb-sucking baby sat across from
them. He stared wide-eyed and solemn at Whitney
before reaching out with a pudgy hand to grab her

braid. Embarrassed, his mother yanked him away, rattling a quick stream of Malagasy.

'No, no, it's all right.' Laughing, Whitney stroked the baby's cheek. His fingers closed around hers like a small vise. Amused, she signed for the mother to pass him to her. After a few moments of hesitation and persuasion, Whitney took the baby on to her lap. 'Hello, little man.'

'I'm not sure the natives have heard of Pampers,' Doug said mildly.

She merely wrinkled her nose at him. 'Don't you like children?'

'Sure, I just like them better when they're housebroken.'

Chuckling, she gave her attention to the baby. 'Let's see what we've got,' she told him and reaching in her purse came up with a compact. 'How about this? Want to see the baby?' She held the mirror up for him, enjoying the gurgling laughter. 'Pretty baby,' she crooned, rather pleased with herself for amusing him. Just as amused as she, the baby pushed the mirror toward her face.

'Pretty lady,' Doug commented, earning a laugh from Whitney.

'Here, you try it.' Before he could protest, she'd passed the baby to him. 'Babies are good for you.'

If she'd expected him to be annoyed or to be awkward, she was wrong. As if he'd spent his life doing it, Doug straddled the baby on his lap and began to entertain him.

That was interesting, Whitney noted. The thief had a sweet side. Sitting back, she watched Doug bounce the baby on his knee and make foolish noises. 'Ever thought about going straight and opening a day-care center?'

He lifted a brow and snatched the mirror from her. 'Look here,' he told the baby, holding the mirror at an angle that had the sunlight flashing off it. Squealing, the baby grabbed the compact and pushed it toward Doug's face.

'He wants you to see the monkey,' Whitney said with a bland smile.

'Smartass.'

'So you've said.'

To satisfy the baby, Doug made faces in the mirror. Bouncing with delight, the baby knocked at the mirror, angling it back so that Doug had a quick view of the rear of the train. He tensed and, angling the mirror again, took a longer scan.

'Holy shit.'

'What?'

Still juggling the baby, he stared at her. Sweat pooled in his armpits and ran down his back. 'You just keep smiling, sugar, and don't look behind me. We've got a couple of friends a few seats back.'

Though her hands tensed on the arms of the seat, she managed to keep her gaze from darting back over Doug's shoulder. 'Small world.'

'Ain't it just.'

'Got any ideas?'

'I'm working on it.' He measured the distance to the door. If they got off at the next stop, Remo would be on them before they'd crossed the platform. If Remo was here, Dimitri was close. He kept his men on a short leash. Doug gave himself a full minute to fight the panic. What they needed was a diversion and an unscheduled departure.

'You just follow my lead,' Doug told her in undertones. 'And when I say go, you grab the knapsack and run toward the doors.'

Whitney glanced down the length of the train. There were women, children, old people jammed into seats. Not the place for a showdown, she decided. 'Do I have a choice?'

'No.'

'Then I'll run.'

The train slowed for the next stop, brakes squeaking, engine puffing. Doug waited until the crowd of incoming and outgoing passengers was at its thickest. 'Sorry old man,' he murmured to the baby, then gave his soft butt a hard pinch. On cue, the baby set up a yowling scream that had the concerned mother hopping up in alarm. Doug rose as well and set about causing as much confusion as possible in the crowded center aisle.

Sensing the game, Whitney stood and jostled the man at her right hard enough to dislodge the packages in his arms and send them scattering on the floor. Grapefruit bounced and squashed.

When the train began to move again, there were six people between Doug and where Remo sat, crowding the aisle and arguing among themselves in Malagasy. In a gesture of apology, Doug raised his arms and upended a net bag of vegetables. The baby sent up long, continuous howls. Deciding it was the best he could do, Doug slipped a hand down and gripped Whitney's wrist. 'Now.'

Together, they streaked toward the doors. Doug glanced up long enough to see Remo spring from his seat and begin to fight his way through the still-arguing group blocking the aisle. He caught a glimpse of another man wearing a panama tossing a newspaper aside and jumping up before he, too, was encircled by the crowd. Doug only had a second to wonder where he'd seen the face before.

'Now what?' Whitney demanded as she watched the ground begin to rush by beneath them.

'Now, we get off.' Without hesitating, Doug jumped, dragging her with him. He wrapped himself around her, tucking as they hit the ground so that they rolled together in a tangled heap. By the time they'd stopped, the train was yards away and picking up speed.

'Goddamn it!' Whitney exploded from on top of him. 'We could've broken our necks.'

'Yeah.' Winded, he lay there. His hands had worked up under her skirt to her thighs, but he barely noticed. 'But we didn't.'

Unappeased, she glowered at him. 'Well, aren't we lucky. Now what do we do?' she demanded, blowing loose hair out of her eyes. 'We're in the middle of nowhere, miles from where we're supposed to be and with no transportation to get there.'

'You've got your feet,' Doug tossed back at her.

'So do they,' she said between her teeth. 'And they'll be off at the next stop and doubling back for us. They've got guns and we've got mangos and a folding tent.'

'So the sooner we stop arguing and get going the better.' Unceremoniously, he pushed her from him and stood up. 'I never told you it'd be a picnic.'

'You never mentioned tossing me off a moving train either.'

'Just get your ass in gear, sweetheart.'

Rubbing a bruised hip, she rose until she stood toe to toe with him. 'You're crude, arrogant, and very dislikable.'

'Oh, excuse me.' He swept her a mock bow. 'Would you mind stepping this way so we can avoid getting a bullet in the brain, duchess?'

She stormed away and dragged up the backpack that had been knocked out of her hands on impact. 'Which way?'

Doug slipped his own pack over his shoulders. 'North.'

# CHAPTER FIVE

Whitney had always been fond of mountains. She could look back with pleasure on a two-week skiing vacation in the Swiss Alps. In the mornings, she'd ridden to the top of the slopes, admiring the view from a lift. The swishing rush of the ride down had always delighted her. A great deal could be said about a cozy après-ski with hot buttered rum and a crackling fire.

Once she'd enjoyed a lazy weekend in a villa in Greece, high on a rocky slope overlooking the Aegean. She'd appreciated the height, the view, and the quality of nature and antiquity—from the comfort of a terra-cotta balcony.

However, Whitney had never been big on mountain climbing—sweaty, leg-cramping mountain climbing. Nature wasn't all it was cracked up to be when it worked its way under the tender balls of your feet and dug in.

North, he'd said. Grimly she kept pace with him, up tough, rocky slopes and down again. She'd continue to keep pace with Lord, she promised herself as sweat dribbled down her back. He had the envelope. But while she'd hike with him, sweat with him, pant with him, there was absolutely no reason she had to speak to him.

No one, absolutely no one, told her to get her ass in gear and got away with it.

It might take days, even weeks, but she'd get him for it. There was one basic business rule she'd learned from her father. Revenge, chilled a bit, was much more palatable.

North. Doug looked around at the rugged, steep hills that surrounded them. The terrain was a monotony of high grass that fanned in the breeze and rough red scars where erosion had won. And rock, endless, unforgiving rock. Further up were a few sparse, spindly trees, but he wasn't looking for shade. From his vantage point there was nothing else, no huts, no houses, no fields. No people. For now, it was exactly what he wanted.

The night before while Whitney had slept, he'd studied the map of Madagascar he'd ripped from the stolen library book. He couldn't stand to mar a book of any kind, because books had given his imagination an outlet as a child, and kept him company through lonely nights as a man. But it had been necessary in this case. The ragged piece of paper fit nicely in his pocket while the book stayed in his pack. It was only there for backup. In his mind's eye, Doug separated the terrain into the three parallel belts he'd studied. The western lowlands didn't matter. As he strode up a rocky, rough path he hoped they'd detoured as far west as they'd have to. They'd stick to the highlands, avoid the river banks and open areas as long as they could. Dimitri was closer than he'd anticipated. Doug didn't want to guess wrong again.

The heat was already oppressive, but their water supply should last until morning. He'd worry about replenishing it when he had to. He wished he could be certain just how far north they should travel before they dared swing east to the coast and easier ground.

Dimitri might be waiting in Tamatave, soaking up wine and sunshine, dining on the fresh local fish.

Logically, that should be their first stop, so logically they had to avoid it. For the time being.

Doug didn't mind playing a game of wits, the bigger the odds the better. The sweeter the pot, as he'd once told Whitney. But Dimitri. . .Dimitri was a different story.

He hitched at the straps of his backpack until the weight settled more comfortably on his shoulders. And there wasn't only himself to think of this time. One of the reasons he'd avoided partnerships for so long was because he preferred having one body to worry about. His own. He shot a look across at Whitney, who'd been cooly silent since they'd left the train tracks and headed toward the highlands.

Damn woman, he thought for lack of anything better. If she thought the cold-shoulder routine was going to shake him up, she was dead wrong. It might make some of her fancy patent-leather jerks beg for a word of forgiveness, but as far as he was concerned, she was a hell of a lot more attractive when her mouth was shut anyway.

Imagine complaining because he'd gotten her off the train in one piece. Maybe she had a few bruises, but she was still breathing. Her problem was, he decided, she wanted everything all nice and pretty, like that high-class apartment of hers. . .or the tiny little piece of silk she was wearing under that skirt.

Doug shook away that particular thought in a hurry and concentrated on picking his way over the rocks.

He'd like to keep to the hills for a while—two days, maybe three. There was plenty of cover, and the going was rough. Rough enough, he was certain, to slow Remo and some of Dimitri's other trained hounds down. They were more accustomed to tramping down back alleys and into sleazy motel rooms than over rocks and hills. Those used to being hunted acclimated with more ease.

Pausing on a crest, he drew out the field glasses and took a long, slow sweep. Below and slightly west, he spotted a small settlement. The cluster of tiny red houses and wide barns bordered a patchwork of fields. Rice paddies, he decided, because of their moist emerald green color. He saw no power lines and was grateful. The farther away from civilization, the better. The settlement would be a Merina tribe, if his memory of the guidebook was accurate. Just beyond was a narrow winding river. Part of the Betsiboka.

Eyes narrowed, Doug followed its trail while an idea formed. True, the river flowed northwest, but the notion of traveling by boat had some appeal. Crocodiles or not, it was bound to be faster than going on foot, even for a short distance. Traveling by river was something he'd have to decide on when the time came. He'd take an evening or two to read up on it—what rivers would suit his purpose best and how the Malagasy traveled by them. He remembered skimming over something that had reminded him of the flatbed canoes the Cajuns used. Doug had traveled through the bayous on one himself after nearly bungling a job in a stately old house outside of Lafayette.

How much had he gotten for those antique pearl-handled dueling pistols? He couldn't remember. But the chase through the swamp where he'd had to pole his way across cypress trees and under dripping moss—that had been something. No, he wouldn't mind traveling by river again.

In any case, he'd keep an eye out for more settlements. Sooner or later, they'd need more food and have to bargain for it. Remembering the woman beside him, he decided that Whitney might just come in handy there.

Disgusted, and aching from bruises, Whitney sat on the ground. She wasn't going another step until she'd rested and eaten. Her legs felt entirely too much like they had the one and only time she'd tried the electric jogging track at the gym. Without giving Doug a glance she dug into her pack. The first thing she was going to do was change her shoes.

Replacing the glasses, Doug turned to her. The sun was straight up. They could make miles before dusk. 'Let's go.'

Cooly silent, Whitney found a banana and began to peel it in long, slow strips. Just let him tell her to move her ass this time. With her eyes on Doug's she bit into the fruit and chewed.

Her skirt was hiked up past her knees as she sat cross-legged on the ground. Damp with perspiration, her blouse clung to her. The neat braid she'd fashioned while he'd watched that morning had loosened so that pale, silky hair escaped to tease her cheekbones. Her face was as cool and elegant as marble.

'Let's move.' Desire made him edgy. She wasn't going to get to him, he promised himself. No way. Every time he let a woman get under his skin, he ended up losing. Maybe, just maybe, he'd get to her before they were finished, but there was no way this cool-eyed, skinny lady was going to shake his priorities. Money, the good life.

He wondered what it would be like to have her under him, naked, hot, and completely vulnerable.

Whitney leaned back against a rock and took another bite of fruit. A rare breeze moved hot air over her. Idly, she scratched the back of her knee. 'Up yours, Lord,' she suggested in perfectly rounded tones.

God, he'd like to make love with her until she was limp and slick and malleable. He'd like to murder her. 'Listen, sugar, we've got a lot of ground to cover today. Since we're on foot—'

'Your doing,' she reminded him.

He crouched down until they were at eye level. 'It was my doing that kept your empty head on your sexy shoulders.' Full of fury and frustration, of unwanted needs, he gripped her chin in his hand. 'Dimitri would just love to get his pudgy little hands on a classy number like you. Believe me, he's got a unique imagination.'

A quick thrill of fear went through her, but she kept her eyes level. 'Dimitri's your boogeyman, Doug, not mine.'

'He won't be selective.'

'I won't be intimidated.'

'You'll be dead,' he tossed back. 'If you don't do what you're told.'

Firmly, she pushed his hand away. Gracefully, she rose. Though the skirt was smudged with red dust and rent with a hole at the hip, it billowed around her like a cloak. The rough Malagasy shoes might have been glass slippers. He had to admire the way she pulled it off. It was innate, he was sure. No one could have taught her. If she'd been the peasant she looked like at that moment, she'd still have moved like a duchess.

One brow rose as she dropped the banana peel into his hand. 'I never do what I'm told. In fact, I often make a point not to. Do try to keep that in mind in the future.'

'Keep it up, sugar, and you're not going to have one.'

Taking her time, she brushed some of the dust from her skirt. 'Shall we go?'

He tossed the peel into a ravine and tried to convince himself he'd have preferred a woman who whimpered and trembled. 'If you're sure you're ready.'

'Quite sure.'

He took out his compass for another check. North. They'd keep heading north for a while yet. The sun might beat down unmercifully with no shade to fight it, and the ground might be misery itself to hike on, but the rocks and slopes offered some protection. Whether it was instinct or superstition, something was prickling at the back of his neck. He wouldn't stop again until sundown.

'You know, duchess, under different circumstances I'd admire that class of yours.' He began to walk in a steady, ground-eating pace. 'Right now you're in danger of becoming a pain in the ass.'

Long legs and determination kept her abreast with him. 'Breeding,' she corrected, 'is admirable under any circumstances.' She sent him an amused glance. 'And enviable.'

'You keep your breeding, sister, I'll keep mine.'

With a laugh, she tucked her arm through his. 'Oh, I intend to.'

He looked down at her neat, manicured hand. He didn't think there was another woman in the world who could make him feel as though he were escorting her to a ball when they were fighting their way up a rocky slope in the full afternoon sun. 'Decided to be friendly again?'

'I decided rather than sulk, I'd keep my eye open for the first opportunity to pay you back for the bruises. In the meantime, just how far are we going to walk?'

'The train ride would've taken about twelve hours, and we've got to follow a less direct route. You figure it out.'

'No need to be testy,' she said mildly. 'Can't we find a village and rent a car?'

'Let me know when you see the first Hertz sign. It'll be my treat.'

'You really should eat something, Douglas. Lack of food always puts me in a bad mood.' Turning away from him, she offered her pack. 'Go ahead, have a nice mango.'

Fighting a grin, he loosened the strap and reached in. The fact was he could use something warm and sweet at the moment. His fingers brushed over the net bag that held the fruit and touched something soft and silky. Curious, he drew it out and examined the tiny, lace-trimmed pair of bikini briefs. So she hadn't worn them yet. 'Great looking mangoes they have here.'

Whitney looked over her shoulder and watched him run the material between his fingers. 'Get your hands out of my pants, Douglas.'

He only grinned and held them up so that the sun beamed through them. 'Interesting phrasing. How come you bother wearing something like this anyway?'

'Modesty,' she said primly.

With a laugh, he stuffed them back in the pack. 'Sure.' Pulling out a mango, he took a big, greedy bite. Juice trickled wonderfully down his dry throat. 'Silk and lace always make me think of modest little nuns in underdeveloped countries.'

'What an odd imagination you have,' she observed as she half skidded down a slope. 'They always make me think of sex.'

With this she lengthened her stride to a marching pace and whistled smartly.

They walked. And walked. They slapped sunscreen on every inch of exposed skin and accepted the fact that they'd burn anyway. Flies buzzed and swooped, attracted by the scent of oil and sweat, but they learned to ignore them. Other than insects, they had no company.

As the afternoon waned Whitney lost her interest in the rolling, rocky highlands and the stretches of valley below. The earthy smells of dirt and sun-baked grass lost their appeal when she was streaked with both. She watched a bird fly overhead, caught in a current. Because she was looking up, she didn't see the long, slim snake that passed inches in front of her foot, then hid itself by a rock.

There wasn't anything exotic about dripping with sweat or slipping over pebbles. Madagascar would have held more appeal from the cool terrace of a hotel room. Only the thin edge of pride kept her from demanding that they stop. As long as he could walk, so, by God, could she.

From time to time she spotted a small village or settlement, always cupped near the river and spread out into fields. From the hills, they could see cook smoke, and when the air was right, hear the sounds of dogs or cattle. Voices didn't carry. Distance and fatigue gave Whitney a sense of unreality. Perhaps the huts and fields were only part of a stage.

Once, through Doug's field glasses, she watched workers bending over the swamplike paddies, many of the women with babies strapped in lambas papoose-style on their backs. She could see the moist ground shiver and give under the movement of feet.

In all her experience, her treks through Europe, Whitney had never seen anything quite like it. But then Paris, London, and Madrid offered the glitter and cosmopolitan touches she was accustomed to. She'd never strapped a pack on her back and hiked over the countryside before. As she shifted the weight yet again, she told herself there was always a first time—and a last. While she might enjoy the color, the terrain, and the openness, she'd enjoy it a hell of a lot more off her feet.

If she wanted to perspire, she wanted to do it in a sauna. If she wanted to exhaust herself, she wanted to do it trouncing someone in a few fast games of tennis.

Aching and sticky with sweat, she put one foot in front of the other. She wouldn't come in second place to Doug Lord or anyone else.

Doug watched the angle of the sun and knew they'd have to find a place to camp. Shadows were lengthening. To the west, the sky was already taking on streaks of red. Normally he did his best maneuvering at night but he didn't think the highlands of Madagascar was a good place to try his luck in the dark.

He'd traveled the Rockies at night once and had nearly broken his leg in the process. It didn't take much effort to remember his slide over the rocks. The unplanned trip down the cliff had masked his trail, but he'd had to limp his way into Boulder. When the sun set, they'd park and wait for dawn.

He kept waiting for Whitney to complain, to wail, to demand—to act in general as he considered a woman would act under the circumstances. Then again, Whitney hadn't acted the way he'd expected from the first moment they had set eyes on one another. The truth was, he wanted her to grumble. It would make it easier to justify dumping her at the first opportunity. After he'd skimmed her of most of her cash. If she complained, he could do both without a qualm. As it was, she wasn't slowing him down, and she was carrying her share of the load. It was only the first day, he reminded himself. Give her time. Hothouse flowers wilted quickly when they were exposed to real air.

'Let's take a look at that cave.'

'Cave?' Shielding her eyes, Whitney followed his gaze. She saw a very small arch and a very dark hole. 'That cave?'

'Yeah. If it isn't occupied by one of our four-legged friends, it'll make a nice hotel for the night.'

*Inside?* 'The Beverly Wilshire's a nice hotel.'

He didn't even spare her a glance. 'First we'd better see if there's a vacancy.'

Swallowing, Whitney watched him go over, strip off his pack, and crawl in. Just barely, she resisted the urge to call him out.

Everyone's entitled to a phobia, she reminded herself as she walked a bit closer. Hers was a terror of small, closed-in spaces. As tired as she was, she'd have walked another ten miles rather than crawl into that tiny arch of darkness.

'It ain't the Wilshire,' Doug said as he crawled back out. 'But it'll do. They have our reservations.'

Whitney sat down on a rock and took a long look around. There was nothing but more rock, a few scrubby pines, and pitted dirt. 'I seem to remember paying an exorbitant amount of money for that tent that folds up like a handkerchief. The one you insisted we had to have,' she reminded him. 'Haven't you ever heard of the pleasure of sleeping under the stars?'

'When someone's after my hide—and they've come close to peeling it a number of times—I like having a wall to keep my back to.' Still kneeling, he picked up his pack. 'I figure Dimitri's looking for us east of here, but I'm not taking any chances. It cools down in the highlands at night,' he added. 'In there we can risk a small fire.'

'A campfire.' Whitney examined her nails. If she didn't have a manicure soon, they'd look very tacky.

'Charming. In a little place like that, the smoke would suffocate us in minutes.'

Doug pulled a small hatchet out of his pack and unsnapped the leather sheath. 'After about five feet, the place opens up. I can stand.' Moving to a scrawny pine, he began hacking at a branch. 'Ever go spelunking?'

'I beg your pardon?'

'Cave exploring,' he explained, grinning. 'I knew this geology major once. Her daddy owned a bank.' As he recalled, he'd never been able to soak her for much more than a couple of memorable nights in a cave.

'I've always found better things to explore than holes in the ground.'

'Then you've missed a lot, sugar. This might not be a tourist attraction, but it has some first-class stalactites and stalagmites.'

'How exciting,' she said dryly. When she looked toward the cave, all she saw was a very small, very dark hole in the rock. Just looking made the sweat bead cold on her forehead.

Annoyed, Doug began to chop a respectable pile of firewood. 'Yeah, I guess a woman like you wouldn't find rock formations very exciting. Unless you could wear them.' They were the same, women who wore French dresses and Italian shoes. That's why for pleasure he'd go for a fan dancer or a pro. You got honesty there, and some spine.

Whitney stopped staring at the opening long enough to narrow her eyes at him. 'Just what do you mean, a woman like me?'

'Spoiled,' he said, bringing his hatchet down with a thwack. 'Shallow.'

'Shallow?' She rose from the rock. Accepting the spoiled wasn't a problem. Whitney figured truth was truth. 'Shallow?' she repeated. 'You've a hell of a nerve calling me shallow, Douglas. I didn't steal my way to easy street.'

'You didn't have to.' He tilted his head so that their eyes met. His cool, hers hot. 'That's about all that separates us, duchess. You were born with a silver spoon in your mouth. I was born to take it out and hock it.' Tucking the firewood under his arm, he walked back to the cave. 'You wanna eat, lady, then get your high-class buns inside. You won't get any room service here.' Agile and quick, he grabbed his pack by the straps, crawled inside, and disappeared.

How dare he! With her hands on her hips, Whitney stared at the cave. How dare he speak to her that way after she'd walked miles and miles? Since she'd met him, she'd been shot at, threatened, chased, and pushed from a train. And it had cost her thousands of dollars to date. How dare he talk to her as though she were a simpering, empty-headed debutante? He wouldn't get away with it.

Briefly, she thought of simply going on herself, leaving him to his cave like any bad-tempered bear. Oh no. She took a long, deep breath as she stared at the opening in the rock. No, that was just what he'd like. He'd be rid of her and have the treasure all to himself. She wouldn't give him the satisfaction. If she killed herself in the process, she was sticking with him until she got every dime he owed her. And a lot more.

A hell of a lot more, she added as she gritted her teeth. Getting down on her hands and knees, Whitney started into the cave.

Pure anger carried her the first couple of feet. Then the cold sweat of fear broke out and riveted her to the spot. As her breath began to hitch, she couldn't move forward, she couldn't move back. It was a box, airless, dark. The lid was already closed to suffocate her.

She felt the walls, the dark, damp walls closing in, squeezing the air out of her. Laying her head down on the hard dirt, she fought back hysteria.

No, she wouldn't give in to it. Couldn't. He was just ahead, just ahead. If she whimpered, he'd hear. Pride was every bit as strong as fear. She wouldn't have his scorn. Gasping for air, she inched forward. He'd said the cave opened up. She'd be able to breathe if she could just crawl in a few more feet.

Oh God, she needed light. And room. And air. Balling her hands into fists, she fought off the need to scream. No, she wouldn't make a fool of herself in front of him. She wouldn't be his entertainment.

While she lay prone, waging her own war, she caught a glimpse of a flicker of light. Staying perfectly still, she concentrated on the sound of crackling wood, the light smell of pine smoke. He'd started the fire. It wouldn't be dark. She had only to pull herself a few more feet and it wouldn't be dark.

It took all her strength, and more courage than she'd known she had. Inch by inch, Whitney worked her way in until the light played over her face and the walls spread out around her. Drained, she lay for a moment, just breathing.

'So you decided to join me.' With his back to her, Doug drew out one of the clever folding pans to heat water. The thought of hot, strong coffee had kept him going the last five miles. 'Dinner's Dutch treat, sugar. Fruit, rice, and coffee. I'll handle the coffee. Let's see what you can do with the rice.'

Though she was still shaking, Whitney brought herself into a sitting position. It would pass, she told herself. In moments, the nausea, the light-headedness would pass. Then somehow, she'd make him pay.

'Too bad we didn't pick up a little white wine, but. . .' When he turned to her, he trailed off. Was it a trick of the light, or was her face gray? Frowning, he set the water on the heat, then went to her. No trick of the light, he decided. She looked as though she'd dissolve if he touched her. Unsure of himself, Doug crouched down. 'What's wrong?'

Her eyes were hot and hard when she looked at him. 'Nothing.'

'Whitney.' Reaching out, he touched her hand. 'Jesus, you're like ice. Come on over to the fire.'

'I'm fine.' Furious, she snatched her hand away. 'Just leave me alone.'

'Hold on.' Before she could spring to her feet, he had her by the shoulders. He could feel her tremble under his palms. She wasn't supposed to look so young, so defenseless. Women with blue-chip stocks and watery diamonds had all the defense they needed. 'I'll get you some water,' he murmured. In silence, he reached for the canteen and opened it for her. 'It's a little warm, take it slow.'

She sipped. It was indeed warm and tasted like iron. She sipped again. 'I'm all right.' Her voice was tense, fretful. He wasn't supposed to be kind.

'Just rest a minute. If you're sick—'

'I'm not sick.' She thrust the canteen back in his hands. 'I have a little problem with closed-in places, okay? I'm in now and I'll be just fine.'

Not a little problem, he realized as he took her hand again. It was damp, cold and trembling. Guilt hit him, and he hated it. He hadn't given her a break since they'd started. Hadn't wanted to. Once she made him soften, made him care, he'd lose his edge. It had happened before. But she was trembling.

'Whitney, you should've told me.'

She angled her chin in a gesture he couldn't help but admire. 'I have a bigger problem with being a fool.'

'Why? It never bothers me.' Grinning, he brushed the hair away from her temples. She wasn't going to cry. Thank Christ.

'People who're born fools rarely notice.' But the sting had gone out of her voice. Her lips curved. 'Anyway, I'm in. It might take a crane to get me back out again.' Breathing slowly, she glanced around at the wide cave with the pillars of rock he'd spoken of. In the firelight, the rocks shone, rising up or plunging down. Here and there, the cave floor was littered with dung. She saw, with a shudder, a snake skin curled against the wall. 'Even if it is decorated in early Neanderthal.'

'We've got a rope.' He ran his knuckles quickly back and forth over her cheek. Her color was coming back. 'I'll just haul you out when the time comes.' Glancing back, he saw the water beginning to simmer. 'Let's have some coffee.'

When he turned away, Whitney touched her cheek where it was warmed from his hand. She hadn't thought he could be so unexpectedly sweet when there wasn't an angle.

Or was there?

With a sigh, she stripped off her pack. She still held the bankroll. 'I don't know anything about cooking rice.' Opening her bag, she took out the mesh bag of fruit. More than a few had suffered bruises and the scent was hot and ripe. No seven-course dinner had ever looked so good.

'Due to our current facilities, there's nothing to do

but boil and stir. Rice, water, fire—' He glanced over his shoulder. 'You should be able to handle it.'

'Who does the dishes?' she wanted to know as she poured water into another pan.

'Cooking's a joint effort, so's cleaning.' He shot her a fast, appealing grin. 'After all, we're partners.'

'Are we?' Smiling sweetly, Whitney set the pot to heat and drew in the scent of coffee. The cave, full of dung and damp, was immediately civilized. 'Well, partner, how about letting me see the papers?'

Doug handed her a metal mug filled with coffee. 'How about letting me hold half the money?'

Over the rim, her eyes laughed at him. 'Coffee's good, Douglas. Another of your many talents.'

'Yeah, I was blessed.' Drinking half his cup down, he let it run hot and strong through him. 'I'll leave you in the kitchen while I see to our sleeping arrangements.'

Whitney hauled out the sack of rice. 'Those sleeping bags better feel like feather beds after what I paid for them.'

'You've got a dollar fixation, sugar.'

'I've got the dollars.'

He mumbled under his breath as he cleared spaces for their bags. While Whitney couldn't catch the words, she caught the drift. Grinning, she began to scoop out rice. One handful, two. If rice was to be their main dish, she mused, they might as well eat hearty. She dug into the bag again.

It took her a moment to figure out the mechanics of the spoon that folded into itself. By the time she had it opened, the water was beginning to boil rapidly. Rather pleased with herself, Whitney began to stir.

'Use a fork,' Doug told her while he unrolled the sleeping bags. 'A spoon mashes the grains.'

'Picky, picky,' she mumbled, but went through the same process on the fork as she had on the spoon. 'How do you know so much about cooking anyway?'

'I know a lot about eating,' he said easily. 'I don't often find myself in the position where I can go out and enjoy the kind of food I'm entitled to.' He unrolled the second bag next to the first. After a moment's consideration, he moved them about a foot apart. He was better off with a little distance. 'So I learned to cook. It's satisfying.'

'As long as someone else is doing it.'

He only shrugged. 'I like it. Brains and a few spices and you can eat like a king—even in a ratty motel room with bad plumbing. And when things get tough, I'll work in a restaurant for awhile.'

'A job? I'm disillusioned.'

He let the light sarcasm pass over him. 'The only one I've ever been able to tolerate. Besides, you eat good, and it gives you a chance to check out the clientele.'

'For a possible mark.'

'No opportunity should ever go undeveloped.' Spreading the lower half of his body on one of the bags, he leaned against the cave wall and drew out a cigarette.

'Is that a Boy Scout motto?'

'If it isn't, it should be.'

'I bet you'd've just raked in the merit badges, Douglas.'

He grinned, enjoying the quiet, the tobacco, the coffee. He'd learned long ago to enjoy what he could when he could, and plan for more. Much more. 'One way or the other,' he agreed. 'How's dinner?'

She swiped through the rice with the fork again. 'It's coming.' As far as she could tell.

He stared up at the ceiling, idly studying the formation of rock that had dripped down over centuries into long spears. He'd always been drawn to antiquity, to heritage, perhaps because he didn't have much of one himself. He knew that it was part of the reason he was driving himself north, toward the jewels and the stories behind them. 'Rice is better sautéed in butter, with mushrooms and a few slivers of almonds.'

She felt her stomach groan. 'Eat a banana,' she suggested and tossed him one. 'Any idea how we're going to replace our water?'

'I think we might slip down to the village below in the morning.' He blew out a cloud of smoke. The only thing that was missing, he decided, was a nice hot tub and a pretty, scented blonde to scrub his back. It would be one of the first things he saw to when the treasure was in his hands.

Whitney crossed her legs under her and chose another piece of fruit. 'Do you think it's safe?'

He shrugged and finished off his coffee. It was always more a matter of need than safety. 'We need water, and we might bargain for some meat.'

'Please, you'll get me excited.'

'The way I figure it, Dimitri knew the train was going to Tamatave, so that's where he'll be looking for us. By the time we get there, I'm hoping he's looking someplace else.'

She bit into the fruit. 'So he doesn't have any idea where you're ultimately going?'

'No more than you do, sugar.' He hoped. But the itch between his shoulder blades had yet to let up. Taking a last deep drag, Doug flicked the stub of the cigarette into the fire. 'As far as I know, he's never seen the papers, at least not all of them.'

'If he's never seen them, how did he find out about the treasure?'

'Faith, sugar, same as you.'

She lifted a brow at his smirk. 'This Dimitri doesn't strike me as a man of faith.'

'Instinct then. There was a man named Whitaker who figured to sell the papers to the highest bidder and make a nice profit without having to dig for it. The idea of a treasure, a documented one, caught Dimitri's imagination. I told you he had one of those.'

'Indeed. Whitaker. . .' Turning the name over in her mind, Whitney forgot to stir. 'George Allan Whitaker?'

'The same.' Doug blew out smoke. 'Know him?'

'Casually. I dated one of his nephews. It's thought he made his money from bootlegging among other things.'

'Smuggling, among other things, especially in the last ten years or so. Remember the Geraldi sapphires that were stolen, let's see, in seventy-six?'

She frowned a minute. 'No.'

'You should keep up with current events, sugar. Read that book I lifted in DC.'

'*Missing Gems through the Ages*?' Whitney moved her shoulders. 'I prefer fiction when I read.'

'Broaden your outlook. You can learn anything there is to learn from books.'

'Really?' Interested, she studied him again. 'So you like to read?'

'Next to sex, it's my favorite pastime. Anyway, the Geraldi sapphires. The sweetest set of rocks since the crown jewels.'

Impressed, she lifted a brow. 'You stole them?'

'No.' He settled his shoulders against the wall. 'I was on a down swing in seventy-six. Didn't have the fare to get to Rome. But I've got connections. So did Whitaker.'

'*He* stole them?' Her eyes widened as she thought of the skinny old man.

'Arranged,' Doug corrected. 'Once he hit sixty Whitaker didn't like getting his hands dirty. He liked to pretend he was an expert in archeology. Didn't you catch any of his shows on public television?'

So he watched PBS too. A well-rounded thief. 'No, but I heard he wanted to be a land-locked Jacques Cousteau.'

'Not enough class. Still, he got pretty good ratings for a couple of years. Bullshitting a lot of hotshots with big bank accounts into financing digs. He had a real smooth game going.'

'My father said he was full of shit,' Whitney said idly.

'Your father's got more on the ball than fudge ripple. Anyway, Whitaker played middleman for a lot of rocks and art objects that crossed from one side of the Atlantic to the other. About a year ago, he conned some English lady out of a bunch of old documents and correspondence.'

Her interest peaked. 'Our papers?'

He didn't care for the plural pronoun but shrugged it off. 'The lady considered it all part of art or history—cultural value. She'd written a lot of books on stuff like that. There was some general involved who'd nearly worked a deal with her, but it seemed Whitaker knew more about flattering matrons. And Whitaker had a more basic train of thought. Greed. Trouble was, he was broke and had to do some campaigning for funds for the expedition.'

'That's where Dimitri came in.'

'Exactly. Like I said, Whitaker threw the bidding open. It was supposed to be a business deal. Partners,' he added with a slow smile. 'Dimitri decided he didn't like the competitive market and made an alternate proposition.' Doug crossed his ankles and peeled the banana. 'Whitaker could let him have the papers, and Dimitri'd let Whitaker keep all his fingers and toes.'

Whitney took another nibble of fruit but it wasn't easy to swallow. 'Sounds like a forceful businessman.'

'Yeah, Dimitri loves to wheel and deal. Trouble was, he used a little too much persuasion on Whitaker. Apparently the old man had a heart problem. Keeled over before Dimitri had the papers or his jollies—I'm not sure which pissed him off more. An unfortunate accident, or so Dimitri said when he hired me to steal them.' Doug bit into the banana and savored it. 'He went into graphic detail on how he'd planned to change Whitaker's mind—for the purpose of putting the fear of God into me so I wouldn't get any ideas myself.' He remembered the tiny pair of silver pliers Dimitri had fondled during the interview. 'It worked.'

'But you took them anyway.'

'Only after he'd double-crossed me,' he told her over another bite of banana. 'If he'd played it straight, he'd have the papers. I'd've taken my fee and a little vacation in Cancun.'

'But this way, you have them. And no opportunity should go undeveloped.'

'You got it, sister. Jesus Christ!' Doug bolted up and scrambled to the fire. In automatic defense, Whitney curled up her legs, expecting anything from a slimy snake to a hideous spider. 'Damn, woman, how much rice did you put in here?'

'I—' She broke off and stared as he grabbed at the pan. Rice was flowing over the sides like lava. 'Just a couple of handfuls,' she said as she bit her lip to keep from laughing.

'My ass.'

'Well, four.' She pressed the back of her hand to her mouth as he dug for a plate. 'Or five.'

'Four or five,' he muttered while scooping rice on to the plates. 'How the hell did I end up in a cave in Madagascar with "I Love Lucy"?'

'I told you I couldn't cook,' she reminded him as she studied the brownish, sticky mass on the plate. 'I simply proved it.'

'In spades.' When he heard her muffled chuckle, he glanced over. She sat Indian style, her skirt and blouse filthy, the ribbon at the end of her braid dangling free. He remembered how she'd looked the first time he'd seen her, cool and sleek in a white fedora and lush furs. Why was it she looked every bit as appealing now? 'You laugh,' he tossed back, shoving a plate at her. 'You're going to have to eat your share.'

'I'm sure it's fine.' With the fork she'd used for cooking, she poked into the rice. Bravely, he thought, she took the first bite. The flavor was nutty and not altogether unpleasant. With a shrug, Whitney ate more. Though she'd never been in the position of being a beggar, she'd heard they couldn't be choosers. 'Don't be a baby, Douglas,' she told him. 'If we can get our hands on some mushrooms and almonds, we'll fix it your way next time.' With the enthusiasm of a child over a bowl of ice cream, she dug in. Without fully realizing it, Whitney had had her first experience of real hunger.

Eating at a slower pace, and with less enthusiasm, Doug watched her. He'd been hungry before, and figured he'd be hungry again. But she. . . . Perhaps she was dining on rice off a tin plate, in a skirt that was streaked with grime, but class shone through. He found it fascinating, and intriguing enough to make it worth-while discovering if it always would. The partnership, he mused, might be more interesting than he'd bargained for. For as long as it lasted.

'Douglas, what about the woman who gave Whitaker the map?'

'What about her?'

'Well, what happened to her?'

He swallowed a lump of rice. 'Butrain.'

When she glanced up, he saw the fear come and go in her eyes and was glad. Better for both of them if she understood this was the big league. But her hands were steady when she reached for the coffee.

'I see. So you're the only one alive who's seen those papers.'

'That's right, sugar.'

'He'll want you dead, and me too.'

'That's also right.'

'But I haven't seen them.'

Casually, Doug dug for more rice. 'If he gets his hands on you, you can't tell him anything.'

She waited a minute, studying him. 'You're a firstclass bastard, Doug.'

This time he grinned because he'd heard the light trace of respect. 'I like first class, Whitney. I'm going to live there the rest of my life.'

Two hours later, he was cursing her again, though only to himself. They'd let the fire burn down to embers so that the light in the cave was dim and red. Somewhere, deeper, water dripped in a slow, musical plop. It reminded him of a pricey, innovative little bordello in New Orleans.

They were both exhausted, both aching from the demands of a very long, very arduous day. Doug stripped off his shoes with his only thought one of the pleasures of unconsciousness. He never doubted he'd sleep like a rock.

'You know how to work that thing?' he asked idly as he opened his own bag.

'I think I can handle a zipper, thanks.'

Then he made the mistake of glancing over—and not looking away again.

Without any show of self-consciousness, Whitney drew off her blouse. He remembered just how thin the material of her teddy had looked in the morning light. When she pulled off her skirt, his mouth watered.

No, she wasn't self-conscious, she was nearly comatose with fatigue. It never occurred to her to make a play at modesty. Even if she'd thought it out, Whitney would have considered the teddy adequate cover. She wore a fraction of that on a public beach. Her only thought was of getting horizontal, of closing her eyes, and of oblivion.

If she hadn't been so tired, she might have enjoyed the discomfort she was causing in the region of Doug's loins. It might have given her some pleasure to know his muscles had tensed as he watched the subtle flicker of firelight play over her skin as she bent to unzip her bag. She'd have gotten pure feminine satisfaction knowing he sucked in his breath as the thin material rose up at her thighs and pulled over her bottom with her movements.

Without giving it a thought, she climbed into the sleeping bag and pulled up the zipper. Nothing was visible but a cloud of pale hair untangled from the braid. With a sigh, she pillowed her head on her hands. 'Good night, Douglas.'

'Yeah.' He pulled off his shirt, then gripped the edge of adhesive and held his breath. Ruthlessly he ripped and the fire snaked across his chest. Whitney never budged as his curse bounced off the cave walls. She was already asleep. Cursing her, cursing the pain, he snapped the envelope into his knapsack before he climbed into his own bag. In sleep, she sighed, low and quiet.

Doug stared at the ceiling of the cave, wide awake and aching from more than bruises.

# CHAPTER SIX

Something tickled the back of her hand. Fighting to cling to sleep, Whitney flicked her wrist in a lazy, back-and-forth action and yawned.

She had always kept her own hours. If she wanted to sleep until noon, she slept until noon. If she wanted to get up at dawn, she did. When the mood struck her, she could work for an eighteen-hour stretch. With a similar enthusiasm, she could sleep for the same length of time.

At the moment, she wasn't interested in anything but the vague, rather pretty dream she was having. When she felt the feathery brush on her hand again, she sighed, only slightly annoyed, and opened her eyes.

In all probability, it was the biggest, fattest spider she'd ever seen. Big, black, and hairy, it probed and skiddled with its bowed legs. Her hand only inches from her face, Whitney watched as it loomed full in her vision, moving lazily across her knuckles in a direct line to her nose. For a moment, dazed with sleep, she just stared at it in the dim light.

Her knuckles. Her nose.

Realization came loud and clear. Muffling a yelp, she knocked the spider off and several feet into the air. It landed with an audible plop on the cave floor, then meandered drunkenly away.

The spider hadn't frightened her. She never considered the possibility that it might have been poisonous. It was simply ugly, and Whitney had a basic disrespect for the ugly.

Sighing in disgust, she sat up and combed her fingers through her tangled hair. Well, she supposed when one slept in a cave, one could expect a visit from ugly neighbors. But why hadn't it visited Doug instead? Deciding there was no reason why he should sleep when she'd been so rudely awakened, Whitney turned with the full intention of giving him a hard shove.

He was gone, and so was his sleeping bag.

Uneasy, but not yet alarmed, she looked around. The cave was empty, with the rock formations Doug had spoken of giving it the look of an abandoned and slightly dilapidated castle. The cook fire was only a pile of glowing embers. The air smelled ripe. Some of the fruit was already turning. Doug's pack, like his sleeping bag, was gone.

The bastard. The rotten bastard. He had taken himself off, with the papers, and left her stuck in a damn cave with a couple of pieces of fruit, a sack of rice, and a spider as big as a dinner plate.

Too furious to think twice, she dashed across the cave and began to crawl through the tunnel. When her breath clogged up, she pushed on. The hell with phobias, she told herself. No one was going to double-cross her and get away with it. To catch him, she had to get out. And when she caught him. . .

She saw the opening and concentrated on it, and revenge. Panting, shuddering, she pulled herself into the sunshine. Scrambling up, she drew in all of her breath and let it out on a shout.

'*Lord!* Lord, you sonofabitch!' The sound rang out and bounced back at her, half as loud but twice as angry. Impotently, she looked around at red hills and rock. How was she supposed to know which way he'd gone?

North. Damn north, he had the compass. And he

had the map. After gritting her teeth, Whitney shouted again. 'Lord, you bastard, you won't get away with it!'

'With what?'

She spun on her heel and nearly bumped into him. 'Where the hell were you?' she demanded. In a blaze of relief and anger, she gripped his shirt and yanked him against her. 'Where the hell did you go?'

'Easy, sugar.' Companionably, he patted her bottom. 'If I'd known you wanted to get your hands on me, I'd've stuck around longer.'

'Around your throat.' With a jerk, she released him.

'Gotta start somewhere.' He set his pack near the mouth of the cave. 'D'you think I'd ditch you?'

'At the very first opportunity.'

He had to admit, she was sharp. The idea had occurred to him, but after a quick look around that morning, he hadn't been able to justify leaving her in a cave in the middle of nowhere. Still, the opportunity was bound to come up.

In an attempt to keep her from getting a step ahead of him, he poured on the charm. 'Whitney, we're partners. And. . .' He lifted a hand and ran a fingertip down her cheek. 'You're a woman. What kind of man would I be if I left you alone in a place like this?'

She met his engaging smile with one of her own. 'The kind of man who'd sell the hide off the family dog if the price was right. Now, where were you?'

He wouldn't have sold the hide, but he might have hocked the whole dog if it had been necessary. 'You're a hard lady. Look, you were sleeping like a baby.' As she had all night, while he'd spent a good part of it tossing, turning, and fantasizing. He wouldn't forgive her for that easily, but there was a time and place for payback. 'I wanted to do a little scouting around, and I didn't want to wake you.'

She let out a long breath. It was reasonable, and he was back. 'Next time you want to play Daniel Boone, wake me up.'

'Whatever you say.'

Whitney saw a bird fly overhead. She watched it for a moment until she was calm. The sky was clear, so was the air—and it was cool. The heat was a few hours off. There was a quality of silence she'd only heard a few times in her life. It soothed.

'Well, since you've been scouting, how about a report?'

'Everything's quiet down in the village.' Doug drew out a cigarette which Whitney plucked from his fingers. Pulling out another, he lit them both. 'I didn't go close enough to get any real particulars, but it looks like business as usual. The way I see it, since everybody's calm and easy, it's a good time to drop in for a visit.'

Whitney looked down at her grime-smeared teddy. 'Like this?'

'I've already told you it's a nice dress.' And it had a certain appeal with one strap hanging down her shoulder. 'Anyway, I didn't pass a local beauty parlor and boutique.'

'You might go visiting looking sleazy.' Whitney cast one long look up his body, then down. 'In fact, I'm sure you do. I, on the other hand, intend to wash and change first.'

'Suit yourself. There's probably enough water left to get some of the dirt off your face.'

When she reached up automatically to brush at her cheeks, he grinned. 'Where's your pack?'

She looked back at the mouth of the cave. 'It's in there.' Her gaze was defiant, her voice firm when she looked back at him. 'I'm not going back in there.'

'Okay, I'll get your gear. But you're not going to be

able to primp all morning. I don't want to lose any time.'

Whitney merely lifted a brow as he started to crawl back in. 'I never primp,' she said mildly. 'It's not necessary.'

With an indistinguishable grunt, he was gone. Nibbling on her lip, she glanced at the cave, then at the pack he'd left beside it. She might not have a second chance. Without hesitation, she crouched down and began to root through it.

There was cooking gear to paw through, and his clothes. She came upon a rather elegant man's brush that had her pausing a moment. When had he gotten that? she wondered. She knew every item down to his shorts that she'd paid for. Light fingers, she decided, and dropped the brush back in.

When she found the envelope, she took it out carefully. This had to be it. She glanced back at the cave again. Quickly, she drew out a thin, yellowed sheet sealed in plastic and skimmed it. It was written in French in a trim, feminine hand. A letter, she thought. No, part of a journal. And the date—my God. Her eyes widened as she studied the neat, faded writing. September 15, 1793. She was standing in the blazing sunlight, on a wind- and weather-torn rock, holding history in her hand.

Whitney scanned it again, quickly, catching phrases of fear, of anxiety, and of hope. A young girl had written it, of that she was all but certain because of references to Maman and Papa. A young aristocrat, confused and afraid by what was happening to her life and her family, Whitney reflected. Did Doug have any idea just what he was carrying in a canvas sack?

It wouldn't do to take the chance to read it thoroughly now. Later. . .

Carefully, Whitney closed his pack again and set it down next to the mouth of the cave. Thinking, she tapped the envelope against her open palm. It was very satisfying to beat a man at his own game, she decided, then heard the sounds of his return.

Holding the envelope in one hand, she looked down at herself. Dumbly, she passed the other hand from her breast to her waist. Just where the hell was she supposed to hide it? Mata Hari must've had a sarong at least. Frantic, she started to slip it down the bodice of the teddy, then realized the absurdity. She might as well pin it to her forehead. With seconds to spare, she slipped it down her back and left the rest to luck.

'Your luggage, Ms MacAllister.'

'I'll catch you later with your tip.'

'That's what they all say.'

'Good service is its own reward.' She gave him a smug smile. He gave one right back to her. Whitney had taken the pack from his hand when a sudden thought occurred to her. If she could lift the envelope so easily, then he. . .Opening the pack, she dug for her wallet.

'You'd better get moving, sugar. We're already late for our morning call.' He started to take her arm when she shoved the pack into his stomach. The hiss of air coming from his lungs gave her great satisfaction. 'My wallet, Douglas.' Taking it out, she opened it and saw he'd been generous enough to leave her with a twenty. 'It appears you've had your sticky fingers on it.'

'Finders, keepers—partner.' Though he'd hoped she wouldn't find him out quite so soon, he only shrugged. 'Don't worry, you'll get your allowance.'

'Oh, really?'

'You could say I'm a traditionalist.' Satisfied with

the new situation, he started to heft his pack on to his back. 'I feel a man should handle the money.'

'You could say you're an idiot.'

'Whatever, but I'm handling the money from here on.'

'Fine.' She gave him a sweet smile he immediately mistrusted. 'And I'm holding the envelope.'

'Forget it.' He handed her back her pack. 'Now go change like a good girl.'

Fury leapt into her eyes. Nasty words scrambled on her tongue. There was a time for temper, Whitney reminded herself, and there was a time for cool heads. Another of her father's basic rules of business. 'I said I'm holding it.'

'And I said. . .' But he trailed off at the expression on her face. A woman who'd just been neatly ripped off shouldn't look smug. Doug glanced down at his pack. She couldn't have. Then he looked back at her. Like hell she couldn't.

Tossing down his pack, he dug into it. It only took a moment. 'All right, where is it?'

Standing in the full sunlight, she lifted her hands, palms up. The brief teddy shifted over her like air. 'It doesn't appear necessary to search me.'

He narrowed his eyes. It wasn't possible to keep them from sweeping down her. 'Hand it over, Whitney, or you'll be buck naked in five seconds.'

'And you'll have a broken nose.'

They faced each other, each determined to come out on top. And each with no choice but to accept a standoff.

'The papers,' he said again, giving masculine strength and dominance one last shot.

'The money,' she returned, relying on guts and feminine guile.

Swearing, Doug reached in his back pocket and took out a wad of bills. When she reached for them, he jerked them back out of range. 'The papers,' he repeated.

She studied him. He had a very direct gaze, she decided. Very clear, very frank. And he could lie with the best of them. Still, in some areas, she'd trust him. 'Your word,' she demanded. 'Such as it is.'

His word was worth only what he chose it to be worth. With her, he discovered, that would be entirely too much. 'You've got it.'

Nodding, she reached behind her, but the envelope had slipped down out of range. 'There're a lot of reasons I don't like to turn my back on you. But. . .' With a shrug, she did so. 'You'll have to get it out yourself.'

He ran his gaze down the smooth line of her back, over the subtle curve of hip. There wasn't much of her, he thought, but what there was, was excellent. Taking his time, he slipped his hand under the material and worked his way down.

'Just get the envelope, Douglas. No detours.' She folded her arms under her breasts and stared straight ahead. The brush of his fingers over her skin aroused every nerve. She wasn't accustomed to being moved by so little.

'It seems to have slipped down pretty low,' he murmured. 'It might take me awhile to find it.' It occurred to him that he could indeed have her out of the teddy in five seconds flat. What would she do then? He could have her beneath him on the ground before she'd taken the breath to curse him. Then he'd have what he'd sweated about the night before.

But then, he thought as his fingers brushed the edge of the envelope, she might have a hold over him he couldn't afford. Priorities, he reminded himself as his fingers touched both the stiff manila and the soft skin. It was always a matter of priorities.

It took all her concentration to hold perfectly still. 'Douglas, you've got two seconds to get it out, or lose the use of your right hand.'

'A little jumpy, are you?' At least he had the satisfaction of knowing she was churning even as he was. He hadn't missed the huskiness in her voice or the slight tremor. With the tip between his finger and thumb, he pulled out the envelope.

Whitney turned quickly, hand outstretched. He had the map, he had the money. He was fully dressed, she was all but naked. He didn't doubt she could make her way down to the village and wangle herself transportation back to the capital. If he was going to ditch her, there would never be a better time.

Her eyes stayed on his, calm and direct. Doug didn't doubt she'd read every thought in his head.

Though he hesitated, Doug found in this case his word was indeed his word. He slapped the wad of bills into her hand.

'Honor among thieves—'

'—is a major cultural myth,' she finished. There'd been a moment, just a moment, when she hadn't been sure he'd come through. Picking up her pack and the canteen, she walked toward the pine. It was cover of a sort. Though at the moment, she'd have preferred a steel wall with a heavy bolt. 'You might consider shaving, Douglas,' she called out. 'I hate my escort to look rangy.'

He ran a hand over his chin and vowed not to shave for weeks.

\* \* \*

Whitney found it was easier going when the destination was in sight.

One memorable summer in her early teens she'd stayed on her parents' estate on Long Island. Her father had developed an acute obsession with the benefits of exercise. Every day that she hadn't been quick enough to escape, she'd been railroaded into jogging with him. She remembered her determination to keep up with a man twenty-five years her senior, and the trick she'd developed of looking for the stately white dormers of the house. Once she saw them, she could lope ahead, knowing the end was in sight.

In this case, the destination was only a huddle of buildings adjoining green, green fields and a brown, westward-flowing river. After a day of hiking and a night in a cave, it looked as tidy as New Rochelle to Whitney.

In the distance, men and women worked in the rice paddies. Forests had been sacrificed for fields. The Malagasy, a practical people, worked diligently to justify the exchange. They were islanders, she remembered, but without the breezy laziness island life often promoted. As she looked at them, Whitney wondered how many had ever seen the sea.

Cattle, with bored eyes and swishing tails, milled in paddocks. She saw a battered jeep, wheelless, propped on a stone. From somewhere came the monotonous ring of metal against metal.

Women hung clothes on a line, bright, flowery shirts that contrasted with their plain, workday clothes. Men in baggy pants hoed a long, narrow garden. A few sang as they worked, a tune not so much cheerless as purposeful.

At their approach, heads turned and work stopped.

No one came forward except a skinny black dog who ran in circles in front of them and sent up a clatter.

East or West, Whitney knew curiosity and suspicion when she saw it. She thought it a pity she wore nothing more cheerful than a shirt and slacks. She cast a look at Doug. With his unshaven face and untidy hair, he looked more like he'd just come from a party—a long one.

As they drew closer, she made out a smatter of children. Some of the smaller ones were carried on the backs and hips of men and women. In the air was the smell of animal dung and of cooking. She ran a hand over her stomach, scrambling down a hill behind Doug who had his nose in the guidebook.

'Do you have to do that now?' she demanded. When he only grunted, she rolled her eyes. 'I'm surprised you didn't bring one of those little clip-on lights so you could read in bed.'

'We'll pick one up. The Merina are of Asiatic stock—they're the upper crust of the island. You'd relate to that.'

'Of course.'

Ignoring the humor in her voice, he read on. 'They have a caste system that separates the nobles from the middle class.'

'Very sensible.'

When he shot her a look over the top of the book, Whitney only smiled. 'Sensibly,' he returned, 'the caste system was abolished by law, but they don't pay much attention.'

'It's a matter of legislating morality. It never seems to work.'

Refusing to be drawn, Doug glanced up, squinting. The people were drawing together, but it didn't look like a welcome committee. According to everything he'd read, the twenty or so tribes or groups of the Malagasy had packed up their spears and bows years ago. Still. . .he looked back at dozens of dark eyes. He and Whitney would just have to take it one step at a time.

'How do you think they'll respond to uninvited guests?' More nervous than she wanted to admit, Whitney tucked her arm into his.

He'd slid his way without invitation into more places than he could count. 'We'll be charming.' It usually worked.

'Think you can pull it off?' she asked and strode by him to the flatland at the base of the hill.

Though Whitney felt uneasy, she continued to walk forward, shoulders back. The crowd grumbled, then parted, making a path for a tall, lean-faced man in a stark black robe over a stiff white shirt. He might have been the leader, the priest, the general, but she knew with only a glance that he was important. . .and he was displeased with the intrusion.

He was also six-four if he was an inch. Abandoning pride, Whitney took a step back so that Doug was in front of her.

'Charm him,' she challenged in a mutter.

Doug scanned the tall black man with the crowd behind him. He cleared his throat. 'No problem.' He tried his best grin. 'Morning. How's it going?'

The tall man inclined his head, regal, aloof, and disapproving. In a deep, rumbling voice he tossed out a spate of Malagasy.

'We're a little short on the language, Mister, ah. . .' Still grinning, Doug stuck out his hand. It was stared at, then ignored. With the grin still plastered on his face, he took Whitney's elbow and shoved her forward. 'Try French.'

'But your charm was working so well.'

'This isn't a good time to be a smartass, sugar.'

'You said they were friendly.'

'Maybe he hasn't read the guidebook.'

Whitney studied the rock-hard face several long inches above hers. Maybe Doug had a point. She smiled, swept up her lashes, and tried a formal French greeting.

The man in black robes stared at her for ten pulsing seconds, then returned it. She nearly giggled in relief. 'Okay, good. Now apologize,' Doug ordered.

'For what?'

'For butting in,' he said between his teeth as he squeezed her elbow. 'Tell him we're on our way to Tamatave, but we lost our way and our supplies are low. Keep smiling.'

'It's easy when you're grinning like my idiot brother.'

He swore at her, but softly, with his lips still curved. 'Look helpless, the way you would if you were trying to fix a flat on the side of the road.'

She turned her head, brow raised, eyes cool. 'I beg your pardon?'

'Just do it, Whitney. For Chrissake.'

'I'll tell him,' she said with a regal sniff. 'But I won't look helpless.' When she turned back, her expression changed to a pleasant smile. 'We're very sorry to have intruded on your village,' she began in French. 'But we're traveling to Tamatave, and my companion—' She gestured toward Doug and shrugged. 'He's lost his way. We're very low on food and water.'

'Tamatave is a very long way to the east. You go on foot?'

'Unfortunately.'

The man studied Doug and Whitney again, cooly, deliberately. Hospitality was part of the Malagasy heritage, their culture. Still, it was extended discriminately. He saw nerves in the eyes of the strangers, but no ill will. After a moment, he bowed. 'We are pleased to receive guests. You may share our food and water. I am Louis Rabemananjara.'

'How do you do?' She extended her hand and this time, he accepted the gesture. 'I'm Whitney Mac-Allister and this is Douglas Lord.'

Louis turned to the waiting crowd and announced they would have guests in the village. 'My daughter, Marie.' At his words a small, coffee-skinned young woman with black eyes stepped forward. Whitney eyed her intricate braided hairstyle and wondered if her own stylist could match it.

'She will see to you. When you have rested, you will share our food.' With this, Louis stepped back into the crowd.

After a quick survey of Whitney's periwinkle shirt and slim pants, Marie lowered her eyes. Her father would never permit her to wear anything so revealing. 'You are welcome. If you will come with me, I will show you where you can wash.'

'Thank you, Marie.'

They moved in Marie's wake through the crowd. One of the children pointed at Whitney's hair and spilled out with an excited babble before being shushed by his mother. A word from Louis sent them back to work before Marie had reached a small, one-story house. The roof was thatched and pitched steeply to spread shade. The house was built of wood and some of the boards were bowed and curled. The windows sparkled. Outside the door was a square woven mat bleached nearly white. When Marie opened the door, she stepped back to allow her guests to enter.

Everything inside was neat as a pin, every surface

polished. The furniture was rough and plain, but bright cushions were plumped in every chair. Yellow daisylike flowers stood in a clay pot by a window where wooden slats held back the intense light and heat.

'There is water and soap.' She led them farther inside where the temperature seemed to drop ten degrees. From a small alcove, Marie produced deep wooden bowls, pitchers of water, and cakes of brown soap. 'We will have our midday meal soon, with you as our guests. Food will be plentiful.' She smiled for the first time. 'We have been preparing for *fadamihana*.'

Before Whitney could thank Marie, Doug took her arm. He hadn't followed the French, but the one phrase had rung a bell. 'Tell her we, too, honor their ancestors.'

'What?'

'Just tell her.'

Humoring him, Whitney did so and was rewarded with a beaming smile. 'You are welcome to what we have,' she said before she left them alone.

'What was that about?'

'She said something about *fadamihana*.'

'Yes, they're preparing for it, whatever it is.'

'Feast of the dead.'

She stopped examining a bowl to turn to him. 'I beg your pardon?'

'It's an old custom. Part of Malagasy religion is ancestor worship. When somebody dies, they're always brought back to their ancestral tombs. Every few years they disentomb the dead and hold a party for them.'

'Disentomb them?' Immediate revulsion took over. 'That's disgusting.'

'It's part of their religion, a gesture of respect.'

'I hope no one respects me that way,' she began, but her curiosity got the better of her. She frowned as

Doug poured water into the bowl. 'What's the purpose?'

'When the bodies are brought up, they're given a place of honor at the celebration. They get fresh linen, palm wine, and all the latest gossip.' He dipped both hands in the bowl of water and splashed it over his face. 'It's their way of honoring the past, I guess. Of showing respect for the people they descended from. Ancestor worship's the root of Malagasy religion. There's music and dancing. A good time's had by all, living or otherwise.'

So the dead weren't mourned, Whitney mused. They were entertained. A celebration of death, or perhaps more accurately of the bond between life and death. Suddenly she felt she understood the ceremony and her feelings about it changed.

Whitney accepted the soap Doug offered and smiled at him. 'It's beautiful, isn't it?'

He lifted a small, rough towel and scrubbed it over his face. 'Beautiful?'

'They don't forget you when you die. You're brought back, given a front-row seat at a party, filled in on all the town news, and drunk to. One of the worst things about dying is missing out on all the fun.'

'The worst thing about dying is dying,' he countered.

'You're too literal. I wonder if it makes it easier to face death knowing you've got something like that to look forward to.'

He'd never considered anything made it easier to face death. It was just something that happened when you couldn't con life any longer. He shook his head, dropping the towel. 'You're an interesting woman, Whitney.'

'Of course.' Laughing, she lifted the soap and

sniffed. It smelled of crushed, waxy flowers. 'And I'm starving. Let's see what's on the menu.'

When Marie came back, she had changed into a colorful skirt that skimmed her calves. Outside, villagers were busily loading a long table with food and drink. Whitney, who'd been expecting a few handfuls of rice and a fresh canteen, turned to Marie again with thanks.

'You are our guests.' Solemn and formal, Marie lowered her eyes. 'You have been guided to our village. We offer the hospitality of our ancestors and celebrate your visit. My father has said we will have today as holiday in your honor.'

'I only know we're hungry.' Whitney reached out to touch her hand. 'And very grateful.'

She stuffed herself. Though she didn't recognize anything but the fruit and rice, she didn't quibble. Scents flowed on the air, spicy, exotic, different. The meat, without aid of electricity, had been cooked over open fires and in stone kilns. It was gamey and rich and wonderful. The wine, cup after cup of it, was potent.

Music began, drums and rough wind and string instruments that formed thready, ancient tunes. The fields, it seemed, could wait one day. Visitors were rare, and once accepted, prized.

A little giddy, Whitney swirled into a dance with a group of men and women.

They accepted her, grinning and nodding as she mimicked their steps. She watched some of the men leap and turn as the rhythm quickened. Whitney let her head fall back with her laugh. She thought of the smoky, crowded clubs she patronized. Electric music, electric lights. There, each one tried to outshine the other. She thought of some of the smooth, self-absorbed men who'd partnered her—or tried to. Not one of them would be able to hold up against a Merina. She whirled until her head spun and then turned to Doug.

'Dance with me,' she demanded.

Her skin was flushed, her eyes bright. Against him, she was warm and impossibly soft. Laughing, he shook his head. 'I'll pass. You're doing enough for both of us.'

'Don't be a stick-in-the-mud.' She poked a finger into his chest. 'The Merina know a party pooper when they see one.' She linked her hands behind him and swayed. 'All you have to do is move your feet.'

On their own power, his hands slipped down to her hips to feel the movement. 'Just my feet?'

Tilting her head, she aimed a deadly look from beneath her lashes. 'If that's the best you can do—' She let out a quick whoop when he swung her in a circle.

'Just try to keep up with me, sugar.' In a flash, he had an arm hooked behind her, and extending the other, gripped her hand. He held the dramatic tango pose for a moment, then moved smoothly forward. They broke, turned, and came back together.

'Damn, Douglas, I think you might be a fun date after all.'

As they continued, stepping, swaying, then moving forward, their dance caught the crowd's approval. They turned so their faces were close, their bodies facing, hand extended to hand as Doug guided her backward.

Her heart began to drum pleasantly, both from the pleasure of being foolish and the constant brush of his body against hers. His breath was warm. His eyes, so unusual and clear, stayed on hers. It wasn't often she thought of him as a strong man, but now, caught close, she felt the ripple of muscle in his back, along his shoulders. Whitney tilted her head back in challenge. She'd match him, step for step.

He whirled her so quickly her vision blurred. Then she felt herself being flung back. Freely, she let her body go so that her head nearly brushed the ground in the exaggerated dip. Just as quickly, she was upright and caught against him. His mouth was only a whisper from hers.

They had only to move—only a slight shift of their heads would bring their lips together. Both were breathing quickly, from the exertion, from the excitement. She could smell the muskiness of light sweat, the hint of wine and rich meat. He'd taste of all of them.

They had only to move—a fraction closer. And what then?

'What the hell,' Doug muttered. Even as his hand tightened at her waist, even as her lashes fluttered down, he heard the roar of an engine. His head swiveled around. He tensed like a cat so quickly that Whitney blinked.

'Shit.' Grabbing her hand, Doug ran for cover. Because he had to make do, he pushed her up against the side of a house and pressed himself against her.

'What the hell're you doing? One tango, and you turn into a crazy man.'

'Just don't move.'

'I don't. . .' Then she heard it too, loud and clear above them. 'What is it?'

'Helicopter.' He prayed the overhang of the steeply pitched roof and the shade it spread would keep them from view.

She managed to peer over his shoulder. She could hear it, but she couldn't see it. 'It could be anyone.'

'Could be. I don't risk my life on could be's. Dimitri

doesn't like to waste time.' And dammit, he thought as he looked for shelter and escape, how could he have found them in the middle of nowhere? Cautiously, he glanced around. There would be no running. 'That mop of blonde hair would stand out like a road sign.'

'Even under pressure, you're full of charm, Douglas.'

'Let's just hope he doesn't decide to land to get a closer look.' The words were hardly out of his mouth when the sound grew louder. Even on the far side of the house, they felt the wind from the blades. Dust billowed up.

'You had to give him the idea.'

'Shut up a minute.' He glanced behind him, poised to run. Where? he asked himself in disgust. Where the hell to? They were cornered as neatly as if they'd run down a blind alley.

At the whisper of a sound, he whirled, fists lifted. Marie stopped, raising her hand for silence. Gesturing, she hurried along the side of the house. With her back pressed against the wall, she moved along the west side to the door. Though it meant putting his luck into the hands of a woman again, Doug followed, keeping Whitney's hand in his.

Once inside, he signaled to them both to remain still and silent before he moved to the window. Keeping well to the side, he peered out.

The helicopter was some distance away on the flatland at the base of the hills. Already Remo was striding toward the crowd of celebrants.

'Sonofabitch,' Doug muttered. Sooner or later, it was going to come down to dealing with Remo. He had to make certain he had house advantage. At the moment, he had nothing more lethal than a penknife in the pocket of his jeans. It was then he remembered that both he and Whitney had left their packs outside, near the spread of food and drink.

'Is it—'

'Stay back,' he ordered when Whitney crept up behind him. 'It's Remo and two more of Dimitri's toy soldiers.' And sooner or later, he admitted as he wiped a hand over his mouth, it was going to come down to dealing with Dimitri. He'd need more than luck when the time came. Racking his brain, he looked around the room for something, anything to defend himself with. 'Tell her these men are looking for us and ask her what her people are going to do.'

Whitney looked over at Marie, who stood quietly by the door. Briefly, she followed Doug's instructions.

Marie folded her hands. 'You are our guests,' she said simply. 'They are not.'

Whitney smiled and told Doug. 'We've got sanctuary, for what it's worth.'

'Yeah, that's good, but remember what happened to Quasimodo.'

He watched as Remo faced down Louis. The village leader stood steely-eyed and implacable, speaking briefly in Malagasy. The sound, if not the words, came through the open window. Remo pulled something out of his pocket.

'Photographs,' Whitney whispered. 'He must be showing him pictures of us.'

Him, Doug agreed silently, and every other villager between here and Tamatave. If they got out of this one, there'd be no more parties along the way. He'd been stupid to believe he could take time to breathe with Dimitri after him, he realized.

Along with the pictures, Remo produced a wad of bills and a smile. Both were met with awesome silence.

While Remo tried his bargaining powers on Louis,

another of the helicopter crew wandered to the spread of food and began sampling. Helpless, Doug watched him come closer and closer to the packs.

'Ask her if she has a gun in here.'

'A gun?' Whitney swallowed. She hadn't heard him use that tone of voice before. 'But Louis won't—'

'Ask her. Now.' Remo's companion poured himself a cup of palm wine. He had only to look down to the left. It wouldn't make any difference whose side the villagers ranged themselves on if he saw the packs. They were unarmed. Doug knew what would be tucked into a leather holster under Remo's coat. He'd felt it prod into his ribs not too many days before. 'Dammit, Whitney, ask her.'

At Whitney's question, Marie nodded expressionlessly. After slipping into the adjoining room, she came back carrying a long, deadly looking rifle. When Doug took it, Whitney grabbed his arm.

'Doug, they'll have guns too. There're babies out there.'

Grimly, he loaded the gun. He'd just have to be fast, and accurate. Damn fast. 'I'm not going to do anything until I have to.' He crouched down, rested the barrel on the windowsill and focused the site. His finger was damp before he placed it on the trigger.

He hated guns. Always had. It didn't matter which side of the barrel he was on. He had killed. In Nam he'd killed because a quick mind and clever hands hadn't kept him out of the draft or the stinking jungles. He had learned things there he hadn't wanted to learn, and things he'd had to use. Survival, that was always number one.

He had killed. There had been one miserable night in Chicago when his back had been against the wall and a knife whizzed at his throat. He knew what it was to look at someone as the life eased out of them. You had to know the next time, anytime, it could be you.

He hated guns. He held the rifle steady.

One of Whitney's dance partners let out a high-pitched laugh. Holding a pitcher of wine over his head, he grabbed the man beside the packs. As the Merina whirled, leaping with the wine, the packs slid away into the crowd and disappeared.

'Stop acting like an idiot,' Remo shouted as his partner lifted his cup for more wine. Turning back to Louis again, he gestured with the photos. He got nothing but a hard stare and a rumble of Malagasy.

Doug watched Remo stuff the photos and money back in his pocket and stride off toward the waiting copter. With a roar and a whirl, it started up. When it was ten feet off the ground, he felt his shoulder muscles loosen.

He didn't like the feel of a gun in his hand. As the sound of the copter died away, he unloaded it.

'You might've hurt somebody with that,' Whitney murmured when he'd handed it back to Marie.

'Yeah.'

When he turned, she saw a ruthlessness she hadn't gauged before. There was an edge there that had nothing to do with fear, and everything to do with cunning. A thief, yes, that she understood and accepted. But she saw now that in his own way, he was just as tough, just as hard as the men who searched for them. She wasn't certain she could accept that as easily.

The look vanished from his eyes when Marie came back into the room. Taking her hand, Doug lifted it to his lips as gallantly as royalty. 'Tell her we owe her our lives. And we won't forget it.'

Though Whitney said the words, Marie continued to stare up at Doug. Woman to woman, Whitney recog-

nized the look. A glance at Doug showed he recognized
it too, and loved every minute of it.

'Maybe you two would like to be alone,' she said
dryly. Crossing the room, she pulled open the door.
'After all, three's a crowd.' She let it slam with more
force than necessary.

'Nothing?' A puff of fragrant smoke rose up in front of
a high-backed, brocade chair.

Remo shifted his feet. Dimitri didn't care for nega-
tive reports. 'Krentz, Weis, and me covered the whole
area, stopped at every village. We've got five men here
in town watching for them. There's not a sign.'

'Not a sign.' Dimitri's voice was mild, with richness
beneath. Diction, among other things, had been taught
relentlessly by his mother. The three-fingered hand
tapped the cigarette into an alabaster tray. 'When one
has eyes to look, there's always a sign, my dear Remo.'

'We'll find them, Mr Dimitri. It's just going to take
a little more time.'

'It worries me.' From the table to the right, he
plucked up a faceted glass half filled with deep ruby
wine. On his unmarred hand he wore a ring—thick,
glossy gold around a hard diamond. 'They've eluded
you three. . .' He paused as he sipped, letting the wine
lie on his tongue. He had a taste for the sweet. 'No,
dear me, four times now. It's becoming a very disturb-
ing habit of yours to fail.' While his voice flowed softly,
he flicked on his lighter so that the flame rose straight
and thin. Behind it, his gaze locked on Remo's. 'You
know how I feel about failures?'

Remo swallowed. He knew better than to make
excuses. Dimitri dealt harshly with excuses. He felt the
sweat begin on the nape of his neck and roll slowly
down.

'Remo, Remo.' The name came out in a sigh. 'You've been like a son to me.' The lighter clicked off. Smoke plumed again, thin and rich. He never spoke quickly. A conversation, stretched to the last word, was more frightening than a threat. 'I'm a patient man and generous.' He waited for Remo's comment, pleased when there was only silence. 'But I expect results. Do succeed next time, Remo. An employer, like a parent, must exercise discipline.' A smile moved his lips, but not his eyes. They were flat and passionless. 'Discipline,' he repeated.

'I'll get Lord, Mr Dimitri. You'll have him on a platter.'

'An enjoyable thought, I'm sure. Get the papers.' His voice changed, iced. 'And the woman. I find myself more and more intrigued with the woman.'

In reflex, Remo touched the thin scar on his cheek. 'I'll get the woman.'

# CHAPTER SEVEN

They waited until an hour before dusk. With great ceremony, food, water, and wine were wrapped and presented to them for the journey ahead. The Merina seemed to feel themselves highly entertained by the visit.

In a gesture of generosity that made Doug wince, Whitney pressed bills into Louis's hands. His relief when they were refused was short-lived. For the village, she insisted, then on a stroke of inspiration added that the money was to express their respect and good wishes for the ancestors.

The bills disappeared into the folds of Louis's shirt.

'How much did you give him?' Doug demanded as he picked up his newly replenished pack.

'Only a hundred.' At his expression, she patted his cheek. 'Don't be a piker, Douglas. It's unbecoming.' Humming, she took out her notebook.

'Oh no, you shelled it out, not me.'

Whitney noted the amount in her book with a flourish. Doug's tab was definitely adding up. 'You play you pay. Anyway, I have a surprise for you?'

'What, a ten-percent discount?'

'Don't be crass.' She looked over at the sputtering sound of an engine. 'Transportation.' Her arm waved out in a wide gesture.

The jeep had definitely seen better days. Though it shone from a fresh washing, the engine spit and missed as a Merina with a bright, rolled headband drove it up the rutted road.

As a getaway car, he figured it came in a poor second to a blind mule. 'It won't go twenty miles.'

'It'll be twenty miles we don't use our feet. Say thank you, Douglas, and stop being rude. Pierre's going to drive us to the Tamatave province.'

It only took one look at Pierre to see that he'd freely imbibed palm wine. They'd be lucky if they didn't end up sunk in a rice paddy. 'Terrific.' Pessimistic, and dealing with a headache from his own free use of wine, Doug said a formal good-bye to Louis.

Whitney's was much lengthier and more elaborate. Doug climbed into the back of the jeep and stretched out his legs. 'Get your ass in gear, sweetheart. It'll be dark in an hour.'

Smiling at the Merina who crowded around the jeep, she stepped in. 'Up yours, Lord.' Settling the pack on the floor at her feet, she leaned back and swung one arm jauntily over the back of the seat. '*Avant*, Pierre.'

The jeep lurched forward, bucked, then rattled down the road. Doug felt his headache explode in tiny, unmerciful blasts. He closed his eyes and willed himself to sleep.

Whitney took the teeth-rattling ride in stride. She'd been wined, dined, and entertained. The same could be said about dinner at the 21 Club and a Broadway show. And this had been unique. Perhaps this wasn't a hansom-cab ride through the park, but anyone with twenty dollars could have one of those. She was bouncing along a road in Madagascar in a jeep driven by a Merina native with a thief snoring lightly in the back. It was entirely more interesting than a sedate ride through Central Park.

For the most part, the scenery was monotonous. Red hills, almost treeless, wide valleys patched with fields. It had cooled now that the sun was hanging low, but the day's baking left the road dusty. It plumed under the wheels and coated the just-washed jeep. There were mountains that rose up sharply, but again, pines were sparse. It was rock and earth. Though there was a sameness, it was the basic space that caught Whitney's imagination.

Miles of it, she mused. Miles and miles with nothing to block the sky, nothing to impede the vision. She felt it would be possible to find here a sense of self that a city dweller would never understand.

From time to time in New York, she missed the sky. When the feeling came upon her, she would simply hop a plane and go wherever the spirit moved her, staying until her mood swung again. Her friends accepted it because they couldn't do anything about it. Her family accepted it because they were still waiting for her to settle down.

Perhaps it was the aloneness, perhaps it was a full stomach and a clear head, but she felt a strange contentment. It would pass. Whitney knew herself too well to think otherwise. She hadn't been fashioned for long periods of contentment, but rather for darting around the next corner to see what was waiting.

For now, though, she leaned back in the jeep and enjoyed the serenity. Shadows shifted, lengthened, thickened. Something small and fast dashed across the road just in front of the jeep. It was over the rocks and gone before Whitney could fully focus on it. The air began to take on that pearly hush that lasts only moments.

The sun set, spectacularly. She had to turn and kneel on her seat to watch the western sky explode with color. Part of her profession dealt with incorporating tints and hues into fabrics and paints. As she watched, she thought about doing a room in the colors of sunset.

Crimsons, golds, deep jewel blues, and softening mauves. An interesting and intense combination. Her gaze lowered and rested on Doug as he slept. It would suit him, she decided. The flash of brilliance, the spark of power, the underlying intensity.

He wasn't a man to take lightly, nor was he a man to trust. Still, she was beginning to think he was a man who could fascinate. Like a sunset, he could shift and change before your eyes, then vanish while you were still looking. The moment he'd taken that rifle in his hands, she'd seen he had a ruthlessness he could pull out and slip on at a moment's notice. If and when he found it necessary, he'd be just as ruthless with her.

She needed more leverage.

Catching her tongue between her teeth, Whitney looked from him to the floor. The pack—and the envelope—sat at his feet. While she kept her eyes on his face for any signs of wakefulness, she leaned over. The pack was well out of reach. The jeep jostled as she rose up enough to bend over the seat from the waist. Doug continued to snore lightly. Her fingers gripped the strap of the pack. Gingerly, she began to lift it up.

There was a bang loud enough to make her gasp. Before she had time to fumble for a good hold, the jeep veered, sending her tumbling into the back.

Doug woke up with the air knocked out of him and Whitney sprawled over his chest. She smelled of wine and fruit. Yawning, he ran a hand down her hip. 'Just can't keep your hands off me.'

Blowing the hair out of her eyes she scowled at him. 'I was watching the sunset out the back.'

'Uh-huh.' His hand closed over hers, still on the strap of his pack. 'Sticky fingers, Whitney.' He clucked his tongue. 'I'm disappointed.'

'I don't know what you're talking about.' With a

huff, she struggled up and called to Pierre. Though the spate of French went over his head, Doug needed no translation when the native kicked the front right tire.

'A flat. Figures.' Doug started to climb out, then glanced over his shoulder, located his pack and took it with him. Whitney reached for her own before she followed him. 'What're you going to do?' Doug asked.

She glanced at the spare Pierre rolled out. 'Just stand here and look helpless, of course. Unless you'd like me to phone Triple A.'

Swearing, Doug crouched down and began to loosen lug nuts. 'The spare's bald as a baby's ass. Tell our chauffeur that we'll walk from here. He'll be lucky if this gets him back to the village.'

Fifteen minutes later, they stood in the middle of the road and watched the jeep bounce over ruts. Cheerful, Whitney linked her arm with Doug's. Insects and small birds had begun to sing as the first stars came out. 'A little evening stroll, darling?'

'As much as I hate to turn you down, we find cover and camp. In another hour, it'll be too dark to see. Over there,' he decided, pointing to a jumble of rocks. 'We'll pitch the tent behind them. We can't do anything about them spotting us from the air, but we'll be out of sight from the road.'

'So, you think they'll be back.'

'They'll be back. All we have to do is not be there.'

Because she had begun to wonder if there were trees in any quantity in Madagascar, Whitney was pleased when they came to the forest. It helped ease the annoyance of being awakened at dawn. The only courtesy he'd given her had been a cup of coffee shoved in her face.

The hills going east were steep, peaking up and

dropping down so that walking had become a chore she was ready to swear off for good.

Doug looked at the forest as welcome cover. Whitney looked at it as a welcome change.

Though the air was mild, after an hour of climbing, she was sticky and cut of sorts. There were better ways to hunt for treasure, she was certain. An air-conditioned car would be the first choice.

The forest might not have been air-conditioned, but it was cool. Whitney stepped in among fanning fern trees. 'Very pretty,' she decided, looking up and up.

'Travelers' trees.' He broke off a leaf stalk and poured clear water into the palm from the sheath. 'Handy. Read the guidebook.'

Whitney poked her finger into the puddle in his hand, then laid it on her tongue. 'But it's so good for your ego to spout off knowledge.' At a rustle, she glanced over and saw a furry white shape and long tail disappear into the brush. 'Why, it's a dog.'

'Uh-uh.' Doug grabbed her arm before she could race after it. 'A sifaka—you've just seen your first lemur. Look.'

As she followed his pointing finger, Whitney caught a glimpse of the snow-white-bodied, black-headed lemur as it dashed through the top of the trees. She laughed and strained for another look. 'They're so cute. I was beginning to think we'd see nothing but hills and grass and rock.'

He liked the way she laughed. Maybe just a bit too much. Women, he thought. It had been too damn long since he'd had one. 'This ain't no guided tour,' he said briefly. 'Once we have the treasure, you can book one. Right now, we've got to move.'

'What's the hurry?' Shifting her pack, Whitney

trooped along beside him. 'It seems to me the longer we take, the less chance Dimitri has to find us.'

'I get itchy—not knowing where he is. In front of us, or behind.' It made him think of Nam again, where the jungle hid too much. He preferred the dark streets and mean alleys of the city.

Whitney glanced over her shoulder and grimaced. The forest had already closed in behind them. She wanted to take comfort in the deep greens, the moistness, and the cool air, but Doug was making her see gnomes. 'Well, there's no one in the forest but us. So far we've been one step ahead of them every time.'

'So far. Let's keep it that way.'

'Why don't we pass the time with conversation. You could tell me about the papers.'

He'd already decided she wouldn't let it go and that he'd give her enough information to stop her from nagging him. 'Know much about the French Revolution?'

She shifted the hateful pack as she walked. It would be best, Whitney calculated, not to mention the quick look she'd had at the one page already. The less Doug thought she knew, the more he might tell her.

'Enough to get me through a French history class in college.'

'How about rocks?'

'I passed on geology.'

'Not limestone and quartz. Real rocks, sugar. Diamonds, emeralds, rubies as big as your fist. Put them together with the Reign of Terror and fleeing aristocrats and you have a lot of potential. Necklaces, earrings, unset stones. A hell of a lot was stolen.'

'And more hidden or smuggled out.'

'Right. When you think about it, there's more still

missing than anyone will ever find. We're going to find a little part. It's all I need.'

'The treasure's two hundred years old,' she said quietly and thought again of the paper she'd skimmed. 'Part of French history.'

'Royal antiques,' Doug murmured, already seeing them gleam in his hands.

'Royal?' The word had her glancing up. He was looking off into middle distance, dreaming. 'The treasure belonged to the king of France?'

It was close enough, Doug decided. Closer than he'd intended her to get this soon. 'It belonged to the man who was smart enough to get his hands on it. It's going to belong to me. Us,' he corrected, anticipating her. But she fell silent.

'Who was the woman who gave Whitaker the map?' she asked at length.

'The English lady? Ah—Smythe-Wright. Yeah, Lady Smythe-Wright.'

As the name hit home, Whitney stared into the forest. Olivia Smythe-Wright was one of the few members of the gentry who fully deserved the title. She'd devoted herself to the arts and charity with a near-religious fervor. Part of the reason, or so she'd often said, was that she was a descendant of Marie Antoinette's. Queen, beauty, victim—a woman some historians deemed a selfish fool and others called a victim of circumstance. Whitney had been to some of Lady Smythe-Wright's functions and had admired her.

Marie Antoinette and lost French jewels. A page of a journal dating from 1793. It made sense. If Olivia had believed the papers were history. . .Whitney remembered reading of her death in the *Times*. It had been a ghastly murder. Bloody and without apparent motive. The authorities were still investigating.

Butrain, Whitney thought. He'd never be brought to justice now or have a trial by his peers. He was dead and so was Whitaker, Lady Smythe-Wright, and a young waiter named Juan. The motive for all sat in Doug's pocket. How many more had lost their lives for a queen's treasure?

No, she couldn't think of it that way. Not now. If she did, she'd turn around and give up. Her father had taught her many things, but the first, the most important, was to finish no matter what. Perhaps it had the edges of pride, but it was her breeding. She'd always been proud of it.

She'd go on. She'd help Doug find the treasure. Then she'd decide what to do about it.

He found himself looking around at every rustle. According to his guidebook, the forests abounded with life. Nothing very dangerous, he recalled. This wasn't the land of safaris. In any case, it was two-legged carnivores he worried about.

By this time, Dimitri would be very annoyed. Doug had heard some graphic stories about what happened when Dimitri was annoyed. He didn't want any first-hand knowledge.

The forest smelled of pine and morning. The large, leafy trees cut the glare of the sun he and Whitney had lived with for days. Instead, it came in shafts, white, shimmering, and lovely. There were flowers underfoot that smelled like expensive women, flowers in trees overhead that spread out and promised fruit. Passion-flower, he thought, spotting a flaring violet blossom. He remembered the one he'd handed Whitney in Antananarivo. They hadn't stopped running since.

Doug let his muscles relax. The hell with Dimitri. He was miles away and running in circles. Even he couldn't track them through uninhabited forest. The itch at the back of his neck was just sweat. The envelope was safe, tucked in the pack. He'd slept with it digging into his back the night before, just in case. The treasure, the end of the rainbow, was closer than ever.

'Nice place,' he decided, glancing up to see some fox-faced lemurs scrambling in the treetops.

'So glad you approve,' Whitney returned. 'Maybe we can stop and have the breakfast you were in too much of a hurry for this morning.'

'Yeah, soon. Let's work up an appetite.'

Whitney pressed a hand to her stomach. 'You've got to be kidding.' Then she saw a swarm of large butterflies, twenty, perhaps thirty, flow by. It was like a wave, swelling, then dipping, then swirling. They were the most beautiful, most brilliant blue she'd ever seen. As they passed, she felt the light breeze their wings had ruffled on the air. The sheer strength of color almost hurt her eyes. 'God, I'd kill for a dress that color.'

'We'll shop later.'

She watched them move, scatter, and regroup. The sight of something lovely helped her forget the hours of walking. 'I'd settle for some of that mystery meat and a banana.'

Though he knew he should have been immune to her quick smile and her sweep of lashes by this time, Doug felt himself softening. 'We'll have a picnic.'

'Wonderful!'

'In another mile.'

Taking her hand in his, he continued through the forest. It smelled soft, he thought. Like a woman. And like a woman, it had shadows and cool corners. It paid to stay on your feet and keep your eyes open. No one traveled here. From the looks of the undergrowth, no one had traveled here in some time. He had the compass to guide him and that was all.

'I don't understand why you have this obsession about covering miles.'

'Because every one takes me that much closer to the pot of gold, sugar. We're both going to have penthouses when we get home.'

'Douglas.' Shaking her head, she reached down and scooped up a flower. It was pale, watery pink, delicate as a young girl. Its stem was thick and tough. Whitney smiled and tucked it into her hair. '*Things* shouldn't be that important.'

'Not nearly so much when you've got them all.'

Shrugging, she plucked another flower to twirl under her nose. 'You worry too much about money.'

'What?' He stopped and gaped at her. 'I worry? *I* worry? Just who keeps marking down every solitary penny in her little book? Just who sleeps with her wallet under her pillow?'

'That's business,' Whitney said easily. She touched the flower in her hair. Pretty petals and a tough stem. 'Business is entirely different.'

'Bullshit. I've never seen anyone so bent on counting their change, tallying every cent. If I were bleeding, you'd charge me a goddamn dime for a Band-Aid.'

'No more than a nickel,' she corrected. 'And there's absolutely no need to shout.'

'I have to shout to be heard over all that racket.'

They both stopped, brows drawing together. The sound they'd just begun to notice was like an engine. No, Doug decided even as he tensed to run, it was too steady and deep for an engine. Thunder? No. He took her hand again.

'Come on. Let's go see what the hell that is.'

It grew louder as they walked east. Louder, it lost all

resemblance to the sound of a motor. 'Water against rock,' Whitney murmured. When they stepped into the clearing, she saw she'd nearly been right. Water against water.

The falls plunged down twenty feet into a clear, gurgling lagoon. The white agitated water was struck by the sun on its journey down, then turned to a deep crystal blue. The falls made a sound of rushing, of power and speed, and yet it was a picture of serenity. Yes, the forest was like a woman, Doug thought again. Intensely beautiful, powerful, and full of surprises. Without realizing it, Whitney rested her head against Doug's shoulder.

'It's lovely,' she murmured. 'Absolutely lovely. Just as though it were waiting for us.'

He gave in and slipped an arm around her. 'Nice spot for a picnic. Aren't you glad we waited?'

She had to match his grin. 'A picnic,' she agreed with her eyes dancing. 'And a bath.'

'Bath?'

'A wonderful, cool, wet bath.' Catching him by surprise, she gave him a quick, smacking kiss, then dashed to the side of the lagoon. 'I'm not passing this up, Douglas.' She dropped her pack and began to dig inside. 'Just the thought of getting my body into water and washing off the dirt of the past couple of days makes me crazy.' She brought out a cake of French milled soap and a small bottle of shampoo.

Doug took the soap and held it under his nose. It smelled like her—feminine, fresh. Expensive. 'Gonna share?'

'All right. And in this case, because I'm feeling generous, no charge.'

His grin tilted as he tossed the soap back to her. 'Can't take a bath with your clothes on.'

She met the challenge in his eyes and undid her top button. 'I've no intention of keeping them on.' Slowly, she undid the range of buttons, waiting while his gaze followed the trail. A light breeze ruffled the edges and tickled the line of bare skin. 'All you have to do,' she said softly, 'is turn around.' When he lifted his gaze to hers and smiled, she gestured with the cake in her hand. 'Or no soap.'

'Talk about spoilsports,' he mumbled, but turned his back.

In seconds, Whitney stripped and dove cleanly into the pool. Breaking the surface, she trod water. 'Your turn.' With the simple pleasure of having water against her skin, she dipped her head back and let it flow through her hair. 'Don't forget the shampoo.'

The water was clear enough to give him a tempting silhouette of her body from the shoulders down. Water lapped over her breasts. Her feet kicked gently. Feeling the stir, the dull, dangerous stir of desire, he concentrated on her face. It didn't help.

It glowed with laughter, washed clean of the light, sophisticated makeup she put on every morning. Her hair was sleek, turned dark with water and sun as it framed the elegant bones that would keep her a beauty even when she was eighty. Doug picked up the little plastic bottle of shampoo and tossed it in his hand.

Under the circumstances, he thought it wise to look at the humor in the situation. He had a ticket to a million-dollar prize literally at his fingertips, a determined and very clever enemy breathing down his throat, and he was about to skinny-dip with an ice-cream princess.

After pulling his shirt over his head, he reached for the snap of his jeans. 'You're not going to turn around are you?'

Dammit, she liked it when he grinned that way. The cheerful cockiness was just plain appealing. Lavishly, she began to soap one arm. She hadn't realized how much she'd missed that cool, slick feeling. 'Want to brag, do you, Douglas? I'm not easily impressed.'

He sat down to remove his shoes. 'Leave me my share of the soap.'

'Move a little faster then.' She began to soap her other arm in the same long, smooth stroke. 'God, this is better than Elizabeth Arden's.' With a sigh, she lay back and lifted one leg out of the water. When he stood and dropped his jeans, she gave him a thorough, critical study. Her expression was bland, but she didn't miss the lean, muscled thighs, the taut stomach, the narrow hips just covered with low, snug briefs. He had the clean, sleek build of a runner. And that, she supposed, was what he was.

'Adequate,' she said after a moment. 'Since you apparently like to pose, it's a pity I didn't bring my Polaroid.'

Unstung, he pulled off his briefs. For a moment, he was poised, naked—and she was forced to admit, magnificent—at the edge of the lagoon. His dive was sharp before he surfaced a foot away from her. What he'd seen underwater made his mouth go dry with desire.

'Soap,' he said, as cool as she, and offered the shampoo in trade.

'Don't forget behind the ears.' Using a generous hand, she poured shampoo into her palm.

'Hey, half's mine, remember.'

'You'll get it. Anyway, I've more hair than you.' She worked it into a lather while she scissored her feet to keep above water.

He gestured with the soap before rubbing it over his chest. 'And I've more body.'

With a smile, she sank below the surface, leaving a frothy trail of suds where her hair fanned out. The beat of water sucked them down and away. Unable to resist, she swam down, deeper. She could hear the vibrations of the falls, drumming, drumming, see rocks sparkling a foot beneath her, taste the clear, sweet water that was kissed by the sun. Glancing up, she saw the strong, lean body of the man who was now her partner.

The idea of danger, or men with guns, of being pursued seemed ludicrous. This was paradise. Whitney didn't believe in cunning-snakes behind luscious flowers. When she surfaced, she was laughing.

'This is fabulous. We should book in for the weekend.'

He saw the sun shoot sparks into her hair. 'Next time. I'll even spring for the soap.'

'Yeah?' He looked attractive, dangerously so. She discovered she preferred a touch of danger in a man. The word boredom, the only word she considered a true obscenity, wouldn't apply to him. Unexpected. That was the word. She found it had a sensuous ring.

Testing him, and perhaps herself, she trod slowly until their bodies were too close for safety. 'Trade,' she murmured, keeping her eyes on his as she held out the bottle.

His fingers tightened on the slick soap so that it nearly slid out of them. Just what the hell was she up to? he asked himself. He'd been around enough to recognize that look in a woman's eyes. It said—maybe. Why don't you persuade me? The trouble was, she wasn't anything like the women he'd known. He wasn't entirely sure of his moves.

Instead, he equated her to a job, a high-class, luxury

apartment complex that took careful casing, meticulous planning, and intricate legwork before he took it down. Better that he be the thief with her. He knew the rules, because he'd made them.

'Sure.' He opened his palm so that she had to slide the wet cake of soap from it. In response, she tossed the bottle high, laughing as she retreated. Doug plucked it inches above the water.

'I hope you don't mind a touch of jasmine.' Lazily she lifted her other leg and began to run the soap up and down her calf.

'I can handle it.' He poured the shampoo directly on his hair, rescrewed the cap, then tossed it on the ground beside the lagoon. 'Ever been to a public bath?'

'No.' Curious, she glanced back over. 'Have you?'

'I was in Tokyo a couple years back. It's an interesting experience.'

'I usually like to keep the quantity in my tub down to two.' She ran the soap up a thigh. 'Cozy, but not crowded.'

'I'll bet.' He ducked under to rinse off, and to cool off. She had legs that went all the way up to her waist.

'Convenient, too,' she said when he'd surfaced. 'Especially when you need your back scrubbed.' With a smile, she held out the soap again. 'Would you mind?'

So she wanted to play games, he decided. Well, he rarely turned one down—as long as he'd figured the odds. Taking the soap from her, he began to run it over her shoulder blades. 'Marvelous,' she said after a moment. It wasn't easy to keep her voice even when her stomach had begun to tighten, but she managed. 'But then I suppose a man in your line of work has to have clever hands.'

'It helps. I suppose all that ice cream could buy million-dollar skin.'

'It helps.'

His hand ran lower, down her spine, then slowly up again. Unprepared for the jolt it brought her, Whitney shuddered. Doug grinned.

'Cold?'

Just who had she managed to push anyway? she wondered. 'The water gets chilly unless you move around.' Telling herself it wasn't a retreat, she gently sidestroked away. Not that easy, sugar, Doug thought. He tossed the soap on to the grass beside the shampoo. In a quick move, he grabbed her ankle.

'Problem?'

Effortlessly, he pulled her back toward him. 'As long as we're playing games—'

'I don't know what you're talking about,' she began, but the sentence ended on a quick gasp as her body collided with his.

'The hell you don't.'

He found he enjoyed it—the uncertainty, the annoyance, and the flare of awareness that came and went in her eyes. Her body was long and slim. Deliberately, he tangled her legs with his so that she was forced to grab his shoulders to stay afloat.

'Watch your step, Lord,' she warned.

'Water games, Whitney. I've always been a sucker for them.'

'I'll let you know when I want to play.'

His hands slid up to just under her breasts. 'Didn't you?'

She'd asked for it. Knowing it didn't improve her temper one whit. Yes, she'd wanted to play with him, but on her terms, in her own time. She discovered she was over her head in more ways than one, and she didn't care for it. Her voice became very cool; her eyes were equally chilly.

'You don't really consider we're in the same league, do you?' Long ago, she'd discovered insults, given coldly, were the most successful of defenses.

'No, but then I've never paid much attention to caste systems. You want to play duchess, go ahead.' He slid his thumbs up, over her nipples, and heard her breath shudder in, then out. 'As I recall, royalty always had a penchant for taking commoners to bed.'

'I've no intention of taking you to mine.'

'You want me.'

'You're flattering yourself.'

'You're lying.'

Temper flared. The warm liquid pull in her stomach battled with it. 'The water's getting cold, Douglas. I want to get out.'

'You want me to kiss you.'

'I'd sooner kiss a toad.'

He grinned. She'd practically hissed at him. 'I won't give you warts.'

Making up his mind on the instant, he covered her mouth with his.

She stiffened. No one ever kissed her without her consent, and without jumping through the hoops she tossed out first. Who the hell did he think he was?

And her heart pounded against his. Her pulses raced. Her head swam.

She didn't give a damn who he was.

With a spurt of passion that rocked them both, she moved her mouth on his. Tongues met. His teeth scraped her lower lip while he slid his arms around her back to mold them closer together. Surprises, he thought as he began to lose himself in her. The lady was full of them.

He tasted cool, fresh, different, so excitingly different. Passion took them beneath the surface. Wrapped together, they came up again, mouths fused, water cascading off skin.

There'd never been anything like him in her life. He didn't ask, but took. His hands moved over her body with an intimacy she'd always doled out stingily. She chose a lover, sometimes impulsively, sometimes calculatingly, but *she* chose. This time, she'd been given no choice. The moment of helplessness was as exhilarating as anything she'd ever experienced.

He'd bring her madness in bed. If he could take her so far with a kiss. . . He'd take her, up, over, beyond, whether she wanted to go or not. And oh, now, with the water lapping over her, with his hands stroking and his mouth growing hotter, hungrier, she wanted to go.

And then, she thought, he'd give her a salute, a cocky grin, and slip off into the night. Once a thief, always a thief, whether it was gold or a woman's soul. Perhaps she hadn't chosen this beginning, but she'd hold on long enough to choose her own end.

She pushed regrets aside. Pain was something to be avoided at all costs. Even if the cost was pleasure.

Whitney let her body go limp, as in total surrender. Then quickly, she lifted her hands to his shoulders and pushed. Hard.

Doug went under without a chance to gulp in air.

Before he'd surfaced, Whitney was at the side of the lagoon and climbing out. 'Game's over. My point.' She grabbed up her blouse and pulled it on without bothering to dry.

Fury. He'd thought he knew precisely what it felt like. Women. He had thought he'd known what buttons to push. Doug discovered he was just learning.

Swimming to the side, he hauled himself out. Whitney was already pulling on her slacks.

'A nice diversion,' she said, letting out a quiet, relieved breath when she was fully clothed. 'Now I think we'd better have that picnic. I'm starving.'

'Lady. . .' Keeping his eyes on her, Doug picked up his jeans. 'What I've got in mind for you is no picnic.'

'Really?' On solid ground again, she reached in her pack and found her brush. She began to pull it slowly through her hair. Water rained out in gemlike drops. 'You look like you could use a bit of raw meat at the moment. Is that the look you use to scare little old ladies out of their purses?'

'I'm a thief, not a mugger.' He snapped his jeans, and tossing wet hair out of his eyes, approached her. 'But I might make an exception in your case.'

'Don't do anything you'd regret,' she said softly.

He gritted his teeth. 'I'm going to love every minute of it.' When he gripped her shoulders, she stared up at him solemnly.

'You simply aren't the violent sort,' she told him. 'However. . .'

Her fist connected with his stomach, hard and fast. Gasping, he bent double.

'I am.' Whitney dropped her brush back in the pack and hoped he was too dazed to see her hand shake.

'That does it.' Holding his sore stomach, he sent her a look that might've made Dimitri step back and reconsider.

'Douglas. . .' She held up a hand as she might to a lean, vicious dog. 'Take a few deep breaths. Count to ten.' What else was there? she wondered frantically. 'Jog in place,' she hazarded. 'Don't lose control.'

'I'm in complete control,' he said between his teeth as he stalked her. 'Let me show you.'

'Some other time. Let's have some wine. We can. . .' She broke off as his hand closed over her throat. 'Doug!' It came out in a squeak.

'Now,' he began, then looked up at the whirl of engines. 'Sonofabitch!'

He wouldn't mistake the sound of the helicopter a second time. It was almost overhead and they were in the open. Wide fucking open, he thought on a surge of fury. Releasing her, he began to grab up gear. 'Move ass,' he shouted. 'Picnic's over.'

'If you tell me to move ass one more time—'

'Just move it!' He shoved the first pack at her even as he hauled up the other. 'Now get those pretty long legs moving, sugar. We ain't got much time.' He locked his hand over hers and headed for the trees in a dead run. Whitney's hair flowed out behind them.

Above, in the small cabin of the copter, Remo lowered his binoculars. For the first time in days, a grin moved under his moustache. Lazily, he stroked the scar that marred his cheek. 'We've spotted them. Radio Mr Dimitri.'

# CHAPTER EIGHT

'Do you think they saw us?'

At top speed, Doug headed dead east and kept to the thickest part of the forest. Roots and vines snatched at their feet, but he never lost his footing. He ran instinctively, through a foreign forest crowded with bamboo and eucalyptus just as he had through Manhattan. Leaves swung out and lashed back as they pushed through. Whitney might've complained when they swatted into her face, but she was too busy saving her breath.

'Yeah, I think they saw us.' He didn't waste time on fury, on frustration, on panic, though he felt all. Every time he thought they'd gained some time, he found Dimitri on his heels like some well-groomed English hound who'd tasted blood. He needed to rework his strategy, and he'd have to do it on his feet. Through experience he'd come to believe it was the best way. If you had too much time to think, you thought too much about consequences. 'There's no place for them to put that copter down in this forest.'

It made sense. 'So we stay in the forest.'

'No.' He was loping along like a marathon runner, smoothly, breath even. Whitney could detest him for it even as she admired it. Overhead lemurs chattered in wild fear and excitement. 'Dimitri'll have men combing this area within the hour.'

That made sense as well. 'So we get out of the forest.'

'No.'

Exhausted from the run, Whitney stopped, leaned her back against a tree, and just slid down to the mossy ground beneath. She'd once, arrogantly, considered herself in shape. The muscles in her legs screamed in revolt. 'What're we going to do?' she demanded. 'Disappear?'

Doug frowned, not at her, nor at the steady, whirling sound of blades and engine overhead. He looked off into the forest while the plan formed in his mind.

It was risky. In fact, it was undoubtedly foolhardy. He glanced up to where a canopy of leaves was all that separated them from Remo and a .45.

Then again, it might work.

'Disappear,' he murmured. 'That's what we're going to do.' Crouching down, he opened a pack.

'Looking for your fairy dust?'

'I'm looking to save that alabaster skin of yours, sugar.' He pulled out the lamba Whitney had bought in Antananarivo. While she sat, he draped it over her head, going more for coverage than style. 'Good-bye Whitney MacAllister, hello Malagasy matron.'

Whitney blew pale blonde hair out of her eyes. One elegant, fine-boned hand folded over the other. 'You've got to be kidding.'

'Got a better idea?'

She sat for a moment. The forest was no longer quiet with the intrusion of helicopter blades overhead. Its shade and spreading trees and mossy scent no longer equalled protection. In silence, she crossed the lamba under her chin and tossed the ends back. A lousy idea was better than none at all. Usually.

'Okay, let's move.' Taking her hand he hauled her to her feet. 'We've got work to do.'

Ten minutes later, he found what he'd been looking for.

Near the bottom of a rocky, uneven slope was a clearing with a handful of bamboo huts. The grass and vegetation on the incline had been slashed and burned, then planted with hill rice. Below gardens had been cleared and hoed so that the leafy vines of beans wound up around poles. She could see an empty paddock and a small lean-to where chickens scratched for whatever they could find.

The hill was steep so that the small buildings rose on stilts to compensate for the irregular terrain. Roofs were thatched but even with the distance looked in need of repair. A line of crude steps dug directly into the hill ran down to a narrow, rutted path below them. The path went east. Doug kept low behind the cover of small, scrubby bushes and watched for any sign of life.

Balancing herself with a hand on his shoulder, Whitney looked over his head. The cluster of houses looked cozy. Remembering the Merina, she felt a certain safety.

'Are we going to hide down there?'

'Hiding's not going to do us much good for very long.' Taking out his field glasses, he lay down on his belly and took a closer look at the huddle of houses. There was no cook smoke, no movement at any of the windows. Nothing. Making up his mind quickly, he handed the glasses to Whitney. 'Can you whistle?'

'Can I what?'

'Whistle.' He made a low steady sound through his teeth.

'I can whistle better than that,' she said with a sniff.

'Terrific. You watch through the glasses. If you see anyone coming back toward the huts, whistle.'

'If you think you're going down there without me—'

'Look, I'm leaving the packs here. Both of them.'

He grabbed her hair so that he could pull her face close. 'I figure you want to stay alive more than you want to get your hands on the envelope.'

She nodded, coolly. 'Staying alive's become quite a priority lately.'

It had always been his. 'So stay put.'

'Why're you going down there?'

'If we're going to pass ourselves off as a couple of Malagasy, we need to acquire a few more things.'

'Acquire.' She lifted a brow. 'You're going to steal them.'

'That's right, sugar, and you're the lookout.'

After a moment's thought, Whitney decided she rather liked the idea of being a lookout. Perhaps in another time and place, it might've had a crude·ring, but she'd always believed in enjoying each experience within its own frame.

'If I see anyone coming back, I whistle.'

'You got it. Now stay down, out of sight. Remo could come buzzing by in the 'copter.'

Getting into the spirit, Whitney shifted on to her stomach and scanned with the glasses. 'Just do your job, Lord. I'll do mine.'

With a quick glance toward the heavens, Doug began to scramble his way down the steep slope behind the huts. The steps, such as they were, would leave him in the open for too long. He avoided them. Loose pebbles bounced against his calves, and once the eroded slope gave out under him and sent him sliding five feet before he could gain another foothold. Already he was working out an alternate plan, in case he ran into someone. He couldn't speak the language, and his French interpreter was now his lookout. God help him. But he had a few—very few, he thought grimly—dollars in his pocket. If worse came to worst, he might buy most of what they needed.

Pausing a moment, straining to hear any sound, he dashed into the open toward the first hut.

He'd have liked it better if the lock had had more character. Doug had always found a certain satisfaction in outwitting a clever lock—or a clever woman. He glanced up and around toward where Whitney waited. He hadn't finished with her yet, but in the case of the lock, he had to make do with what there was. In seconds, he was inside.

Comfortable on the soft ground of the forest, Whitney watched him through the glasses. He moved very well, she decided. Because she'd been running with him almost since the moment they'd met, she hadn't been able to appreciate the smoothness with which he moved. Impressive, she decided, and touched her tongue on her top lip. She remembered the way he'd held her in the water of the lagoon.

And much more dangerous, she reminded herself, than she'd initially believed.

When he disappeared into the hut, she began a slow sweep with the field glasses. Twice she caught a movement, but it was only that of animals in the trees. Something resembling a hedgehog waddled out into the sunlight, lifted its head to scent, then slipped back into the bush. She heard flies buzzing and the whine of insects. That's what reminded her the sound of the 'copter had ceased. She kept her mind set on Doug, willing him to hurry.

Though the settlement below seemed sparse and dingy, this was a much lusher Madagascar than the one she'd passed through over the last two days. It was green and wet, thriving with life. She knew there were birds or animals overhead as she listened to the leaves rustle. Once through the field glasses she thought she spotted a fat partridge fly low over the clearing.

She could smell grass and the light fragrance of flowers that grew in the shade. Her elbows pushed through the springy moss to where the ground was dark and rich. A few yards away the hill sloped steeply, and erosion had washed soil down to rock. As she lay still, a fresh hush fell over the forest, a humming silence that was touched with the mystery she'd first anticipated when Doug had mentioned the country's name.

Had it really only been a matter of days, she mused, since they'd been in her apartment, him pacing, impatient, trying to wheedle a stake out of her? Already, everything that had come before that night seemed like a dream. She hadn't even unpacked from Paris, yet she could remember nothing exciting from her trip there. She couldn't think of a dull moment since Doug had jumped into her car in Manhattan.

Definitely more interesting, she decided. She looked back at the huts, but they were as quiet now as they'd been before Doug had scrambled down the hill. He'd be very good, she thought, at his chosen profession. His hands were quick, his eye keen, and he was light, very light, on his feet.

Though she wasn't looking for a career change herself, she thought it might be fun to have him teach her a few tricks of his trade. She was a quick study and good with her hands. That, and a certain steel-coated charm had helped her achieve success in her business without the help of her influential family. Weren't the same basic abilities required in Doug's field?

Perhaps, just for the experience naturally, she could try her hand at being a thief. After all, black was one of her best colors.

She had a trim little angora sweater that would do

very nicely, she thought. And, if she remembered right, she owned a pair of black jeans. Yes, she was certain of it, snug black jeans with a row of silver studs down one leg. Really, she could be outfitted in no time if she picked up a pair of black sneakers.

She could try the family estate on Long Island for starters. The security system there was complex and intricate. So intricate, her father set it off regularly, then bellowed at the servants to shut it down again. If she and Doug could manage to get through it. . .

There was the Rubens, the pair of T'ang horses, the perfectly hideous solid-gold salver her grandfather had given to her mother. She could take a few choice pieces, box them up, and ship them back to her father's New York offices. It would drive him crazy.

Amused at the thought, Whitney scanned again. Day-dreaming, she nearly missed the movement to the east. With a jerk, she brought the glasses back to the right and focused.

The three bears were coming back, she thought. And Goldilocks was going to be caught with his fingers in the porridge.

She drew in her breath to whistle when a voice close behind her had her gulping instead.

'We flush 'em out in here, or we drive 'em out.' Leaves rustled smartly behind her and just overhead. 'Either way, Lord's luck's running out.' The man who spoke hadn't forgotten having a bottle of whiskey swung into his face. As he spoke, he touched the nose Doug had broken in the bar in Manhattan. 'I want first shot at Lord myself.'

'I want first shot at the woman,' another voice piped up, high and whiny. Whitney felt as though something slimy had passed over her skin.

'Pervert,' the first man grumbled as he pushed his

way through the forest. 'You can play with her, Barns, but remember, Dimitri wants her in one piece. As for Lord, the boss doesn't care how many pieces he's in.'

Whitney lay still on the ground, eyes wide, mouth dry. She'd read somewhere that true fear mists over hearing and sight. She could now verify it firsthand. It occurred to her that the woman they spoke of so casually was herself. All they had to do was look over the rise they were approaching and they'd see her spread out on the forest floor like goods in a marketplace.

Frantic, she looked back toward the huts. A hell of a lot of good Doug would do her, she thought grimly. He could come out into the open at any moment. From their position on the rise, Dimitri's men would simply pick him off like a bear in a shooting gallery. If he stayed where he was much longer, the Malagasy who were trooping home might create a bit of a scene when they found him systematically looting their hut.

First things first, Whitney cautioned herself. She needed better cover, and she needed it quickly. Moving only her head, she looked from side to side. Her best shot seemed to be a wide, downed tree between her and a thicket of bushes. Without giving herself time to consider, she gathered both packs and scrambled for it on all fours. Scraping her skin on the bark, she rolled over the tree and hit the ground with a thud.

'Hear something?'

Holding her breath, Whitney flattened herself against the trunk. Now she couldn't even see down to the huts and Doug. But she could see an army of tiny, rust-colored insects burrowing into the dead tree an inch from her face. Fighting revulsion, she kept still. Doug was on his own now, she told herself. And so was she.

Overhead came a rustling that might have been thunder by the way it echoed in her head. Fear gripped, followed by a wave of giddiness. How the hell was she going to explain to her father that she'd been kidnapped by a couple of thugs in a forest in Madagascar on her way to find lost treasure with a thief?

He didn't have much of a sense of humor.

Because she knew her father's wrath and didn't know Dimitri, the idea of the first worried her a great deal more than the second. She nearly crawled into the tree.

The rustling came again. There was no more casual conversation between the men. Stalking was done in silence. She tried to imagine them walking toward her, around her, beyond her, but her mind iced over with fear. Silence dragged on until sweat pearled on her forehead.

Whitney screwed her eyes shut as though, like a child, she believed the idea of *I can't see you, you can't see me*. It seemed easy to hold her breath when her blood was slowed and thickened with terror. There was a quiet thump on the trunk directly above her head. Resigned, she opened her eyes. Staring at her with intense eyes out of a black face was a smooth-coated Lemur.

'Jesus.' The word came out on a trembling breath, but there wasn't time for relief. She could hear the men approaching, more cautiously now. She wondered if being stalked in Central Park brought the same chilling fear. 'Get!' she hissed at the lemur. 'Go on.' She lay there, making faces at him, not daring to move. Obviously more amused than intimidated, he began making faces back at her. Whitney shut her eyes on a sign. 'Sweet Christ.' The lemur sent up a chatter that brought both men rushing to the rise.

She heard a high-pitched whoop and the retort of a

gun, then watched the wood splinter and fly no more
than six inches above her face. At the same moment,
the lemur leaped off the trunk and into the thicket.

'Idiot!' Whitney heard the quick, hard sound of a
slap, then incredibly, a giggle. It was the giggle more
than the shot, more than the stalking, that had her
body limp with terror.

'Almost got him. Another inch and I'd've plugged
the little bastard.'

'Yeah, and that gunshot probably has Lord running
like a rabbit.'

'I like shooting rabbits. Little fuckers freeze and look
right at you when you pull the trigger.'

'Shit.' She recognized disgust when she heard it and
nearly sympathized. 'Get going. Remo wants us
moving north.'

'Nearly got me a monkey.' The giggle sounded again.
'Never shot a monkey before.'

'Pervert.'

The word and the echoing laughter drifted away.
Moments passed. Whitney lay still and silent as a stone.
The insects had decided to explore her arm as well as
the tree, but she didn't move. She decided she might
have found a very good place to spend the next few
days.

When a hand closed over her mouth, she jerked like
a spring.

'Taking a nap?' Doug whispered in her ear. Watching her eyes he saw surprise turn to relief and relief to
fury. As a precaution, he held her down a moment
longer. 'Take it easy, sugar. They aren't that far away
yet.'

The moment her mouth was free, she started. 'I
nearly got shot,' she hissed at him. 'By some whiny
little creep with a cannon.'

He saw the fresh splinters in the tree above her head, but shrugged. 'You look okay to me.'

'No thanks to you.' She brushed at the sleeve of her blouse, allowing the disgust as insects scattered into the moss. 'While you were down there playing Robin Hood, two nasty men with equally nasty guns came strolling by. Your name was mentioned.'

'Fame's a burden,' he murmured. It had been close, he thought with a glance at the splintered tree again. Too close. No matter how he maneuvered, no matter how often he shifted direction and tactics, Dimitri hung on. Doug knew the sensation of being tracked. He also knew the sweaty, gut-fluttering feeling of the hunted when the hunter was closing in. He wasn't going to lose. He looked into the forest and forced himself to stay calm. He wasn't going to lose when he'd almost won.

'By the way, you're a lousy lookout.'

'You'll have to excuse the fact that I was preoccupied and couldn't whistle.'

'I nearly had to talk my way out of a very sensitive situation.' Back to business, he told himself. If Dimitri was close, they'd just have to move faster and jazz up their footwork. 'However, I managed to pick up a few things and get out before it got crowded.'

'It figures.' It didn't matter that she was relieved he was in one piece, and that she was more than pleased to have him with her again. She wouldn't let him know it. 'There was this lemur, and. . .' Whitney broke off when she saw one of the things he'd brought with him. 'What,' she began, in a tone that was obviously as offended as it was curious, 'is that?'

'A present.' Doug picked up the straw hat and offered it. 'I didn't have time to wrap it.'

'It's unattractive and has absolutely no style.'

'It has a wide brim,' he returned and dropped it on her head. 'Since it isn't possible for me to stick a bag over your head, this has to do.'

'How flattering.'

'I picked you up a little outfit to go with it.' He tossed her a stiff, shapeless cotton dress the color of sun-bleached dung.

'Douglas, really.' Whitney picked up a sleeve between her thumb and fingertip. She felt a revulsion nearly identical with that she'd experienced the morning she'd woken with the spider. Ugly was ugly, after all. 'I wouldn't be caught dead in this.'

'That's just what we're shooting for, sugar.'

She remembered the wood splintering a few inches above her nose. Perhaps the dress would pick up a bit of style when it was worn. 'And while I'm wearing this fetching little number, what about you?'

He picked up another straw hat, this one with a slightly peaked cap.

'Very chic.' She smothered her laughter when he held up a long plaid shirt and wide cotton pants.

'Our host obviously likes his rice,' Doug commented as he spread the generous waist of the pants. 'But we'll manage.'

'I hate to bring up the previous success of your disguises, but—'

'Then don't.' He rolled the clothes into a ball. 'In the morning, you and I are going to be a loving Malagasy couple on their way to market.'

'Why not a Malagasy woman and her idiot brother on their way to market?'

'Don't press your luck.'

Feeling a bit more confident, Whitney examined her slacks. They'd been torn at the knee on the bark. The hole annoyed her a great deal more than the bullet had. 'Just look at this!' she demanded. 'If this keeps up, I won't have a decent outfit left. I've already ruined a skirt and a perfectly lovely blouse, and now this.' She could stick three fingers in the hole. 'I just bought these slacks in DC.'

'Look, I brought you a new dress, didn't I?'

Whitney glanced at the ball of clothes. 'How droll.'

'Bitch later,' he advised. 'Right now tell me if you overheard anything I should know.'

She sent him a smoldering look, reached in her pack, and pulled out her notebook. 'These slacks are on your tab, Douglas.'

'Isn't everything?' Twisting his head, he looked down at the amount she noted. 'Eighty-five dollars? Who the hell pays eighty-five bucks for a pair of cotton pants?'

'You do,' she said sweetly. 'Just be grateful I'm not adding on the tax. Now. . .' Satisfied, she dropped the notebook back in her pack. 'One of the men was a creep.'

'Only one of them?'

'I mean a first-class creep with a voice like a slug. He giggled.'

Doug momentarily forgot his growing tab. 'Barns?'

'Yes, that's it. The other man called him Barns. He tried to shoot one of those cute little lemurs and nearly took off the tip of my nose.' As an afterthought she dug in her pack for her compact to make certaiin there was no damage.

If Dimitri had set his pet dog loose, Doug knew he was feeling confident. Barns wasn't on the payroll because of his brains or cunning. He didn't kill for profit or for practicality. He killed for fun. 'What'd they say? What'd you hear?'

Satisfied, she patted on a bit of powder. 'It came through loud and clear that the first man wanted to get his hands on you. It sounded personal. As for Barns. . .' Nervous again, she reached in Doug's pocket and pulled out a cigarette. 'He prefers me. Which, I suppose, shows some discrimination.'

He felt a well of fury rise up so quickly he nearly choked on it. While he battled it back, Doug took a pack of matches and lit the cigarette. Since he was running low, they'd have to share awhile. Saying nothing, he took the cigarette from Whitney and drew smoke in deeply.

He'd never seen Barns in action, but he'd heard. What he'd heard wasn't pretty, even up against some of the obscenities that happened with regularity in places Whitney'd never heard of.

Barns had a penchant for women, and small, fragile things. There was a particularly gruesome story about what he'd done to a sharp little hooker in Chicago—and what had been left of her after he'd done it.

Doug watched Whitney's slender, elegant fingers as she took the cigarette again. Barns wouldn't get his sweaty hands on her. Not if he had to cut them off at the wrist first.

'What else?'

She'd only heard that tone of voice from him once or twice before—when he'd held a rifle in his hand and when his fingers had closed around her throat. Whitney took a long pull on the cigarette. It was easier to play the game when Doug seemed half-amused and half-frustrated. When his eyes went cool and flat in just that way, it was a different story.

She remembered a hotel room in Washington and a young waiter with a red stain spreading over the back of his neat white jacket.

'Doug, can it be worth it?'

Impatient, he kept his eyes trained on the rise above their heads. 'What?'

'Your end of the rainbow, your pot of gold. These men want you dead—you want to jingle some gold in your pocket.'

'I want more than jingles, sugar. I'm going to drip with it.'

'While you're dripping, they'll be shooting at you.'

'Yeah, but I'll have something.' His gaze shifted and locked on hers. 'I've been shot at before. I've been running for years.'

She met the look, as intense as he. 'When do you plan to stop?'

'When I have something. And this time, I'm going to get it. Yeah.' He blew out a long stream of smoke. How could he explain to her what it was like to wake up in the morning with twenty dollars and your wits? Would she believe him if he told her he knew he'd been born for more than two-bit hustling? He'd been given a brain, he'd honed the skill, all he needed was a stake. A big one. 'Yeah, it's worth it.'

She was silent a moment, knowing she'd never really understand the need to have. You had to be without first. It wasn't as simple as greed, which she would have understood. It was as complex as ambition and as personal as dreams. Whether she was still following her first impulse, or something deeper, she was with him.

'They were heading north—the first man said Remo'd told them to. They figure to flush us out in here, or drive us out where they can pick us up.'

'Logical.' As if it were pricey Columbian, they passed the Virginian tobacco back and forth. 'So for tonight, we stay put.'

'Here?'

'As close to the huts as we can without being spotted.' With regret, he stubbed out the cigarette as it burned into the filter. 'We'll start out just after dawn.'

Whitney took his arm. 'I want more.'

He gave her a long look that reminded her of a moment by the waterfall. 'More what?'

'I've been chased and shot at. A few minutes ago I lay behind that tree wondering how much longer I was going to live.' She had to take a deep breath to keep her voice steady, but her gaze never faltered. 'I stand to lose every bit as much as you do, Doug. I want to see the papers.'

He'd wondered when she'd back him into a corner. He'd only hoped they could be closer before she did. Abruptly, he realized he'd stopped looking for opportunities to ditch her. It seemed he'd taken a partner after all.

But it didn't have to equal fifty-fifty. Going to his pack, he searched through the envelope until he came to a letter that hadn't been translated. If it hadn't been, his deduction was it wasn't as vital as those which had. On the other hand, he couldn't read it. Whitney might pass on something useful.

'Here.' He handed her the carefully sealed page before he sat on the ground again.

They looked each other over, wary, distrustful, before Whitney lowered her gaze to the sheet. It was dated October, 1794.

'Dear Louise,' she read. 'I pray as I write this letter will reach you and find you well. Even here, so many miles away, word comes to us of France. This settlement is small, and many people walk with their eyes regarding the ground. We have left one war for the threat of another. Political intrigue can never be escaped, it seems. Every day we search for French troops, the exile of another queen, and my heart is divided as to whether I would welcome them or hide.

'Still, there is a certain beauty here. The sea is close and I walk in the mornings with Danielle and gather shells. She has grown so in these last months, seen more, heard more than any mother can bear for her daughter. Yet from her eyes the fear is fading. She picks flowers—flowers such as I have never seen grow in any place. Though Gerald still mourns the queen, I feel, in time, we can be happy here.

'I write you, Louise, to get you to reconsider to join us. Even in Dijon you cannot be safe. I hear the stories of homes burned and looted, of people dragged to prison and to death. There is here a young man who received word that his parents were driven from their home near Versailles and hanged. At night I dream of you and fear desperately for your life. I want my sister with me, Louise, safe. Gerald will open a store and Danielle and I have planted a garden. Our lives are simple, but there is no guillotine, and no Terror.

'There is so much I need to talk with you about, sister. There are things I dare not write in a letter. I can tell you only that Gerald received a message, and an obligation from the queen only months before her death. It burdens him. In a plain wooden box he holds a part of France and Marie which will not release him. I beg you, do not cling to what has turned against you. Do not tie your heart as my husband has to what is surely over. Depart from France and what is past, Louise. Come to Diégo-Suarez. Your devoted sister, Magdaline.'

Slowly, Whitney handed the sheet back to him. 'Do you know what that is?'

'A letter.' Because he hadn't been unaffected, Doug slipped it back into the envelope. 'The family came here to escape the Revolution. According to other documents, this Gerald was some sort of manservant to Marie Antoinette.'

'It's important,' she murmured.

'Damn right. Every paper in here's important because every one adds a piece to the puzzle.'

She watched him secure the envelope in his pack. 'And that's all?'

'What else?' He shot her a look. 'Sure I feel sorry for the lady, but she's been dead quite a while. I'm alive.' He put his hand on the pack. 'This is going to help me live exactly the way I've been waiting to.'

'That letter is nearly two centuries old.'

'That's right, and the only thing in it that still exists is what's in a little wooden box. It's going to be mine.'

She studied him a moment, the intense eyes, the sensitive mouth. With a sigh, she shook her head. 'Life's not simple, is it?'

'No.' Because he needed to take the lonely look from her face, he smiled. 'Who wants it to be?'

She'd think later, Whitney decided. She'd demand to see the rest of the papers later. For now she wanted only to rest, body and mind. She rose, 'What now?'

'Now. . .' He scanned the immediate area. 'We make do with our accommodations.'

Making a primitive camp deep in the trees on the hill, they ate Merina meat and drank palm wine. They built no fire. Through the night they took turns keeping watch and sleeping. For the first time since they began the journey together, they barely spoke. Between them was the breath of danger and the memory of a wild, mindless moment under a waterfall.

Dawn in the forest brought streams of gold, shafts of rose, misty greens. The scent was like that of a hothouse with its doors just flung open. The light was dreamy, the air soft, carrying the cheerful sound of birds greeting the sunlight. Dew skimmed over the ground and clung to leaves. A shaft of sunlight turned tiny drops into rainbows. There were corners of paradise in the world.

Lazy, content, Whitney cuddled closer to the warmth beside her. She sighed when a hand stroked down her hair. Pleased with the feelings drifting through her, she settled her head on a male shoulder and slept.

It wasn't difficult to lose time watching her this way. Doug gave himself a moment of pleasure after a long, tense night. She was a stunner. And when she slept there was a softness about her that her tart wit concealed when she was in gear. Her eyes often dominated her face. Now, with them closed, it was possible to appreciate the sheer beauty of her bone structure, the flawless purity of her skin.

A man could fall very quick and very deep with a woman like this. Though he was sure-footed, Doug had already had a stumble or two himself.

He wanted to make love with her, slowly, luxuriously, on a soft, springy bed piled with pillows, lined with silk, lit by candles. His imagination had no trouble setting the scene for him. He wanted it, but he'd wanted many things in his life. Doug considered one of the highest marks of success the ability to separate what you wanted from what you could get, and what you could get from what would pay off. He wanted Whitney, and had a good chance of having her, but instinct warned him it wouldn't pay off.

A woman like her had a way of tossing out strings on a man—then tugging on them when they were good and tight. He had no intention of being tied down, or tied to. Take the money and run, he reminded himself.

That was the name of the game. In sleep, Whitney stirred and sighed. Awake, so did he.

It was time for a little distance, he decided. Reaching across her, he shook her by the shoulder. 'Rise and shine, duchess.'

'Hmmm?' She simply curled into him, as warm and sinuous as a napping cat. He was forced to let out a very long, very slow breath.

'Whitney, get your ass in gear.'

The phrase penetrated the fogs of sleep. Frowning, she opened her eyes. 'I'm not sure fifty percent of a pot of gold's worth having to hear your charming voice every morning.'

'We ain't growing old together. Anytime you want to back out, just say the word.'

It was then it occurred to her that their bodies were pressed close, like lovers after a night of passion—and compassion. One thin, arched, and elegant brow lifted. 'And what do you think you're doing, Douglas?'

'Waking you up,' he told her easily. 'You're the one who started crawling all over me. You know what a hard time you have resisting my body.'

'No, but I do know what a hard time I have resisting putting a few dents in it.' Pushing him away, she sat up and shook her hair back. 'Oh, God!'

His reflexes were quick. He had her under him again in a move swift enough to knock her breathless. Though neither of them realized it, he'd made one of the few purely unselfish gestures in his life. He'd shielded her body with his without a second thought to his own safety, or to profit. 'What?'

'Christ, must you habitually manhandle me?' Resigned, she sighed and pointed straight up. Cautiously, he followed the line of her finger.

Above their heads dozens of lemurs stood in the tops

of the trees. Their slim arching bodies were upright, their long, thin arms reaching up and up toward the sky. With their bodies stretched, lining the branches, they resembled a row of ecstatic pagans at sacrifice.

Doug let out an oath and relaxed. 'You're going to be seeing a lot of those little fellas,' he told her as he rolled aside. 'Do me a favor and don't shout every time we run into one.'

'I didn't shout.' She was much too charmed to be annoyed as she pulled up her knees and circled them with her arms. 'It looks as though they're praying, or worshipping the sunrise.'

'So the legend goes,' Doug agreed as he began to strike camp. Sooner or later, Dimitri's men would double back. Doug wasn't going to leave them a sign. 'Actually, they're just warming themselves.'

'I prefer the mystique.'

'Good. You'll have plenty of mystique in your new dress.' He tossed it to her. 'Put it on, there's one more thing I want to get from below.'

'While you're shopping, why don't you look for something a bit more attractive. I'm fond of silk, raw or refined. Something in blue with a bit of drape at the hips.'

'Just put it on,' he ordered and disappeared.

Huffing, and far from pleased, Whitney stripped off the soft, expensive, and ruined clothes she'd bought in Washington and pulled the shapeless tunic over her head. It fell lifelessly to her knees.

'Maybe with a nice wide leather belt,' she muttered. 'Something in scarlet with a really flashy buckle.' She ran a hand down the nubby cotton and scowled.

The hemline was all wrong and the color was simply hopeless. She absolutely refused to look like a dowd, whether she was attending the ballet or running from bullets. Sitting on the ground, she dug out her makeup case. At least she could do something about her face.

When Doug returned, she was trying and rejecting several different styles of wrapping the lamba over her shoulders. 'Nothing,' she said in disgust, 'absolutely nothing works with this sack. I think I'd rather wear your shirt and pants. At least. . .' She broke off as she turned around. 'Good God, what's that?'

'A pig,' he said precisely as he struggled with the squirming bundle.

'Of course it's a pig. What's it for?'

'More cover.' He fastened the rope he'd slipped around the pig's neck to a tree. With a few indignant squeaks, it subsided in the grass. 'The packs'll go in those baskets I lifted, so it looks like we're carrying our wares to market. The pig's a little more insurance. Lots of farmers in this region take livestock to market.' He stripped off his shirt as he spoke. 'What'd you put that stuff on your face for? The important thing is for nobody to see any more of it than absolutely necessary.'

'I might have to wear this shroud, but I refuse to look like a hag.'

'You've got a real problem with vanity,' he told her as he pulled on his newly acquired shirt.

'I don't see vanity as a problem,' she countered. 'When it's justified.'

'Pile your hair under that hat—all of it.'

She did, turning slightly away while he peeled off his jeans and replaced them with the cotton pants. To make up for the wide gap of inches, he cinched them with another piece of rope. When she turned, they studied each other.

The pants gathered generously at his waist, billowing down over his hips and riding to several inches above his ankles. The lamba he'd draped over his shoulders and back hid his build. The hat shadowed his face and covered most of his hair.

He might get away with it, as long as no one looked too closely, Whitney decided.

The long wide dress concealed every dip and curve of her body. It left her feet and ankles exposed. Much too elegant ankles, Doug observed, and decided they'd have to be coated with dust and dirt. The lamba, draped around her throat, over her shoulders and down her arms, was a good touch. For the most part, her hands would be hidden.

The straw hat had none of the style and flash of the white fedora she'd once worn, yet despite the fact that it thoroughly covered her hair, it did nothing to disguise the classic and very Western beauty of her face.

'You won't get a mile,' he muttered.

'What do you mean?'

'Your face. Christ, do you have to look like something that just stepped off the cover of *Vogue*?'

Her lips curved ever so slightly. 'Yes.'

Dissatisfied, Doug rearranged her lamba. With a bit of ingenuity, he brought it further up to her throat so that her chin was nearly buried in the folds, then pulled her hat down further on her head, tilting down the front brim.

'Just how the hell am I supposed to see?' She blew at the lamba. 'And breathe?'

'You can fold the brim back when nobody's around.' With his hands on his hips, he stood back to take a long, critical look. She looked shapeless, sexless, and overwhelmed by the circling shawl. . .until she looked up and shot him a glare.

There was nothing sexless about those eyes, he thought. They reminded him that there was indeed a shape under all that cotton. He shoved the packs into the baskets and covered them with the handfuls of fruit and food they had left. 'When we get out on the road, you keep your head down and walk behind me, like a properly disciplined wife.'

'Shows what you know about wives.'

'Let's get moving before they decide to backtrack this part of the forest.' He hefted a basket on each shoulder and started back down the steep, uncertain path.

'Didn't you forget something?'

'You get the pig, lover.'

Deciding her choices were limited, Whitney untied the rope from the tree and began to tug the uncooperative pig behind her. Eventually, she found it simpler to bundle him up in her arms like a recalcitrant child. He squirmed, oinked, and subsided.

'Come along, Little Douglas, Daddy's taking us to market.'

'Smartass,' Doug grumbled, but grinned as they cleared the trees.

'There is a bit of a resemblance,' she said as she skidded to a stop at the bottom. 'Around the snout.'

'We'll take this road east,' he said, ignoring her. 'With any luck, we'll make it to the coast by nightfall.'

Struggling with the pig, Whitney navigated down the steep dirt steps.

'For Chrissake, Whitney, put the damn pig down. He can walk.'

'I don't think you should swear in front of the baby.' Gently, she set him down, tugging on the rope so that he swayed along beside them. Mountain, brush, and cover were left behind. From a helicopter, she mused, they'd probably look enough like farmers to get away with it. Up close. . . 'What if we run into our hosts?'

she began, casting a quick look at the huts behind them. 'They might recognize this designer original.'

'We'll take our chances.' Doug started down the narrow road and decided Whitney's feet would be dirty enough within a mile. 'They'd be a lot easier to deal with than Dimitri's ape patrol.'

Because the road ahead looked endless and the day was only beginning, Whitney decided to take his word for it.

# CHAPTER NINE

After thirty minutes, Whitney knew the lamba was going to smother her. It was the kind of day where she felt it best to wear as little as possible while doing as little as possible. Instead, she was trapped inside a long-sleeved, long-skirted sack, wound inside yards of lamba, and assigned to a thirty-mile hike.

This one would be great for her memoirs, she decided. *Travels with My Pig.*

In any case, she was becoming rather fond of the little fellow. He had a princely kind of waddle, trooping along with his head swiveling from side to side now and again, as though he were leading a procession. She wondered how he'd like an overripe mango.

'You know,' Whitney decided, 'he's rather sweet.'

Doug glanced down at the pig. 'He'd be sweeter barbecued.'

'That's revolting.' She shot him a long, critical look. 'You wouldn't.'

No, he wouldn't, only because he didn't have the stomach for it. But there was no reason to let Whitney know he had a certain delicacy. If he was going to eat ham, he wanted it all nicely cured and packaged first.

'I've got this recipe for sweet-and-sour pork. Worth its weight in gold.'

'Just keep it filed,' she said smartly. 'This little piggy's under my protection.'

'I did three weeks in a Chinese restaurant in San Francisco. Before I left town, I had the classiest ruby necklace outside of a museum, a black pearl tiepin as

big as a robin's egg, and a pad full of great recipes.' All
he had left were the recipes. They satisfied him. 'You
marinate the pork overnight. It's so tender, it practically dissolves on the plate.'

'Stuff it.'

'Herb sausage in a very thin casing. Grilled.'

'Your IQ's all in your stomach.'

The road became more even, smoother, and wider
as they left the hills behind. The eastern plane was lush
and green and humid. And much too open for Doug's
thinking. He glanced overhead at power lines. A
disadvantage. Dimitri could issue orders quickly over
the phone. From where? Was he south, following the
trail Doug so desperately tried to cover? Behind, just
behind and closing in?

They were being followed, of that he was certain.
He recognized the feeling, and hadn't been able to
shake it since they'd left New York. And yet. . .Doug
shifted the basket. He couldn't lose the notion that
Dimitri knew the destination and was waiting patiently
to close the net. Doug glanced around again. He'd
have slept easier knowing from which direction he was
being hunted.

Though they didn't dare risk the use of his field
glasses, they could see wide, well-tended planta-
tions—with long stretches of flatland that could accom-
modate the landing of a helicopter. Flowers sprang up
everywhere to bake in the heat. Dust from the road
coated petals but didn't make them any less exotic.
The view was excellent, the day clear. All the easier to
spot two people and one pig traveling down the eastern
road. He kept the pace steady, hoping to come across
a group of travelers they could blend with. One glance
at Whitney reminded him that blending wasn't a simple
matter.

'Do you have to walk as though you were strolling toward Bloomingdale's?'

'I beg your pardon?' She was getting the hang of leading the pig and wondered if it would make a more interesting pet than a dog.

'You walk rich. Try for humble.'

She heaved a long-suffering sigh. 'Douglas, I might have to wear this very unattractive outfit and lead a pig on a rope, but I won't be humble. Now, why don't you stop griping and enjoy the walk. Everything's pretty and green and the air smells like vanilla.'

'There's a plantation over there. They grow it.' And on a plantation were vehicles. He wondered just how risky it would be to attempt to liberate one.

'Really?' She squinted as she looked into the sun. The fields were wide and very green, dotted with people. 'It grows in a little bean, doesn't it?' she asked idly. 'I've always been fond of the scent in those slim white candles.'

He shot her a mild look. White candles, white silk. That was her style. Ignoring the image, he gave his attention back to the fields they were passing. There were too many people working in them and too much open space to try hot-wiring a pickup at the moment.

'The weather's certainly become tropical, hasn't it?' Sweltering, she dabbed at her forehead with the back of her hand.

'Trade winds bring in the moisture. It's hot and humid till around next month, but we've missed the cyclone season.'

'There's good news,' she murmured. She thought she could actually see the heat rising from the road in waves. Oddly, it brought a flash of nostalgia for New York in high summer, where the heat bounced up off the sidewalks and you could choke on the smell of sweat and exhaust.

A late brunch at the Palm Court would be nice, with strawberries in cream and a tall iced coffee. She shook her head and ordered herself to think of something else.

'On a day like this, I'd like to be in Martinique.'

'Who wouldn't?'

Ignoring his testy tone of voice, she went on. 'I've a friend with a villa there.'

'I bet.'

'Perhaps you've heard of him—Robert Madison. He writes spy thrillers.'

'Madison?' Surprised, Doug gave her his attention again. '*The Pisces Symbol?*'

Impressed that he'd named what she considered Madison's best work, she looked at him under the brim of her hat. 'Why, yes, you've read him?'

'Yeah.' Doug shifted the bags on his shoulders. 'I've managed to get a bit beyond "see Spot run."'

She'd already gauged that for herself. 'Don't be cranky. It just happens that I'm a rather avid fan. We've known each other for years. Bob moved to Martinique when the IRS made it uncomfortable for him in the States. His villa's quite lovely, with a spectacular view of the sea. Right now, I'd be sitting beside the pool on the terrace with an enormous frozen margarita, watching half-naked people play on the beach.'

That was her style all right, he thought, incomprehensibly annoyed. Terraced pools and sultry air, little white-suited houseboys serving drinks on silver platters while some jerk with more looks than brains rubbed oil on her shoulder blades. He'd done both the serving and the rubbing in his time and couldn't say he preferred one to the other as long as the haul was rich.

'If you had nothing to do on a day like this, what would you choose?'

He struggled against the image of Whitney, lying half-naked on a lounge, skin slick with oil. 'I'd be in bed,' he told her. 'With a clever redhead with green eyes and big—'

'A rather ordinary fantasy,' Whitney interrupted.

'I've rather ordinary urges.'

She feigned a yawn. 'So, I'm sure, does our pig. Look,' she went on before he could retort, 'something's coming.'

He saw the dust plume in the road ahead. Muscles tense, he looked right and left. If necessary, they could make a run for it over the fields, but it wasn't likely they'd get far. If their impromptu costuming didn't work, it could all be over within minutes.

'Just keep your head down,' he told Whitney. 'And I don't care how much it goes against the grain, look humble and subservient.'

She tilted her head so that she looked at him from under the brim of her hat. 'I wouldn't have the least idea how.'

'Keep your head down and walk.'

The truck's engine sounded well-tuned and powerful. Though the paint was splashed with dirt, Doug could see it was fairly new. He'd read that many of the plantation owners were well-off, growing wealthy through the sale of vanilla, coffee, and clovers that thrived in this region. As the truck drew closer, he shifted the bag on his shoulder slightly so that most of his face was hidden. His muscles tingled and tensed. The truck barely slowed as it passed them. All he could think of was how quickly they could get to the coast if he could get his hands on one.

'It worked.' Whitney lifted her head and grinned. 'He drove right by us without a glance.'

'Mostly if you give people what they expect to see, they don't see anything.'

'How profound.'

'Human nature,' he tossed back, still regretting that he wasn't behind the wheel of the truck. 'I've gotten into plenty of hotel rooms wearing a red bellman's jacket and a five-dollar smile.'

'You rob hotels in broad daylight?'

'For the most part, people aren't in their rooms during the day.'

She thought about it a moment, then shook her head. 'It doesn't sound nearly as thrilling. Now, stalking around in the dead of night in a black suit with a flashlight, while people are sleeping right in the same room. That's exciting.'

'And that's how you get ten to twenty.'

'Risk adds to the excitement. Have you ever been to jail?'

'No. It's one of the small pleasures in life I've never experienced.'

She nodded. It confirmed her opinion that he was good at what he did. 'What was your biggest heist?'

Though the sweat was running freely down his back, he laughed. 'Christ, where do you get your terminology? "Starsky and Hutch" reruns?'

'Come on, Douglas, this is called passing the time.' If she didn't pass the time, she'd collapse on the road in a puddle of dripping exhaustion. Once she'd thought she'd never be any more hot and uncomfortable than she'd been hiking over the highlands. She'd been wrong. 'You must've had one big haul in your illustrious career.'

He said nothing for a moment as he looked down the straight, endless road. But he wasn't seeing the dust, the ruts, the short shadows cast by the piercing noontime sun. 'I had my hands on a diamond as big as your fist.'

'A diamond?' It so happened she had a weakness for them, the icy glitter, the hidden colors, the ostentation.

'Yeah, not just any rock; a big, glittery granddaddy. The prettiest piece of ice I've ever seen. The Sydney Diamond.'

'The Sydney?' She stopped, gaping. 'God, it's forty-eight and a half carats of perfection. I remember it was on exhibition in San Francisco about three, no four years ago. It was stolen. . .' She broke off, astonished and deeply impressed. 'You?'

'That's right, sugar.' He enjoyed the fascinated surprise on her face. 'I had that sonofabitch in my hand.' In memory, he looked down at his empty palm. It was scratched now from the flight through the forest, but he could see the diamond in it, gloating up at him. 'I swear, you could feel the heat from it, see a hundred different pictures by putting it up to the light. It was like holding a cool blonde while her blood ran hot.'

She could feel it, the arousal, the pure physical thrill. Since she'd received her first string of pearls, Whitney had often pinned and draped on diamonds and other glitters. It pleased her. But the pleasure of imagining holding the Sydney was much deeper, of plucking it out of its cold glass case and watching light and life gleam in your hand.

'How?'

'Melvin Feinstein. The Worm. The little bastard was my partner.'

Whitney saw from the set of his mouth that the story wasn't going to have a happy-ever-after ending. 'And?'

'The Worm earned his name in more ways than one. He was four-foot-six. I swear, he could slip under the crack of a door. He had the blueprints of the museum, but he didn't have the brains to handle the security. That's where I came in.'

'You handled the alarms.'

'Everybody's got a specialty.' He looked back, back over the years in San Francisco where the days had been misty and the nights cool. 'We cased that job for weeks, calculating every possible angle. The alarm system was a beauty, the best I'd ever come across.' That memory was pleasant, the challenge of it, and the logic by which he'd outwitted it. With a computer and figures, you could find more interesting answers than the balance of your checkbook.

'Alarms're like women,' he mused. 'They bait you, wink at you. With a little charm and the right skill, you figure out what makes them tick. Patience,' he murmured, nodding to himself. 'The right touch, and you've got them just where you want them.'

'A fascinating analogy, I'm sure.' She watched him cooly from under the brim of her hat. 'One might even say they have a habit of going off when provoked.'

'Yeah, but not if you keep a step ahead.'

'You'd better go on with your story before you get in any deeper, Douglas.'

His mind was back in San Francisco on a chilled night where the fog came in long fingers to sweep the ground. 'We got in through the ducts, easier for the Worm than me. Had to shoot out a line and go hand over hand because the floors were wired. I lifted it; the Worm has clumsy hands and he wasn't long enough to reach the display anyway. I had to hang down over the case. It took me six and a half minutes to cut through the glass. Then I had it.'

She could see it—Doug hanging by his feet over the display, dressed in black, while the diamond glinted up at him.

'The Sydney was never recovered.'

'That's right, sugar. It's one of the little entries in the book in my pack.' There was no way he could explain to her the pleasure and frustration he felt reading about it.

'If you had it, why aren't you living in a villa in Martinique?'

'Good question.' With something between a smile and a sneer, he shook his head. 'Yeah, that's a damn good question. I had it,' he murmured, half to himself. He angled his hat forward but still squinted against the sun. 'For a minute I was one rich sonofabitch.' He could still picture it, still feel the near-sexual pull of hanging over the display case, holding the glittering piece of ice in his hand, the world under his feet.

'What happened?'

The image and the feeling shattered, like a diamond split carelessly. 'We started back out. Like I said, the Worm could squirm through the ducts like a slug. By the time I got through, he was gone. The little bastard'd lifted the rock right out of my bag and vanished. To top it off, he put an anonymous call through to the police. They were crawling all over my hotel when I got back. I hopped a freighter with the shirt on my back. That's when I spent some time in Tokyo.'

'What about the Worm?'

'Last I heard he had himself a cozy yacht and was running a high-class floating casino. One of these days. . .' He relished the fantasy a moment, then shrugged. 'Anyway, that was the last time I took a partner.'

'Until now,' she reminded him.

He looked down at her, his eyes narrowed. He was back in Madagascar and there was no chilling fog. There was only sweat, aching muscles, and Whitney. 'Until now.'

'In case you have any notion of imitating your friend, the Worm, Douglas, remember, there isn't a hole deep enough for you to slide into.'

'Sugar—' He pinched her chin. 'Trust me.'

'I'll pass, thanks.'

For a time they walked in silence, Doug reliving every step of the Sydney Diamond job—the tension, the cool-headed concentration that kept the blood very still and the hands very steady, the thrill of holding the world in his hands, if only for a moment. He'd have it again. That much he promised himself.

It wouldn't be the Sydney this time, but a box of jewels that would make the Sydney look like a prize in a Cracker Jack box. This time nobody'd take it from him, no bowlegged midget, and no classy blonde.

Too many times he'd had the rainbow in his hands and watched it vanish. It wasn't so bad if you blew it yourself on foolishness and chances. But when you were stupid enough to trust someone. . . That had always been one of his big problems. He might steal, but he was honest. Somehow he figured other people were as well. Until he ended up with empty pockets.

The Sydney, Whitney mused. No second-class hood would've attempted to steal it, or have succeeded. The story confirmed for her what she'd thought all along. Doug Lord was a class act, in his own fashion. And there was one more thing—he'd be very possessive

with the treasure when and if they found it. That was
something she'd have to think about carefully.

Absently, she smiled at two children racing across
the field to her left. Perhaps their parents were working
on the plantation, perhaps they owned it. Still, their
lives would be simple, she thought. It was interesting
how appealing simplicity could be from time to time.
She felt the cotton dress rub uncomfortably over her
shoulder. Then again, there was something to be said
for luxury. Lots of it.

They both jolted at the sound of an engine behind
them. When they turned, the truck was practically on
top of them. If they'd had to run, they wouldn't have
gotten ten yards. Doug cursed himself, then cursed
again when the driver leaned out and called to them.

It wasn't a new model like the truck that had passed
them earlier, nor was it quite as rickety as the Merina
jeep. The engine ran smoothly enough as it idled in the
middle of the road. The back was loaded with wares,
from pots and baskets to wooden chairs and tables.

A traveling salesman, Whitney decided, already
eyeing what he had to offer. She wondered how much
he wanted for the colorful clay pot. It would look
rather nice on a table with a collection of cacti.

The driver would be a Betsimisaraka, Doug calculated, both from the region they were traveling in and
the European touch of his derby. He grinned, showing
a mouthful of healthy white teeth as he gestured for
them to approach the truck.

'Well, what now?' Whitney asked under her breath.

'I think we've just hitched a ride, sugar, whether we
want to or not. We'd better give your French and my
charm another try.'

'Let's simply use my French, shall we?' Forgetting to
look humble, she walked to the truck. While she

peered from under the brim of her hat, she gave the driver her best smile and made up a story as she went along.

She and her husband, though she had to swallow a bit on that one, were traveling from their farm in the hills to the coast where her family lived. Her mother, she decided on the spot, was ill. She noticed that his curious dark eyes roamed her face, pale and regal under the simple straw hat. Without breaking rhythm, Whitney rattled off an explanation. Apparently satisfied, the driver gestured to the door. He was traveling to the coast, they were welcome to a ride.

Stooping, Whitney gathered up the pig. 'Come on, Douglas, we've got a new chauffeur.'

Doug secured the baskets in the back, then climbed in beside her. Luck would play either way, he knew that well enough. This time he was willing to believe it had played on his side.

Whitney laid the pig on her lap as though it were a small, weary child. 'What'd you tell him?' he asked her as he nodded to the driver and grinned.

Whitney sighed, absorbing the luxury of being driven. 'I told him we're going to the coast. My mother's ill.'

'Sorry to hear it.'

'It's very like a deathbed scene, so don't look too happy.'

'Your mother never liked me.'

'That's beside the point. Besides, it's merely that she wanted me to marry Tad.'

He paused in the act of offering one of their few cigarettes to the driver. 'Tad who?'

She enjoyed the scowl on his face and smoothed the skirt of her dress. 'Tad Carlyse IV. Don't be jealous, darling. After all, I chose you.'

'Lucky me,' he muttered. 'How'd you get around the fact that we aren't natives?'

'I'm French. My father was a sea captain who settled on the coast. You were a teacher on holiday. We fell madly in love, married against our family's wishes, and now work a small farm in the hills. By the way, you're British.'

Doug played back the story in his head and decided he couldn't have done better. 'Good thinking. How long've we been married?'

'I don't know, why?'

'I just wondered if I should be affectionate or bored.'

Whitney narrowed her eyes. 'Kiss ass.'

'Even if we're newlyweds, I don't think I should be that affectionate in front of company.'

Barely smothering a chuckle, Whitney closed her eyes and pretended she was in a plush limo. Within moments, her head was snuggled on Doug's shoulder. The pig snored gently in her lap.

She dreamed she and Doug were in a small, elegant room washed with candlelight that wafted the scent of vanilla. She wore silk, white and thin enough to show the silhouette of her body. He was all in black.

She recognized the look in his eyes, the sudden darkening of that clear, clear green before his clever hands ran up her body and his mouth covered hers. She was weightless, floating, unable to touch the ground with her feet—yet she could feel every plane and line as his body pressed against hers.

Smiling he drew away from her and reached for a bottle of champagne. The dream was so clear that she could see the beads of water on the glass. He pried the cork. It opened with an ear-splintering blast. When she looked again, he held only a jagged bottle in his hand.

At the door was the shadow of a man and the glint of a sun.

They were crawling through a small, dark hole. Sweat rolled from her. Somehow she knew they were winding through ducts, yet it was like the tunnel to the cave—dark, dank, suffocating.

'Just a little bit farther.'

She heard him speak and saw something glitter up ahead. It was light beaming off the facets of an enormous diamond. For a moment, it filled the darkness with a wild, almost religious light. Then it was gone, and she was standing alone on a barren hill. 'Lord, you sonofabitch!'

'Rise and shine, sugar. This is our stop.'

'You worm,' she muttered.

'That's no way to talk to your husband.'

Opening her eyes, she looked into his grinning face. 'You sonofa—'

He cut the oath off, kissing her hard and long. With his lips only a breath from hers, he pinched her. 'We're supposed to be in love, sugar. Our friendly chauffeur might have a grasp of some of the cruder English expressions.'

Dazed, she squeezed her eyes shut, then opened them again. 'I was dreaming.'

'Yeah. And it sounds like I didn't come off very well.' Doug hopped out to retrieve the baskets in the back.

Whitney shook her head to clear it, then looked through the windshield. A town. It was small by any standard and the air had a scent that brought fish to mind rather sharply. But it was a town. As thrilled as if she'd woken in Paris on an April morning, Whitney jumped from the truck.

A town meant a hotel. A hotel meant a tub, hot water, a real bed.

'Douglas, you're wonderful!' With the pig sandwiched and squealing between them, she hugged him.

'Jesus, Whitney, you're getting pig all over me.'

'Absolutely wonderful,' she said again and gave him a loud, exuberant kiss.

'Well, yeah.' He found his hand could settle comfortably at her waist. 'But a minute ago I was a worm.'

'A minute ago I didn't know where we were.'

'You do now? Why don't you fill me in?'

'In town.' Hugging the pig against her, she whirled away. 'Hot and cold running water, box springs and mattresses. Where's the hotel?' Shading her eyes, she began to scan.

'Look, I wasn't planning on staying—'

'There!' she said triumphantly.

It was clean and without frills, more along the lines of an inn than a hotel. It was a town of seamen, fishermen, with the Indian Ocean close at its back. A seawall rose high as protection against the floods that came every season. Here and there, nets were spread over to dry in the sun. There were palm trees and fat orange flowers growing in vines against clapboard. A gull nestled at the top of a telephone pole and slept. The straight lines of the coast prevented it from being a port, but the little seaside town obviously enjoyed a smatter of tourist trade now and then.

Whitney was already thanking the driver. Though it surprised him, Doug didn't have the heart to tell her they couldn't stay. He'd planned to replenish supplies and see about transportation up the coast before they went on. He watched her smile at their driver.

One night couldn't hurt, he decided. They could start out fresh in the morning. If Dimitri was close, at

least Doug would have a wall at his back for a few
hours. A wall at his back and a few hours to plan the
next step. He swung a basket over each shoulder. 'Give
him the pig and say good-bye.'

Whitney smiled at the driver a last time, then started
across the street. There were shells crushed underfoot
mixed with dirt and a stingy spread of gravel. 'Abandon
our first-born son to a traveling salesman? Really,
Douglas, it'd be like selling him to the gypsies.'

'Cute, and I understand you might've formed a bit
of an attachment.'

'So would you if you hadn't been thinking with your
stomach.'

'But what the hell are we going to do with it?'

'We'll find him a decent home.'

'Whitney.' Just outside the inn, he took her arm.
'That's a slab of bacon, not a Pomeranian.'

'Ssh!' Cuddling the pig protectively, she walked
inside.

It was marvelously cool. There were ceiling fans
lazily circling that made her think of Rick's Place in
*Casablanca*. The walls were whitewashed, the floors
dark wood, scarred but scrubbed. Someone had tacked
bleached, woven mats to the walls, the only decoration.
A few people sat at tables drinking a dark gold liquid
in thick glasses. Whitney caught the scent of something
unidentifiable and wonderful drifting through an open
door in the back.

'Fish stew,' Doug murmured as his stomach yearned.
'Something close to bouillabaisse with a touch
of—rosemary,' he said, closing his eyes. 'And a little
garlic.'

Because her mouth watered, Whitney was forced to
swallow. 'It sounds like lunch to me.'

A woman came through the door, wiping her hands

on a big white apron that was colored like a parade flag
from her cooking. Though her face was creased deeply,
and her hands showed work as well as age, she wore
her hair in gay braided rings like a young girl. She
scanned Whitney and Doug, looked at the pig for only
a moment, then spoke in quick, heavy accented English. So much for Doug's disguises.

'You wish a room?'

'Please.' Struggling to keep her eyes from drifting
beyond the woman to the doorway where scents poured
out, Whitney smiled.

'My wife and I would like a room for the night, a
bath, and a meal.'

'For two?' the woman said, then looked again at the
pig. 'Or for three?'

'I found the little pig wandering on the side of the
road,' Whitney improvised. 'I didn't like to leave it.
Perhaps you know someone who'd care for it.'

The woman eyed the pig in a way that had Whitney
hugging it tighter. Then she smiled. 'My grandson will
take care of it. He is six, but he is responsible.' The
woman held out her arms, and reluctantly Whitney
handed her erstwhile pet over. Hefting the pig under
one arm, the woman reached in her pocket for keys.
'This room is ready, up the stairs and two doors on the
right. You are welcome.'

Whitney watched her go back into the kitchen with
the pig under her arm.

'Now, now, sugar, every mother has to let her
children go one day.'

She sniffed and started for the stairs. 'He'd better
not be on the menu tonight.'

The room was a great deal smaller than the cave
they'd slept in. But it had a few cheerful seaside
paintings on the wall and a bed covered in a flashy

floral print that had been meticulously patched. The bath was no more than an alcove separated from the bedroom by a bamboo screen.

'Heaven,' Whitney decided after one look and flopped facedown on the bed. It smelled, only lightly, of fish.

'I don't know how celestial it is'—he checked the lock on the door and found it sturdy—'but it'll do until the real thing comes along.'

'I'm going to crawl into the tub and wallow for hours.'

'All right, you take the first shift.' Without ceremony, he dumped the baskets on the floor. 'I'm going to do a little checking around and see what kind of transportation we can get heading up the coast.'

'I'd prefer a nice, stately Mercedes.' Sighing, she pillowed her head on her hands. 'But I'd settle for a wagon and a three-legged pony.'

'Maybe I can find something in between.' Taking no chances, he pulled the envelope out of his pack and secured it under the back of his shirt. 'Don't use all the hot water, sugar. I'll be back.'

'Be sure to check on room service, won't you? I hate it when the canapés are late.' Whitney heard the door click shut and stretched luxuriously. As much as she'd like just to sleep, she decided, she wanted a bath more.

Rising, she stripped off the long cotton dress and let it fall in a heap. 'My sympathies to your former owner,' she murmured, then threw the straw hat like a Frisbee across the room. Over her naked skin, her hair cascaded like sunlight. Cheerful, she turned the hot tap on full and searched through her pack for her cache of bath oil and bubbles. In ten minutes, she was steeped in steaming, fragrant, frothy water.

'Heaven,' she said again and shut her eyes.

Outside, Doug took in the town quickly. There were a few little shops with handicrafts arranged in the windows. Colorful hammocks hung on hooks from porch rails and a row of shark's teeth were lined on a stoop. Obviously, the people were accustomed to tourists and their odd penchant for the useless. The scent of fish was strong as he wandered down toward the wharf. There, he admired the boats, the coils of rope, and the nets spread out to dry.

If he could figure out a way to keep some fish on ice, he'd bargain for it. Miracles could be accomplished with a fish over an open fire if one had the right touch. But first, there was a matter of the miles he had yet to travel up the coast, and how he was going to go about it.

He'd already decided that going by water would be the quickest and most practical way. From the map in the guidebook, he'd seen that the Canal des Pangalanes could take them all the way to Maroantsetra. From there, they'd have to travel through the rain forest.

He'd feel safer there, with the heat, the humidity, and the plentiful cover. The canal was the best route. All he needed was a boat, and someone with the skill to guide it.

Spotting a small shop, he wandered over. He hadn't seen a paper in days and decided to buy one even if he had to depend on Whitney to translate. As he reached for the door, he felt a quick flash of disorientation. From within, he heard the unmistakable tough-rock sound of Pat Benatar.

'Hit me with your best shot!' she challenged as he pushed the door open.

Behind the counter stood a tall, lanky man whose dark skin gleamed with sweat as he moved to the beat pouring out of a small, expensive portable stereo.

While his feet shuffled, he polished the glass in the windows to the side of the counter and belted out the lyrics with Benatar.

'Fire awaaay!' he shouted, then turned as the door slammed behind Doug. 'Good afternoon.' The accent was decidedly French. The faded T-shirt he wore read City College of New York. The grin was youthful and appealing. On the shelves behind him were trinkets, linens, cans, and bottles. A general store in Nebraska wouldn't have been better stocked.

'May I interest you in some souvenirs?'

'CCNY?' Doug questioned as he crossed the bare wood floor.

'American!' Reverently, the man turned Benatar down to a muffled roar before he held out his hand. 'You are from the States?'

'Yeah. New York.'

The young man lit up like a firecracker. 'New York! My brother'—he tugged on the T-shirt—'he goes to college there. Student exchange. Going to be a lawyer, yes sir. A hotshot.'

It was impossible not to grin. With his hand still caught in the man's grasp, Doug shook lightly. 'I'm Doug Lord.'

'Jacques Tsiranana. America.' Obviously reluctant, he released Doug's hand. 'I go there myself next year to visit. You know Soho?'

'Yeah.' And until that moment, he hadn't realized just how much he missed it. 'Yeah, I know Soho.'

'I have a picture.' Digging in behind the counter, he brought out a bent snapshot. It showed a tall, muscular man in jeans standing in front of Tower Records.

'My brother, he buys the records and puts them on the tapes for me. American music,' Jacques pronounced. 'Rock and roll. How about that Benatar?'

'Great pipes,' Doug agreed, handing the snapshot back.

'So what are you doing here, when you could be in Soho?'

Doug shook his head. There had been times he'd asked himself the same question. 'My, ah, lady and I are traveling up the coast.'

'Vacation?' He took a quick glimpse at Doug's clothes. He was dressed like the humblest Malagasy peasant, but there was a look of sharp authority in his eye.

'Yeah, like a vacation.' If you didn't count the guns and the running. 'I thought it might give her a kick to go up the canal, you know, scenic.'

'Pretty country,' Jacques agreed. 'How far?'

'To here.' Doug drew the map out of his pocket and ran a finger along the route. 'All the way to Maroantsetra.'

'Some kick,' Jacques murmured. 'Two days, two long days. In places the canal is hard to navigate.' His teeth shone. 'Crocodiles.'

'She's tough,' he claimed, thinking of that very sensitive, very soft skin. 'You know the kind who digs camping out and open fires. What we need is a good guide and a strong boat.'

'You pay in American dollars?'

Doug narrowed his eyes. It looked like luck was indeed playing on his side. 'It can be arranged.'

Jacques poked his thumb into the printing on his shirt. 'Then I take you.'

'Got a boat?'

'The best boat in town. Built it myself. Got a hundred?'

Doug looked down at his hands. They appeared

competent and strong. 'Fifty up front. We'll be ready to go in the morning. Eight o'clock.'

'Bring your lady here at eight o'clock. We'll give her a kick.'

Unaware of the pleasures in store for her, Whitney half dozed in the tub. Each time the water had cooled a bit, she had let in another stream of hot. As far as she was concerned, she could spend the night there. Her head rested against the back lip, her hair fell behind, wet and shining.

'Trying for a world's record?' Doug asked from behind her.

With a gasp, she jerked up so that the water lapped dangerously near the edge. 'You didn't knock,' she accused. 'And I locked the door.'

'I picked it,' he said easily. 'Need to keep in practice. How's the water?' Without waiting for an answer, he dipped in a finger. 'Smells good.' His gaze skimmed over the surface. 'Looks like your bubbles're starting to give out.'

'They've got a few minutes left in them. Why don't you get rid of that ridiculous outfit?'

Grinning, he began to unbutton his shirt. 'Thought you'd never ask.'

'On the other side of the screen.' Smiling, she examined her toe just above the water's surface. 'I'll get out so you can have your turn.'

'Shame to waste all that pretty hot water.' Putting a hand on either side of the tub, he leaned over her. 'Since we're partners, we should share.'

'You think so?' His mouth was very close, and she was very relaxed. Reaching up she trailed a damp finger down his cheek. 'Just what did you have in mind?'

'A little'—gently, he brushed her lips with his—'unfinished business.'

'Business?' She laughed and let her hand roam over his neck. 'Want to negotiate?' On impulse she pulled, and off-balance, he slid into the tub. Water heaved over the side. Giggling like a schoolgirl, she watched as he swiped bubbles from his face. 'Douglas, you never looked better.'

Tangled with her, he struggled to keep from submerging. 'She likes games.'

'Well, you looked so hot and sweaty.' Generous, she offered the soap, then laughed again when he rubbed it over the shirt that clung to him.

'Why don't I give you a hand?' Before she could avoid it, he ran the soap down from her throat to her waist. 'I seem to remember you owe me a back scrub.'

Aware, and still amused, she took the soap from him. 'Why don't you—'

Both of them tensed at the knock at the door.

'Don't move,' Doug whispered.

'I wasn't going to.'

Untangling himself, he climbed out of the tub. Water ran everywhere. It swished in his shoes as he went to his pack and dug out the gun he'd buried in it. He hadn't had it in his hands since their flight from Washington. He didn't like the feel of it any more now.

If Dimitri had found them, he couldn't have cornered them more neatly. Doug glanced at the window behind him. He could be out and down in seconds. Then he glanced at the bamboo screen. In a tub of cooling water, Whitney sat naked and completely vulnerable. Doug gave a last regretful look at the window and escape.

'Shit.'

'Doug—'

'Quiet.' Holding it close, barrel up, he moved to the door. It was time to try his luck again. 'Yeah?'

'Captain Sambirano, police. At your service.'

'Shit.' Looking around quickly, Doug stuck the gun in the back waistband of his pants. 'Your badge, Captain?' Coiled to spring, Doug opened the door a crack and examined the badge, then the man. He could spot a cop ten miles away. Reluctantly, he opened the door. 'What can I do for you?'

The captain, small, rotund, and very Western in dress stepped inside. 'I seem to have interrupted you.'

'Having a bath.' Doug saw the puddle forming at his feet and reached for a towel behind the screen.

'I beg your pardon, Mr—'

'Wallace, Peter Wallace.'

'Mr Wallace. It is my custom to greet anyone who passes through our town. We have a quiet community.' The captain gently tugged on the hem of his jacket. Doug noticed his nails were short and polished. 'From time to time we entertain tourists who are not fully aware of the law or our customs.'

'Always happy to cooperate with the police,' Doug said with a wide smile. 'As it happens, I'm moving on tomorrow.'

'A pity you can't extend your stay. You are perhaps in a hurry?'

'Peter. . .' Whitney poked her head and one naked shoulder around the screen. 'Excuse me.' She did her best to blush as she swept her lashes down, then up again.

Whether the blush worked or not, the captain took off his hat and bowed. 'Madam.'

'My wife, Cathy. Cath, this is Captain Sambirano.'

'How do you do?'

'Charmed.'

'I'm sorry I can't come out just now. You see I'm. . .' She trailed off and smiled.

'Of course. You must forgive the interruption, Mrs Wallace. Mr Wallace. If I can be of any help to you during your stay, please do not hesitate.'

'How sweet.'

Halfway out the door, the captain turned back. 'And your destination, Mr Wallace?'

'Oh, we're following our noses,' Doug claimed. 'Cathy and I are graduate students. Botany. So far we've found your country fascinating.'

'Peter, the water's getting cold.'

Doug glanced over his shoulder, looked back, and grinned. 'It's our honeymoon, you understand.'

'Naturally. May I congratulate you on your taste? Good afternoon.'

'Yeah, see you.'

Doug closed the door, leaned back against it and swore. 'I don't like it.'

Wrapped in a towel, Whitney came out from behind the screen. 'What do you think that was all about?'

'I wish I knew. But one thing, when cops start nosing around, I look for other accommodations.'

Whitney took a long look at the gaily covered bed. 'But, Doug.'

'Sorry, sugar. Get yourself dressed.' He began to strip off his own dripping clothes. 'We're catching a boat, a little ahead of schedule.'

'You have something new?' After fondling a glass chess piece, Dimitri moved bishop's pawn.

'We think they headed toward the coast.'

'Think?' At the snap of Dimitri's fingers a dark-suited man placed a crystal goblet in his hand.

'There was a little settlement in the hills.' Remo

watched Dimitri drink and swallowed on his own dry throat. He hadn't had a decent night's sleep in a week. 'When we checked it out, the family was in an uproar. Somebody'd ripped them off while they were in the fields.'

'I see.' The wine was excellent, but, of course, he'd brought his own stock with him. Dimitri enjoyed traveling, but not inconvenience. 'And what precisely was acquired from these people?'

'A couple hats, some clothes, baskets. . .' He hesitated.

'And?' Dimitri prompted, too gently for comfort.

'A pig.'

'A pig,' Dimitri repeated and chuckled. Remo nearly let his shoulders relax. 'How ingenious. I begin to regret Lord must be disposed of. I could put a man like him to good use. Go on, Remo. The rest.'

'A couple kids saw a peddlar in a truck pick up a man and woman—and a pig—late this morning. They headed east.'

There was a long silence. Remo wouldn't have broken it if there'd been a knife in his back. Dimitri studied the wine in his goblet then sipped, drawing the moment out. He could hear Remo's nerves stretching, stretching. His gaze came up.

'I suggest you also head east, Remo. I, in the meantime, will move on.' He ran his fingers over another chess piece, admiring the craftsmanship, the detail. 'I've calculated the area our quarries are headed for. While you track them, I shall wait.' He brought the goblet to his lips again, breathing deeply of the bouquet of the wine. 'I grow weary of hotels, though the service here is quite excellent. When I entertain our guest, I'd like to do so with more privacy.'

Setting down the wine, he picked up the white knight and its queen. 'Yes, I do love to entertain.' In a quick move, he smashed the pieces together. The shards tinkled lightly as they fell on to the table.

# CHAPTER TEN

'We didn't eat.'

'We'll eat later.'

'You're always saying that. And another thing,' Whitney said, 'I still don't understand why we have to check out this way.' She gave a quick grimace to the pile of 'borrowed' clothes in a heap on the floor. Whitney wasn't accustomed to seeing anyone move quite so fast as Doug had in the last five minutes.

'Ever heard of an ounce of prevention, sugar?'

'With a little salt, I'd *eat* an ounce of prevention at the moment.' Whitney scowled down at his fingertips on the window ledge. In a flash they were gone and she held her breath as she watched him drop to the ground below.

Doug felt his legs sing briefly. A quick glance around showed him that no one had seen his leap but a fat, battle-scarred cat dozing in a patch of sunshine. Looking up, he signaled to Whitney. 'Toss down the packs.' She did, with an enthusiasm that nearly knocked him off his feet. 'Take it easy,' he said between his teeth. Setting them aside, Doug braced himself beneath the window. 'Okay, now you.'

'Me?'

'You're all that's left, lover. Come on, I'll catch you.'

It wasn't that she doubted him. After all, she'd taken the precaution of slipping her wallet out of her pack—and making certain he saw her—before he'd climbed through the window. In the same way, she remembered that he'd switched the envelope to the pocket of his jeans. Trust among thieves was obviously the same sort of myth as honor.

Whitney thought it rather strange that the drop looked so much longer now than it had when he'd hung by his fingers. She frowned down at him.

'A MacAllister always leaves a hotel by the front door.'

'We ain't got time for family traditions. For Chrissake come on before we draw an audience.'

Setting her teeth, she swung a leg over. Agilely, but very slowly, she twisted herself around and lowered. It only took her an instant to discover she didn't like the sensation of hanging from the window ledge of an inn in Madagascar one bit. 'Doug. . .'

'Drop,' Doug ordered.

'I'm not sure I can.'

'You can, unless you want me to start throwing rocks.'

He might. Whitney closed her eyes, held her breath, and let go.

She fell free for hardly more than a heartbeat before his hands clamped around her hips, then slid up to her armpits. Even so, the abrupt stop took the breath from her.

'See?' he told her when he placed her lightly on the ground. 'Nothing to it. You've got real potential as a cat burglar.'

'Goddamn it.' Turning, she examined her hands. 'I broke a nail. Now what am I supposed to do?'

'Yeah, that's tragic.' He bent to pick up the packs. 'I guess I could shoot you and put you out of your misery.'

She snatched her pack out of his hands. 'Very droll. I happen to think walking around with nine fingernails is extremely tacky.'

'Put your hands in your pockets,' he suggested and started to walk.

'Just where are you going now?'

'I've arranged for a little trip by water.' He slid his arms through the straps until the pack rested comfortably on his back. 'All we have to do is get to the boat. Unobtrusively.'

Whitney followed as he wound his way around, keeping to the backs of houses, away from the street. 'All this because some fat little policeman dropped by to say hello.'

'Fat little policemen make me nervous.'

'He was very polite.'

'Yeah, fat little polite policemen make me more nervous.'

'We're being very rude to the nice lady who took our pig.'

'What's the matter, sugar, never skip out on a bill before?'

'Certainly not.' She sniffed, racing along behind him as he crossed a narrow side street. 'Nor do I intend to begin. I left her twenty.'

'Twenty!' Grabbing her, Doug stopped behind a tree beside Jacques's store. 'What the hell for? We didn't even use the bed.'

'We used the bath,' she reminded him. 'Both of us.'

'Christ, I didn't even take my clothes off.' Resigned, he studied the little faded frame building beside them.

While she waited for Doug to move again, Whitney glanced back wistfully toward the hotel. Another complaint sprang to her mind before she saw a man in a white panama crossing the street. Idly she watched him until sweat began to pool at the base of her spine.

'Doug.' Her throat had gone dry with an anxiety she couldn't explain. 'Doug, that man. Look.' She grabbed his hand, turning only slightly. 'I swear he's the same one I saw at the zoma, then again on the train.'

'Jumping at shadows,' Doug muttered but glanced back.

'No.' Whitney gave his arm a quick tug. 'I saw him. I saw him twice. Why should he turn up again? Why should he be here?'

'Whitney. . .' But he broke off as he watched the man stroll down to meet the captain. And he remembered with sudden clarity a man jolting him out of his seat on the train in the middle of the confusion, dropping a newspaper on to the ground, and looking him straight in the eye. Coincidence? Doug pulled Whitney back behind the tree. He didn't believe in them.

'Is it one of Dimitri's men?'

'I don't know.'

'Who else could he be?'

'Dammit, I don't know.' Frustration tore through him. He felt he was being chased from all sides. Knew it, but couldn't understand it. 'Whoever he is, we're getting out.' He looked back at Jacques's shop. 'Better go in the back way. He might have customers and the less people that see us, the better.'

The back door was locked. Crouching down, Doug took out his penknife and went to work. Within five seconds, the lock clicked open. Whitney counted.

Impressed, she watched him pocket the knife again. 'I'd like you to teach me how to do that.'

'A woman like you doesn't have to pick locks. People open doors for you.' While she thought this over, he slipped in the back.

It was part storage room, part bedroom, part kitchen. Beside the narrow, neatly made bunk was a collection of half a dozen cassette tapes. Upbeat Elton

John music seemed to pour through the wallboards. Tacked to them was a full-color poster of a pouting, sexy Tina Turner. Beside her was an ad for Bud-weiser—the King of Beers, a New York Yankees pennant, and an evening shot of the Empire State Building.

'Why do I feel as though I've just walked into a room on Second Avenue?' And because she did, she felt ridiculously safe.

'His brother's an exchange student at CCNY.'

'That explains everything. Whose brother?'

'Shh!' Padding silently on the balls of his feet like a cat, Doug moved to the door that connected with the shop. He opened it a crack and peered through.

Jacques leaned over the counter, in the midst of a transaction that involved what was obviously a detailed exchange of town gossip. The bony, dark-eyed girl had apparently come in to flirt more than she'd come in to buy. She poked among the spools of colored thread and giggled.

'What's going on?' Whitney maneuvered herself so that she could peek through the crack under Doug's arm. 'Ah, romance,' she proclaimed. 'I wonder where she got that blouse. Just look at the embroidery work.'

'We'll have a fashion show later.'

The girl bought two spools of thread, giggled for another moment or two, then left. Doug opened the door another inch and made a hissing sound through his teeth. It was no competition for Elton John. Jacques continued to swivel his hips as he picked up on the lyrics. With a glance to the window that opened on to the street, Doug eased the door open a bit more and called Jacques by name.

Jolting, Jacques nearly upset the display of spools he was rearranging. 'Man, you gave me a scare.' Still cautious, Doug crooked a finger and waited for Jacques to saunter over. 'What are you doing hiding back here?'

'A change of schedule,' Doug told him. Taking Jacques's hand, he jerked him inside. He realized Jacques smelled of English Leather. 'We want to take off now?'

'Now?' Narrowing his eyes, Jacques studied Doug's face. He might have lived in a small seaside village all of his life, but he wasn't a fool. When a man was on the run, it showed in his eyes. 'You got trouble?'

'Hello, Jacques.' Stepping forward, Whitney held out her hand. 'I'm Whitney MacAllister. You must forgive Douglas for neglecting to introduce us. He's often rude.'

Jacques took the slim white hand in his and was instantly in love. He'd never seen anything so beautiful. As far as he could tell, Whitney MacAllister outshone Turner, and Benatar, and the high priestess Ronstadt put together. His tongue quite simply tied itself in knots.

She'd seen the look before. In a slick, three-piece-suited professional on Fifth Avenue it bored her. In a trendy club on the West Side, it amused her. In Jacques, she found it sweet. 'We have to apologize for barging in on you this way.'

'It's. . .' He had to search for the Americanisms that were usually on the tip of his tongue. 'Okay,' he managed.

Impatient, Doug laid a hand on Jacques's shoulder. 'We want to move.' His sense of fair play wouldn't allow him to drag the young man blindly into the mess they were in. His sense of survival prevented him from telling all. 'We had a little visit from the local police.'

Jacques managed to drag his gaze away from Whitney. 'Sambirano?'

'That's right.'

'Asshole,' Jacques proclaimed, rather proud of the way the word rolled off his tongue. 'You don't worry about him. He's just nosey, like an old woman.'

'Yeah, maybe, but we've got some people who'd like to find us. We don't want to be found.'

Jacques took a moment to look from one to the other. A jealous husband, he thought. He needed nothing more to trigger his sense of romance. 'We Malagasy don't worry about time. The sun rises, the sun sets. You want to leave now, we leave now.'

'Terrific. We're a little low on supplies.'

'No problem. You wait here.'

'How'd you manage to find him?' Whitney asked when Jacques went through to the front again. 'He's wonderful.'

'Sure, just because he was making bug-eyes at you.'

'Bug-eyes?' She grinned and sat down on the edge of Jacques's bed. 'Really, Douglas, wherever do you dig up some of your quaint expressions?'

'His eyes nearly fell out of his head.'

'Yes.' She brushed a hand through her hair. 'They did, didn't they?'

'You really eat it up, don't you?' Annoyed, he paced the small room and wished he could do something. Anything. He could smell trouble, and it wasn't as far away as he'd have liked. 'You just love it when men drool.'

'You weren't exactly offended when little Marie all but kissed your feet. As I recall, you strutted around like a rooster with two tails.'

'She helped save our skins. That was simple gratitude.'

'With a touch of simple lust thrown in.'

'Lust?' He stopped directly in front of her. 'She couldn't've been more than sixteen.'

'Which made it all the more disgusting.'

'Yeah, well old Jacques here must be pushing twenty.'

'My, my.' Whitney pulled out her emery board and began to repair her chipped nail. 'That sounds distinctly like jealousy.'

'Shit.' He paced from one door to the other. 'This is one man who won't drool over you, duchess. I've got better things to do.'

Giving him a half smile Whitney continued to file and hum along with Elton John.

A few moments later there was silence. When Jacques came back in, he was carrying a good-size sack in one hand and his portable stereo in the other. With a grin, he packed the rest of his tapes. 'Now we're ready. Rock and roll.'

'Won't anyone wonder why you closed up early?' Doug opened the back door a crack and peered out.

'Close up then, close up now. Nobody cares.'

Nodding, Doug opened the door for him. 'Then let's go.'

His boat was docked less than a quarter mile away and Whitney had never seen anything like it. It was very long, perhaps fifteen feet, and no more than three feet wide. She thought of a canoe she'd paddled at summer camp in upstate New York. This was along the same lines if one stretched it out. Light on his feet, Jacques hopped in and began to stow the gear.

The canoe was traditional Malagasy, his hat was a New York Yankees fielder's cap, and his feet were bare. Whitney found him an odd and endearing combination of two worlds.

'Nice boat,' Doug murmured, wishing he saw an engine somewhere.

'I built her myself.' In a gesture she found very smooth and very courtly, he held out a hand for Whitney. 'You can sit here,' he told her, indicating a spot in the center. 'Very comfortable.'

'Thank you, Jacques.'

When he saw she was settled opposite where he would sit, he handed a long pole to Doug. 'We pole out here when the water's shallow.' Taking one himself, Jacques pushed off. The boat glided out like a swan on a lake. Relaxing, Whitney decided the boat trip had possibilities—the scent of the sea, feathery leaves dancing in the breeze, the gentle movement beneath her. Then, two feet away, she saw the ugly leathery head skim the surface.

'Ah. . .' It was all she could manage.

'Yes, indeed.' With a chuckle Jacques continued to pole. 'Those crocks, they're everywhere. You have to watch out for them.' He made a sound somewhere between a hiss and a roar. The round, sleepy eyes at the surface came no closer. Without a word, Doug reached in his pack, dug out the gun, and hitched it in his belt again. This time Whitney made no objection.

When the water deepened enough for them to use the paddles, Jacques switched on his stereo. Vintage Beatles blasted out. They were on their way.

Jacques paddled tirelessly, with a smooth energy and enthusiasm Whitney admired. Through the hour and a half Beatle extravaganza, he sang along in a clear tenor, grinning when Whitney joined in with him.

From the stores Jacques had brought aboard, they had a late impromptu lunch of coconut meat, berries, and cold fish. When he passed Whitney the canteen, she drank deeply, expecting plain water. Tilting the canteen down again, she swished the liquid around in her mouth. It wasn't unpleasant, but it wasn't plain water either.

'*Rano vola*,' Jacques told her. 'Good for traveling.'

Doug's paddle cut through the water smoothly. 'They make it by adding water to rice that sticks to the bottom of the cooking pot.'

Whitney swallowed, trying to do it graciously. 'I see.' Shifting a bit, she passed the canteen down to Doug.

'You come from New York, too?'

'Yes.' Whitney popped another berry into her mouth. 'Doug tells me your brother goes to college there.'

'Law school.' The letters on his T-shirt nearly trembled with pride. 'He's going to be a hotshot. He's been to Bloomingdale's.'

'Whitney practically lives there,' Doug said under his breath.

Ignoring him, she spoke to Jacques. 'Do you plan to go to America?'

'Next year,' he told her, resting his paddle across his lap. 'I visit my brother. We're going to do the town. Times Square, Macy's, McDonald's.'

'I want you to call me.' As if she were in a plush East-Side restaurant, Whitney drew a card out of her wallet and handed it to him. Like its owner, the card was smooth, classy, and slender. 'We'll have a party.'

'Party?' His eyes lit up. 'A New York party?' Visions of glittering dance floors, wild colors, and wilder music raced in his head.

'Absolutely.'

'With all the ice cream you can eat.'

'Don't be cranky, Douglas. You can come too.'

Jacques was quiet a moment while his imagination worked out all the fascinations of a party in New York.

His brother had written about women with dresses that came high above the knee and cars as long as the canoe he rowed. There were buildings as high as the mountains to the west. Once his brother had eaten in the same restaurant as Billy Joel.

New York, Jacques thought, awed. Maybe his new friends knew Billy Joel and would invite him to the party. He fondled Whitney's card before tucking it into his pocket.

'You two are. . .' He wasn't quite sure of the American term for what he meant. Not a polite one anyway.

'Business partners,' Whitney provided, smiling.

'Yeah, we're all business.' Scowling, Doug cut through the water with his pole.

Jacques might've been young, but he hadn't been born yesterday. 'You have business? What kind?'

'At the moment, we're into travel and excavation.'

Whitney lifted a brow at Doug's terminology. 'In New York, I'm an interior designer. Doug's a—'

'Freelancer,' he finished. 'I work for myself.'

'Best way,' Jacques agreed while his feet tapped out the beat. 'When I was a boy, I worked on a coffee plantation. Do this, do that.' He shook his head and smiled. 'Now, I have my own shop. I say do this, do that. But I don't have to listen.'

Chuckling, Whitney stretched her back while the music reminded her of home.

Later, the sunset reminded her of the Caribbean. The forest on either side of the canal had become denser, deeper, more junglelike. Reeds grew along the verge, thin and brown, before they gave way to dense foliage. At the sight of her first flamingo, all pink-feathered and fragile-legged, she was charmed. She saw the iridescent blue flash in the brush and heard the quick, repetitive song Jacques identified as the coucal's.

Once or twice she thought she'd caught sight of a fast, agile lemur. The water, becoming shallow enough now and then to require the poles, was washed with red and skimmed with insects. Through the trees to the west, the sky was lit up like a forest fire. She decided a ride in an outrigger canoe had a lot more allure than punting on the Thames, though it was just as relaxing—except for the occasional crocodile.

Over the quiet dusk and jungle silence, Jacques's stereo poured out what any self-respecting DJ would have called hit after hit—commercial-free. She could've floated for hours.

'We'd better camp.'

Turning her eyes away from the sunset, she smiled at Doug. He'd long before stripped off his shirt. His chest gleamed in the dim light with a light sheen of sweat. 'So soon?'

He bit back a retort. It wasn't easy to admit that his arms felt like rubber and his palms burned. Not when young Jacques was still bopping with the beat, looking as though he could row until midnight without slackening pace.

'It'll be dark soon,' was all he said.

'Okay.' Jacques's lean, limber muscles rippled as he stroked. 'We'll find an A-Number-One campsite.' He turned his shy smile on Whitney. 'You should rest,' he told her. 'Long day on the water.'

Mumbling under his breath, Doug rowed toward shore.

Jacques wouldn't allow her to carry a pack. Hefting hers and his sack, he entrusted her with his stereo. Single file, they walked into the forest where the light was rose-colored, touched with mauve. Birds they couldn't see sang to the darkening sky. Leaves shimmered green, damp with the moisture that was always

present. Now and then Jacques would stop and hack at
vines and bamboo with a small sickle. The scent was
rich: vegetation, water, flowers—flowers that climbed
through vines and burst through bush. She'd never
seen so many colors in one place, nor had she expected
to. Insects hovered, humming and whining in the
twilight. On a frantic rustle of leaves a heron rose out
of the bush and glided toward the canal. The forest was
hot, wet, and close and had all the tastes of the exotic.

They set up camp to the tune of Springsteen's *Born
in the USA*.

By the time they had a fire started and coffee
heating, Doug found something to be cheerful about.
Out of Jacques's sack came a few small containers of
spice, two lemons, and the rest of the carefully wrapped
fish. With them, he found two packs of Marlboros. At
the moment, they meant nothing compared with the
other loot.

'At last.' He held a container that smelled something
like sweet basil up to his nose. 'A meal with style.' He
might have been sitting on the ground, surrounded by
thick vines and insects just beginning to bite, but he
liked the challenge. He'd eaten with the best of them,
in the kitchens and under chandeliers. Tonight would
be no different. Breaking out the cooking utensils, he
prepared to enjoy himself.

'Doug's quite the gourmand,' Whitney told Jacques.
'I'm afraid we've had to make do with what's been
available so far. It hasn't been easy for him.' Then she
sniffed the air. Mouth watering, she turned to see him
sautéing the fish over the fire. 'Douglas.' His name
came out on a sultry breath. 'I think I'm in love.'

'Yeah.' Eyes intense, hands firm, he gave the fish an
expert flick. 'That's what they all say, sugar.'

That night the three of them slept deeply, replete with rich food, plum wine, and rock and roll.

When the dark sedan pulled into the small seaside town an hour past dawn, it drew quite a crowd. In charge, impatient and out of sorts, Remo stepped out and brushed through a huddle of children. Having the instinct of the young and the vulnerable, they made way for him. With a jerk of his head, he signaled the two other men to follow.

They didn't deliberately try to look out of place. If they'd come into town on mules, dressed in lambas, they'd still have looked like hoods. The way they'd lived, the way they intended to live—badly—oozed through their pores.

The townspeople, though inherently wary of strangers, were also inherently hospitable. Still no one approached the three men. The island term for taboo was *fady*. Remo and company, though trim in their crisp summer suits and glossy Italian shoes, were definitely *fady*.

Remo spotted the inn, and signaling his men to circle the sides of the building, approached the front.

The woman of the inn had on a fresh apron. Breakfast smells came from the rear though only two tables were occupied. She looked at Remo, sized him up, and decided she had no vacancies.

'Looking for some people,' he told her, though he didn't expect anyone on that godforsaken island to speak English. He simply pulled out the glossies of Doug and Whitney and waved them under her nose.

Not by a flicker did she show any recognition. Perhaps they'd left abruptly, but there'd been twenty dollars American money on the dresser. Their smiles hadn't reminded her of a lizard. She shook her head.

Remo peeled a ten-dollar bill from the wad he carried. The woman simply shrugged and handed him back the photos. Her grandson had spent an hour the evening before playing with his new pig. She preferred his smell to Remo's cologne.

'Look, Grandma, we know they got off here. Why don't you make this easy on everybody.' As incentive, he peeled back another ten.

The innkeeper gave him a blank look and another shrug. 'They are not here,' she said, surprising him with her precise English.

'I'll just take a look myself.' Remo started for the stairs.

'Good morning.'

Like Doug, Remo had no trouble recognizing a cop, in a one-horse town in Madagascar or in an alley in the lower Forties.

'I am Captain Sambirano.' Stiffly proper, he offered his hand. He admired Remo's taste in clothes, noticed the still-puffy scar on his cheek and the cool grimness in his eye. Neither did he miss the healthy wad of bills in his hand. 'Perhaps I can be of some assistance.'

He didn't like dealing with cops. Remo considered them basically unstable. In a year, he could make approximately three times what the average police lieutenant pulled in, for doing the same thing. Backwards.

But more, he didn't like the thought of going back to Dimitri with empty hands. 'I'm looking for my sister.'

Doug had said he had brains. Remo put them to use.

'She ran off with this guy, nothing but a two-bit thief. The girl's infatuated, if you know what I mean.'

The captain nodded politely. 'Indeed.'

'Dad's worried sick,' Remo improvised. He pulled

out a thin Cuban cigar from a flat gold case. Offering one, he noticed the captain's appreciation of the fragrance and the glint of classy metal. He knew which approach to take. 'I've managed to track them this far, but. . .' He let the sentence trail off and tried to look like a concerned brother. 'We'll do anything to get her back, Captain. Anything.'

While he let that sink in, Remo pulled out the photos. The same photos, the captain noted silently, that the other man had shown him only the day before. His story had been that of a father seeking his daughter as well, and as well, he'd offered money.

'My father's offering a reward to anyone who can help us. Understand that my sister's my father's only daughter. And the youngest,' he added for clout. He remembered, without much affection, how pampered his own kid sister had been. 'He's prepared to be generous.'

Sambirano looked down at the pictures of Whitney and Doug. The newlyweds who'd left town rather abruptly. He glanced over at the innkeeper who kept her lips folded in disapproval. Those eating breakfast understood the look and went back to their meal.

The captain wasn't impressed by Remo's story anymore than he'd been impressed by Doug's the day before. Whitney beamed up at him. She, however, had impressed him, then and now. 'A lovely woman.'

'You can imagine how my father feels, Captain, knowing she's with a man like him. Scum.'

There was enough passion in the word to let the captain know the animosity wasn't feigned. If one man found the other, one would die. It mattered little to him, as long as neither died in his town. He saw no reason to mention the man in the panama with a similar set of pictures.

'A brother,' he said slowly as he drew the cigar under his nose, 'is responsible for the welfare of his sister.'

'Yeah, I'm worried sick about her. God knows what he'll do when her money runs out or when he just gets tired of her. If there's anything you can do. . .I promise to be very grateful, Captain.'

The captain had chosen law enforcement in the quiet little town because he hadn't much ambition. That is, he didn't care to sweat in the fields or callous his hands on a fishing boat. But he did believe in making a tidy profit. He handed Remo the photographs. 'I sympathize with your family. I have a daughter myself. If you'll come with me to my office, we can discuss this further. I believe I can help you.'

Dark eyes met dark eyes. Each recognized the other for what he was. Each accepted that business was indeed business. 'I'd appreciate that, Captain. I'd appreciate that very much.'

As he walked through the door, Remo touched the scar on his cheek. He could almost taste Doug's blood. Dimitri, he thought with a flood of relief, was going to be very pleased. Very pleased.

# CHAPTER ELEVEN

Over her breakfast coffee, Whitney added Jacques's fifty-dollar advance and retotaled the list of Doug's expenses. A treasure hunt, she decided, had quite an overhead.

While the others had slept during the night, Doug beside her in the tent, Jacques content under the stars, Whitney had lain awake for some time, going over the journey. In many ways it had been a lark, an exciting, somewhat twisted vacation complete with souvenirs and a few exotic meals. If they never found the treasure, she would've written it off just that way—except for the memory of a young waiter who'd died only because he'd been there.

Some people are born with a certain comfortable naiveté that never leaves them, mainly because their lives remain comfortable. Money can provoke cynicism or cushion it.

Perhaps her wealth had sheltered her to some extent, but Whitney had never been naive. She counted her change not because she had to worry about pennies, but because she expected value for value. She accepted compliments with grace, and a grain of salt. And she knew to some, life was cheap.

Death could be a means to an end, something accomplished for revenge, for amusement, or for a fee. The fee might vary—the life of a statesman was certainly worth more on the open market than the life of a ghetto drug dealer. One might be worth no more than the price of a syringe full of heroin, the other hundreds of thousands of cool, clean Swiss francs.

A business, some had taken the exchange of life for gain to the height and routine of a brokerage firm. She'd known it before, considered it the way one considered many of the daily social ills. Aloofly. But now she'd dealt with it personally. An innocent man had died, and she might very well have killed a man herself. There was no telling how many other lives had been lost, or bought and sold, in the quest for this particular pot of gold.

Dollars and cents, she mused as she looked down at her neat columns and totals on the notepad. But it had become much more than that. Perhaps like many of the carelessly wealthy, she'd often skimmed over the surface of life without seeing the eddies and currents the less fortunate had to pit themselves against. Perhaps she'd always taken such things as food and shelter for granted until the last few weeks. And perhaps Whitney's own personal view of right and wrong often depended on circumstances and her own whims. But she had a strong sense of good and bad.

Doug Lord might be a thief, and in his life he might've done innumerable things that were wrong by society's standards. She didn't give a hang about society's standards. He was, she'd come to believe, intrinsically good, just as she believed Dimitri was intrinsically bad. She believed it, not naively, but completely, with all the healthy intelligence and instinct she'd been born with.

She'd done something more while the others had slept. Restless, Whitney had finally decided to glance through the books Doug had taken from the Washington library. To pass the time, she'd told herself as she flicked on a flashlight and located the books. As she'd begun to read about the jewels, the gems lost over the centuries, she'd become caught up. The illustrations hadn't particularly moved her. Diamonds and rubies meant more in three dimensions. But they'd made her think.

Reading through the history of this necklace, that diamond, she'd understood, personally, that what men and women craved for adornment, others had died for. Greed, desire, lust. They were things Whitney could understand, but passions she felt too shallow to die for.

But what of loyalty? Whitney had gone back over the words she'd read in Magdaline's letter. She's spoken of her husband's grief over the queen's death, but more, his obligation to her. How much had the man Gerald sacrificed for loyalty and what had he kept in a wooden box? The jewels. Had he kept his heritage in a wooden box and mourned a way of life that could never be his again?

Was it money, was it art, was it history? As she'd closed the book she had been left uncertain. Whitney had respected Lady Smythe-Wright, though she'd never quite comprehended her fervor. Now she was dead for little more than having a belief that history, whether it was written in dusty volumes or glittered and shone, belonged to everyone.

Antoinette had lost her life, along with hundreds of others, with rough justice on the guillotine. People had been driven from their homes, hunted and slaughtered. Others had starved in the streets. For an ideal? No, Whitney doubted people often died for ideals any more than they truly fought for them. They'd died because they'd been caught up in something that had swept over them and carried them along whether they wanted to go or not. What would a handful of jewels have meant to a woman walking up the steps to the guillotine?

It made a treasure hunt seem foolish. Unless—unless it had a moral. Maybe it was time Whitney discovered her own.

Because of this, and because of a young waiter named Juan, Whitney was determined to find the treasure, and to kick dust in Dimitri's face when she did.

She faced the morning confidently. No, she wasn't naive. Still Whitney held to the basic belief that good would ultimately outdo bad—especially if good was very clever.

'What the hell're you going to do when the batteries on that thing run down?'

Whitney smiled up at Doug before she slipped the thin, hand-held calculator and her notepad back in her bag. She wondered what he would think if he knew she'd spent several hours during the night analyzing him and what they were doing. 'Duracell,' she said sweetly. 'Would you like some coffee?'

'Yeah.' He sat down, a bit leery of the way she poured and served so cheerfully.

She looked exquisite. He'd figured a few days on the road would leave her a bit haggard, a little rough around the edges. He scraped his palm over the stubble on his own chin. Instead, she looked radiant. Her pale, angel-blonde hair shone as it rippled down her back. The sun had warmed her skin, bringing up touches of rose that only accentuated its flawlessness and the classic line of bone. No, she looked anything but haggard at the moment.

Doug accepted the coffee and drank deeply.

'This is a lovely spot,' Whitney said, bringing up her knees and circling them with her arms.

He glanced around. Moisture dripped from leaves in quiet plip-plops. The ground was damp and spongy. He slapped at a mosquito and wondered how long the repellent would hold out. The mist rose off the ground in little fingers, like steam in a Turkish bath. 'If you like saunas.'

Whitney cocked a brow. 'Woke up on the wrong side of the bedroll, didn't we?'

He only grunted. He'd woken up itchy, as any healthy man would after spending the night next to a healthy woman without having the luxury of taking things to their natural conclusion.

'Look at it this way, Douglas. If there were an acre of this in Manhattan, people would be scrambling for it, piling in on top of each other.' She lifted her hands, palms up. Birdsong burst out in an ecstasy of sound. A chamelion crawled on to a dull gray rock and slowly faded into it. Flowers seemed to pour out of the ground and the green, green of leaves and ferns still damp with dew gave everything a lushness. 'We've got it all to ourselves.'

He poured a second cup of coffee. 'I figured a woman like you would prefer crowds.'

'A time and place, Douglas,' she murmured. 'A time and place.' Then she smiled, so simply, so exquisitely, he felt his heart stop. 'I like being here, with you.'

The coffee had scalded his tongue, but he didn't notice. He swallowed it, still staring at her. He'd never had any problem with women, pouring on the rough-edged, cocky charm that he'd learned very young they found appealing. Now, when he could've used a surplus of what came so handily to him, he couldn't find any at all. 'Oh yeah?' he managed.

Amused that he could be thrown off so easily, she nodded. 'Yeah. I've given it some thought.' Leaning over, she kissed him very, very lightly. 'Just what do you think of that?'

He might stumble, but years of experience had taught him how to land on his feet. Reaching out, he gathered her hair in his hand. 'Well, maybe we should—' he nipped at her lip—'discuss it.'

She liked the way he kissed without quite kissing, the way he held her without really holding her. She remembered what it had been like when he'd done both, thoroughly. 'Perhaps we should.'

Their lips did no more than tease each other's. Eyes open, they nibbled, testing, tempting. They didn't touch. Each was used to leading, to being in control. To lose the edge—that was the primary mistake, in matters of love and money, to both of them. As long as the reins were held, even loosely, then neither of them felt they would go where they didn't lead.

Lips warmed. Thoughts clouded. Priorities shifted.

His hand tightened on her hair, hers gripped his shirtfront. In that rare instant that moves timelessly, they were caught close. Need became the leader, and desire, the map. Each surrendered without hesitation or regret.

Beyond the thick, moist leaves came a bright, bubbling blast of Cyndi Lauper.

Like children caught with their fingers deep in the cookie jar, Whitney and Doug sprang apart. Jacques's clear tenor echoed with Cyndi's cheery voice. Both of them cleared their throats.

'Company's coming,' Doug commented and reached for a cigarette.

'Yes.' Rising, Whitney brushed at the seat of her thin, baggy slacks. They were a bit damp with dew, but the heat was already drying the ground. She watched sunbeams slash through the tops of cypress. 'As I said, a spot like this seems to draw people. Well, I think I'll. . .' She trailed off in surprise when his hand circled her ankle.

'Whitney.' His eyes were intense, as they became when least expected. His fingers were very firm. 'One day, we're going to finish this.'

She wasn't used to being told what she'd do, and saw no reason to begin now. She sent him a long, neutral look. 'Perhaps.'

'Absolutely.'

The neutral look became a hint of a smile. 'Douglas, you're going to find out I can be very contrary.'

'You're going to find out I take what I want.' He said it softly, and her smile faded. 'It's my profession.'

'Man oh man, we got ourselves some coconuts.' Coming through the bush, Jacques shook the net bag he carried.

Whitney laughed when he pulled one out and tossed it to her. 'Anyone got a corkscrew?'

'No problem.' Making use of a rock, Jacques slammed the coconut against it sharply. The chamelion scrambled away without a sound. With a grin, he broke the fruit apart and handed the two pieces to Whitney.

'How clever.'

'A little rum and you could have piña coladas.'

Brow arched, she handed a half to Doug. 'Don't be testy, darling. I'm sure you could've climbed up a palm tree too.'

Grinning, Jacques carved out a piece of the meat with a small knife. 'It's *fady* to eat anything white on Wednesdays,' he said with a simplicity that caused Whitney to study him more carefully. He popped the coconut into his mouth with a kind of guilty relish. 'It's worse not to eat at all.'

She looked at the fielder's cap, the T-shirt, and the

portable radio. It was difficult for her to remember that he was Malagasy, and part of an ancient tribe. With Louis of the Merina it had been easy. He'd looked the part. Jacques looked like someone she'd pass crossing Broadway and Forty-second.

'Are you superstitious, Jacques?'

He moved his shoulders. 'I apologize to the gods and spirits. Keep them happy.' Reaching in his front pocket, he drew out what looked like a small shell on a chain.

'An *ody*,' Doug explained, both amused and tolerant. He didn't believe in talismans, but in making your own luck. Or cashing in on someone else's. 'It's like an amulet.'

Whitney studied it, intrigued by the contrasts between Jacques's Americanized dress and speech and his deep-seated belief in taboos and spirits. 'For luck?' she asked him.

'For safety. The gods have bad moods.' He rubbed the shell beween his fingers, then offered it to Whitney. 'You carry it today.'

'All right.' She slipped the chain over her neck. After all, she thought, it wasn't so odd. Her father carried a rabbit's foot that had been tinted baby blue. The amulet fell along the same lines—or perhaps more along the lines of a St Christopher's medal. 'For safety.'

'You two can carry on the cultural exchange later. Let's get moving.' As he rose, Doug tossed the fruit back to Jacques.

Whitney winked at Jacques. 'I told you he was often rude.'

'No problem,' Jacques said again, then reached into his back pocket where he'd carefully secured the stem of a flower. Pulling it out, he offered it to Whitney.

'An orchid.' It was white, pure, spectacular white

and so delicate it seemed as though it would dissolve in her palm. 'Jacques, it's exquisite.' She touched it to her cheek before she threaded the stem through the hair above her ear. 'Thank you.' When she kissed him, she heard the audible click of his swallow.

'Looks nice.' He began to gather gear quickly. 'Lots of flowers here in Madagascar. Any flower you want, you find it here.' Still chattering, he began to cart gear to the canoe.

'You wanted a flower,' Doug muttered, 'all you had to do was bend over and yank one up.'

Whitney touched the petals above her ear. 'Some men understand sweetness,' she commented, 'and others don't.' Picking up her pack, she followed Jacques.

'Sweetness,' Doug grumbled as he struggled with the rest of the gear. 'I've got a pack of wolves after me and she wants sweetness.' Still muttering, he kicked out the campfire. 'I could've picked her a damn flower. A dozen of them.' He glanced over his shoulder at the sound of Whitney's laughter. 'Oh Jacques, it's exquisite,' he mimicked. With a snort of disgust, Doug checked the safety on his gun before he secured it in his belt. 'And I can open a goddamn coconut too.' He gave the fire one last kick before hefting the remaining gear and starting toward the canoe.

When Remo nudged one expensively shod toe into the campfire, it was no more than a pile of cold ash. The sun was straight up and streaming; there was no relief from the heat in the shade. He'd removed his suit jacket and tie—something he'd never have done in front of Dimitri during working hours. His once-crisp Arrow shirt was limp with sweat. Tracking Lord was becoming a pain in the ass.

'Looks like they spent the night here.' Weis, a tall, bankerish-looking man who'd had his nose broken by a whiskey bottle swiped sweat from his forehead. He had a line of insect bites on his neck that constantly plagued him. 'I guess we're about four hours behind them.'

'What're you, part Apache?' Giving the fire a last violent kick, Remo turned. His gaze rested on Barns, whose round moon face was creased in smiles. 'What're you grinning at, you little asshole!'

But Barns hadn't stopped grinning since Remo had told him to take care of the Malagasy captain. He knew Barns had, but even a man of Remo's experience didn't want to hear the details. It was common knowledge that Dimitri had an affection for Barns, the way one had an affection for a half-witted dog who dropped mutilated chickens and small mangled rodents at your feet. He also knew that Dimitri often let Barns take care of employees on their way out. Dimitri didn't believe in unemployment benefits.

'Let's go,' he said briefly. 'We'll have them before sundown.'

Whitney had herself nestled comfortably between the packs. Lengthening shadows from cypress and eucalyptus fell on the dunes alongside the canal and on the thick brush on the opposing side. Thin brown reeds waved in the current. From time to time a startled egret folded in its legs and lifted off into the brush with a whoosh of wings and rush. Flowers poked out, profuse in places, red, orange and melting yellow. Orchids grew as haphazardly as poppies in a meadow. Butterflies, sometimes alone, sometimes in troups, swooped and fluttered around the petals. Their color was a blaze against vegetation and the dung brown of the canal. Here and there crocodiles stretched on sloping banks and took in the sun. Most barely turned a head as the canoe rowed by. The fragrance lifting over the scent of the river was lazily rich.

With the brim of Jacques's cap shielding her eyes, she lay crossways in the canoe, her feet resting on the edge. The long fishing pole Jacques had fashioned rested loosely in her hands as she half dozed.

She decided she'd discovered just what Huck Finn had found so appealing about floating down the Mississippi. A good deal of it was bone laziness and the rest was wide-eyed adventure. It was, Whitney reflected, a delightful combination.

'And just what do you plan to do if a fish reaches up and bites on that bent safety pin?'

Taking her time, Whitney stretched her shoulders. 'Why I'd drop him right in your lap, Douglas. I'm sure you'd know exactly what to do with a fish.'

'You cook 'em up good.' Jacques paddled with the long steady strokes that would've made a Yale alumnus's heart patter with pride. Tina Turner helped him keep the rhythm. 'My cooking. . .' He shook his head. 'Pretty bad. When I get married, I have to make sure my wife cooks good. Like my mama.'

Whitney made a snorting sound from under the cap. A fly landed on her knee but it was too much effort to brush it aside. 'Another man whose heart's in his stomach.'

'Look, the kid's got a point. Eating's important.'

'To you it's more like a religion. Do it with the proper tradition and respect or not at all.' She shifted the brim of her cap so that she could see Jacques more clearly. Young, she thought, with a good-humored, good-looking face and well-muscled body. She didn't think he'd have any trouble attracting the girls. 'So you're putting your stomach on the same level with your heart. What happens if you fall for a girl who can't cook.'

Jacques considered this. He was only twenty, and answers were as easy and basic as life. The smile he gave her was young, innocent, and cocky enough to make her chuckle. 'I'd take her to my mother so she could learn.'

'Very sensible,' Doug agreed. He broke rhythm to pop a piece of coconut into his mouth.

'I don't suppose you ever considered learning to cook.' Whitney watched Jacques mull this over while his lean, strong arms worked the paddles. Smiling at him, she ran a finger over the shell that nestled just above her breasts.

'A Malagasy wife cooks the meals.'

'In between the times she takes care of the house, the children, and tills the fields, I imagine.' Whitney put in.

Jacques nodded and grinned. 'But she takes care of the money too.'

Whitney felt the lump of her wallet in her back pocket. '*That's* very sensible,' she agreed, smiling at Doug.

He had the envelope secure in his own pocket. 'I thought you'd like that.'

'Again, it's a simple matter of people doing what they're best suited for.' She started to settle back again when her line jerked. With her eyes wide, she sat straight up. 'Oh God, I think I've got one.'

'One what?'

'A fish!' Gripping the pole fiercely, she watched the line bob. 'A fish,' she said again. 'A big goddam fish.'

A grin split Doug's face as she saw the improvised fishing line grow taut. 'Sonofabitch. Now take it easy,' he advised as she scrambled to her knees and rocked the boat. 'Don't lose it, that's tonight's main course.'

'I'm not going to lose it,' she said between gritted teeth. And she wouldn't, but she didn't have any idea what to do next. After another moment of struggle, she turned to Jacques. 'What now?'

'Pull him up easy. It's a big bastard.' Drawing his paddle into the canoe, he went to her with light movements that kept the boat steady. 'Yessirree, we eat tonight. He's going to fight.' He rested a hand on her shoulder while he looked over the side. 'He's thinking about the frying pan.'

'Come on, sugar, you can do it.' Doug left the oars behind to creep in the center and root. 'Just bring 'im up.' And he'd fillet him, sauté him, and serve him on a bed of fluffy rice.

Giddy, excited, determined, Whitney caught her tongue between her teeth. If either man had offered to take the pole from her, she'd have snarled. Using arm muscles she only remembered during an occasional brief set of tennis, she brought the fish out of the water.

Wiggling on the end of the line, he caught the glint of the late afternoon sun. It was only a simple trout, flopping frantically, but for a moment, he looked regal, a flash of silver caught against the deepening blue of the sky. Whitney gave out a war whoop and fell back on her rump.

'Don't drop him now!'

'She won't.' Reaching out, Jacques caught the line between his thumb and fingers, drawing it gently in. The fish waved back and forth like a flag in the breeze. 'She's caught herself one big, fat fish.' In a quick move, he drew out the hook and held up the catch. 'How about that? Some luck.' He grinned, fish in hand, while

Tina Turner gritted out a tune from the tape player behind him.

It happened so fast. Still, as long as she lived Whitney would remember the instant as though it had been captured frame by frame on film. One moment, Jacques was standing, glistening with healthy sweat and triumph. Her laughter was still hanging on the air. The next, he was tumbling into the water. The explosion never even registered in her mind.

'Jacques?' Dazed, she scrambled to her knees.

'Down.' Doug had her pinned beneath him so that her breath came in gasps. He held her down while the boat rocked and he prayed they wouldn't capsize.

'Doug?'

'Lie still, understand?' But he wasn't looking at her. Though his head was only inches above hers, he scanned the shore on either side of the canal. The brush was thick enough to hide an army. Where the hell were they? Keeping his movements slow, he reached for the gun in his belt.

When Whitney saw it, she shifted her head to look for Jacques. 'Did he fall? I thought I heard a—' When she saw the answer in Doug's eyes, she arched like a bow. '*No!*' She struggled, nearly knocking the gun from Doug's hand as she tried to get up. 'Jacques! Oh God.'

'Stay down.' He gave the order between his teeth as he locked his legs around hers. 'There's nothing you can do for him now.' When she continued to fight, he dug his fingers in hard enough to bruise her. 'He's dead, dammit. Dead before he hit the water.'

Her eyes were wide, swimming, as she stared up at him. Without a word she closed them and lay still.

If he felt guilt, if he felt grief, he'd deal with them later. Now it was back to the first priority. Staying alive.

He could hear nothing but the gentle lap of water as the boat drifted in the current. They could be on either side, that he knew. What he didn't know was why they hadn't simply riddled the canoe with bullets. The thin outer skin would be no protection.

They had orders to take them alive. Doug glanced down at Whitney. She remained still and passive, eyes shut. Or to take one of them alive, he realized.

Dimitri would be curious about a woman like Whitney MacAllister. He'd know everything there was to know about her by now. No, he wouldn't want her dead. He'd want to entertain her for a time—be entertained by her—then ransom her back. The first order of business was to find out where they were waiting. Doug could already feel the sweat pooling between his shoulder blades.

'That you, Remo?' he shouted. 'You're still using too much of that fancy cologne. I can smell you out here.' He waited a moment, straining to hear any sound. 'Dimitri know I've had you running around in circles?'

'You're the one who's running, Lord.'

On the left. He didn't know how he was going to do it yet, but he knew they'd have to get to the opposite shore.

'Yeah, maybe I'm slowing down.' Checking off different angles, Doug kept talking. The birds that had fled skyward screaming at the sound of the shot were calm again. A few had resumed their lazy chatter. He saw that Whitney had opened her eyes again, but she wasn't moving. 'Maybe it's time we talked deal. You and me, Remo. With what I got, you could fill a swimming pool with that French cologne. Ever think about branching out on your own, Remo? You got brains. Aren't you getting tired of taking orders and doing somebody else's dirty work?'

'You want to talk, Lord. Paddle over. We'll have a nice little business meeting.'

'Paddle over and you'll put a bullet in my brain, Remo. Come on, let's not insult each other's intelligence.' Maybe, just maybe, he could angle one of the poles in the water and guide the boat. If he could wait until dusk, they might have a chance.

'You're the one who wants to deal, Lord. What do you have in mind?'

'I got the papers, Remo.' Gently he tugged open his pack. He also had a box of bullets. 'And I got me a classy lady. They're both worth a hell of a lot more money than you've ever seen.' He shot Whitney a look. She was staring at him, pale and dry-eyed. 'Dimitri tell you I got me a heiress, Remo? MacAllister. You know, MacAllister's ice-cream? Best goddamn fudge ripple in the States. You know how many million they made off fudge ripple alone, Remo? You know how much her old man'd pay to get her back in one piece?'

He slid the box of bullets into his pocket while Whitney watched. 'Play along with me, sugar,' he told her as he checked to see that his gun was fully loaded. 'We both might get out breathing. I'm going to give him a list of your attributes. When I do, I want you to start swearing at me, rock the boat, kick up a scene. While you're doing it, grab that pole. Okay?'

Expressionless, she nodded.

'There ain't much meat on her but she really warms up the sheets, Remo. And she ain't too particular about who she warms them up with. Know what I mean? I got no problem sharing the wealth.'

'You rotten sonofabitch.' With a screech that would've done a fishwife proud, Whitney reared up.

He hadn't meant for her to put herself in range and grabbed for her. Wound up, she swung at his hand and knocked it away. 'You've absolutely no style,' she shouted, standing straight. 'Absolutely no class. I'd as soon sleep with a slug as let you into my bed.'

In the lowering light she was magnificent, passionate, hair streaming behind her, eyes dark. He didn't have any doubt that Remo's attention was fixed on her.

'Grab the pole and don't get so damn personal,' he muttered.

'You think you can talk to me that way, you worm?' Snatching up the pole, Whitney raised it over her head.

'Good, good now. . .' He trailed off when he saw the expression on her face. He'd seen vengeance in a woman's eyes before. Automatically he lifted a hand. 'Hey, wait a minute,' he began as the pole smashed down. He rolled aside in time to see Weis come tumbling into their boat from a small, dark raft. They'd have capsized then if Whitney hadn't lost her balance and fallen half over the opposite end, righting their boat again. 'Jesus, get down.' But the warning ended on a whoosh of air as he started to struggle with Weis.

Whitney's blow had caught the big man on the shoulder, knocking his gun aside, but annoying him more than harming him. And he remembered the sensation of having his nose shatter. Whitney lifted the pole again and would have brought it down but Doug rolled on top of him. The boat swayed, taking in water. She saw Jacques's body floating on the surface of the canal before she froze her heart to fight for her life.

'For God's sake give me a clear shot,' she shouted, then tumbled backward when the boat rocked violently.

On shore, Remo pushed Barns aside. 'Lord's mine,

you little bastard. Remember it.' Taking out his gun, he focused and waited.

It looked like a game. Whitney thought as she shook her head to clear it. Two overgrown boys wrestling in a boat. Any moment one might cry uncle, then they'd brush themselves off and go on to other amusements.

She tried to stand again, but nearly tipped over the side. She could see the gun still in Doug's hand, but the other man outweighed him by at least fifty pounds. Balancing herself on her knees, she gripped the pole again. 'Damn it, Doug, how can I smash him if you're laying on top of him? Move!'

'Sure.' Panting, Doug managed to pry Weis's hand from around his throat. 'Just give me a minute.' Then his head jerked back as Weis caught him on the jaw. Doug tasted blood.

'You broke my fucking nose,' Weis said as he dragged Doug to his feet.

'Was that you?'

They stood, legs braced as Weis began slowly to turn Doug's gun hand so that the barrel pointed at his face.

'Yeah. And I'm going to blow yours off.'

'Look, don't take it personally.' Planting his feet, Doug was certain he felt something rip inside his left shoulder. It was something to think about later when the barrel of a gun wasn't staring him in the face.

Sweat ran from him as he fought to keep Weis's finger from slipping over the trigger. He saw the smile and cursed that it was the last thing he'd ever see. Abruptly, Weis's eyes widened and air whooshed out of his mouth as Whitney shoved the pole smartly into his stomach.

Gripping Doug for balance, Weis shifted. In the next instant his body jerked. He'd become Doug's shield at the instant Remo had fired from shore. With a look of surprise, he fell like a stone against the side of the canoe. The next thing Whitney knew, she was swallowing water.

On the first panic, she surfaced, choking and thrashing.

'Grab the packs,' Doug shouted, shoving them at her as he treaded beside the overturned canoe. Two bullets struck the water inches from his head. 'Holy shit.' He saw the jaws of the first crock open and close over Weis's torso. And he heard the sickening sound of ripping flesh and breaking bone. Making one frantic grab, he locked his fingers over the strap of one pack. The other floated just out of range. 'Go!' he shouted again. 'Just go. Get to shore.'

She too saw what remained of Weis and struck out blindly. A dull red mist floated over the brown river water. What she didn't see until it was nearly on top of them was the second crock.

'*Doug!*'

He turned in time to see jaws open. He fired five shots point blank before they closed again and sunk in a pool of red.

There were more. Doug fumbled for the box of bullets, knowing he'd never get them all. In a desperate move, he propelled himself between Whitney and an oncoming crock, lifting the gun butt first. He waited for the impact, the pain. He was braced, lips pulled back in a snarl. The top of the crock's head exploded when he was less than an arm's length away. Before Doug could react, three more crocks went under, tails swishing. Blood swirling around him.

The shots hadn't come from Remo. Even as Doug turned toward shore he knew it. They'd come from farther south. Either they had a fairy godmother or someone else was on their trail. He caught a movement and a glimpse of a white panama. When he saw Whitney just behind him, he didn't stop to think about it.

'Go, dammit.' He grabbed her arm and pulled her toward the bank. Whitney didn't look back but simply forced her legs to kick her through the water to shore.

Doug half dragged her over the wet reeds on the edge of the canal and into the bush. Panting, aching, he propped himself on the trunk of a tree.

'I've still got the papers, you sonofabitch!' he shouted across the canal. 'I've still got them. Why don't you take a little swim across the canal and try to take them from me?' For a moment he closed his eyes and just worked on getting his breath back. He could hear Whitney heaving up canal water beside him. 'You tell Dimitri I've got them and you tell him I owe him one.' He wiped the blood from his mouth, then spat. 'You got that, Remo? You tell him I owe him. And by God, I'm not finished yet.' Wincing, he rubbed the shoulder he'd wrenched during the struggle with Weis. His clothes were plastered to him, wet, bloody, and stinking with mud. A few yards away in the canal, crocodiles were in a frenzy of feeding. The gun was still in his hand, empty. Deliberately, Doug took out the box of bullets and reloaded.

'Okay, Whitney, let's. . .'

She was curled into a ball beside him, her head on her knees. Though she made absolutely no sound, he knew she was weeping. At a loss, he ran a hand through his dripping hair. 'Hey, Whitney, don't.'

She didn't move, she didn't speak. Doug looked down at the gun in his hand. Violently, he shoved it back in his belt. 'Come on, honey. We've got to move.' He started to put his arms around her, but she jerked back. Though tears ran freely down her face, her eyes burned when she looked at him.

'Don't touch me. You've got to move, Lord. That's what you're made for. Moving, running. Why don't you just take that all-important envelope and get lost. Here.' Reaching in her pocket, she struggled to pull her wallet out of her clinging slacks. She threw it at him. 'Take this too. It's all you care about, all you think about. Money.' She didn't bother to wipe at the tears, but watched him through them. 'There's not much cash in there, only a few hundred, but there's plenty of plastic. Take it all.'

It was what he'd wanted all along, wasn't it? The money, the treasure, and no partner. He was closer than ever, and alone, he'd get there faster and have the whole pot to himself. It was what he'd wanted all along.

Doug dropped the wallet back in her lap and took her hand. 'Let's move.'

'I'm not going with you. You go after your pot of gold alone, Douglas.' Nausea heaved in her stomach, rising in her throat. She swallowed it down. 'See if you can live with it now.'

'I'm not leaving you here alone.'

'Why not?' she tossed back. 'You left Jacques back there.' She looked over toward the river and the shaking started. 'You left him. Leave me. What's the difference?'

He grabbed her shoulders hard enough to make her wince. 'He was dead. There was nothing we could do.'

'We killed him.'

The thought had already rammed into him. Perhaps because of it he gripped her harder. 'No. I got enough baggage to carry around without that. Dimitri killed him the same way he'd swat a fly off the wall. Because it doesn't mean any more to him than that. He killed him without even knowing his name, because killing doesn't make him sweat, it doesn't make him sick. It doesn't even make him wonder when it's going to be his turn.'

'Do you?'

He went very still a moment, while water dripped from his hair. 'Yeah, dammit, I do.'

'He was so young.' Her breath hitched as she grabbed his shirt. 'All he wanted was to go to New York. He'll never get there.' More tears spilled over, but this time she began to sob with them. 'He'll never get anywhere. And all because of that envelope. How many people have died for it now?' She felt the shell, Jacques's *ody*—for safety, for luck, for tradition. Whitney wept until she ached from it, but the pain didn't cleanse. 'He died because of those papers, and he didn't even know they existed.'

'We're going to follow this thing through,' Doug told her as he pulled her closer. 'And we're going to win.'

'Why the hell does it matter so much?'

'You want reasons?' He drew her back so that his face was inches from hers. His eyes were hard, his breath fast. 'There're plenty of them. Because people've died for it. Because Dimitri wants it. We're going to win, Whitney, because we're not going to let Dimitri beat us. Because that kid's dead, and he's not going to have died for nothing. It's not just the money now. Shit, it's never just the money, don't you see? It's the winning. It's always the winning, and making Dimitri sweat because we did.'

She let Doug draw her into his arms, cradle her there. 'The winning.'

'Once you don't care about winning, you're already dead.'

That she understood because the need was in her as well. 'There'll be no *fadamihana* for Jacques,' she murmured. 'No festival for him.'

'We'll give him one.' He stroked her hair, remembering the way Jacques had looked when he'd held the fish. 'A real New York party.'

She nodded, turning her face into his throat a moment. 'Dimitri isn't going to get away with this, Doug. Not with this. We're going to beat him.'

'Yeah, we're going to beat him.' Drawing her away, he rose. They'd lost his pack in the canal so they'd lost the tent and cooking utensils. Hefting hers, Doug secured it to his back. They were wet, tired, and still grieving. He held out his hand. 'Get your ass in gear, sugar.'

Wearily, she stood and tucked the wallet back in her pocket. She sniffed, inelegantly. 'Up yours, Lord.'

They walked north in the lowering evening light.

# CHAPTER TWELVE

They had eluded Remo, but they knew he was hot on their heels, and so they did not stop. They walked as the sun set and the forest took on lights only artists and poets fully understand. In twilight when the air turned pearly gray with mist as the dew fell, they walked still. The sky darkened, went black before the moon rose, a majestic ball, white as bone. Stars glittered like jewels of another age.

Moonlight turned the forest into a fairy tale. Shadows lowered and shifted. Flowers closed their petals and slept as animals that knew only night stirred. There was a flutter of wings, a thrash of leaves, and something screamed in the bush. They walked.

When Whitney wanted to drop into a ball of mindless exhaustion, she thought of Jacques. Gritting her teeth, she went on.

'Tell me about Dimitri.'

Doug paused only long enough to pull the compass out of his pocket to check their direction. He saw her fingering the shell as she had off and on during the hike but he'd run dry of comforting words. 'I already did.'

'Not enough. Tell me more.'

He recognized the tone of voice. She wanted revenge. And revenge, Doug knew, was a dangerous ambition. It could blind you to priorities—like staying healthy. 'Just take my word for it, you don't want a personal acquaintance.'

'But you're wrong.' Though breathless, her voice was soft and firm. She wiped sweat from her forehead with the back of her hand. 'Tell me about our Mr Dimitri.'

He'd lost track of the miles they'd covered, even the hours. He was only sure of two things. They had put distance between themselves and Remo, and they needed to rest. 'We'll camp here. We should be deep enough in the haystack.'

'Haystack.' She sank down gratefully on the soft, springy ground. If it'd been possible, her legs would've wept with relief.

'We're the needle, this is the haystack. Got anything in here we can use?'

Whitney pulled makeup out of her pack, lacy underwear, clothes already rent, filthy, or ruined, and what was left of the bag of fruit she'd brought in Antananarivo. 'A couple of mangoes and a very ripe banana.'

'Think of it as a portable Waldorf salad.' Doug advised as he plucked up one of the mangoes.

'All right.' Whitney followed suit and stretched out her legs. 'Dimitri, Douglas. Tell me.'

He'd hoped to set her mind on some other scene. He should've known better. 'Jabba the Hutt in an Italian suit,' he said as he bit into the fruit. 'Dimitri could make Nero look like a choirboy. He likes poetry and porno flicks.'

'Eclectic taste.'

'Yeah. He collects antiques—specializes in torture instruments. You know, thumbscrews.'

Whitney felt the little pulse in her right thumb throb. 'Fascinating.'

'Sure, Dimitri's a real fascination. He has an affection for soft, pretty things. Both of his wives were stunners.' He gave her a long, level look. 'He'd like your style.'

She tried not to shudder. 'So he's married.'

'Married twice,' Doug explained. 'And tragically widowed twice if you catch the drift.'

She did, and bit into the fruit thoughtfully. 'What makes him so. . .successful,' she decided for lack of a better term.

'Brains and a streak of ice-cold mean. I've heard he can quote Chaucer while he's sticking pins between your toes.'

She lost her appetite for the fruit. 'Is that his style? Poetry and torture?'

'He doesn't simply kill, he executes, and he executes with ceremony. He keeps a first-class studio where he tapes his victims before, during, and after.'

'Oh God.' She studied Doug's face, wanting to believe he was weaving a tale. 'You're not making that up.'

'I ain't got that much imagination. His mother was a school-teacher I hear, with a few wires crossed.' Juice dribbled down his chin and he wiped at it absently. 'Story goes that when he couldn't recite some poem, Byron or somebody, I think, she hacked off his pinky.'

'She—' Whitney choked, then forced herself to swallow. 'His mother cut off his finger because he couldn't recite?'

'That's the story on the streets. Seems she was religious and got her poetry and theology a little mixed. Figured if the kid couldn't quote Byron, he was being sacrilegious.'

For the moment she forgot the horror and death Dimitri had been responsible for. She thought of a young boy. 'That's horrible. She should've been taken away.'

He wanted her to shy away from revenge, but he didn't want to replace it with pity. One was as dangerous as the other. 'Dimitri saw to that, too. When he left home to start his own—business, he went out in a blaze. He torched the whole damn apartment building where his mother lived.'

'He killed his own mother?'

'He got her—and twenty or thirty other people. He didn't have anything against them, you understand. They just happened to be there at the time.'

'Revenge, amusement, or gain,' she murmured, remembering her earlier thoughts on killing.

'That about sums it up. If there's such a thing as a soul, Whitney, Dimitri's is black with boils running on it.'

'If there's such a thing as a soul,' she repeated, 'we're going to help his into hell.'

He didn't laugh. She'd said it too quietly. He studied her face, pale and tired in the bright moonlight. She meant what she said. He was already indirectly responsible for the death of two innocents. In that moment, he took responsibility for Whitney. Another first for Doug Lord.

'Sugar.' He shifted so that he sat next to her. 'The first thing we have to do is stay alive. The second is to get to the treasure. That's all we have to do to make Dimitri pay.'

'It's not enough.'

'You're new at this. Listen, you get in a kick when you can, then you back off. That's the way to stay in business.' She wasn't listening. Uncomfortable, Doug came to a decision. 'Maybe it's time you got a look at the papers.' He didn't have to see her face to know she was surprised. He could feel it in the way her shoulder moved against him.

'Well, well,' she said softly. 'Break out the champagne.'

'Get smart and I might change my mind.' Relieved

by her grin, he reached in his pocket. Reverently he held the envelope. 'This is the key,' he said. 'The goddamn key. And I'm using it to get through the lock I've never been able to pick.' Drawing out papers, one by one, Doug smoothed them.

'Mostly in French like the letter,' he murmured. 'But someone already translated a good bit.' He hesitated another moment, then handed her a yellowed sheet enclosed in clear plastic. 'Look at the signature.'

Whitney took it, skimming down the text. 'My God.'

'Yeah. Let 'em eat cake. Looks like she sent this message a few days before she was taken prisoner. The translation's here.'

But Whitney was already reading the leader written in the tragic queen's own hand. 'Leopold has failed me,' she murmured.

'Leopold II. Holy Roman emperor and Marie's brother.'

She lifted her gaze to Doug's. 'You've done your homework.'

'I like to know the facts on any job. I've been boning up on the French Revolution. Marie was playing politics and struggling to secure her position. She didn't pull it off. By the time she wrote that, she knew she was almost finished.'

With only a nod, Whitney went back to the letter. 'He is more emperor than brother. Without his help, I have few to turn to. I cannot tell you, my dear valet, of the humiliation of our forced return from Varennes. My husband, the king, disguised as a common servant and ¬myself—it is too shameful. To be arrested, arrested, and returned to Paris like criminals with armed soldiers. The silence was like death. Even though we breathed, it was a funeral procession. The Assembly had said that the king had been kidnapped and has already revised the constitution. This ploy was the beginning of the end.

'The king has believed that Leopold and the Prussian king would intervene. He communicated to his agent, Le Tonnelier, that things would be the better for it. A foreign war, Gerald, should have extinguished the fires of this civil unrest. The Girondist bourgeoisie has proved incapable, and they fear the people who follow Robespierre, the devil. You understand that though war was declared on Austria, our expectations were not met. The military defeats of the past spring have demonstrated the Girondins do not comprehend how it is to conduct a war.

'Now there is talk of a trial—your king on trial, and I fear for his life. I fear, my trusted Gerald, for all our lives.

'Now I must beg your help, depend on your loyalty and friendship. I am not able to flee, so I must wait and trust. I beg you, Gerald, to receive that which my messenger brings you. Guard it. Your love and loyalty I must depend upon now that everything is crumbling around me. I have been betrayed, time and time again, but it is sometimes possible to turn the betrayal into advantage.

'This small portion of what is mine as queen, I entrust to you. It perhaps will be needed to pay for the lives of my children. Even if the bourgeois are successful, they too will fall. Take what is mine, Gerald Lebrun, and guard it for my children, and theirs. The time will come when we again take our rightful place. You must wait for it.'

Whitney looked down at the words written by a stubborn woman who had plotted and maneuvered herself to her own death. But still, she'd been a woman, a mother, a queen. 'She had only a few months to live,'

Whitney murmured. 'I wonder if she knew.' And it occurred to her that the letter itself belonged safely behind glass in some tidy corner of the Smithsonian. That's what Lady Smythe-Wright would have felt. That's why she'd been foolish enough to give it and the rest to Whitaker. Now they were both dead.

'Doug, do you have any idea just how valuable this is?'

'That's just what we're going to find out, sugar,' he muttered.

'Stop thinking in dollar signs. I mean culturally, historically.'

'Yeah, I'm going to buy a boatload of culture.'

'Contrary to popular belief, one can't buy culture. Doug, this belongs in a museum.'

'After I've got the treasure, I'll donate every sheet. I'm going to be needing some tax write-offs.'

Whitney shook her head and shrugged. First things first, she decided. 'What else is there?'

'Pages from a journal, looks like it was written by this Gerald's daughter.' He'd read the translated parts, and they were grim. Without a word he handed a page to Whitney. It was dated October 17, 1793 and in the young hand and simple words were a black fear and a confusion that was ageless. The writer had seen her queen executed.

'She appeared pale and plain, and so old. They brought her in a cart through the streets, like a drab. She revealed no fear as she mounted the steps. Maman has said she was a queen to the end. People crowded around and merchants sold wares as though at a fair. It smelled like animals and flies came in clouds. I have seen other people pulled in carts through the streets, like sheep. Mademoiselle Fontainebleu was among them. Last winter she ate cakes with Maman in the salon.

'When the blade descended on the queen's neck, people cheered. Papa wept. Never have I seen him weep before and I could only stand, holding his hand. Seeing his tears I was afraid, more afraid than when I saw the carts or watched the queen. If Papa wept, what would happen to us? That same night we left Paris. I think perhaps I will never see it again, or my pretty room that looks over the garden. Maman's beautiful necklace of gold and sapphire has been sold. Papa tells me we will go on a long journey and must be brave.'

Whitney turned to another sheet, dated three months later. 'I have been sick unto death. The boat sways and rocks and stinks from the filth of the wretched below-decks. Papa also has been ill. For a time we feared he would die and we would be alone. Maman prays and sometimes, when he is feverish, I remain and hold his hand. It seems so long ago that we were happy. Maman grows thin and Papa's beautiful hair more gray every day.

'While he lay in his bed, he had me bring to him a little wooden chest. It appeared plain, as one in which a peasant girl might hide her trinkets. He told us that the queen had sent it to him, enlisting his trust. One day, we would return to France and release the contents to the new king in her name. I was tired and ill and wished to lie down, but Papa made both Maman and me swear we would bide by his oath. When we had sworn, he opened the box.

'I have seen the queen wear such things, with her hair piled high and her face glowing with laughter. In the simple box, the emerald necklace I had seen once upon her breasts seemed to catch the light of the candles and throw it upon the other jewels. There was a ruby ring with diamonds like a starburst and a bracelet of emeralds to match the necklace. There were stones yet to be set.

'But as I looked, my eyes were dazzled. I saw a diamond necklace more beautiful than all the rest. It was set in tiers, but each stone, some bigger than I have ever seen, seemed alive of its own. I remembered Maman speaking of the scandal of Cardinal de Rohan and the necklace of diamonds. Papa had told me the cardinal had been tricked, the queen used, and that the necklace itself had disappeared. Still I wondered as I looked into the box if the queen had contrived to find it.'

Whitney set the paper down but her hands weren't steady. 'The diamond necklace was supposed to have been broken up and sold.'

'Supposed,' Doug repeated. 'But the cardinal was banished, and the Comtesse de La Motte was caught, tried, and sentenced. She escaped to England, but I've never read anything that proved she had the necklace.'

'No.' Whitney studied the page of the journal. The paper itself would've made any museum curator worth his salt drool. As for the treasure, 'That necklace was one of the catalysts for the Revolution.'

'It was worth a pretty penny then.' Doug handed her another page. 'Care to estimate what it might be worth today?'

Priceless, Whitney thought, but knew he wouldn't understand her meaning. The sheet he'd given her listed in detailed inventory what the queen had entrusted to Gerald. Jewels were described and valued. As with the pictures in the book, Whitney found them unexciting. Still, one shone out among the rest. A diamond necklace valued at more than a million livres.

Doug would understand that, Whitney mused, then set the paper aside and took up the journal again.

More months had passed and Gerald and his family were settled on the northeast coast of Madagascar. The young girl wrote of long, harsh days.

'I yearn for France, for Paris, for my room and the gardens. Maman says we must not complain and sometimes goes with me for walks along the shore. Those are the best times, with the birds flying and shells to find. Maman looks happy then, but sometimes she looks out to sea and I know she too longs for Paris.

'Winds blow in from the sea and ships come. News from home is of death. The Terror rules. The merchants say that there are thousands of prisoners and many have faced the guillotine. Others have been hung, even burned. They talk of the Committee of Public Safety. Papa says that Paris is unsafe because of them. If one mentions the name of Robespierre, he will not speak at all. So while I long for France, I begin to understand that the home I knew is gone forever.

'Papa works hard. He has opened a store and trades with other settlers. Maman and I have a garden, but we grow only vegetables. Flies plague us. We have no servants and must fend for ourselves. I regard it as an adventure, but Maman tires easily now she is with child. I look forward to the baby coming and wonder when I will have my own. At night we sew, though we have few coins for extra candles. Papa is constructing a cradle. We do not speak of the little box hidden under the floor in the kitchen.'

Whitney set the page aside. 'How old was she, I wonder.'

'Fifteen.' He touched another paper sealed in plastic. 'Her record of birth, her parents' marriage lines.' He handed it to Whitney. 'And death certificates. She died when she was sixteen.' He picked up a last page. 'This gives us the rest of it.'

'To my son,' Whitney began and glanced up at Doug. 'You sleep in the cradle I made you, and wearing the little blue gown your mother and sister sewed. They are departed now, your mother giving you life, your sister from a fever striking so quickly there was no time for a doctor. I have discovered your sister's journal and read it, wept over it. One day, when you are older, it too will be yours. I have done what I thought I must, for my country, my queen, my family. I have saved them from the Terror only to lose them in this strange, foreign place.

'I have not the will to continue. The sisters will care for you as I cannot. I can give to you only these pieces of your family, the words of your sister, your mother's love. With them, I add the responsibility I took for our queen. A letter will be left with the sisters, instructions for passing you this package when you are of age. You inherit my responsibility and my oath to the queen. Though it will be buried with me, you will again take it up and fight for the cause. When the time is right, come to where I rest and find Marie. I pray you do not fail as I have done.'

'He killed himself.' Whitney set the letter down with a sigh. 'He'd lost his home, his family, and his heart.' She could see them, French aristocrats displaced by politics and social unrest, floundering in a strange country, struggling to adjust to a new life. And Gerald, living and dying by his promise to a queen. 'What happened?'

'As best I can make out, the baby was taken into a convent.' He shifted through more papers. 'He was adopted and emigrated with his family to England. It looks like the papers were stored away and just forgotten until Lady Smythe-Wright unearthed them.'

'And the queen's box?'

'Buried,' Doug said with a faraway look in his eye. 'In a cemetery in Diégo-Suarez. All we have to do is find it.'

'And then?'

'Then we take a stroll on easy street.'

Whitney looked down at the papers in her lap. There were lives scattered there, dreams, hopes, and loyalty. 'Is that all?'

'Isn't it enough?'

'This man made a promise to his queen.'

'And she's dead,' Doug pointed out. 'France is a democracy. I don't think anyone would back us up if we decided to use the treasure to restore the crown.'

She started to speak, then found herself too tired to argue. She needed time to take it all in, evaluate her own standards. In any case, they'd yet to find it. Doug had said it was the winning. After he'd won, she'd talk to him about morals. 'So you think you can find a cemetery, stroll in, and dig up a queen's treasure.'

'Damn right.' He gave her a quick, dashing smile that made her believe him.

'It might already have been found.'

'Uh-uh.' He shook his head and shifted. 'One of the pieces the girl described, the ruby ring. There was a whole section on it in the library book. That ring had been passed down through royal succession for a hundred years before it was lost—during the French Revolution. If that or any of the other pieces had turned up, underground or otherwise, I'd've heard about it. It's all there, Whitney. Waiting for us.'

'It's plausible.'

'The hell with plausible. I've got the papers.'

'We've got the papers.' Whitney corrected as she leaned back against a tree. 'Now all we have to do is find a cemetery that's been around for two centuries.' She closed her eyes and went instantly to sleep.

It was hunger that woke her, the deep, hollow kind she'd never experienced. On a moan, she rolled over and found herself nose to nose with Doug.

'Morning.'

She ran her tongue around her teeth. 'I'd kill for a croissant.'

'A Mexican omelette.' He closed his eyes as he pictured it. 'Cooked to a deep gold and just busting with peppers and onions.

Whitney let that lie in her imagination, but it didn't fill her stomach. 'We have one brown banana.'

'Around here, it's serve yourself.' Rubbing his hands over his face, Doug sat up. It was well past dawn. The sun had already burned off the mist. The forest was alive with sound and movement and the smells of morning. He glanced up to the treetops where birds hid and sang. 'The place is loaded with fruit. I don't know what lemur meat tastes like, but—'

'No.'

He grinned as he rose. 'Just a thought. How about light fare? Fresh fruit salad.'

'Sounds delightful.' When she stretched, the lamba slipped off her shoulder. Fingering it, Whitney realized Doug must have spread it over her the night before. After all that had happened, all they'd seen, he could still manage to surprise her. As if it were the most elegant of silks. Whitney folded and repacked it.

'You get the fruit, I'll get the coconuts.'

Whitney reached up into the branches. 'These look like stunted bananas.'

'Pawpaws.'

Whitney picked three and grimaced at them. 'What I wouldn't give for one lowly apple, just as a change of pace.'

'Take her out to breakfast and she complains.'

'Least you could do is buy me a Bloody Mary,' she began, then turned to see him halfway up a palm tree. 'Douglas,' she said, moving cautiously closer, 'do you know what you're doing?'

'I'm climbing a goddamn tree,' he managed as he shinnied up another foot.

'I hope you're not planning on falling and breaking your neck. I hate to travel alone.'

'All heart,' he muttered under his breath. 'It's not so different from climbing into a third-story window.'

'A nice brick building isn't likely to give you splinters in sensitive places.'

Reaching up, he yanked off a coconut. 'Stand back, sugar, I might be tempted to aim for you.'

Lips curved, she did so. One, then two, then three coconuts landed at her feet. Taking one up, she smacked it against a tree trunk until it cracked. 'Well done,' she told Doug when he dropped to the ground. 'I believe I'd like a chance to watch you work.'

He accepted the coconut she offered and, sitting on the ground, pulled out his pocketknife to carve out the meat. It reminded her of Jacques. Whitney touched the shell she still wore, then pushed back the grief.

'You know, most people in your position wouldn't be so—tolerant,' he decided, 'of somebody in my line of work.'

'I'm a firm believer in free enterprise.' Whitney dropped down beside him. 'It's also a matter of checks and balances,' she concluded with her mouth full.

'Checks and balances?'

'Say you steal my emerald earrings.'

'I'll keep it in mind.'

'Let's keep this hypothetical.' She shook the hair back from her face and gave a fleeting thought to digging out her brush. Food came first. 'Well, the insurance company's stuck with shelling out the cash. I've been paying them outrageous premiums for years and I never wear the emeralds because they're too gaudy. You hock the emeralds, someone else buys them who finds them attractive, and I have the cash to buy something entirely more suitable. In the long run, everyone's happy. It could almost be considered a public service.'

He broke off a piece of coconut and chewed. 'I guess I never thought about it that way.'

'Of course the insurance company's not going to be happy,' she added. 'And some people might not appreciate losing some particular piece of jewelry or the family silver, even if it was too ornate. You're not always doing a good deed by breaking into their house, you know.'

'Guess not.'

'And I suppose I have more respect for straight, honest stealing than computer crimes and white-collar swindling. Like the crooked stockbrokers,' she continued as she sampled coconut. 'Fooling around with some little old lady's portfolio until they've pocketed the profits and she's left with nothing. That's not on the same level with picking someone's pocket or lifting the Sydney Diamond.'

'I don't want to talk about the Sydney,' he mumbled.

'In one way it does keep the cycle going, then again. . .' She paused to dig out more fruit. 'I don't think robbery has a very good occupation potential. An interesting hobby, certainly, but as a career, it has its limitations.'

'Yeah. I've been thinking about retiring—when I can do it in style.'

'When you get back to the States, what's the first thing you're going to do?'

'Buy a silk shirt and have my initials monogrammed on the cuffs. I'm going to have an Italian suit to go over it and a sleek little Lamborghini to set it all off.' He sliced a mango in half, wiped the blade on his jeans, and offered her a piece. 'What about you?'

'I'm going to stuff myself,' Whitney told him with her mouth full. 'I'm going to make a career out of eating. I think I'll start out with a hamburger, smothered with cheese and onions, and work my way up to lobster tails, lightly broiled and drowned in melted butter.'

'For somebody so preoccupied with eating, I don't see how you're so skinny.'

She swallowed mango. 'It's lack of occupation that leads to preoccupation,' she told him. 'And I'm slender, not skinny. Mick Jagger's skinny.'

Grinning, he popped another piece of fruit into his mouth. 'You forget, sugar, I've had the privilege of seeing you naked. Yours ain't exactly an hourglass figure.'

With a brow lifted, she licked juice from her fingers. 'I've a very delicate build,' she said, and when he continued to grin, she moved her gaze up and down him. 'And you'll remember, I also have had the fascination of seeing you stripped. It wouldn't hurt you to pump a little iron, Douglas.'

'Obvious muscles get in the way. I'd rather be subtle.'

'You certainly are.'

He shot her a look as he tossed a coconut shell aside.

'You like biceps and triceps bulging out of a sleeveless T-shirt?'

'Masculinity,' she said lightly, 'is very arousing. A confident male doesn't find it necessary to ogle an overendowed woman who chooses to wear tight sweaters to disguise the fact she has a very small brain.'

'I guess you don't like being ogled.'

'Certainly not. I prefer style to cleavage.'

'Good thing.'

'There's no need to be insulting.'

'Just being agreeable.' He remembered too well the way she'd wept in his arms the day before and how helpless he'd felt. Now, he found he wanted to touch her again, watch her smile, feel the softness. 'Anyway,' he said, working his way back from a long drop. 'You might be skinny, but I like your face.'

Her lips curved in that cool, aloof smile he found maddeningly alluring. 'Really? What about it?'

'Your skin.' Going with the impulse, he ran the back of his knuckles down her jawline. 'I came across this alabaster cameo once. It wasn't big,' he remembered as he traced a finger down her cheekbone. 'Probably wasn't worth more than a few hundred, but it was the classiest thing I'd ever picked up.' He grinned, then let his hands roam into her hair. 'Until you.'

She didn't move away, but kept her eyes on his as his breath feathered over her skin. 'Is that what you did, Douglas? Pick me up?'

'You could look at it that way, couldn't you?' He knew he was making a mistake. Even as his lips brushed over hers he knew he was making a very big mistake. He'd made them before. 'Since I did,' he murmured, 'I haven't known exactly what to do with you.'

'I'm not an alabaster cameo,' she murmured as her

arms wound around his neck. 'Or the Sydney Diamond or a pot of gold.'

'I'm not a member of the country club and I don't have a villa in Martinque.'

'It would seem. . .' She traced the outline of his mouth with her tongue. 'We have very little in common.'

'Nothing in common,' he corrected as his hands slid up her back. 'People like you and me can't bring each other anything but trouble.'

'Yeah.' She smiled and the eyes beneath the fringe of long, luxurious lashes were dark and amused. 'When do we start?'

'We already have.'

When their lips met, they were no longer a lady and a thief. Passion was a great equalizer. Together they rolled on to the soft forest floor.

She hadn't meant for it to happen, but she had no regrets. Attraction that she'd felt from the moment he'd removed the sunglasses in her elevator and looked at her with his clear, direct eyes had been edging toward something deeper, broader, more unsettling. He'd begun to touch something in her, and now with passion, he released a great deal more.

Her mouth was as hot and hungry as his. That had happened before. Her pulse raced—no new experience. Her body stretched and arched at the touch of a man's hands. She'd felt those sensations before. But this time, this first and only time, she let her mind go and experienced lovemaking as it was meant to be. Mindless, liberating pleasure.

Though the surrender of her best defense, her mind, was complete, she wasn't passive. Her need was as great as his, as primitive, as overwhelming, as elemental. When they undressed each other in a frenzy, her hands were as quick as his.

Flesh against flesh, warm, firm, sleek. Mouth against mouth, open, hot, hungry. They rolled over the soft ground with no more inhibitions than children, but with passion full-grown and straining.

She couldn't get enough of him and tasted, touched, as if she'd never known a man before. In that moment, she could remember no others. He filled her, heart, mind, threatening to stay so that there would never be room for another. She understood, and after the first fear, accepted.

He'd wanted women before, desperately. Or so he'd thought. Until now he hadn't known the full meaning of desperation. Until now, he hadn't known what it was to want. She was seeping into him, pore by pore. Women were allowed to pleasure and be pleasured, but they weren't allowed intimacy. Intimacy meant complications a man on the run couldn't afford. But there was no stopping her.

His hands might run along her skin, clever, skilled, strong, but it was she who led. He knew a man was at his most vulnerable when in a woman's arms—mother, wife, or lover—yet he forgot anything but the need to be there. She melted into him, dangerously warm, dangerously soft, but he took and cursed the consequences.

Naked, agile, exquisite, she moved under him, wrapped around him. With his face buried in her hair, Doug heard the door lock behind him. He heard the bolt slide quietly into place. He didn't give a damn.

Taking his time, he ran kisses down her face, forehead, nose, mouth, chin. He felt her smile answer his. Her elegant pampered fingers slid down to his hips.

They both had their eyes open when he plunged into her.

He filled her and moaned at the exquisite heat and softness that encompassed him. Her face was dappled with sun and shade, her eyes half-closed as she matched him stroke for stroke, pulse for pulse.

Speed built, needs whirled. As his thoughts began to tumble and skid, his last rational flash was that perhaps he'd already found the end of the rainbow.

They lay in silence. Neither were children, neither were without experience. Both knew they'd never made love before. Both were wondering what the hell they were going to do about it.

Gently, she ran a hand up and down his back. He drew in the scent of her hair.

'I guess we knew this would happen,' she said after a moment.

'I guess we did.'

She looked up at the canopy of trees overhead and the pure blue beyond them. 'What now?'

It wasn't practical to think beyond the present. If her question dealt with the future, Doug thought it best to pretend otherwise. He kissed her shoulder. 'We get to the nearest town, beg, borrow, or steal transportation, and head to Diégo-Suarez.'

Whitney closed her eyes briefly, then opened them again. She had, after all, walked into this with them open. She'd keep them that way. 'The treasure.'

'We're going to get it, Whitney. It's only a matter of days now.'

'And then?'

The future again. Propping himself on his elbows, he looked down at her. 'Anything you want,' he said because he couldn't think of anything but how beautiful she was. 'Martinique, Athens, Zanzibar. We'll buy a farm in Ireland and raise sheep.'

She laughed because it seemed so simple just now. 'We could plant wheat in Nebraska with about the same rate of success.'

'Right. What we should do is open an American restaurant right here in Madagascar. I'll cook and you do the books.'

Abruptly, he sat up, gathering her with him. Somehow, he'd stopped being alone and hadn't fully realized it until that moment. Stopped being alone when alone had always seemed the best angle. He wanted to share, to belong, to have someone there right beside him. It wasn't smart, but it was.

'We're going to get that treasure, Whitney. After we do, nothing can stop us. Anything we want, anytime we want. I can shower diamonds in your hair.' He ran a hand through it, forgetting for the moment that she could have her pick of diamonds now if she chose.

She felt a twinge of regret, and of something like grief. He could see no further than his pot of gold. Not now, perhaps not ever. Smiling, she ran a hand over his cheek. Yet she'd known that all along. 'We'll find it.'

'We'll find it,' he agreed, drawing her closer. 'And when we do, we'll have it all.'

They walked through another day to dusk while Whitney's stomach rumbled and her legs went to rubber. Like Doug, she fixed her mind on the goal of Diégo-Suarez. It helped keep her feet moving and her mind from questioning. They'd come this far for the treasure. Whatever happened before, after, or in between, they'd find it. The time for thinking, questioning, analyzing would come after.

She shook her head at the fruit Doug offered. 'My system would punish me if I sent any more mango down.' As if to soothe it, she placed her hand over her stomach. 'I thought McDonald's had franchises everywhere. Do you realize how far we've walked without seeing one golden arch?'

'Forget the fast food. When we're finished with this, I'll fix you a five-course dinner that'll make you think you've gone to heaven.'

'I'd settle for a hot dog with everything.'

'For somebody who thinks like a duchess, you've got the stomach of a peasant.'

'Even serfs had a leg of mutton now and again.'

'Look, we'll—' Then he grabbed her and shoved her into the bush.

'What is it?'

'A light, up ahead. See it?'

Cautiously, she looked over his shoulder and angled her head. It was there, faint and white through the dim light and thick foliage. Automatically, she dropped her voice to a whisper. 'Remo?'

'I don't know. Maybe.' He went silent as he thought of and rejected a half dozen ideas. 'We'll take it slow.'

It took them fifteen minutes to reach the tiny settlement. By then, it was fully dark. They could see the light through the window of what seemed to be a small stove or trading post. Moths as big as the palm of her hand batted against the glass. Outside was a jeep.

'Ask and you shall receive,' Doug said under his breath. 'Let's have a look.' Crouching, he made his way over to the window. What he saw inside made him grin.

Remo, his tailored shirt stained and limp, sat at a table scowling into a glass of beer. Across from him was Barns, balding, molelike, and grinning at nothing in particular.

'Well, well,' Doug breathed. 'Looks like our lucky day.'

'What're they doing here?'

'Running in circles. Remo looks like he needs a shave and a husky Norwegian masseuse.' Doug counted three others in the bar, all giving the Americans a wide berth. He also saw two bowls of steaming soup, a sandwich, and what looked like a bag of potato chips. Saliva pooled in his mouth.

'A shame we can't order something to go.'

Whitney'd seen the food as well. She barely stopped herself from pressing her nose up against the glass. 'Can't we wait until they leave and then go in and eat?'

'They leave, so does the jeep. Okay, sugar, you're going to be lookout again. This time do a better job.'

'I told you I couldn't whistle last time because I was busy staying alive.'

'We're both going to stay alive, and we're going to liberate ourselves a set of wheels. Come on.'

Moving quickly, he circled the hut. With whispers and hand signals, he positioned Whitney near the front window while he crept to the jeep and went to work.

She watched, gasping when Remo rose and began to pace. Eyes wide, she looked back at the jeep. Sprawled on the floor, Doug was hidden from view. She gritted her teeth and pressed her back to the all as Remo passed the window.

'Make it fast,' she hissed to Doug. 'He's getting restless.'

'Don't rush me,' he muttered as he freed wires. 'These things take a delicate touch.'

She glanced inside in time to see Remo shove Barns

to his feet. 'You better get your delicate touch moving, Douglas. They're coming.'

Swearing, he wiped sweat from his fingers. Another minute. All he needed was another minute. 'Pile in, sugar, we're almost there.' When she didn't respond, he looked up to see the little front porch of the hut was empty. 'Sonofabitch.' Struggling with the wires, he searched for her. 'Whitney? Goddammit, this is no time to take a walk.'

Still swearing, fingers working, he scanned the settlement. Nothing.

He jolted at the sound of squeals, barks, and confusion as the engine roared in life. As he started to leap out of the jeep, gun raised, Whitney raced around the side of the hut and jumped inside.

'Hit the gas, sugar,' she panted. 'Or we'll have company.'

The words weren't out of her mouth before he had the jeep roaring down the narrow dirt road. A low-hanging branch swiped against the windshield and broke with a crack like a gunshot. Glancing over his shoulder, he saw Remo running around the side of the hut. He pushed Whitney's face into the seat and the gas pedal to the floor before the first of three shots rang out.

'Where'd you go?' Doug demanded as they left the light of the settlement behind. 'A hell of a lookout you made when I nearly get myself shot looking for you.'

'That's gratitude.' She shook back her hair as she sat up. 'If I hadn't created a diversion, you'd never have gotten the jeep hot-wired in time.'

He slowed down only enough to assure himself he wouldn't smash the jeep against the tree. 'What're you talking about?'

'When I saw Remo was coming out, I figured you needed a diversion—like in the movies.'

'Terrific.' He negotiated a bend, bumped over a rock, and kept on going.

'So I ran around back and let the dog into the pigsty.' Whitney brushed the hair out of her eyes and revealed a very smug smile. 'It was quite entertaining, but I couldn't hang around to watch. It did, however, work perfectly.'

'Lucky you didn't get your head shot off,' he mumbled.

'I continue to prevent you from having yours shot off and you resent it,' she returned. 'Typical male ego. I don't know why I. . .' She trailed off and sniffed the air.

'What's that smell?'

'What smell?'

'That smell.' It wasn't grass, damp, or animal, odors to which they had become accustomed. She sniffed again, then turned and kneeled on the seat. 'It smells like. . .' She lowered so that when Doug turned his head he saw only her slim, well-shaped bottom. 'Chicken!' Triumphant, Whitney leapt up again, holding a drumstick. 'It's chicken,' she said again, taking an enormous bite. 'They have a whole cold chicken back here and a pile of cans—cans with food in them. Olives,' she announced, digging in the back again. 'Big, fat Greek olives. Where's the can opener?'

While she dug, head down, Doug plucked the drumstick from her hand. 'Dimitri believes in eating well,' he said over a healthy bite. He could have sworn he felt it slide all the way down. 'Remo's smart enough to raid the larder when he's going to be on the road.'

'I'll say.' With a light in her eyes, she flopped back on the seat again. 'Beluga.' She held the small tin between her thumb and finger. 'And there's a bottle of Pouilly-Fuissé, '79.'

'Any salt?'

'Of course.'

Grinning, he handed her the half-eaten drumstick. 'Looks like we're traveling to Diégo-Suarez in style, sugar.'

Whitney retrieved the bottle of wine and drew out the cork. 'Sugar,' she drawled. 'I never travel any other way.'

# CHAPTER THIRTEEN

They made love in the jeep like giddy teenagers, high on exhaustion and wine. The moon was white, the night still. There was music from night birds, insects, and frogs. With the jeep pulled deep into the bush they feasted on caviar and one another while the forest sang around them. Whitney laughed as they struggled to have more of each other on the small, uncooperative front seat of the jeep.

With her clothes half on, half off, her mind light, and her hunger satisfied, Whitney rolled on top of him and grinned. 'I haven't had a date like this since I was sixteen.'

'Oh yeah?' He ran a hand up her thigh to her hip. Her eyes were dark, glazed with a combination of weariness, wine, and passion. Doug promised himself he'd see them like that again, when they were in some cozy hotel on the other side of the world. 'So a guy could get you in the back seat with a little wine and caviar?'

'Actually it was crackers and beer.' She sucked beluga from her finger. 'And I ended up punching him in the stomach.'

'You're a fun date, Whitney.'

She tipped the last drops from the bottle into her mouth. Around them, the forest was full of insects rubbing their wings and singing. 'I am, and have always been, selective.'

'Selective, huh?' He shifted so that she lay across

him as he supported himself against the door of the jeep. 'What the hell're you doing here with me then?'

She'd asked herself the same question and the simplicity of the anwer left her uneasy. She wanted to be. For a moment she was silent, nestling her head against his shoulder. It felt right there, and though it was foolish, safe. 'I suppose I fell for your charm.'

'They all do.'

Whitney tilted her head, smiled, then sunk her teeth, not so gently, into his bottom lip.

'Hey!' While she laughed, he pinned her arms to her side. 'So, she wants to play rough.'

'You don't scare me, Lord.'

'No?' Enjoying himself, he gripped both her wrists in one hand and circled her neck with the other. Her eyes never flickered. 'Maybe I've been too easy on you so far.'

'Go ahead,' she challenged. 'Do your worst.'

She looked up at him with that cool half smile, her whiskey eyes dark and sleepy. Doug did what he'd avoided all his life, what he'd avoided more cleverly, more carefully than small-town sheriffs and big-city cops. He fell in love.

'Jesus, you're beautiful.'

There was something in the tone of his voice. Before she could analyze it, or the look that had come into his eyes, his mouth was on hers. They both fell into passion.

It was as the first time. He hadn't expected it to be. The feelings, the needs that swam through him were just as intense, just as overwhelming. He was just as helpless.

Under his hands, her skin flowed like water. Under his mouth, her lips were strong, more potent than sweet. The light-headed weariness passed into a light-headed power. With her, he could do and have anything.

The night was hot, and the air moist and heavy with the scent of dozens of heat-soaked flowers. Night-feeding insects rubbed their wings and whined. He wanted candlelight for her, and a soft, cool feather bed with silk-covered pillows. He wanted to give, something new for a man who, while generous, always took first.

Her body was so delicate. It captivated him in a way all the others—the flamboyant, the obvious, the professional—never had. Her curves were subtle, her bones long and elegant. Her skin was soft in a way that spoke of daily pampering. He told himself there'd be a time when he'd have the luxury of exploring every inch of her, slowly, thoroughly, until he knew her like no other man ever had, like no other man ever would.

There was something different about him. He was no less passionate, but she knew there was something. . . .

Her senses were tangled, layered one on top of the other so that she was caught in a delicious mass of sensation. She could feel, but what she felt came from him. The stroke of a fingertip, the brush of lips. She could taste, but it was his flavor which filled her, warm, male, exciting. She heard him murmur to her, and her own whispered answer floated on the air. His scent reached her, muskier, more intoxicating than the hothouse that surrounded them. Until now, she hadn't understood what it meant to be steeped in someone. Until now, she hadn't wanted to.

She opened. He filled. He gave. She absorbed.

From the beginning, they'd raced together. This was no different. Heart pounding against heart, bodies close, they crossed the line all lovers seek.

They slept lightly, only an hour, but it was a luxury they took greedily, curled together on the seat of the jeep. The moon was lower now. Doug watched its position through the trees before he nudged her.

'We've got to move.' Remo might still be scrambling for transportation, then again, he might already be on the road behind them. Either way, he wouldn't be cheerful.

Whitney sighed and stretched. 'How much farther?'

'I don't know—another hundred, maybe hundred and twenty miles.'

'Okay.' Yawning, she began to dress. 'I'll drive.'

He snorted as he pulled on his jeans. 'The hell you will. I've driven with you before, remember?'

'I certainly do.' After a brief inspection, Whitney decided the wrinkles in her clothes were permanent. She wondered if there was any chance of finding a dry cleaner. 'Just as I remember I saved your life then, too.'

'Saved it?' Doug turned to see her rooting out her brush. 'You nearly got us both killed.'

Whitney flicked the brush through her hair. 'I beg your pardon. Through my superior skill and maneuvering, I not only saved your ass, but detained Remo and his band of merry men.'

Doug turned on the ignition. 'I guess it's all a matter of perspective. Anyway, I'll drive. You've had too much to drink.'

Whitney cast him a long, withering look. 'The MacAllisters never lose their wits.' She grabbed the door handle as they bumped through the brush and on to the road.

'All that ice cream,' Doug decided as he set a steady speed. 'It coats the stomach so the booze neutralizes.'

'Very droll.' She released the door handle, propped

her feet on the dash, and watched the night whiz by. 'It occurs to me that you're quite aware of my family history and background. What about yours?'

'Which story do you want?' he asked lightly. 'I keep a variety, depending on the occasion.'

'Everything from the destitute orphan to the misplaced aristocrat, I'm sure.' Whitney studied his profile. Who was he? she wondered. And why did she care? She didn't have the first answer, but the time had passed when she could pretend she didn't have the second. 'What about the real one, just for variety?'

He could have lied. It would have been a simple matter for him to have given her the story of a homeless little boy sleeping in alleys and running from a vicious stepfather. And he could have made her believe it. Settling back, Doug did what he did rarely. He told the unvarnished truth.

'I grew up in Brooklyn, a nice, quiet neighborhood. Blue-collar, plain and settled. My mother kept house and my father fixed drains. Both my sisters were cheerleaders. We had a dog named Checkers.'

'It sounds very normal.'

'Yeah, it was.' And sometimes, rarely, he could bring it back in focus and enjoy it. 'My father belonged to the Moose and my mom made the best blueberry pie you ever tasted. They both still do.'

'And what about young Douglas Lord?'

'Because I was, ah, clever with my hands, my father thought I'd make a good plumber. It just didn't seem like my idea of a good time.'

'The hourly rate of a union plumber's quite impressive.'

'Yeah, well I've never been into working by the hour.'

'So instead you decided to—how do you term it—freelance?'

'A vocation's a vocation. I had this uncle, the family always kept kind of quiet about him.'

'A black sheep?' she asked, interested.

'I guess you wouldn't have called him lily white. Seems he'd done some time. Anyway, to keep it short, he came to live with us for awhile and worked for my dad.' He shot Whitney a quick, appealing grin. 'He was good with his hands, too.'

'I see. So you came by your talent, dare I say, honestly.'

'Jack was good. He was real good except he had a weakness for the bottle. When he gave into it he got sloppy. Get sloppy, you get caught. One of the first things he taught me was never to drink on the job.'

'I don't imagine you're referring to unstopping pipes.'

'No. Jack, was a second-rate plumber, but he was a first-class thief. I was fourteen when he taught me to pick a lock. Never been real sure why he took to me. One thing was I liked to read and he liked to hear stories. He wasn't much on sitting down with a book, but he'd sit there for hours if you'd tell him the story of *The Man in the Iron Mask* or *Don Quixote*.'

She'd been aware from the beginning of a sharp intellect and a varied kind of taste. 'So young Douglas liked to read.'

'Yeah.' He moved his shoulders and negotiated a curve. 'First thing I stole was a book. We weren't poor, really, but we couldn't afford to stock the kind of library I wanted.' Needed, he corrected. He needed the books, the escape from the everyday the same way he'd needed food. No one had understood.

'Anyway, Jack liked hearing stories. I remember what I read.'

'Authors hope readers do.'

'No. I mean I remember almost line for line. It's just the way it is. Got me through school.'

She thought about the ease with which he'd spouted off facts and figures from the guidebook. 'You mean you have a photographic memory?'

'I don't see it in pictures, I just don't forget, that's all.' He grinned, thinking. 'It got me a scholarship to Princeton.'

Whitney sat up straight. 'You went to Princeton?'

His grin widened at her reaction. Until then, he'd never considered the truth more interesting than fiction. 'No. I decided rather than college I wanted on-the-job training.'

'You're telling me you turned down a Princeton scholarship?'

'Yeah. Pre-law seemed pretty cut and dried.'

'Pre-law,' she murmured and had to laugh. 'So, you might've been a lawyer. Ivy League at that.'

'I'd've hated it just as much as I'd've hated unstopping johns. There was Uncle Jack. He always said he didn't have any kids and wanted to pass on his trade.'

'Ah, a traditionalist.'

'Yeah, well, in his way, he was. I caught on quick. I had a hell of a lot more fun tripping a lock than I did conjugating verbs, but Jack had this thing about education. He wouldn't take me on a real job until I had my high-school diploma. And a little math and science come in handy when you're dealing with security systems.'

With his talent, she imagined Doug could've been one of the top engineers in the business. She let it pass. 'Very sensible.'

'We went on the road. Did pretty well for ourselves for about five years. Small, clean jobs. Hotels mostly. One memorable night we picked up ten thousand at the Waldorf.' He smiled, reminiscently. 'We went to Vegas and dropped most of it, but it was a hell of a time.'

'Easy come, easy go?'

'If you can't have fun with it, there's no use taking it.'

She had to smile at that. Her father was fond of saying if you couldn't have fun with it, there was no use making it. She supposed he'd appreciate Doug's slight variation on the theme.

'Jack had this idea about hitting this jewelry store. Would've set us up for years. We only had a few details to work out.'

'What happened?'

'Jack fell off the wagon. He tried to pull the job on his own, what you might call an ego thing. I was getting better, and he was slipping a bit. I guess it was hard to take. Anyway, he got sloppy. It wouldn't have been so bad if he hadn't broken the rules and taken a gun with him.' Doug swung his arm back on the seat and shook his head. 'That little flourish cost him ten good years.'

'So Uncle Jack went up the river. And you?'

'Up the river,' he murmured, amused. 'I hit the streets. I was twenty-three and a hell of a lot greener than I thought I was. But I learned fast enough.'

He'd given up a Princeton scholarship to climb in second-story windows. The education might have brought him some of the luxury he seemed to crave. And yet. . . And yet, Whitney couldn't see him choosing the well-trod road.

'What about your parents?'

'They tell the neighbors I work for General Motors.

My mother keeps hoping I'll get married and settle down. Maybe become a locksmith. By the way,' he added as one thought led to another, 'who's Tad Carlyse IV?'

'Tad?' Whitney noticed that the sky in the east was beginning to lighten. She might've closed her eyes and slept if her eyelids hadn't felt filled with grit. 'We were sort of engaged for a time.'

He immediately and completely detested Tad Carlyse IV. 'Sort of engaged?'

'Well, let's say Tad and my father considered us engaged. I consider it a matter for debate. They were both rather annoyed when I opted out.'

'Tad.' Doug visualized a blond with a weak jaw in a blue blazer, white deck shoes, and no socks. 'What does he do?'

'Do?' Whitney fluttered her lashes. 'Why I suppose you'd say Tad delegates. He's the heir to Carlyse and Fitz, they manufacture everything from aspirin to rocket fuel.'

'Yeah, I've heard of them.' More megamillions, he thought and hit the next three ruts rather violently. The kind of people who stepped on an ordinary man without ever noticing the bump. 'So why aren't you Mrs Tad Carlyse IV?'

'Probably for the same reason you didn't become a plumber. It didn't seem like a great deal of fun.' She crossed her feet at the ankles. 'You might want to back up, Douglas. I believe you missed that last pothole.'

It was full morning when they stood on the rise of a mountain overlooking Diégo-Suarez. From that distance, the water in the bay was achingly blue. But the pirates who'd once roamed there wouldn't have recognized it. The ships that dotted the water were gray and sturdy. There were no sleek sails billowing, no wooden hulls rolling.

The bay that had once been a pirate's dream and an immigrant's hope was now a major French naval base. The town that had once been the pride of buccaneers was a tidy modern city of some fifty thousand Malagasy, French, Indian, Oriental, British, and American. Where there had once been thatched huts stood steel and concrete buildings.

'Well, here we are.' Whitney linked her arm with his. 'Why don't we go down, book into a hotel, and have a hot bath?'

'We're here,' he murmured. He thought he could feel the papers growing warm in his pocket. 'First we find it.'

'Doug.' Whitney turned so that she faced him, her hands on his shoulders. 'I understand this is important to you. I want to find it, too. But look at us.' She glanced down at herself. 'We're filthy. We're exhausted. Even if it didn't matter to us, people are bound to notice.'

'We aren't going to socialize.' He looked over her head to the town below. To the end of the rainbow. 'We'll start with the churches.'

He went back to the jeep. Resigned, Whitney followed.

Fifty miles behind, jolting along the northern road in a '68 Renault with a bad exhaust, were Remo and Barns. Because he needed to think, Remo let Barns drive. The little molelike man gripped the wheel with both hands and grinned straight ahead. He liked to drive, almost as much as he liked to run over whatever furry little thing might dash out on the road.

'When we catch 'em, I get the woman, right?'

Remo shot Barns a look of mild disgust. He considered himself a fastidious man. He considered Barns a slug. 'You better remember Dimitri wants her. If you mess her up, you might just piss him off.'

'I won't mess her up.' His eyes gleamed a moment as he remembered the photo. She was so pretty. He liked pretty things. Soft, pretty things. Then he thought of Dimitri.

Unlike the others, he didn't fear Dimitri. He adored him. The adoration was simple, basic, in much the same way a small ugly dog might adore his master, even after a few good kickings. What few brains Barns had been blessed with had been rattled well over the years. If Dimitri wanted the woman, he'd bring the woman to him. He gave Remo an amiable smile because in his own fashion Barns liked Remo.

'Dimitri wants Lord's ears,' he said with a giggle. 'Want me to cut 'em off for you, Remo?'

'Just drive.'

Dimitri wanted Lord's ears, but Remo was well aware he might settle for a substitute. If he'd had any hope that he would've gotten away with it, he'd have headed the car in the opposite direction. Dimitri would find him because Dimitri believed an employee remained an employee until death. Premature or otherwise. Remo could only pray he still had his own ears after he reported to Dimitri at his temporary headquarters in Diégo-Suarez.

Five churches in two hours, she thought, and they'd found nothing. Their luck had to come in soon, or run out. 'What now?' she demanded as they pulled up in front of yet another church. This one was smaller than the others they'd been to. And the roof needed repair.

'We pay our respects.'

The town was built on a promontory, jutting out over the water. Though it was still morning, the air was hot and sticky. Overhead, palm fronds barely moved in the slight breeze. With a little imagination, Doug could picture the town as it had once been, rowdy, simple, protected by mountains on one side and the man-made wall on the other. As he strode away from the jeep, Whitney caught up with him.

'Care to guess how many churches, how many cemeteries there are around here? Better yet, how many there were that've been built over?'

'You don't build over cemeteries. Makes people nervous.' He liked the layout here. The front door was hanging crooked on its hinges, making him think no one used the church with any regularity. Around the side, a bit overgrown and canopied by palms, were groups of headstones. He had to crouch down to read the inscriptions.

'Doug, don't you feel a bit ghoulish.' Skin chilled, Whitney rubbed her arms and looked over her shoulder.

'No.' The answer was simple as he peered closely at headstone after headstone. 'Dead's dead, Whitney.'

'Don't you have any thoughts on what happens after?'

He shot her a look. 'Whatever I think, what's buried six feet down doesn't have any feelings at all. Come on, give me a hand.'

It was pride that had her crouching down with him and tugging vines from headstones. 'The dates are good. See—1790, 1793.'

'And the names are French.' The tingle at the back of his neck told him he was closing in. 'If we could just—'

'*Bonjour.*'

Whitney sprang to her feet, poised to run before she saw the old priest step through the trees. She fought to keep guilt off her face as she smiled and answered him in French. 'Good morning, Father.' His black cassock was a stark contrast to his pale hair, pale eyes, pale face. His hands, when he folded them, were spotted with age. 'I hope we're not trespassing.'

'Everyone is welcome to God's house.' He took in their bedraggled appearance. 'You're traveling?'

'Yes, Father.' Doug stood up beside her but said nothing. Whitney knew it was up to her to spin the tale, but she found she couldn't tell a direct lie to a man in a white collar. 'We've come a long way, looking for the graves of family who immigrated here during the French Revolution.'

'Many did. Are they your ancestors?'

She looked into the priest's calm, pale eyes. She thought of the Merina who worshipped the dead. 'No. But it's important we find them.'

'To find what is gone?' His muscles, weary with age, trembled with the simple movement of linking his hands. 'Many look, few find. You've come a long way?'

His mind, she thought as she struggled with impatience, was as old as his body. 'Yes, father, a long way. We think the family we're looking for may be buried here.'

He thought, then accepted. 'Perhaps I can help you. You have the names?'

'The Lebrun family. Gerald Lebrun.'

'Lebrun.' The priest's withered face closed in as he thought. 'There are no Lebrun in my parish.'

'What's he talking about?' Doug muttered in her ear but Whitney merely shook her head.

'They immigrated here from France two hundred years ago. They died here.'

'We must all face death in order to have everlasting life.'

Whitney gritted her teeth and tried again. 'Yes, Father, but we have an interest in the Lebruns. An historical interest,' she decided, thinking it wasn't actually a lie.

'You've come a long way. You need refreshment. Madame Dubrock will fix tea.' He put his hand on Whitney's arm as if to lead her down the path. She started to refuse, then felt his arm tremble.

'That would be lovely, Father.' She braced herself against his weight.

'What's going on?'

'We're having tea,' Whitney told Doug and smiled at the priest. 'Try to remember where you are.'

'Jesus.'

'Exactly.' She helped the aging priest up the narrow path to the tiny rectory. Before she could reach for the door it was opened by a woman in a cotton housedress whose face sagged with wrinkles. The smell of age was like old paper, thin and dusty.

'Father.' Madame Dubrock took his other arm and helped him inside. 'Did you have a pleasant walk?'

'I brought travelers. They must have tea.'

'Of course, of course.' The old woman led the priest down a dim little hall and into a cramped parlor. A black-bound Bible with yellowed pages was opened to the Book of David. Candles burned low were set on each table and on an old upright piano that looked as though it had been dropped more than once. There was a statue of the Virgin, chipped and faded and somehow lovely in its place by the window. Madame Dubrock murmured and fussed with the priest as she settled him in a chair.

Doug looked at the crucifix on the wall, pitted with

age, stained with the blood of redemption. He dragged a hand through his hair. He always felt a bit uneasy in church, and this was worse. 'Whitney, we haven't got time for this.'

'Ssh! Madame Dubrock,' she began.

'Please sit, I will bring tea.'

Compassion and impatience warred as Whitney looked back at the priest. 'Father—'

'You're young.' He sighed and worried his rosary. 'I have said Mass in the Church of our Lord for more years than you have lived. But so few come.'

Again, Whitney was drawn to the pale eyes, the pale voice. 'Numbers don't matter, do they, Father?' She sat in the chair beside him. 'One is enough.'

He smiled, closed his eyes and dozed.

'Poor old man,' she murmured.

'And I'd like to live just as long,' Doug put in. 'Sugar, while we're waiting to have tea, Remo's making his merry way into town. He's probably a little annoyed that we stole his jeep.'

'What was I supposed to do? Tell him to back off, we have a hired gun at our backs?' He saw the look in her eyes when she flared at him, the look that meant her heart was attached.

'Okay, okay.' Twinges of pity had been working on him as well and he didn't care for it. 'We did our good deed and now he's having a nap. Let's do what we came for.'

She crossed her arms over her chest and felt like a ghoul. 'Listen, maybe there are records, ledgers we could look through rather than. . .' She broke off and glanced toward the cemetery. 'You know.'

He rubbed his knuckles over her cheek. 'Why don't you stay here and I'll have a look?'

Wanting to agree made her feel like a coward. 'No,

we're in this together. If Magdaline or Gerald Lebrun are out there, we'll find them together.'

'There was a Magdaline Lebrun who died in childbirth, and her daughter, Danielle, who succumbed to fever.' Madame Dubrock shuffled back into the room with a tray of tea and hard biscuits.

'Yes.' Whitney turned to Doug and took his hand. 'Yes.'

The old woman smiled as she saw Doug watch her suspiciously. 'I have many hours in the evening to myself. It's my hobby to read and study church records. The church itself is three centuries old. It's withstood war and hurricane.'

'You remember reading of the Lebruns?'

'I'm old.' When Doug took the tray from her she gave a little sigh of relief. 'But my memory is good.' She cast a look at the slumbering priest. 'That too will go.' But she said it with a kind of pride. Or perhaps, Whitney thought, a kind of faith. 'Many came here to escape the Revolution, many died. I remember reading of the Lebruns.'

'Thank you, Madame.' Whitney dug in her wallet and pulled out half of the bills she had left. 'For your church.' She looked over at the priest and added more bills. 'For his church, in the name of the Lebrun family.'

Madame Dubrock took the money with a quiet dignity. 'If God wills it, you'll find what you seek. If you need refreshment, come back to the rectory. You'll be welcomed.'

'Thank you, Madame.' On impulse Whitney stepped forward. 'There are men looking for us.'

She looked Whitney straight in the eye, patient. 'Yes, my child?'

'They're dangerous.'

The priest shifted in his chair and looked at Doug. So was this man dangerous, he thought, but he felt at peace. The priest nodded to Whitney. 'God protects.' He closed his eyes again and slept.

'They never asked any questions,' Whitney murmured as they walked back outside.

Doug looked over his shoulder. 'Some people have all the answers they need.' He wasn't one of them. 'Let's find what we came for.'

Because of the undergrowth, the vines, and the age of the headstones, it took them an hour to work their way through half the cemetery. The sun rose high so that shadows were thin and short. Even with the distance, Whitney could smell the sea. Tired and discouraged, she sat on the ground and watched Doug work.

'We should come back tomorrow and do the rest. I can barely focus on the names at this point.'

'Today.' He spoke half to himself as he bent over another grave. 'It has to be today, I can feel it.'

'All I can feel is a pain in the lower back.'

'We're close. I know it. Your palms get damp. And there's this feeling in your gut that everything's just about to slide into place. It's like cracking a safe. You don't even have to hear the last click to know it. You just know it. The sonofabitch is here.' He shoved his hands in his pockts and stretched his back. 'I'll find it if it takes the next ten years.'

Whitney looked over at him and, with a sigh, shifted to stand. She propped one hand on a headstone for balance as her foot caught on a vine. Swearing, she bent over to free herself. Feeling her heart jolt, she looked down again and read the name on the stone. She heard the last tumbler click. 'It's not going to take that long.'

'What?'

'It's not going to take that long.' She grinned and the sheer brilliance of it made him straighten. 'We found Danielle.' She blinked back tears as she cleared the stone. 'Danielle Lebrun,' she read. '1779–1795. Poor child, so far from home.'

'Her mother's here.' Doug's voice was soft, without the excited lilt. He slipped his hand into Whitney's. 'She died young.'

'She'd have worn her hair powdered, with feathers in it. And her dresses would have come low on the shoulders and swept the floor.' Whitney rested her head against his arm. 'Then she learned to plant a garden and keep her husband's secret.'

'But where is he?' Doug crouched down again. 'Why isn't he buried beside her?'

'He should—' A thought occurred to her then and she spun away, biting off an oath. 'He killed himself. He wouldn't have been buried here, this is consecrated ground. Doug, he's not in the cemetery.'

He stared at her. 'What?'

'Suicide.' She dragged a hand through her hair. 'He died in sin so he couldn't be buried in the church grounds.' She glanced around, hopelessly. 'I don't even know where to look.'

'They had to bury him somewhere.' He began to pace between the gravestones. 'What did they usually do with the ones they wouldn't let in?'

She frowned a bit and tried to think. 'It would depend. I suppose. If the priest was compassionate, I'd think he'd be buried close by.'

Doug looked down. 'They're here,' he muttered. 'And my palms are still sweating' Taking her hand, he walked over to the low fence that bordered the cemetery. 'We start there.'

Another hour passed while they walked and searched through the brush. The first snake Whitney saw nearly sent her back to the jeep, but Doug handed her a stick and no sympathy. Straightening her spine, she stuck with it. When Doug tripped, stumbled and cursed, she paid no attention to him.

'Holy shit!'

Whitney lifted her stick, ready to strike. 'Snake!'

'Forget the snakes.' He grabbed her hand and pulled her down on the ground with him. 'I found it.'

The marker was small and plain, nearly buried itself. It read simply GERALD LEBRUN. Whitney laid a hand on it, wondering if there'd been anyone to mourn for him.

'And bingo.' Doug tore a vine as thick as his thumb, riddled with trumpet-shaped flowers, from another stone. It read only MARIE.

'Marie,' she murmured. 'It could be another suicide.'

'No.' He took Whitney's shoulders so that they faced each other across the stones. 'He'd guarded the treasure just as he'd promised. He died still guarding it. He must have buried it here before he wrote that last letter. He might have written down a request to be buried in this spot. They couldn't bury him in there with his family, but there wasn't any reason not to give him a last wish.'

'All right, it makes sense.' But her mouth was dry. 'What now?'

'Now, I'm going to go steal a shovel.'

'Doug—'

'No time for sensibilities now.'

She swallowed again. 'Okay, but make it fast.'

'You could hold your breath.' He gave her a quick kiss before he was up and gone.

Whitney sat between the two stones, her knees

drawn up and her heart thudding. Were they really so close, so close to the finish at last? She looked down at the flat, neglected plot of ground beneath her hand. Had Gerald, queen's confident, kept the treasure at his side for two centuries?

And if they found it? Whitney plucked the grass with her fingers. For now she'd only remember that if they found it, Dimitri hadn't. She'd be satisfied with that for the moment.

Doug came back without rustling the grass. Whitney heard him only when he murmured her name. She swore and scrambled forward on her knees. 'Do you have to do that?'

'I'd rather not advertise our little afternoon job.' He held a dented, short-handled shovel in his hand. 'Best I could do on short notice.'

For a moment, he just stared down at the dirt under his feet. He wanted to savor the sensation of standing over the gateway to easy street.

Whitney saw his thoughts in his eyes. Again she felt twin sensations of acceptance and disappointment. Then she put her hand over his on the shovel and gave him a long kiss. 'Good luck.'

He began to dig. For minute after minute, there was no sound but the steady rhythm of metal cutting earth. No breeze blew in from the sea, so that sweat drained off his face like rain. The heat and quiet pressed down on them both. As the hole grew deeper, each remembered the stages of the journey that had brought them this close.

A mad chase through the streets of Manhattan, a frantic leg race in DC. A leap from a moving train and an endless hike over barren, rolling hills. The Merina village. Cyndi Lauper along the Canal des Pangalanes.

Passion and caviar in a stolen jeep. Death and love, both unexpected.

Doug felt the tip of the shovel hit something solid. The muffled sound echoed through the brush as his eyes met Whitney's. On their hands and knees, they began to push the dirt aside with their fingers. Not daring to breathe, they lifted it out.

'Oh God,' she said in a whisper. 'It's real.'

It was no more than a foot long, and not quite as wide. The case itself was moldy with dirt and damp. It was as Danielle had describd, very plain. Even so, Whitney knew that the small chest would be worth a small fortune to a collector or a museum. The centuries made gold out of brass.

'Don't break the lock,' Whitney told him when Doug started to pry it.

Though impatient, he took the extra minute to open it as smoothly as if he'd held the key. When he drew back the lid, neither of them could do anything but stare.

She couldn't have said what she'd been expecting. Half of the time, she'd looked on the entire venture as a whim. Even when she'd caught Doug's enthusiasm, pieces of his dream, she'd never believed they'd find anything like this.

She saw the flash of diamonds, the glint of gold. Breathless, she dipped her hand into them.

The diamond necklace that dripped from her hand was as bright and cold and exquisite as moonlight in winter.

Could it have been the one? Whitney wondered. Was there any chance at all that what she held in her hand had been the necklace used in treachery against Marie Antoinette in the last days before the Revolution? Had she worn it, even once, in defiance, watching how the stones turned ice and fire against her skin? Had greed and power taken over the young woman who loved pretty things, or had she simply been oblivious to the suffering going on outside her palace walls?

Those were questions for historians, Whitney thought, though she could be certain that Marie had inspired loyalty. Gerald had indeed guarded the jewels for his queen and his country.

Doug held the emeralds in his hands, five tiers of them in a necklace so heavy it might have strained the neck. He'd seen it in the book. The name—a woman's. Maria, Louise, he wasn't sure. But as Whitney had once thought, jewels meant more in three dimensions. What glinted in his hand hadn't seen light for two centuries.

There was more. Enough for greed, for passion and lust. The little chest all but spilled over with gems. And history. Gingerly, Whitney reached down and picked up the small miniature.

She'd seen portraits of the queen consort many times. But she'd never held a masterpiece of art in her hand before. Maria Antoinette, frivolous, imprudent, and extravagant smiled back at her as though she were still in full reign. The miniature was no more than six inches, oval-shaped, and framed in gold. She couldn't see the artist's name, and the portrait was badly in need of treatment, but she knew its value. And the moral.

'Doug—'

'Holy Christ.' No matter how high he'd allowed his dreams to swing, he'd never believed there'd be such sweetness at the end. He had fortune at his fingertips, the ultimate success. He held a perfect teardrop diamond in one hand and a bracelet winking with rubies in the other. He'd just won the game. Hardly realizing he did so, he slipped the diamond into his pocket.

'Look at it. Whitney, we've got the whole world right here. The whole goddamn world. God bless the queen.' Laughing, he dropped a string of diamonds and emeralds over her head.

'Doug, look at this.'

'Yeah, what?' He was more interested in the glitters tumbling out of the box than a small dulled painting. 'Frame's worth a few bucks,' he said idly as he dug out a heavy, ornate necklace fashioned with sapphires as big as quarters.

'It's a portrait of Marie.'

'It's valuable.'

'It's priceless.'

'Oh yeah?' Interested, he gave the portrait his attention.

'Doug, this miniature's two hundred years old. No one alive's seen it before. No one even knows it exists.'

'So, it'll bring a good price.'

'Don't you understand?' Impatient, she took it back from him. 'It belongs in a museum. This isn't something you take to a fence. It's art. Doug—' She held up the diamond necklace. 'Look at this. It's not just a bunch of pretty stones that have a high market value. Look at the craftsmanship, the style. It's art, it's history. If it's the necklace of the Diamond Affair, it could throw a whole new light on accepted theories.'

'It's my way out,' he corrected and set the necklace back in the case.

'Doug, these jewels belonged to a woman who lived two centuries ago. Two hundred years. You can't take her necklace, her bracelet to a pawnshop and have them cut up. It's immoral.'

'Let's talk about morals later.'

'Doug—'

Annoyed, he closed the lid on the box and stood. 'Look, you want to give the painting to a museum, maybe a couple of the glitters, okay. We'll talk about it. I risked my life for this box, and dammit, yours, too. I'm not giving up the one chance I have to pull myself out and be somebody so people can gawk at stones in a museum.'

She gave him a look he didn't understand as she rose to stand in front of him. 'You are somebody,' she said softly.

It moved something in him, but he shook his head. 'Not good enough, sugar. People like me need what we weren't born with. I'm tired of playing the game. This takes me over the finish line.'

'Doug—'

'Look, whatever happens to the stuff, first we've got to get it out of here.'

She started to argue further, then subsided. 'All right, but we will discuss this.'

'All you want.' He gave her the charming smile she'd learned never to trust. 'What do you say we take the baby home?'

With a shake of her head, Whitney returned the smile. 'We've come this far. Maybe we'll get away with it.'

They stood, but when he turned to push through the brush, she held back. Pulling blooms from vines, she laid them on Gerald's grave. 'You did all you could.' Turning, she followed Doug to the jeep. With another quick glance around, Doug settled the chest in the back and tossed a blanket over it.

'Okay, now we find a hotel.'

'That's the best news I've had all day.'

When he found one that looked stylish and expensive

enough for his taste, Doug pulled up at the curb.
'Look, you go check in. I'm going to go see about
getting us out of the country on the first plane in the
morning.'

'What about our baggage in Antananarivo?'

'We'll send for it. Where do you want to go?'

'Paris,' she said instantly. 'I have a feeling I won't be
bored this time.'

'You got it. Now how about parting with a little of
that cash so I can take care of things.'

'Of course.' As if she'd never denied him a cent,
Whitney took out her wallet. 'You'd better take some
plastic instead,' she decided and pulled out a credit
card. 'First class, Douglas, if you please.'

'Nothing else. Get the best room in the house, sugar.
Tonight we start living in style.'

She smiled, but leaned over the back seat and
retrieved the blanket-covered chest along with her
pack. 'I'll just take this along with me.'

'Don't you trust me?'

'I wouldn't say that. Exactly.' Hopping out, she blew
him a kiss. In dirt-smeared slacks and a torn blouse,
she walked into the hotel like a reigning princess.

Doug watched three men scramble to open the door
for her. Class, he thought again. She reeked with it.
He remembered she'd once asked him for a blue silk
dress. With a grin, he pulled away from the curb. He
was going to bring her back a few surprises.

She approved of the room and told the bellboy so with
a generous tip. Alone, she uncovered the chest and
opened it again.

She'd never considered herself a conservationist, an
art buff, or a prude. Looking down at the gems, jewels,
and coins of another age, she knew she'd never be able

to turn them into something so ordinary as cash. People had died for what she held in her hand. Some had died for greed, some for principle, some for nothing more than timing. If they were only jewels, the deaths would mean nothing. She thought of Juan, and of Jacques. No, they were more, much more than jewels.

What was here, at her fingertips, wasn't hers or Doug's. The trick would be in convincing him of it.

Letting the lid close, she walked into the bath and turned the water on full. It brought back the memory of the little inn on the coast and Jacques.

He was dead, but perhaps when the miniature and the treasure were in their rightful place, he'd be remembered. A small plaque with his name on it in a museum in New York. Yes. It made her smile. Jacques would appreciate that.

She let the water run as she walked to the window to look at the view. She liked seeing the bay spreading out and the busy little town below her. She'd like to walk along the boulevard and absorb the texture of the seaport. Ships, men of ships. There would be shops crowded with goods, the sort a woman in her profession searched for. A pity she couldn't go back to New York with a few crates of Malagasy wares.

As her mind wandered, a figure on the sidewalk caught her eye and made her strain forward. A white panama hat. But that was ridiculous, she told herself. Lots of men wore panamas in the tropics. It couldn't be. . . Yet as she looked, she was almost certain it was the man she'd seen before. She waited, breathlessly, for the man to turn so that she could be sure. When the hat disappeared into a doorway, she let out a frustrated breath. She was just jumpy. How could anyone have followed the zigzagging trail they'd taken to Diégo-Suarez? Doug better get back soon, she

thought. She wanted to bathe, change, eat, and hop a
plane.

Paris, she thought and closed her eyes. A week of
doing nothing but relaxing. Making love and drinking
champagne. After what they'd been through, it was no
less than what they both deserved. After Paris. . . She
sighed and walked back to the bath. That was another
question.

She turned off the taps, straightened, and reached
down to unbutton her blouse. As she did, her eyes met
Remo's in the mirror over the sink.

'Ms MacAllister.' He smiled, lightly touching the
scar on his cheek. 'It's a pleasure.'

# CHAPTER FOURTEEN

She thought about screaming. Fear bubbled in the back of her throat, hot and bitter. It closed in the pit of her stomach, hard and cold. But there was a look in Remo's eyes, a calm, waiting look, that warned her he'd be only too happy to silence her. She didn't scream.

In the next instant, she thought about running—making a wild, heroic dash past him and out the door. There was always a possibility she'd make it. And a possibility she wouldn't.

She backed up, her hand still poised at the top button of her blouse. In the small bathroom, her fast, uneven breathing echoed back over her. The sound of it made Remo smile. Seeing this, Whitney struggled for control. She'd come so far, worked so hard, and now she was cornered. Her fingers closed over the porcelain of the sink. She wouldn't whine. That she promised herself. And she wouldn't beg.

At the movement behind Remo, Whitney shifted her gaze and looked into Barn's idiotic, amiable eyes. She learned fear could be primitive, mindless, like the terror a mouse feels when a cat begins to playfully bat it with its paws. Instinct told her there was a great deal more danger in him than in the tall, dark man who leveled a pistol at her. There was a time for heroics, a time for fear, and a time for rolling the dice. She forced her fingers to relax, and prayed.

'Remo, I presume. You work fast.' And so did her mind, beginning to rapidly tick off angles and escape routes. Doug had been gone no more than twenty minutes. She was on her own.

He'd hoped she'd scream or try to run so that he could have a reason to put a few bruises on her. His vanity still smarted from the scar on his cheek. Vanity aside, Remo feared Dimitri too much to put a mark on her without provocation. He knew Dimitri liked women brought to him unmarred, whatever condition they were in when he was done with them. Intimidation, however, was different. He put the barrel of the gun under her chin so that it pressed into the soft, vulnerable point of her throat. At her quiver, his smile spread.

'Lord,' he said briefly. 'Where is he?'

She shrugged because she'd never been so frightened in her life. When she spoke her voice was deliberately even, deliberately cool. Every drop of moisture in her mouth had dried up. 'I killed him.'

The lie came so easily, so swiftly, it nearly surprised her. Because it had, and easy lies carried the ring of truth, Whitney went with it. Lifting a finger, she nudged the barrel away from her throat.

Remo stared at her. His intellect rarely dipped below the surface to subtleties, so that he saw the insolence in her eyes without seeing the fear beneath. Grabbing her arm, he dragged her into the bedroom and shoved her roughly into a chair. 'Where's Lord?'

Whitney straightened in the chair, then brushed at the already tattered sleeve of her blouse. She couldn't let him notice her fingers were shaking. It was going to take every ounce of guile at her disposal to pull it off. 'Really Remo, I expected a bit more style from you than from a second-rate thief.'

With a jerk of his head Remo signaled to Barns. Grinning still, he approached her with a small, ugly revolver. 'Pretty,' he said and nearly drooled. 'Soft and pretty.'

'He likes to shoot people in places like kneecaps,' Remo told her. 'Now where's Lord?'

Whitney forced herself to ignore the gun Barns aimed at her left knee. If she looked at it, if she even thought about it, she'd have collapsed in a puddle of pleading. 'I killed him,' she repeated. 'Do you have a cigarette? I haven't had one for days.'

Her tone was so casually regal, Remo was reaching for them before he realized it. Frustrated, he aimed the gun at a point just between her eyes. Whitney felt the light, rapid pounding begin there and spread. 'I'm only going to ask nice once more. Where's Lord?'

She gave a sigh that was short and annoyed. 'I've just told you. He's dead.' She knew Barns was staring at her still, lightly humming. Her stomach rolled once before she glanced critically at her nails. 'I don't suppose you know where I can get a good manicure in this dump?'

'How'd you kill him?'

Her heartbeat accelerated. If he asked how, he was close to believing her. 'I shot him, of course,' she smiled, a bit vaguely and crossed her legs. She saw Remo jerk his head so that Barns lowered his gun. She didn't allow herself a sigh of relief. 'It seemed the most foolproof way.'

'Why?'

'Why?' She blinked. 'Why what?'

'Why'd you kill him?'

'I didn't need him anymore,' she said simply.

Barns stepped forward and ran one pudgy hand down her hair. He made a sound in his throat that might've been approval. She made the mistake of turning her head so that their eyes met. What she saw in his made her blood ice over. Keeping still, Whitney fought not to show the fear, only the revulsion. 'Is this your pet rodent, Remo?' she said mildly. 'I certainly hope you know how to control him?'

'Back off, Barns.'

He stroked her hair down to her shoulder. 'I just wanna touch.'

'Back off!'

She saw the look in Barns's eyes when he turned to Remo. The amiability was gone. The idiocy in them now was dark and vile. She swallowed, unsure whether he'd obey or simply shoot Remo where he stood. If she had to deal with one of them, she didn't want it to be Barns.

'Gentlemen,' she said in a calm, clear voice that had them both looking back at her. 'If we're going to be at this for very long, I'd appreciate that cigarette. It's been a very tiring morning.'

With his left hand, Remo reached in his pocket and offered her a cigarette. Whitney took it, then, holding it between her two fingers, looked at him expectantly. He'd have shot her through the brain without a moment's hesitation. Then again, Remo appreciated old-fashioned manners. Taking out his lighter, he flicked it on for her.

With her gaze resting on his, Whitney smiled and blew out a stream of smoke. 'Thank you.'

'Sure. Just how do you expect me to believe you wasted Lord? He's not a fool.'

Whitney sat back, bringing the cigarette to her lips again. 'There we have a difference of opinion, Remo. Lord was a first-class fool. It's pitifully easy to take advantage of a man whose brains, shall we say, hang below the waist.' A bead of sweat ran down her shoulder blades. It took all her effort not to fidget in the chair.

Remo studied her. Her face was calm, her hands steady. Either she had more guts than he'd expected, or she was telling the truth. Normally, he'd have appreciated someone tidying up for him, but he'd wanted to kill Doug himself. 'Look, babe, you've been with Lord willing. You helped him all along.'

'Naturally. He had something I wanted.' She puffed delicately, grateful that she didn't choke. 'I helped him get out of the country, even backed him financially.' She gave the cigarette a gentle tap in the ashtray beside her. Stalling wasn't possible, she realized. If Doug came back while they were still there, it would be all over. For both of them. 'I have to admit, it was a bit of a kick for awhile, even though Douglas lacked style. He's the kind of man a woman tires of easily, if you know what I mean.' She smiled, looking Remo up and down through a mist of smoke. 'In any case, I saw no reason why I should be stuck with him, or why I should share the treasure with him.'

'So you killed him.'

She noticed he didn't say it with any shade of disgust or revulsion. It was speculation she heard. 'Of course. He became foolishly cocky after we'd stolen your jeep. It was a simple matter to persuade him to stop—pull off the road a bit.' She fiddled idly with her top button and watched Remo's eyes lower to it. 'I had the papers and the jeep. I certainly didn't need him any more. I shot him, dumped him out in the bush, and drove into town.'

'Pretty careless of him to let you get the drop on him.'

'He was. . .' She trailed her fingertip down. 'Occupied.' He wasn't buying, she thought and jerked her shoulders. 'You can waste your time looking for him if you like. However, you're probably aware that I checked in alone. And, since you apparently knew Douglas, you might consider the fact that I have the treasure. Do you really think he'd have trusted me with that?'

She pointed one elegant finger toward the dresser.

Remo moved over and tossed back the lid. What he saw made his mouth water.

'Impressive, isn't it?' Whitney lightly tapped out her cigarette. 'Much too impressive to share with someone of Lord's caliber. However. . .' She trailed off until Remo's gaze came back to her. 'A man of certain class and breeding would be quite different.'

It was tempting. Her eyes were dark and promising. He could almost feel the heat rise from the small treasure chest beneath his fingers. But he remembered Dimitri. 'You're going to change your accommodations.'

'All right.' As if it didn't concern her in the least, Whitney rose. She had to get them out, and out quickly. Going with them was preferable to being shot in the kneecap, or anywhere else.

Remo picked up the treasure chest. Dimitri was going to be pleased, he thought. Very, very pleased. He gave Whitney a thin smile. 'Barns is going to walk you out to the car. I wouldn't try anything—unless you'd like to have all the bones in your right hand broken.'

A look at Barns's grinning face brought on a shudder. 'There's no need to be crude, Remo.'

It didn't take Doug long to arrange for the two one-way tickets to Paris, but the shopping expedition ate up more time. It gave him a great deal of pleasure to buy Whitney the filmy underwear—even if it was her credit-card number that was stamped on the receipt. He spent nearly an hour, much to the saleswoman's delight, choosing a royal blue silk dress with a draping bodice and a sleek, narrow skirt.

Pleased, he treated himself to a casually elegant suit. It was precisely how he intended to live, at least for a time. Casually and elegantly.

By the time he got back to the hotel, he was loaded with boxes and whistling. They were on their way. By the next evening, they'd be drinking champagne in Maxim's and making love in a room overlooking the Seine. No more six-packs and roadside motels for Doug Lord. First class, Whitney had said. He was going to learn to live with it.

It surprised him to find the door not quite latched. Didn't Whitney realize by now he wouldn't need a key for something as basic as a hotel lock?

'Hey, lover, ready to celebrate?' Dumping the boxes on the bed, he hefted the bottle of wine he'd spent the equivalent of seventy-five dollars on. As he walked across to the bath, he began loosening the cork in the bottle. 'Water still hot?'

It was cold, and it was empty. For a moment, Doug stood in the center of the room staring at the still, clear water. Giving into pressure, the cork blew out with a celebratory pop. He barely noticed the overflow of champagne dampening his fingers. His heart in his throat, he dashed back into the bedroom.

Her pack was there where she'd tossed it on the floor. But there was no small wooden box. With speed and precision he searched the room. The box and everything in it was gone. So was Whitney.

His first reaction was of fury. To be double-crossed by a woman with whiskey eyes and a cool smile was worse, a hundred times worse, than being double-crossed by a bow-legged midget. At least the midget had been in the business. Swearing, he slammed the bottle down on the table.

Women! They were and had been his biggest problem since puberty. When would he learn? They smiled, crooned, batted their lashes, and rolled you for every last dollar.

How could he have been such a jerk? He'd actually believed she had feelings for him. The way she'd looked when they'd made love, the way she'd stood by him, fought by him. He'd actually let himself fall for her, like a stone in a cool, deep lake. He'd even made some half-baked plans about the future, and she'd just walked out on him the first chance she got.

He looked down at her pack on the floor. She'd carried it on her back, hiking miles, laughing, bitching, teasing him. And then. . . Without thinking, Doug reached down and picked it up. Inside were pieces of her—the lacy underwear, a compact, a brush. He could smell her.

No. The denial rammed into him, sharp and abrupt. With it, he tossed the pack against the wall. She wouldn't have run out on him. Even if he were wrong about her feelings, she just had too much class to renege on a bargain.

So if she hadn't run, she'd been taken.

He stood there, holding her brush in his hand, as the fear poured into him. Taken. He realized he'd rather have believed the double-cross. He'd rather have believed she was already on a plane, heading to Tahiti, laughing at him.

Dimitri. The brush broke cleanly in two at the pressure of his hands. Dimitri had his woman. Doug threw the two pieces across the room. He wasn't going to have her for long.

He left the room quickly, and he was no longer whistling.

The house was magnificent. But then Whitney supposed she should have expected no less from a man of Dimitri's reputation. On the outside, it was elegant, almost feminine, white and clean with wrought-iron balconies that would provide a lovely view of the bay. The grounds were spacious and well kept, rich with the ornate tropical flowers of the region and shaded with palms. She studied it with a sick, creeping dread.

Remo stopped the car at the end of the crushed white gravel drive. Her courage had begun to fail her, but Whitney fought to find it again. A man who could acquire a place like this had brains. Brains could be dealt with.

It was Barns, with his black, greedy eyes and eager grin who worried her.

'Well, I must say this is preferable to the hotel.' With the air of someone preparing to go to a dinner party, Whitney alighted from the car. She plucked a hibiscus and strolled to the front door twirling it under her nose.

At Remo's knock, the door was opened by another dark-suited man. Dimitri insisted on a neat, business-like appearance in his employees. Every one would wear a tie with their blunt-nose ·45. When the man smiled, he showed a badly chipped front tooth. Whitney had no idea he'd acquired it when he'd smashed through the window of Godiva Chocolatiers.

'So you got her.' Unlike Remo, he looked at the chipped tooth as an occupational hazard. He had to admire a woman who could drive with such nerveless lunacy. But he didn't feel the same tolerance toward Doug. 'Where's Lord?'

Remo didn't even glance at him. He only answered to one man. 'Keep an eye on her,' he ordered and went to report directly to Dimitri. Because he carried the treasure, he walked quickly, with the air of a man in charge. The last time he'd reported in, he'd nearly crawled.

'So what's the story, Barns?' The dark-suited man cast a long look at Whitney. Nice-looking lady. He figured Dimitri had some interesting plans for her. 'You forget Lord's ears for the boss?'

Barns's giggle brought a chill to Whitney's skin. 'She killed him,' he said cheerfully.

'Oh yeah?'

She caught the interested look, then brushed back her hair. 'That's right. Any way to get a drink in this place?'

Without waiting for an answer she walked down the wide white hall and into the first room.

It was obviously a formal parlor. Whoever had decorated it leaned toward the ornate. Whitney would have chosen something a great deal breezier.

The windows, twice as tall as she, were festooned in scarlet brocade. As she strolled across the room, she wondered if it would be possible for her to open them and escape. Doug would be back at the hotel by now, she calculated as she ran her fingertip along an intricately carved drum table. But she couldn't count on him to come charging in like the Seventh Cavalry. Whatever move she made, she made on her own.

Knowing both men were watching her every step, she walked to a Waterford decanter and poured. Her fingers were numb and damp. A little shot of courage wouldn't hurt, she decided. Especially since she didn't

yet know what she was up against. As if she had all the
time in the world, she sat in a high-backed Queen
Anne chair and began to sip some very smooth
vermouth.

Her father had always said you could negotiate with
a man who stocked a good bar. Whitney drank again
and hoped he was right.

Minutes passed. She sat in the chair and drank,
trying to ignore the terror that built inside of her. After
all, she reasoned, if he was simply going to kill her,
he'd have done so by now. Wouldn't he? Wasn't it
more likely he'd hold her for ransom? It might not sit
well with her to be exchanged for a few hundred
thousand dollars, but it was a far better fate than a
bullet.

Doug had spoken of torture as though it were
Dimitri's hobby. Thumbscrews and Chaucer. She swallowed more vermouth, knowing she'd never keep her
wits if she thought too deeply about the man who now
had her life in his hands.

Doug was safe. At least for the moment. Whitney
concentrated on that.

When Remo came back she tensed all over, muscle
by muscle. With deliberate care, she lifted the glass to
her lips again.

'It's terribly rude to keep a guest waiting more than
ten minutes,' she said casually.

He touched the scar on his cheek. She didn't miss
the movement. 'Mr Dimitri would like you to join him
for lunch. He thought you'd like to bathe and change
first.'

A reprieve. 'Very considerate.' Rising, she set her
glass aside. 'However, I'm afraid you rushed me away
without my luggage. I simply haven't a thing to wear.'

'Mr Dimitri's seen to that.' Taking her arm, a little
too firmly for comfort, Remo led her into the hall and

up the sweeping stairs to the second floor. It wasn't just the hallway that smelled like a funeral parlor, she realized, but the entire house. He pushed open the door. 'You got an hour. Be ready, he doesn't like to be kept waiting.'

Whitney stepped inside and heard the lock turn behind her.

She covered her face with her hands a moment because she couldn't stop the shaking. A minute, she told herself as she began to breathe deeply. She only needed a minute. She was alive. That was the point to concentrate on. Slowly, she lowered her hands and looked around.

Dimitri wasn't stingy, she decided. The suite he'd given her was as elegant as the outside of the house had promised. The sitting room was wide and long, with porcelain vases of fresh flowers in abundance. The colors were feminine, roses and pearly grays on the silk wallpaper, picking up the tones in the Oriental rug on the floor. The daybed was a deeper, duskier hue, plumped with hand-worked pillows. All in all, she decided professionally, a neat, stylish job. Then she was at the windows, wrenching them open.

One look told her it was hopeless. The drop was nearly a hundred feet from the ornate little balcony. There'd be no nimble leaping out as there'd been in the coastal inn. Closing the windows again, Whitney began to explore the suite for other possibilities.

The bedroom was perfectly lovely, with a large, polished Chippendale bed and delicate china lamps. The rosewood armoire was already open, showing her a selection of clothes no red-blooded woman would turn her nose up at. She fingered the sheer ivory silk of a sleeve and turned away. It would appear Dimitri expected her to be in residence for some time. She could take it as a good sign, or she could worry about it.

Glancing over, Whitney caught a look at herself in a cheval mirror. She walked closer. Her face was pale, her clothes streaked and rent. Her eyes, she saw, were frightened again. Disgusted, she began to pull off her blouse.

Dimitri wasn't going to see some tattered quivering female over lunch, she determined. If she could do nothing else at the moment, she could take care of that. Whitney MacAllister knew how to dress for any occasion.

She checked every door leading to her suite and found them all firmly locked from the outside. Every window she opened led her to the realization that she was well and truly trapped. For now.

Because it was the next logical step, Whitney gave herself to the luxury of a bath in the deep marble tub scented generously with the oils Dimitri had provided. On the vanity was makeup, from foundation to mascara, all in the brand and shades she preferred.

So, he was thorough, Whitney told herself as she made use of it. The perfect host. A bottle of amethyst crystal held her scent. She brushed her freshly shampooed hair, then drew it back from her face with two mother-of-pearl combs. Another gift from her host.

Going to the closet, she gave her choice of outfit all the care and deliberation a warrior might have given to his choice of armor. In her position, she considered it every bit as important. She chose a mint green sundress with yards of skirt and no back, giving it a bit of flare with a silk scarf wound and knotted at her waist.

This time when she looked in the full-length mirror, she gave a nod of satisfaction. She was ready for anything.

When the knock sounded on the door of the sitting room, she answered it boldly. She gave Remo the cool ice-princess look Doug admired.

'Mr Dimitri's waiting.'

Without a word she swept by him. Her palms were damp, but she resisted the urge to curl her hands into fists. Instead, she ran her fingers lightly over the banister as she descended the stairs. If she was walking toward her execution, she thought, at least she was walking toward it in style. Pressing her lips together only briefly, she followed Remo through the house and out on to a wide, flower-bordered terrace.

'Ms MacAllister, at last.'

She wasn't certain what she'd expected. Certainly after all the horror stories she'd lived through and heard, she expected someone fierce and cruel and larger than life. The man who rose from the smoked-glass and wicker table was pale and small and unimpressive. He had a round, mild face and a thinning thatch of dark hair swept back from it. His skin was pale, so pale it looked as though it never saw the sun. She had a quick, giddy flash that if she poked her finger into his cheek it would collapse like soft, warm dough. His eyes were nearly colorless, a light, watery blue under dark, inoffensive brows. She couldn't decide if he were forty or sixty, or somewhere in between.

His mouth was thin, his nose small, and his round cheeks, unless she missed her guess, had been lightly tinted with blusher.

The white, rather dapper suit he wore didn't quite disguise his paunch. It might've been tempting to pass him off as a foolish little man, but she noticed the nine thinly glossed nails and the stub of his pinky.

Against the chubby, glossy appearance, the deformity clashed and rattled. He held his hand, palm out, in greeting so that she could see where the skin had grown thick and tough over the ridge. The palm was as smooth as a young girl's.

Whatever his appearance, it wouldn't do to forget that Dimitri was as dangerous and shrewd as anything that slithered out from the swamp. The breadth of his power might not have been apparent on the surface, but he dismissed the lean, rangy Remo with no more than a look.

'I'm so pleased to have you join me, my dear. There's nothing so depressing as lunching alone. I've some lovely Campari.' He lifted yet another piece of Waterford. 'Can I persuade you to try some.'

She opened her mouth to speak and nothing came out. It was the glint of pleasure in his eyes that had her stepping forward. 'I'd love it.' Whitney swept up to the table. The closer she came, the more the fear built. It was irrational, she thought. He looked like someone's pompous little uncle. But the fear built. His eyes, she realized, never seemed to blink. He just stared and stared and stared. She had to concentrate on keeping her hand steady as she reached for the glass. 'Your house, Mr Dimitri, is quite a showpiece.'

'I take that as a high compliment from someone with your professional reputation. I was fortunate to find it on short notice.' He sipped, then dabbed at his mouth delicately with white linen. 'The owners were— gracious enough to give it over to me for a few weeks. I'm rather fond of the gardens. A pleasant respite in this sticky heat.' In a courtly gesture he walked over to hold her chair. Whitney had to repress a surge of panic and revulsion. 'I'm sure you must be hungry after your journey.'

She looked over her shoulder and forced herself to

smile. 'Actually, I dined quite well last evening, again due to your hospitality.'

Mild curiosity crossed his face as he walked back to his own chair. 'Indeed?'

'In the jeep Douglas and I acquired from your— employees?' At his nod, she continued. 'There was a lovely bottle of wine and a very enjoyable meal. I'm rather fond of beluga.'

She saw the caviar, black and shiny, heaped on ice beside her. Whitney helped herself.

'I see.'

She wasn't certain if she'd annoyed or amused him. Taking a bite, she smiled. 'Again, I must say your pantry's well stocked.'

'I hope you'll continue to find my hospitality to your liking. You must try the lobster bisque, my dear. Let me serve you.' With a grace and an economy of movement she wouldn't have expected, Dimitri dipped a silver ladle into the soup tureen. 'Remo informs me you've disposed of our Mr Lord.'

'Thank you. It smells marvelous.' Whitney took her time, sipping at the soup. 'Douglas was becoming a bit of a bother.' It was a game, she told herself. And she'd just begun to play. The little shell she wore swung lightly on its chain as she reached for her glass. She was playing to win. 'I'm sure you understand.'

'Indeed.' Dimitri ate slowly and with delicacy. 'Mr Lord's been a bother to me for some time.'

'Stealing the papers from under your nose.' She saw the white, manicured fingers tighten on the soupspoon. A nerve, she thought. He wouldn't take kindly to being made a fool of. She resisted the urge to swallow and smiled instead. 'Douglas was clever, in his own fashion,' she said easily. 'A pity he was so crude.'

'I suppose one must concede his cleverness to a

point,' Dimitri agreed. 'Unless I blame my own staff for ineptitude.'

'Perhaps both are true.'

He acknowledged this with the slightest of nods. 'Then again, he had you, Whitney. I may call you Whitney?'

'Of course, I admit I did help him. I believe in watching how the cards fall.'

'Very wise.'

'There were several times when. . .' She trailed off, going back to her soup. 'I don't like speaking ill of the dead, Mr Dimitri, but Douglas was often rash and illogical. However, he was easily led.'

He watched her eat, admiring the fine-boned hands, the glow of healthy young skin against the green dress. It would be a pity to mar it. Perhaps he could find certain uses for her. He thought of her installed in his house in Connecticut, dignified and elegant over meals, submissive and obedient in bed. 'And young and roughly attractive, wouldn't you agree?'

'Oh yes.' She managed another smile. 'He was an intriguing diversion for a few weeks. On the long run, I prefer a man with style rather than physicality. Some caviar, Mr Dimitri?'

'Yes.' As he accepted the dish from her, he let his skin rub hers and felt her stiffen at the brush of his deformed hand. The small show of weakness excited him. He remembered the pleasure it brought him to watch a praying mantis capture a moth—the way the lean, intelligent insect drew the frantic prey closer, waiting patiently while the struggles slowed, weakened until at last it devoured the bright fragile wings. Sooner or later, the young, the weak, and the delicate always submitted. Like the mantis, Dimitri had patience and style and cruelty.

'I must say I find it difficult to believe a woman of your sensitivity could shoot a man. The vegetables in this salad are quite fresh, I'm sure you'll enjoy it.' As he spoke he began to toss the lettuce in a large serving bowl.

'Perfect for a sultry afternoon,' she agreed. 'Sensitivity,' Whitney continued, studying the liquid in her glass, 'becomes secondary to necessity, don't you think, Mr Dimitri? After all, I am a businesswoman. And as I said, Douglas was becoming a bit of a bother. I believe in opportunities.' She lifted her glass, smiling over the rim. 'I saw the opportunity to be rid of a nuisance and to have the papers. I merely took them. He was, after all, only a thief.'

'Precisely.' He was beginning to admire her. Though he wasn't completely convinced her cool demeanor was fact, there was no denying breeding. Born the illegitimate son of a religious fanatic and an itinerant musician, Dimitri had a deep-rooted respect and envy of breeding. Over the years, he'd had to make do with the closest thing to it. Power.

'So you took the papers and found the treasure yourself?'

'It was simple enough. The papers made it clear. Have you seen them?'

'No.' Again she saw his fingers tighten. 'Only a sample of them.'

'Oh well, they've done the job now in any case.' Whitney dipped into her salad.

'I still haven't seen all of them,' he said mildly, his eyes on hers.

She thought fleetingly that they were tucked away again in the jeep with Doug. 'I'm afraid you never will,' she told him, letting the satisfaction of the truth ease her nerves. 'I destroyed them after I'd finished, I don't care for loose ends.'

'Wise. And what did you plan to do with the treasure?'

'Do?' Whitney glanced up in surprise. 'Why enjoy it, of course.'

'Exactly,' he agreed, pleased. 'And now I have it. And you.'

She waited a beat, meeting his eyes directly. The salad nearly stuck in her throat. 'When one plays, one must accept the prospect of losing, no matter how distasteful.'

'Well said.'

'Now I'm dependent on your hospitality.'

'You see things very clearly, Whitney. That pleases me. It also pleases me to have beauty within arm's length.'

The food rolled uncomfortably in her stomach. She held out her glass, waiting until he'd filled it to within an inch of the rim. 'I hope you won't think me rude if I ask for how long you intend to extend me your hospitality?'

He topped off his own glass and toasted her. 'Not at all. For as long as it pleases me.'

Knowing if she put anything else in her stomach, it might not stay down, she ran a fingertip around the rim of her glass. 'It occurred to me that you might be considering demanding a ransom from my father.'

'Please, my dear.' He gave her a light smile, touched with disapproval. 'I don't consider such things proper luncheon conversation.'

'Just a thought.'

'I must ask you not to worry about such things. I'd much prefer you to simply relax and enjoy your stay. I trust your rooms are adequate?'

'Lovely.' She found she wanted to scream now much more than she'd wanted to when she'd turned and faced Barns. His pale eyes stayed steady and open, like a fish's. Or a dead man's. Briefly she lowered her lashes. 'I haven't thanked you for the wardrobe, which as it happens, I was in desperate need of.'

'Think nothing of it. Perhaps you'd like a stroll through the gardens.' He rose, coming over to draw back her chair. 'Afterward, I imagine you'd like a siesta. The heat here in midafternoon is oppressive.'

'You're very considerate.' She laid her hand on his arm, forcing her fingers not to curl.

'You're my guest, my dear. A very welcome one.'

'A guest.' Her smile was cool again. Her voice, though she was amazed she accomplished it, was ironic. 'Do you make it a habit to lock up your guests in their rooms, Mr Dimitri?'

'I make it a habit,' he said, lifting her fingers to his lips, 'To lock up a treasure. Shall we walk?'

Whitney tossed her hair back. She'd find the way out. Smiling at him, she promised herself she'd find the way out. If she didn't—she still felt the cold brush of his lips on her skin—she'd be dead. 'Of course.'

# CHAPTER FIFTEEN

So far so good. It wasn't a very positive statement, but it was the best Whitney could do. She'd gotten through the first day as Dimitri's 'guest' without any problems. And without any bright ideas of how to check out—in one piece.

He'd been gracious, courteous. Her slightest whim had been at her fingertips. She'd tested it by expressing a mild craving for chocolate soufflé. It had been served to her at the end of a long, extraordinary, seven-course meal.

Though she'd racked her brain during the three hours she'd been locked in her rooms that afternoon, Whitney had come up blank. There was no breaking through the doors, no jumping out the window, and the phone in her sitting room was only good for in-house calls.

She might have considered making a break for it during the afternoon stroll in the gardens. Even as she'd been working out the details, Dimitri had plucked her a blush pink rosebud and confided in her how distressing it was for him to have to arrange for armed guards around the perimeter of the grounds. Security, as he put it, was the burden of the successful.

As they'd reached the edge of the garden, he'd casually pointed out one of his staff. The wide-shouldered man had worn a trim, dark suit, sported a natty moustache, and carried a small, deadly Uzi.

Whitney had decided she'd prefer a more subtle

means of escape than a wild dash across the wide-open grounds.

She tried to think of one during her afternoon confinement. Sooner or later her father would become concerned by her prolonged absence. But it might take another month before that came to pass.

Dimitri would want to leave the island at some point. Probably soon, since he had his hands on the treasure. Whether she went with him or not—and was afforded more opportunities for escape—was dependent on his whim. Whitney didn't care for having her fate rest on the whim of a man who wore blusher and paid others to kill for him.

So she paced the suite through the afternoon, thinking up and rejecting plans as basic as tying the sheets together and climbing out the window, and as complicated as carving her way through the walls with a butter knife.

In the end, she dressed in the sheer ivory silk that clung to every subtle curve and glittered with tiny seed pearls.

For the better part of two hours, she faced Dimitri across a long, elegant mahogany table that gleamed dully under the light of two dozen candles. From the escargot to the soufflé and Dom Pérignon, the meal was exquisite in every detail. Chopin floated quietly in the background while they spoke of literature and art.

There was no denying that Dimitri was a connoisseur of such things, and that he would have fit into the most exclusive club without a ripple. Before it was over, they'd dissected a Tennessee Williams play, discussed the intricacies of the French impressionists, and debated the subtleties of the Mikado.

As the soufflé melted in her mouth, Whitney found

herself yearning for the sticky rice and fruit she'd shared with Doug one night in a cave.

While her conversation with Dimitri ran smoothly, she remembered all the arguments and sniping she'd had with Doug. The silk lay cool on her shoulders. She'd have traded the five-hundred-dollar dress in a heartbeat for the stiff cotton sack she'd worn on the road to the coast.

Under the circumstances, with her life on the line, it might have been difficult to say she was bored. She was, miserably.

'You seem a bit distant this evening, my dear.'

'Oh?' Whitney brought herself back. 'It's an excellent meal, Mr Dimitri.'

'But the entertainment is perhaps a bit lax. A young, vital woman demands something more exciting.' With a benevolent smile, he pressed a button at his side. Almost instantaneously, a white-suited Oriental entered. 'Ms MacAllister and I will have coffee in the library. It's quite extensive,' he added as the Oriental backed out of the room. 'I'm pleased you share my affection for the written word.'

She might have refused, but the idea of seeing more of the house could lead to finding some route of escape. It never hurt to have an edge, she decided. She smiled and nudged her dinner knife into the open evening bag she'd placed by her plate.

'It's always a pleasure to spend the evening with a man who appreciates the finer things.' Whitney rose, clipping the bag shut. She accepted his arm and told herself she would, without compunction, stick the knife into his heart at the first opportunity.

'When a man travels as I do,' he began, 'it's often necessary to take certain things of import along. The right wine, the proper music, a few volumes of literature.' He walked smoothly through the house, smelling lightly of cologne. The formal white dinner jacket fit without a wrinkle.

He was feeling benevolent, tolerant. Too many weeks had passed since he'd had a young, beautiful woman to dine with. He opened the tall double doors of the library and ushered her inside. 'Browse if you like, my dear,' he told her, indicating the two levels of books.

The room had terrace doors. That was something she made note of immediately. If there was any way to get out of her room during the night, this might be the method of escape. All she'd have to do then would be to get past the guards. And the guns.

One step at a time, Whitney reminded herself as she skimmed a fingertip over leather-bound volumes.

'My father has a library like this,' she commented. 'I always found it a cozy place to spend the evening.'

'Cozier with coffee and brandy.' Dimitri poured the brandy himself while the Oriental entered with the silver service. 'Do give Chan your knife, my dear. He's very particular about the washing up.' Whitney turned to see Dimitri watching her with a small smile and eyes that reminded her of a reptile—flat, cold, and dangerously patient.

Without a word she took out the knife and handed it over to the servant. All the oaths that were on her tongue, the temper tantrum she barely held back, weren't going to help her out of this one.

'Brandy?' Dimitri asked when Chan left them alone.

'Yes, thank you.' As cool as he, Whitney crossed the room and held out her hand.

'Did you think to kill me with your dinner knife, my dear?'

She shrugged then downed brandy. It rolled in her stomach, then settled. 'It was a thought.'

He laughed, a long, rumbling sound that was indescribably unpleasant. He was again thinking of the mantis, and the struggles of the moth. 'I admire you, Whitney, I really do.' He touched his glass to hers, swirled brandy, and drank. 'I imagine you'd like to get a good look at the treasure again. After all, you hadn't much time for it today, had you?'

'No, Remo was in quite a hurry.'

'My fault, my dear, truly my fault.' He touched a hand lightly to her shoulder. 'I was impatient to meet you. To make amends, I'll give you all the time you'd like right now.'

He walked to the shelves along the east wall and drew back a section of books. Whitney saw the safe without surprise. It was a common enough camouflage. She wondered only a moment how he'd happened to learn of its presence from the owners. Then she tipped back her brandy again. She was certain there was no aspect of the house they hadn't told him of before they'd. . .given it over to him.

He made no attempt to hide the combination from her as he spun the knob. Damn sure of himself, Whitney decided as she memorized the sequence. A man that sure of himself deserved a good kick in the ass.

'Ah.' The sound was like a sigh over the smell of rich food as he drew out the old box. He'd already had it cleaned so that the wood shone. 'Quite a collector's piece.'

'Yes.' Whitney swirled the brandy. It was as smooth and warm as any she'd ever tasted. She wondered what good it would do to toss it in his face. 'I thought the same thing myself.'

He cradled it in his hands carefully, almost hesitantly, like a new father with an infant. 'It's difficult for me to imagine someone with such delicate hands digging in the ground, even for this.'

Whitney smiled, thinking what her delicate hands had been through over the last week. 'I haven't much aptitude for manual labor, but it was necessary.' She turned her hand over, studying it critically. 'I will admit, I'd planned on a manicure before Remo issued your—invitation. This little venture's been death on my hands.'

'We'll arrange for one tomorrow. In the meantime'—he set the chest down on the wide library table—'enjoy.'

Taking him at his word, Whitney moved over to the box and tossed back the lid. The gems were no less impressive now than they'd been that morning. Reaching in, she drew out the necklace of diamonds and sapphires Doug had admired. No, gloated over, she recalled with a half smile. She'd take her cue from that.

'Fabulous,' she breathed. 'Utterly fabulous. One can grow so weary of neat little strands of pearls.'

'You hold approximately a quarter of a million dollars in your hand.'

Her lips curved. 'A pleasant thought.'

His heart beat a little faster as he watched her holding the jewels close, as the queen might have done, not too long before her humiliation and death. 'Such gems belong against a woman's skin.'

'Yes.' With a laugh she held them up against her. The sapphires glowed like dark, brilliant eyes. Diamonds shivered excitedly. 'It's lovely and undoubtedly expensive but this. . .' She dropped the strand back into the box and chose the many-tiered diamond necklace. 'This makes a statement. How do you suppose Marie managed to get it from the comtesse?'

'So you believe it's the infamous necklace of the Diamond Affair?' She'd pleased him again.

'I prefer to.' Whitney let the necklace drip through her fingers and catch the light. It was, as Doug had once said of the Sydney, like holding heat and ice at the same time. 'I like to believe she was clever enough to turn the tables on the people who'd tried to use her.' She tried a ruby bracelet on for size, considering it. 'Gerald Lebrun lived like a pauper with a queen's ransom under his floor. Odd, don't you think?'

'Loyalty's odd, unless it's enhanced by fear.' He took the necklace from her, examining it. For the first time, she saw the greed without the polish. His eyes glowed, very much as Barns's had when he'd pointed a gun at her kneecap. His tongue came out slowly to run over his lips. When he spoke again, his voice had the resonance, the fervor of an evangelist. 'The Revolution itself, a fascinating time of upheaval, death, retribution. Can't you feel it when you hold these in your hands? Blood, despair, lust, power. Peasants and politicians overthrowing a centuries-old monarchy. How?' He smiled at her with the diamonds gleaming in his hands, and the fever burning in his eyes. 'Fear. What more appropriate name than the Reign of Terror? What more suitable spoils than a dead queen's vanity?'

He relished it. Whitney could see it in his eyes. It wasn't simply the jewels, but the blood on them he coveted. She felt her fear die under waves of revulsion. Doug had been right, she realized. It was the winning that counted. She hadn't lost yet.

'A man like Lord would've fenced all this for a fraction of its value. Peasant.' She lifted her snifter again. 'A man like you would have different plans.'

'Perceptive as well as beautiful.' He'd married his second wife because her skin had been as pure as fresh cream. He'd gotten rid of her because her brain had been about the same consistency. Whitney was becoming more intriguing. Calmer, he ran the necklace through his hands. 'I plan to enjoy the treasure. The cash value means little. I'm a very rich man.' It wasn't said offhandedly, but with relish. Being rich was as important as virility, as intellect. More, he thought, because money could cushion the lack of either.

'Collecting'—he skimmed a finger over the bracelet and on to her wrist—'things has become a hobby. At times, an obsessive one.'

He could call it a hobby, she thought. He'd killed time and time again for the box and its contents, yet it meant no more to him than a handful of brightly colored rocks to a young boy. She fought to keep the revulsion off her face and the accusation from her voice.

'Would you think me a poor sport if I told you I wish you hadn't managed this particular hobby quite so well.' Sighing, she ran a hand over the glittering jewels. 'I'd grown rather fond of the idea of owning all this.'

'On the contrary, I admire your honesty.' Leaving her beside the chest, Dimitri walked over to pour the coffee. 'And I understand you worked very hard for Marie's treasure.'

'Yes, I—' Whitney broke off. 'I'm curious, Mr Dimitri, just how did you learn of the treasure?'

'Business. Cream, my dear?'

'No, thank you. Black.' Fighting to hold back her impatience, Whitney crossed the room to the coffee service.

'Did Lord tell you about Whitaker?' asked her host.

Whitney accepted the coffee then forced herself to

sit. 'Only that he'd acquired the papers and then decided to put them on the market.'

'Whitaker was a bit of a fool, but at times he was clever enough. He'd been, at one time, a business partner with Harold R. Bennett. You recognize the name?'

'Of course.' She said it easily while her mind began to work frantically. Hadn't Doug mentioned a general once? Yes, there'd been a general who'd been negotiating with Lady Smythe-Wright for the papers. 'Bennett's a retired five star general and quite a businessman. He's had some dealings with my father—professionally and on the golf course, which almost amounts to the same thing.'

'I've always preferred chess to golf,' Dimitri commented. In the ivory silk, she shimmered so much that she might have replaced the glass queen that was in shards now. He remembered how well it had fit his hand. 'So you know of General Bennett's reputation.'

'He's well known as a patron of the arts, and a collector of the old and unique. A few years ago he led an expedition in the Caribbean and discovered a sunken Spanish galleon. He recovered somewhere around five and a half million in artifacts, coins, and jewels. What Whitaker pretended to do, Bennett did. And very successfully.'

'You're well informed. I like that.' He added cream and two generous spoonfuls of sugar to his own coffee. 'Bennett enjoys the hunt, shall we say. Egypt, New Zealand, the Congo, he's looked for and found the priceless. According to Whitaker he was in the first stages of working out a deal with Lady Smythe-Wright for the papers she'd inherited. Whitaker had his connections, and a certain amount of charm where women are concerned. He slipped the deal from under Bennett's nose. But unfortunately, he was an amateur.'

With a weak heart, Whitney remembered. 'So you learned from him where the papers were kept, and hired Douglas to steal them.'

'Acquire them,' Dimitri corrected delicately. 'Whitaker refused, even under duress, to tell me the contents of all the documents, but he did inform me that Bennett's interest stemmed primarily from the cultural value of the treasure, its history. Naturally, the idea of acquiring a treasure that had belonged to Marie Antoinette, whom I admired particularly for her opulence and ambition, was irresistible.'

'Naturally. If you don't plan to sell the contents of the box, Mr Dimitri, what do you plan to do with it?'

'Why, have it, Whitney.' He smiled at her. 'Fondle it, gaze upon it. Own it.'

While Doug's attitude had frustrated her, at least she understood it. He'd seen the treasure as a means to an end. Dimitri saw it as a personal possession. A dozen arguments sprang up in her mind. She repressed them. 'I'm sure Marie would have approved.'

As he considered this, Dimitri gazed toward the ceiling. Royalty was another of his fascinations. 'She would have, yes. Greed is looked on as one of the seven deadly sins, but so few understand its basic pleasure.' He dabbed his mouth with a linen napkin before he rose. 'I hope you'll forgive me, my dear, I'm accustomed to retiring early.' He pressed a small button that was worked cleverly into the carving on the mantel. 'Perhaps you'd like to choose a book before you go up?'

'Please don't think you have to entertain me, Mr Dimitri. I'll be quite happy on my own, just browsing.'

With another smile, he patted her hand. 'Perhaps

another time, Whitney. I'm sure you need your rest after your experiences of the last few weeks.' There was a quiet knock at he door. 'Remo will show you to your room. Sleep well.'

'Thank you.' She set down her coffee cup and rose, but had taken no more than two steps when Dimitri's hand clamped over her wrist. She looked down at the lightly polished nails, and the stub. 'The bracelet, my dear.' His fingers pressed hard enough to rub against bone. She didn't wince.

'Sorry,' she said easily, holding her hand out.

Dimitri unhooked the gold and rubies from her wrist. 'You'll join me for breakfast, I hope.'

'Of course.' Whitney swept toward the door, pausing as Dimitri opened it. She stood trapped between him and Remo. 'Goodnight.'

'Goodnight, Whitney.'

She held to cool silence until the door of the sitting room locked behind her. 'Sonofabitch.' Disgusted, she took off the delicate Italian slippers that had been provided for her and threw them at the wall.

Trapped, she thought. Locked up just as tidily as the treasure chest—to be gazed upon, fondled. Owned. 'In a pig's eye,' she said aloud. She wanted to weep and wail and beat her fists against the locked door. Instead, she stripped off the ivory silk and left it in a heap before she marched into the bedroom.

She'd find a way, Whitney promised herself. She'd find a way out, and when she did, Dimitri would pay for every minute she'd been his prisoner.

For a moment she rested her head against the armoire because the urge to weep was almost too strong to resist. After she'd controlled it, Whitney reached inside for a teal blue kimono. She needed to think, that was all. She just needed to think. The scent of flowers permeated the room. Air, she decided, and marched to the French doors that led to the tiny bedroom balcony.

With her teeth set, she yanked open the doors. It was going to rain, she thought. Good, the rain and wind might help clear her head. Resting her hands on the rail, she leaned out, looking toward the bay.

How had she gotten herself in this mess? she demanded. The answer was plain, two words. Doug Lord.

After all, she'd been minding her own business when he'd barged into her life and embroiled her in treasure hunts, killers and thieves. At this moment, instead of being trapped like Rapunzel, she'd have been sitting in some nice smoke-choked club, watching people show off their clothes or their new hairstyles. Normal stuff, she thought grimly.

Now look at her, locked in a house in Madagascar with a smiling middle-aged killer and his entourage. In New York, *she* had an entourage, and no one would have dared turn a key on her.

'Doug Lord,' she muttered aloud, then looked down numbly as a hand clamped over hers on the rail. Whitney drew in her breath to scream when the head popped over.

'Yeah, it's me,' Doug said between his teeth. 'Now help me over, goddammit.'

She forgot everything she'd just been thinking about him and bent over to cover his face with kisses. Who said there wasn't any Seventh Cavalry?

'Look, sugar, I appreciate the welcome, but I'm losing my grip. Give me a hand.'

'How'd you find me?' she demanded as she reached down to help him over the rail. 'I didn't think you'd ever come. There are guards out there with these nasty little machine guns. My doors're all locked from the outside, and—'

'Jesus, if I'd remembered you talked so much I wouldn't have bothered.' He landed lightly on his feet.

'Douglas.' She wanted to cry again but held the tears back. 'It's so nice of you to drop in like this.'

'Yeah?' He strolled through the French doors into the opulent bedroom. 'Well, I wasn't sure you wanted any company—especially after that cozy little dinner you had with Dimitri.'

'Were you watching?'

'I've been around.' Turning, he fingered the rich silk of her lapel. 'He gave you this?'

Her eyes narrowed at the tone, her chin tilted. 'Just what are you implying?'

'Looks like a nice setup.' He wandered to her dresser and drew the top from a crystal decanter of scent. 'All the comforts of home, right?'

'I hate to state the obvious, but you're an ass.'

'And what're you?' He pushed the stopper back into the bottle with a snap. 'Walking around in fancy silk dresses he bought for you, drinking champagne with him, letting him put his hands on you?'

'His hands on me?' She said the words slowly, letting them sink in.

Doug gave her a look that skimmed from her bare legs to the milky skin of her throat. 'You sure know how to smile at a man, don't you, sugar? What's your cut?'

Each step measured, Whitney walked over, reared back, and slapped him as hard as she could. For a long moment, there was nothing but the sound of their breathing and the wind kicking up against the open windows.

'You'll get away with that once,' Doug said softly as

he ran the back of his hand over his cheek. 'Don't try it again. I'm not a gentleman like your Dimitri.'

'Just get out,' Whitney whispered. 'Get the hell out. I don't need you.'

There was an ache in him that far outdid the sting in his cheek. 'Don't you think I can see that?'

'You don't see anything.'

'I'll tell you what I saw, sugar. I saw an empty hotel suite. I saw that you and the box were gone. And I saw you here, nuzzling up to that bastard over a rack of lamb.'

'You'd have rather found me tied to the bedpost with bamboo shoots under my nails.' She turned away. 'Sorry to disappoint you.'

'Well, why don't you tell me what the hell's going on then?'

'Why should I?' Furious, she brushed a tear away with the back of her hand. Damn, she hated to cry. Worse, she hated to cry for a man. 'You've already made up your mind. Your very limited mind.'

Doug dragged a hand through his hair and wished he had a drink. 'Look, I've been going crazy for hours. It took me the better part of the afternoon to find this place, then I had to get through the guards.' And one of them, he didn't add, was lying in the bushes with a slit throat. 'When I get here. I see you dressed like a princess, smiling across the table at Dimitri as though you were the best of friends.'

'What the hell was I supposed to do? Run around naked, spit in his eye? Dammit, my life's on the line. If I have to play the game until I find a way out, then I'll play. You can call me a coward if you like. But not a whore.' She turned back again, her eyes dark, wet and angry. 'Not a whore, do you understand?'

He felt as though he'd just struck something small

and soft and defenseless. He hadn't been sure he'd find her alive, then when he had, she'd looked so cool, so beautiful. And worse, so in control. But shouldn't he know her by now?

'I didn't mean that. I'm sorry.' Edgy, he began to pace. He plucked a rose from a vase and snapped the stem in half. 'Christ, I don't know half of what I'm saying. I've been going nuts ever since I walked into the hotel and you were gone. I imagined all kinds of things—and that I was going to be too late to stop any of them.'

He looked dispassionately at the tiny drop of blood on his finger where a thorn had pierced the skin. He had to take a deep breath, and he had to say it quietly. 'Dammit, Whitney, I care, I really care about you. I didn't know what I'd find when I got here.'

She wiped another tear and sniffed. 'You were worried about me?'

'Yeah.' He shrugged, then tossed the mangled rose on to the floor. There was no explaining to her, even to himself, the sick dread, the guilt, the grief he'd lived with during those endless hours. 'I didn't mean to jump all over you like that.'

'Is that an apology?'

'Yes, dammit.' He spun back, his face a study in frustration and fury. 'You want me to crawl?'

'Maybe.' She smiled and walked toward him. 'Maybe later.'

'Jesus.' His hands weren't quite steady when they reached for her face, but his mouth was firm, and a little desperate. 'I didn't think I'd ever see you again.'

'I know.' She pressed against him, wild with relief. 'Just hold me a minute.'

'After we're out of here, I'll hold you as long as you want.' Taking her shoulders, he drew her away.

'You've got to tell me what happened, and what the setup is here.'

She nodded, then sank down on the edge of the bed. Why were her knees weak now when there was hope? 'Remo and that Barns character came.' He saw the quick, nervous swallow and cursed himself again.

'They hurt you?'

'No. You hadn't been gone very long, I'd just run a bath.'

'Why didn't they hold you there until I got back?'

Whitney lifted a foot and examined her toes. 'Because I told them I'd killed you.'

His face, for a brief instant, was a study of incredulity. 'What?'

'Well, it wasn't difficult to convince them that I was a great deal smarter than you, and that I'd put a bullet in your brain so I could have the treasure to myself. After all, they'd've done the same thing to each other at the first opportunity, and I was convincing.'

'Smarter than me?'

'Don't be offended, darling.'

'They bought it?' Not particularly pleased, he dipped his hands in his pockets. 'They believed that a skinny female got the drop on me. I'm a professional.'

'I hated to tarnish your reputation, but it seemed like a good idea at the time.'

'Dimitri bought it too?'

'Apparently. I opted to play the material-minded, heartless woman with an eye on opportunity. I believe he's quite charmed with me.'

'I'll bet.'

'I wanted to spit in his eye,' she said so fiercely Doug cocked a brow. 'I still want the chance to. I don't even think he's human, he just slides from place to place leaving a slimy trail, spouting off his love for the finer things. He wants to hoarde the treasure like a little boy hoarding chocolate bars. He wants to open the box, look, fondle, and think of the screams of people as the guillotine falls. He wants to relive the fear, see the blood. It means more to him that way. All the lives he took to get it mean nothing to him.' Her fingers closed over Jacques's shell. 'They mean absolutely nothing to him.'

Doug moved over to kneel in front of her. 'We're going to spit in his eye.' For the first time, he closed his fingers over hers on the shell. 'I promise. Do you know where he's stashed it?'

'The treasure?' A cold smile moved over her face. 'Oh yes, he took great pleasure in showing it to me. He's so damn sure of himself, so sure he's got me pinned.'

Doug drew her to her feet. 'Let's go get it, sugar.'

It took him a little under two minutes to trip the lock. With the door open only a crack, he peered out to check for guards in the hall.

'Okay, now we move fast and quiet.'

Whitney slipped her hand in his and stepped into the hall.

The house was silent. Apparently when Dimitri retired, everyone retired. In darkness, they moved down the staircase to the first floor. The funeral-parlor smell, flowers and polish, hung thick. Whitney used a gesture of the hand to show Doug which way. Keeping close to the wall, they made their way slowly toward the library.

Dimitri hadn't bothered to lock the door. Doug was a little disappointed, and a little wary that it was so easy. They slipped inside. Rain began to patter against the windows. Whitney went directly to the shelves on the east wall and drew back the section of books.

'It's in here,' she whispered. 'The combination's fifty-two right, thirty-six left—'

'How do you know the combination?'

'I saw him open it.'

Uneasy, Doug reached for the knob. 'Why the hell isn't he covering his tracks?' he muttered as he began to turn. 'Okay, what's next?'

'Another five to the left, then twelve right.' She held her breath as Doug drew down the handle. The door of the safe opened without a sound.

'Come to Poppa,' Doug murmured as he drew out the box. He checked its weight before he grinned at Whitey. He wanted to open it, to take just one more look. To gloat. There'd be other times. 'Let's get out of here.'

'Sounds like an excellent idea.' Tucking a hand through his arm she started toward the terrace doors. 'Shall we use these so we don't disturb our host?'

'It seems like the considerate thing to do.' As he reached for the knob, the doors swung open. Facing them were three men, guns glittering wet in the rain. In the center, Remo grinned. 'Mr Dimitri doesn't want you to leave until he buys you a drink.'

'Yes, indeed.' The library doors opened. Still in his white dinner jacket, Dimitri strolled through. 'I can't have my guests going out in the rain. Do come back and sit down.' The amiable host, he went to the bar and poured brandy. 'My dear, that color's superb on you.'

Doug felt the barrel of Remo's gun at the base of his spine. 'I don't like to impose.'

'Nonsense, nonsense.' He swirled the brandy as he turned. At his touch, the room flooded with light. Whitney could have sworn at that moment his eyes had no color at all. 'Sit down.' The quiet order had all the charm of the hiss of a snake.

Pressed by the barrel of the gun, Doug came forward, the chest in one hand and Whitney's palm in the other. 'Nothing like a brandy on a rainy night.'

'Precisely.' Graciously, he passed two snifters to them. 'Whitney. . .' Her name came out on a sigh as he gestured toward a chair. 'You disappoint me.'

'I didn't give her much choice.' Doug threw Dimitri an arrogant look. 'A woman like her worries about her skin.'

'I admire chivalry, especially from so unlikely a source.' He tipped his glass at Doug before he drank. 'I'm afraid I was aware of Whitney's unfortunate attachment to you all along. My dear, did you really think I believed you'd shot our Mr Lord?'

She shrugged, and though her hands were damp on the snifter, drank. 'I suppose I have to work on my skill as a liar.'

'Indeed, you have very expressive eyes. "Even in the glasses of thine eyes I see thy grieved heart",' he quoted from *Richard II* in his smooth, poet's voice. 'However, I did enjoy our evening together.'

Whitney brushed a hand over the short skirt of her robe. 'I'm afraid I was a bit bored.'

His lips curled back. Everyone in the room knew it would take only a word from him, only a word, and she'd be dead. Instead, he chose to chuckle. 'Women are such unstable creatures, would you agree, Mr Lord?'

'Some show particularly good taste.'

'It amazes me that someone with Miss MacAllister's inherent style would have an affection for someone of your class. But,' he moved his shoulders, 'romance has always been a mystery to me. Remo, relieve Mr Lord of the box, if you please. And his weapons. Just set them on the table for now.' While his orders were carried out, Dimitri sipped his brandy and seemed to ponder great thoughts. 'I took the risk that you would want to retrieve both Miss MacAllister and the treasure. After all this time, after this very intriguing chess game we've been playing, I must say I'm disappointed to have you checkmated with such ease. I'd hoped for a little more flair at the end.'

'You want to send your boys away, you and I could probably come up with something.'

He laughed again, ice clinking on ice. 'I'm afraid my days of physical combat are over, Mr Lord. I prefer more subtle ways of settling disputes.'

'A knife in the back?'

Dimitri merely lifted a brow at Whitney's question. 'I'm forced to admit that one on one, you'd far outmatch me, Mr Lord. After all, you're young and physically agile. I'm afraid I require the handicap of my staff. Now. . .' He touched his finger to his lips. 'What are we to do about this situation?'

Oh, he's enjoying this, Whitney thought grimly. He's like a spider, merrily spinning a web to catch flies so he can suck the blood from them. He wanted to see them sweat.

Because there was no way out, she slipped her hand into Doug's and squeezed. They wouldn't grovel. And by God, they wouldn't sweat.

'As I see it, Mr Lord, your fate is really quite elemental. In essence, you've been a dead man for weeks. It's simply a matter of method.'

Doug gulped down brandy and grinned. 'Don't let me rush you.'

'No, no, I've been giving the matter a great deal of thought. A great deal. Unfortunately, I haven't the facilities here to carry things out in the style I prefer. But I believe Remo has a strong desire to take care of the matter. Though he did fumble quite a bit on this project. I feel the ultimate success deserves a reward.' Dimitri drew out one of his rich black cigarettes. 'I'll give you Mr Lord, Remo.' He lit the cigarette and looked out through the fine mist of smoke. 'Kill him slowly.'

Doug felt the cool barrel of the gun below his left ear. 'Mind if I finish my brandy first?'

'By all means.' With a gracious nod, Dimitri turned his attention to Whitney. 'As to you, my dear, I might have preferred a few more days in your company. I'd thought perhaps we could share some mutual pleasures. However. . .' He tapped the cigarette in a clear crystal tray. 'Under the circumstances, that would add complications. One of my staff has admired you since I showed him your picture. A case of love at first sight.' He smoothed the thinning hair back from his forehead. 'Barns, take her with my blessing. But do be tidy this time.'

'No!' Doug leapt up from his chair. In an instant his arms were clamped behind him and a gun was lodged against his throat. Hearing Barns's giggle, he struggled despite them. 'She's worth more than that,' he said desperately. 'Her father'd pay you a million, two million, to get her back. Don't be a fool, Dimitri. Give her to this little creep, she's worth nothing to you.'

'Not all of us think in terms of money, Mr Lord,' Dimitri said calmly. 'There's a matter of principle at stake you see. I believe as strongly in reward as I do in discipline.' His gaze flicked down to his mutilated hand. 'Yes, just as strongly. Take him along, Remo, he's creating quite a fuss.'

'Keep your hands off me.' Springing up, Whitney

dashed the contents of her snifter in Barns's face. With fury carrying her, she doubled up her fist and planted it squarely on his nose. His squeak and the squirt of blood gave her momentary satisfaction.

Doug took his cue from her and, bracing himself against the man behind him, reared back and smashed his foot under the chin of the man across from him. They might've been mowed down in that instant if Dimitri hadn't signaled. He enjoyed watching the doomed struggle. Calmly he took the derringer from his inside pocket and fired into the vaulted ceiling.

'That'll do,' he told them, as if speaking to obstreperous adolescents. He watched tolerantly as Doug gathered Whitney to his side. He was particularly fond of Shakespeare's tragedies that dealt with star-crossed lovers—not only because of the beauty of words, but because of their hopelessness. 'I'm a reasonable man, and a romantic at heart. In order to give you a bit more time together, Miss MacAllister is welcome to go along while Remo proceeds with the execution.'

'Execution,' Whitney spat at him with all the venom a desperate woman can gather. 'Murder, Dimitri, doesn't have such a clean, cool ring to it. You delude yourself into believing you're cultured and suave. Do you think a silk dinner jacket can hide what you are, and what you'll never be? You're nothing more than a crow, Dimitri, a crow picking at carrion. You don't even kill for yourself.'

'Normally, no.' His voice had frozen. Those of his men who had heard the tone before tensed. 'In this case, however, perhaps I should make an exception.' He lowered the derringer.

The terrace doors burst open, shattering glass. 'Put up your arms.' The order was authoritative, delivered in English with a classy French accent. Doug didn't

wait for the outcome, but shoved Whitney behind a
chair. He saw Barns grab for his gun. The grin was
blown off his face.

'The house is surrounded.' Ten uniformed men
trooped into the library, rifles at the ready. 'Franco
Dimitri, you are under arrest for murder, conspiracy to
commit murder, kidnapping. . .'

'Holy shit,' Whitney murmured as the list lengthened. 'It really is the cavalry.'

'Yeah.' Doug let out a breath of relief, holding her
warm beside him. It was also the police, he reflected.
He wouldn't exactly come out smelling like a rose
himself.

He saw, with a feeling of inevitability and disgust,
the man with the panama walk through the doors. 'I
should've smelled cop,' he muttered. A man with a
shock of white hair strode into the room with an air of
impatience.

'All right, where is that girl!'

Doug saw Whitney's eyes widen until they seemed
to cover her whole face. Then with a bubbling giggle
she sprang up from behind the chair. 'Daddy!'

# CHAPTER SIXTEEN

It didn't take long for the Malagasy police to clear out the room. Whitney watched the handcuffs being snapped on to Dimitri's wrist below a fat emerald cuff link.

'Whitney, Mr Lord.' Dimitri's voice remained soft, cultured, calm. A man in his position understood temporary setbacks. But his eyes, as his gaze passed over them, were as flat as a goat's. 'I'm sure, yes, quite sure we'll see each other again.'

'We'll catch you on the eleven o'clock news,' Doug told him.

'I owe you,' Dimitri acknowledged with a nod. 'I always pay my debts.'

Whitney's gaze met his briefly, and she smiled. Once again, her fingers trailed down to the shell around her neck.

'For Jacques,' she said softly, 'I hope they find a hole dark enough for you.' Then she buried her face against her father's clean-smelling jacket. 'I'm so glad to see you.'

'Explanations.' But MacAllister held her fiercely for a moment. 'Let's have some, Whitney.'

She drew away, eyes laughing. 'Explain what?'

He struggled with a grin and huffed instead. 'Nothing changes.'

'How's Mother? I hope you didn't tell her you were trailing after me.'

'She's fine. She thinks I'm in Rome working. If I'd told her I was chasing our only daughter all over

Madagascar, she wouldn't have been able to play bridge for days.'

'You're so clever.' She kissed him, hard. 'How did you know to chase me all over Madagascar?'

'I believe you've met General Bennett?'

Whitney turned and faced a tall, rangy man with stern, unsmiling eyes. 'Of course.' She offered her hand as though they were at a well-mannered cocktail party. 'At the Stevensons' year before last. How are you, General? Oh, I don't believe you've met Douglas. Doug. . .' Whitney signaled to him across the room where he was mumbling out a tangled statement to one of the Malagasy officials. Grateful for the respite, he went to her. 'Daddy, General Bennett, this is Douglas Lord. Doug's the one who stole the papers, General.'

The smile turned a little sickly on Doug's face. 'Nice to meet you.'

'You owe Douglas quite a bit,' she told the general and poked in her father's jacket for a cigarette.

'Owe,' the general blustered. 'This thief—'

'Secured the papers, keeping them out of the hands of Dimitri. At the risk of his own life,' she added, holding up the cigarette for a light. Doug obliged her, deciding he'd leave the explanations to her after all. She sent him a wink as she blew out smoke. 'You see, it all started when Dimitri hired Doug to steal the papers. Of course, Doug knew right away that they were priceless and had to be kept out of the wrong hands.' She drew in smoke, then waved the cigarette expressively. 'He virtually took his life in his hands to secure them. I can't tell you how many times he told me if we found the treasure, what a priceless contribution to society it would be. Isn't that so, Doug?'

'Well, I—'

'He's so modest. You really must take credit where

credit's due, darling. After all, securing the treasure for General Bennett's foundation nearly cost you your life.'

'It was nothing,' Doug muttered. He could see the rainbow beginning to fade.

'Nothing?' Whitney shook her head. 'General, as a man of action, you'd appreciate just what Doug went through to prevent Dimitri from hoarding the treasure. Hoarding,' she repeated. 'He intended to keep it to himself. To wallow in it,' she added with a slanted look at Doug. 'When, as we all will agree, it belongs to society.'

'Yes, but—'

'Before you express your gratitude, General,' she interrupted, 'I'd appreciate it if you'd explain to me just how you arrived here. We do owe you our lives.'

Flattered, and confused, the general began an explanation.

Whitaker's nephew, terrified by his uncle's fate, had gone to the general confessing everything he knew. Which was considerable. Once the general had been alerted, he hadn't hesitated. The authorities had been on Dimitri's trail before Whitney and Doug had climbed off the plane at Antananarivo.

Dimitri's trail had led to Doug, and Doug's, because of their ecapades in New York and DC, to Whitney. She had reason to be grateful to the ever-eager paparazzi for several grainy pictures in the tabloids her father's secretary poured over.

After a brief session with Uncle Max in Washington, the general and MacAllister had hired a private detective. The man in the panama hat had picked up their trail, dogging them just as Dimitri had. When they'd jumped from the train heading toward Tamatave, both the general and MacAllister had been on a plane to

Madagascar. The authorities there had been only too happy to cooperate in the capture of an international criminal.

'Fascinating,' Whitney said when it looked like the general's monologue would go on until dawn. 'Simply fascinating. I can see why you earned those five stars.' Hooking her arm through his, she smiled. 'You saved my life, General. I hope you'll give me the pleasure of showing you the treasure.'

With a cocky smile over her shoulder, she led him away.

MacAllister drew out a cigarette case and flipped it open, offering it to Doug. 'Nobody bullshits like Whitney,' he said easily. 'I don't believe you've met Brickman.' He gestured to the man in the panama. 'He's worked for me before, one of the best. He's said the same of you.'

Doug eyed the man in the panama. Each man recognized the other for what he was. 'You were at the canal, just behind Remo.'

Brickman remembered the crocs and smiled. 'My pleasure.'

'Now.' MacAllister looked from one man to the other. He hadn't succeeded in business without knowing what went on in men's minds. 'Why don't we get a drink and you can tell me what really happened?'

Doug flipped his lighter and studied MacAllister's face. It was tanned and smooth, a sure sign of wealth. His voice had the ring of authority. The eyes that looked back at him were dark as whiskey, as amused as Whitney's. Doug's lips tilted.

'Dimitri's a pig, but he stocks a good bar. Scotch?'

It was nearly dawn when Doug looked down on Whitney. She was curled, naked, under the thin sheet.

A slight smile touched her lips as though she were dreaming of the rush of lovemaking they'd shared after they'd returned to the hotel. But her breathing was slow and even as she slept the sleep of the exhausted.

He wanted to touch her, but he didn't. He'd thought of leaving her a note. But he didn't.

He was who he was, what he was. A thief, a nomad, a loner.

For the second time in his life, he'd held the world in his hands, and for the second time, it had vanished. It would be possible, after a time, to convince himself that he'd come across that big break again. The end of the rainbow. Just as it would be possible, after a very long time, to convince himself that he and Whitney had had a fling. Fun and games, nothing serious. He'd convince himself because those damn strings were tightening around him. It was break them now, or not at all.

He still had the ticket to Paris, and a check for five thousand the general had written to him after Whitney had had the retired soldier bubbling with gratitude.

But he'd seen the look in the eyes of the officials, of the private detective who recognized a con and a thief when he saw one. He'd earned a reprieve, but the next dark alley was just around the corner.

Doug glanced at the pack and thought of her notebook. He knew his tab came to more than the five thousand he had at his disposal. Going over, he rummaged through her pack until he found the pad and pencil.

After the final total, which caused him to lift a brow, he scribbled a brief message.

*IOU, sugar.*

Dropping both back in the pack, he took a last look at her while she slept. He slipped from the room like the thief he was, silently and swiftly.

The moment she woke, Whitney knew he was gone. It wasn't a matter of the bed being empty beside her. Another woman might have assumed he'd gone out for coffee or a walk. Another woman might have called his name in a husky, sleepy voice.

She knew he was gone.

It was in her nature to face things directly when there wasn't a choice. Whitney rose, pulled back the blinds, and began to pack. Because silence was unbearable, she switched on the radio without bothering to fiddle with the dial.

She noticed the boxes tumbled on the floor. Determined to keep occupied, she began to open them.

Her fingers slid over the flimsy lingerie Doug had picked out for her. She gave a quick, tilted smile at the receipt with her credit-card imprint. Because she'd decided that cynicism would be her best defense, Whitney slipped into the pale blue teddy. After all, she'd paid for it.

Tossing the box aside, she drew off the lid of the next. The dress was rich, blue, the color, she remembered, of the butterflies she'd seen and admired. Cynicism and all other defenses threatened to crumble. Swallowing tears, she bundled the dress back into the box. It wouldn't travel well, she told herself, and yanked a pair of wrinkled slacks out of her pack.

In a few hours, she'd be back in New York, in her own milieu, surrounded by her own friends. Doug Lord would be a vague, and expensive, memory. That was all. Dressed, packed, and utterly calm, she went out to check out and meet her father.

He was already in the lobby, pacing, impatient.

Deals were cooking. The ice-cream business was dog-eat-dog. 'Where's your boyfriend?' he demanded.

'Daddy, really.' Whitney signed her bill with a flourish and a completely steady hand. 'A woman doesn't have boyfriends. She has lovers.' She smiled at the bellboy and followed him out to the car her father had waiting.

He huffed, not entirely pleased with her terminology. 'So where is he?'

'Doug?' She gave her father an unconcerned look over her shoulder as she climbed into the back seat of the limo. 'Why I have no idea. Paris perhaps—he had a ticket.'

Scowling, MacAllister plopped back against the seat. 'What the hell's going on, Whitney?'

'I think I might spend a few days on Long Island when we get back. I tell you, all this traveling's exhausting.'

'Whitney.' He clamped a hand over hers, using the tone he'd used since she was two. It had never been overly successful. 'Why did he leave?'

She reached in her father's pocket, drew out his cigarette case, and chose one. Staring straight ahead, she tapped the cigarette on the dull gold lid. 'Because that's his style. Slipping out in the middle of the night without a sound, without a word. He's a thief, you know.'

'So he told me last night while you were busy bullshitting Bennett. Dammit, Whitney, by the time he was finished, my hair was standing on end. It was worse than reading the report from the detective. The two of you nearly got yourselves killed half a dozen times.'

'It concerned us a bit at the time, too,' she murmured.

'You'd do my ulcer a world of good if you'd marry that empty-headed, weak-jawed Carlyse.'

'Sorry, then I'd have one.'

He studied the cigarette she'd yet to light. 'I got the impression you were—attached to this young thief you'd picked up.'

'Attached.' The cigarette snapped in her fingrs. 'No, it was strictly business.' Tears welled up and spilled over but she continued to speak calmly. 'I was bored and he provided entertainment.'

'Entertainment?'

'Expensive entertainment,' she added. 'The bastard's gone off owing me twelve thousand, three hundred and fifty-eight dollars and forty-seven cents.'

MacAllister took out his handkerchief and dried her cheeks. 'Nothing like losing a few thousand to bring on the waterworks,' he murmured. 'Often happens to me.'

'He didn't even say good-bye,' she whispered. Curling into her father, she wept because there didn't to be anything else she could do.

New York in August can be vicious. The heat can hang, shimmer, gloat, and roll. When a garbage strike coincided with a heat wave, tempers became as ripe as the air. Even the more fortunate, who could summon an air-conditioned limo at the snap of a finger tended to turn surly after two weeks of ninety-degree-plus weather. It was a time when anyone who could arrange it fled the city for the islands, for the country, for Europe.

Whitney had had her fill of traveling.

She stuck it out in Manhattan when the majority of her friends and acquaintances jumped ship. She turned down offers for a cruise on the Aegean, a week on the

Italian Riviera, and a month-long honeymoon in the country of her choice.

She worked because it was an interesting way to ignore the heat. She played because it was more productive than moping. She considered taking a trip to the Orient, but just to be obstinate—in September, when everyone else trickled back to New York.

When she'd returned from Madagascar, she'd treated herself to a wild, indulgent shopping spree. Half of what she'd bought still hung, unworn, in her already-crowded closet. She'd hit the clubs every night for more than two weeks, hopping from one to the next and tumbling into bed after sunrise.

When she lost interest in that, she threw herself into her work with such vigor her friends began to mutter among themselves.

It was one thing for her to exhaust herself with rounds of parties, quite another to do so during working hours. Whitney did what she did best. She ignored them completely.

'Tad, don't make a fool of yourself again. I simply can't bear it.' Her voice was careless, but more sympathetic than cruel. Over the past few weeks, he'd nearly convinced her that he cared for her almost as much as his collection of silk ties.

'Whitney. . .' Blond, tailored, and a little drunk, he stood in the doorway of her apartment, trying to figure the best way to ease himself inside. She blocked him without effort. 'We'd make a good team. It doesn't matter that my mother thinks you're flighty.'

Flighty. Whitney rolled her eyes at the term. 'Listen to your mother, Tad. I'd make a perfectly dreadful wife. Now, go back down so your driver can take you home. You know you can't drink more than two martinis without losing your grip.'

'Whitney.' He grabbed her, kissing her with passion if not with style. 'Let me send Charles home. I'll spend the night.'

'Your mother would send out the National Guard,' she reminded him, slipping out of his arms. 'Now go home and sleep off that third martini. You'll feel more like yourself tomorrow.'

'You don't take me seriously.'

'I don't take *me* seriously,' she corrected and patted his cheek. 'Now run along and listen to your mother.' She closed the door in his face. 'The old battle-ax.'

Letting out a long breath, she crossed to the bar. After an evening with Tad, she deserved a nightcap. If she hadn't been so restless, so. . .whatever, she'd never have let him convince her that she needed an evening of opera and congenial company. Opera wasn't high on her list of enjoyments, and Tad had never been the most congenial companion.

She splashed a healthy dose of cognac into a glass.

'Make it two, will you, sugar?'

Her fingers tightened on the glass, her heart lodged in her throat. But she didn't flinch, she didn't turn. Calmly, Whitney turned over a second glass and filled it. 'Still slipping through keyholes, Douglas?'

She wore the dress he'd bought her in Diégo-Suarez. He'd pictured her in it a hundred times. He didn't know this was the first time she'd put it on, and that she'd done so in defiance. Nor did he know that because of it, she'd thought of him all evening.

'Out pretty late, aren't you?'

She told herself she was strong enough to handle it. After all, she'd had weeks to get over him. One brow cocked, she turned.

He was dressed in black, and it suited him. Plain black T-shirt, snug black jeans. The costume of his trade, she mused as she held out the glass. She thought his face looked leaner, his eyes more intense, then she tried not to think at all.

'How was Paris?'

'Okay.' He took the glass and restrained the urge to touch her hand. 'How've you been?'

'How do I look?' It was a direct challenge. Look at me, she demanded. Take a good look. He did.

Her hair flowed sleekly down one shoulder, held back with a crescent-shaped pin of diamonds. Her face was as he remembered: pale, cool, elegant. Her eyes were dark and arrogant as she watched him over the rim of her glass.

'You look terrific,' he muttered.

'Thank you. So, to what do I owe this unexpected pleasure?'

He'd practiced what he was going to say, how he was going to say it, two dozen times in the last week. He'd been in New York that long, vacillating between going to her and staying away. 'Just thought I'd see how you were,' he mumbled into his glass.

'How sweet.'

'Look, I know you must think I ran out on you—'

'To the tune of twelve thousand, three hundred and fifty-eight dollars and forty-seven cents.'

He made a sound that might've been a laugh. 'Nothing changes.'

'Did you come to make good on the IOU you left me?'

'I came because I had to, dammit.'

'Oh?' Unmoved, she tossed back her drink. She restrained herself from tossing the glass against the wall as well. 'Do you have another venture in mind that requires some ready capital?'

'You want to get a few shots in, go ahead.' With a snap, he set his glass down.

She stared at him a moment, then shook her head. Turning away, she set down her own glass and rested her palms against the table. For the first time since he'd known her, her shoulders slumped and her voice was weary. 'No, I don't want to get any shots in, Doug. I'm a bit tired. You've seen that I'm fine. Now why don't you leave the same way you came in?'

'Whitney.'

'Don't touch me,' she murmured before he'd taken two steps toward her. The quiet, even voice didn't quite hide the trickle of desperation underneath.

He lifted his hands, palms out, then let them drop. 'Okay.' He wandered the room a moment, trying to find his way back to his original plan of attack. 'You know, I had pretty good luck in Paris. Cleaned out five rooms in the Hotel de Crillon.'

'Congratulations.'

I was on a roll, probably could've spent the next six months picking off tourists.' He hooked his thumbs in his pockets.

'So why didn't you?'

'Just wasn't any fun. You got trouble when the fun goes out of your work, you know.'

She turned back, telling herself it was cowardly not to face him. 'I suppose so. You came back to the States for a change of scene?'

'I came back because I couldn't stay away from you anymore.'

Her expression didn't change, but he saw her link her fingers together in the first outward show of nerves he'd ever observed in her. 'Oh?' she said simply. 'It seems an odd thing to say. I didn't kick you out of the hotel room in Diégo-Suarez.'

'No.' His gaze traveled slowly over her face, as if he needed to find something. 'You didn't kick me out.'

'Then why did you leave?'

'Because if I'd stayed, I'd've done then what I guess I'm going to do now.'

'Steal my purse?' she asked with a flippant toss of her head.

'Ask you to marry me.'

It was the first time, perhaps the only time, he'd seen her mouth fall open and hang there. She looked as though someone had just stomped on her toes. He'd hoped for a bit more emotional reaction.

'I guess that charmed the shit out of you.' Helping himself, he took his glass back to the bar. 'Pretty funny idea, a guy like me proposing to a woman like you. I don't know, maybe it was the air or something, I started getting some funny ideas in Paris about setting up housekeeping, settling in. Kids.'

Whitney managed to close her mouth. 'You did?' Like Doug, she decided another drink was in order. 'You're talking marriage as in till death us do part and joint tax returns?'

'Yeah. I decided I'm traditional. Even down to this.' When he went for something, he went for it completely. The policy didn't always work, but it was his policy. He reached in his pocket and drew out a ring.

The brilliance of the diamond caught the light and exploded with it. Whitney made a conscious effort to keep her mouth from dropping open again.

'Where did you—'

'I didn't steal it,' he snapped. Feeling foolish, he tossed it up and clamped it in his palm. 'Exactly,' he amended and managed a half smile. 'The diamond came out of Marie's treasure. I pocketed it—I guess you'd call it a reflex. I thought about fencing it, but—'

Opening his hand, he stared down at it. 'Had it set in Paris.'

'I see.'

'Look, I know you wanted the treasure to go to museums, and most of it did.' It still hurt. 'There was a hell of a write-up in the Paris papers. Bennett Foundation recovers tragic queen's booty, diamond necklace sparks new theories, and so on.'

He moved his shoulders, trying not to think of all those pretty, shiny stones. 'I decided to settle for the one rock. Even though just a couple of those bangles could've set me up for life.' Shrugging again, he held the ring up by its thin gold band. 'If it itches your conscience, I'll take the damn rock out and ship it off to Bennett.'

'Don't be insulting.' In a deft move, she snatched it out of his hand. 'My engagement ring isn't going in any museum. Besides. . .' And she smiled at him fully. 'I also believe there are pieces of history that should belong to the individual. A hands-on sort of thing.' She gave him her cool, lifted-brow look. 'Are you traditional enough to get down on one knee?'

'Not even for you, sugar.' He gripped her left wrist and, taking the ring from her, slipped it on the third finger. The look he gave her was long and steady. 'Deal?'

'Deal,' she agreed, and laughing, launched herself into his arms. 'Damn you, Douglas, I've been miserable for two months.'

'Oh yeah?' He found he liked the idea, almost as much as he liked kissing her again. 'I see you like the dress I bought you.'

'You have excellent taste.' Behind his back she turned her hand so she could watch the light bounce from the ring. 'Married,' she repeated, trying out the word. 'You mentioned settling in. Does that mean you plan to retire?'

'I've been giving it some thought. You know. . .' He nuzzled into her neck so he could draw in the scent that had haunted him in Paris. 'I've never seen your bedroom.'

'Really? I'll have to give you the grand tour. You're a bit young to retire,' she added, drawing away from him. 'What do you plan to do with your spare time?'

'Well, when I'm not making love to you, I thought I might run a business.'

'A pawnshop.'

He nipped at her lip. 'A restaurant,' he corrected. 'Smartass.'

'Of course.' She nodded, liking the idea. 'Here in New York?'

'A good place to start.' He let her go to pick up his glass. Maybe the end of the rainbow had been closer than he'd thought all along. 'Start with one here, then maybe Chicago, San Francisco. Thing is, I'm going to need a backer.'

She ran her tongue around her teeth. 'Naturally. Any ideas?'

He shot her the charming, untrustworthy grin. 'I'd like to keep it in the family.'

'Uncle Jack.'

'Come on, Whitney, you know I can do it. Forty thousand, no, make it fifty, and I'll set up the slickest little restaurant on the West Side.'

'Fifty thousand,' she mused, moving toward her desk.

'It's a good investment. I'd write up the menu myself, supervise the kitchen. I'd. . . What're you doing?'

'That would come to sixty-two thousand, three hundred and fifty-eight dollars and forty-seven cents, all told.' With a brisk nod, she double-underlined the total. 'At twelve and a half percent interest.'

He scowled down at the figures. 'Interest? Twelve and a half percent?'

'A more than reasonable rate, I know, but I'm a softie.'

'Look, we're getting married, right?'

'Absolutely.'

'A wife doesn't charge her husband interest, for Chrissake.'

'This one does,' she murmured as she continued jotting down numbers. 'I can figure out the monthly payments in just a minute. Let's see, over a period of fifteen years, say?'

He looked down at her elegant hands as she scrawled figures. The diamond winked up at him. 'Sure, what the hell.'

'Now, about collateral.'

He bit back an oath, then smothered a laugh. 'How about our firstborn son?'

'Interesting.' She tapped the pad against her palm. 'Yes, I might agree to that—but we don't have any children as yet.'

He walked over and snatched the notebook from her hand. After tossing it over his shoulder, he grabbed her. 'Then let's take care of it, sugar. I need the loan.'

Whitney noticed with satisfaction that the pad had fallen faceup. 'Anything for free enterprise.'